Comfortably Numb

Books by Deborah Grabien

The JP Kinkaid Chronicles

Rock and Roll Never Forgets
While My Guitar Gently Weeps
London Calling
Graceland
Book of Days
Uncle John's Band
Dead Flowers
Comfortably Numb
Gimme Shelter *

The Haunted Ballads

The Weaver and the Factory Maid
The Famous Flower of Serving Men
Matty Groves
Cruel Sister
New-Slain Knight
Geordie *

Other Novels

Woman of Fire
Fire Queen
Plainsong
And Then Put Out the Light
Still Life With Devils
Dark's Tale

forthcoming

Comfortably Numb

Book #8 of the JP Kinkaid Chronicles

Deborah Grabien

Plus One Press
San Francisco

Plus One Press

COMFORTABLY NUMB. Copyright © 2013 by Deborah Grabien. All rights reserved. Printed in the United States of America. For information, address Plus One Press, 2885 Golden Gate Avenue, San Francisco, California, 94118.

www.plusonepress.com

Book Design by Plus One Press

Publisher's Cataloging-in-Publication Data

Grabien, Deborah.
  Comfortably numb : book #8 of the jp kinkaid chronicles / Deborah Grabien.—1st. Plus One Press ed.
       p. cm.
   ISBN: 0-9860085-1-6
   ISBN: 978-0-9860085-1-1
   1. Rock Musicians—Fiction. 2. Musical Fiction. 3. Murder—Fiction.
I. Title. II. Title: Comfortably Numb
   PS3557.R1145 C66 2013
   813'.54—dc22

                                                          2013908890

First Edition: November, 2013

10 9 8 7 6 5 4 3 2 1

Most of us are addicted to something.
This is for those of us who know it,
those of us who admit it, and
those of us who cope as best we can with those who know.

Acknowledgements

For everyone who gave me needed information about non-traditional, non-twelve step recovery and treatment programs and trends in current thinking, my heartfelt thanks.

All the nice wip-readers who keep it coming, book after book: Anne Weber, Marty Grabien, Sandra Larkin, and you know who you all are.

Deep thanks to the nice experts at Luxury Cars of Los Gatos, for letting me sit in the Bugatti Veyron and fiddle with things. That car goes to eleven.

And an acknowledgement of theft: Sandra Larkin came up with the phrase "Villa Priscilla" and I stole it. There, I said it in public.

Comfortably Numb

Chapter One

For some reason, the last few times I've got called over to the UK with no warning because something's come up that needs me there the day before yesterday, the timing's been absolute rubbish.

It's ridiculous. I always seem to get dragged off to England at just the times of year where anyone who wasn't off their nut would want to be anywhere but London: November, or February. I don't really need reminding as to why I don't live there anymore, but if I did, having to cross the Atlantic in midwinter, and then coping with sleety downpours and skies the colour of a nightmare about oblivion, would do it.

It might not have been quite so bad if we'd been out in the countryside. My last emergency trip over here had been for our long-time manager's funeral, a few years back now. Chris Fallow had been Blacklight's manager from the time he'd first seen Mac

Sharpe and Luke Hedley playing together as a folk duo. That goodbye had been made in a cold wintry garden, with Chris's widow Meg supported by the band and the extended band family. And yeah, the weather had been as miserable as it gets, but there'd been something nice about it, as well: Meg scattering Chris's ashes all over his own rose bushes, feeling he was there with us and watching his own memorial, had taken some of the bite out of the weather.

But this was London N10, a quiet little part of town right at the foot of Muswell Hill, and here it was, November again. Thanks to a heart check-up I hadn't been able to reschedule, I hadn't even been able to get over here with Bree in time for Guy Fawkes—we'd missed Bonfire Night by two days. Actually, now that I gave it some proper thought, Bree would probably find the whole Guy Fawkes thing morbid anyway...

"John?" Bree hadn't bothered glancing at any of the glossy magazines or the nice bland prints on the walls or the espresso machine. She also hadn't said a word about the fresh roses that must have cost someone quite a bit of dosh this time of year, since they had to have come out of a hothouse somewhere, and she loves roses. "Are you okay?"

"Yeah, I'm good." I shifted, trying to ease the tingles in my feet, and smiled at her. She was worrying about my multiple sclerosis or maybe my heart, something she does non-stop, basically. I couldn't complain about the sofa not being comfy; it was just as high-end as the rest of the room, big soft buttery leather, no buttons digging into your back or your arse. "Just still pissy I couldn't get you here in time to see the fireworks, that's all."

She smiled, but didn't say anything. There was no need to—I could practically hear her muttering "is *that* all?", even though she stayed quiet. She sighed, and relaxed. Easy to tell, with Bree: when she's tense, her shoulders go sky-high.

The waiting room was old-school Ye Olde Discreet Gent's

Club enough to set my teeth on edge. No expense spared, you know? It was very weird, realising I was responsible for this place's existence: I'd had the idea for it, paid for the leasehold on the property, funded everything from the staff to the espresso machine, arranged for it to continue to be funded, and told the people handling the details to put my first wife's name over the door, along with the words "Addiction Recovery Centre". The one thing I hadn't done was pay any attention to it, once it was up and running. I'd left that up to Blacklight Corporate. I'd never been near the place before.

"Mr. and Mrs. Kinkaid?" The voice came from behind the sofa. "I'm very sorry to keep have kept you waiting."

Bree and I both turned. We had to crane our necks to peer round the back of the sofa; someone, probably a twenty-year-old art school grad named Ludmilla or Veronique who specialised in designing oxygen bar interiors on the South Bank, had decided to face the sofa away from the main door. We hadn't heard the bloke come in or the door opening, either. The doors were as quiet and unobtrusive as the sofa and the espresso machine and the rest of the decor.

"Yeah, I'm John Kinkaid. This is my wife, Bree." We'd got up and gone round the proper end of the sofa, side by side. I held out my right hand; the left one was busy hanging on to Bree's. "Are you the director?"

He shook hands, nice easy grip, not too hard, not trying to prove anything. Good start, that was; I tend to judge blokes on how macho they think they have to get with a handshake. The ones who've got to show how tough they are, who've got some barnyard rubbish tied up in how hard they can squeeze someone else's hand, those are the ones I tend to avoid.

"Yes, I'm Robert Mourdain. Welcome to the Priscilla Kinkaid Addiction Recovery Centre."

He smiled suddenly, a real smile. Seemed like a pleasant type

3

all around, but you never know, do you? Besides, doing his gig, he'd have to wear a kind of mask, that whole persona thing. It comes with the territory. You can't help wondering how much is real. He looked too young to have the cred to be a director of anything, but that was probably genetics. "It seems rather ridiculous, me or anyone else welcoming you, of all people. I hope you were pointed at the espresso machine while you were waiting? A good cup of coffee on a day as raw as today can't be a bad thing."

"It can at my age, at least if I fancy sleeping." I'd got my right hand back with no damage done. "No caffeine for me past about three in the afternoon, I'm afraid, not unless I'm playing a gig that night."

I was still holding on to Bree's hand, swinging gently. Nice and warm. Good. She's got diabetes and her hands get icy cold even when she's someplace where it isn't pissing down a depressing sleet, or rattling windows with what sounds like icy pebbles whenever the wind kicks up. "No worries, we weren't waiting long at all. Ten minutes, maybe. Thanks for taking the time to show us round the place."

"It's a pleasure." He was holding the door open, but he shot me a sideways look. He'd sounded as if he really meant it, not just blowing the usual public-face smoke. "Actually, more of an honour. I've been a Blacklight fan since before I finished university in 1990—I still remember hearing some stuff on the radio and running out to get 'Backseat Babies'. I must have played that end to end about a hundred times. May I ask, are you going to tour again?"

"Don't know, not at this point." That answered one question about Robert Mourdain: he was older than he looked. If he'd got out of university in 1990, he had to be in his mid-forties at least, a year or two younger than Bree. "That last tour, *Book of Days*, was a killer. Two and a half years on the road, and I was quite ill at the end of it, for rather a long time."

4

"I know." He took a deep breath—it was pretty obvious he was deciding whether to say something. "My son Keith signed you in to hospital as a patient after your heart attack at Wembley. He'd been cursing his bad luck in having to work on the closing night of the tour, but he was damned glad to be there and able to do something, even if it was just handling the paperwork and making sure you were set up."

"Wow. Your son signed us in? Please thank him for us—the entire staff at the hospital was wonderful that night, and I never got a chance to really thank anyone personally."

Except for asking if I was okay, that was the first thing out of Bree's mouth since we'd got out of the hire car. Her hands might have been warm, and so was her tone of voice, but her shoulders were hunched up again, very tense. Most times, I've got no clue what's making her boulder up, but this time, it was pretty obvious: she didn't enjoy any reminders of the worst few weeks of her life, and anyway, it didn't matter how posh the waiting room was or how kind the director was, she was still standing in a building that had been named in memory of my first wife.

It didn't matter that the first wife in question had been a junkie and a panic killer and a suicide, you know? It didn't matter that she'd been dead a good long while, either. It made no difference that she and I had been so estranged for so long before she'd deliberately done enough heroin to take out a street gang, I probably could have passed her on the street and not looked twice. It had taken me a long time to sort out, but I did get it now: Cilla's name, no matter how or why it came up, was never going to mean anything but heartbreaking memories and bad associations for Bree.

We'd moved out of the waiting room, and into a nice long corridor. There was an odd split-personality thing going on there. One half reminded me of the long hallway in our house at 2828

5

Clay Street in San Francisco, all gleaming old wood panelling, but on the outer half, someone had done some serious remodelling or maybe just straight-up new construction: the wood was gone, replaced with glass walls floor to roof, ultra-modern. That let us get a view of what was probably quite a nice garden in the summer, surrounded on all four sides by the rest of the building, all three floors. There was a gardener out there, looking miserable and wet even in his boots and mac, pruning bits off dead things and putting them in a wheeled bin.

"That's the Quad." Mourdain sounded quite proud of it. Odd thing to get your peacock feathers up for, a bit of drab grass with some benches, but whatever. "On sunny days, our clients very often come out here and just think. It's a very nice place to meditate, and we do encourage meditation here, as part of the process. Ah, here we are—to the left, please? I wanted to show you our kitchen."

He pushed open a swinging door with a porthole window. Bree made a noise and I actually found myself grinning, first time since we'd walked in. My wife's a cook, and this kitchen was right up her *cul de sac*: tarted up to the nines, pots in long rows and a sodding huge stove. I counted eight burners.

"It's a very nice kitchen, isn't it?" Mourdain sounded polite, probably wondering why Bree'd reacted to it so hard. "We take food here very seriously. One of the things we stress in the recovery process is learning to love your body without whatever the artificial stimulus is, and that means a return to health. Proper food is a major component of that."

"No, Mr. Mourdain." Bree's red hair swung as she turned away from me. Oh, bloody hell. "Sorry, but you're wrong. It's not a major component, it's *the* major component. I know that if you've got an addictive personality you're going to be addicted to something one way or another, but most of it's negotiable. It's stuff you can do without just fine if you have to, and never really suffer from the lack: sex, sports, money, heroin, tequila, shopping, whatever. But you try going without food for a few days, and you realise just how non-negotiable that is."

She sounded quite fierce, and I was biting back another grin, because Mourdain was blinking and looking as if his professional face might have just had a pie thrown at it. Of course, he didn't know Bree. I do.

"Yes, that's quite right, but I'm afraid I don't –"

"My wife's a chef." I dropped an arm around her. Yeah, so we were in the Priscilla Kinkaid Addiction Recovery Centre—it was Bree Kinkaid rocking the house, as usual. I'm quite proud of my old lady, you know? "She's got a cookbook coming out this year, about making sure people with special needs are properly fed. You ever want to talk food with Bree, you'd best know your stuff, because you're talking with an expert."

"Oh, I see." He'd gone back to doing the smooth thing. "A special needs cookbook? Excellent! Congratulations. Would you like to see the rest of the facility? As you know, we limit our guest residencies to no more than five clients at a time, so that we can give everyone specialised one-on-one care. And of course, our clients do tend to carry a certain weight of celebrity. The smaller list enables us to keep almost absolute control over the privacy concerns..."

We traipsed round the entire place, bedrooms, consultation rooms, public rooms, the lot. I found myself thinking I'd shown decent smarts, letting the staff at Blacklight Corporate handle all the details to do with buying a thirteen-room Victorian house in North London and get it remodelled for medical stuff and licensed for treating people with addictions they wanted to get clear of. The place had been updated to the nines, done to a turn; I'd told the Corporate Finance people handling it to spend whatever they needed to get it right. The staffing looked to be brilliant, as well, if Mourdain was anything to go by.

We finished up the tour, finally. I was beginning to feel a bit rough round the edges, probably from standing too long in one spot a few times too often over the past couple of hours. The multiple sclerosis gets beyond dodgy if I do that, and besides, it was time for my afternoon meds. I was ready to get back to our rented digs and have a cuppa and put my boots up. Bree, on the other hand, was looking and sounding energised.

"So, here's the important question." We were back in the front room, with the espresso machine and the leather sofa, saying our goodbyes and shaking hands. Bree and Mourdain were very much of a height, and they were meeting each other's eye. I'm a few inches shorter, myself, but I had his attention. "Are there any openings at the moment, or are you full up?"

"We do have one space open." He coughed, a delicate little clearing of the throat. "We actually have a waiting list, but when we received the call from Blacklight's corporate office about your visit, they asked us the same thing. We've just had a client check out—she finished her course of treatment—and we've held off on booking the slot. I'd rather assumed there was some need on a personal level."

He let the words trail away. Next to me, Bree'd gone stiff as a board. She'd got what he'd been thinking, all right.

"No, it's not either of us." I might not be eye to eye with him physically, but I know how to make people look at me when I need them to, and I was damned if I was having him thinking I'd fallen off the wagon on either booze or heroin after thirty years. "But yeah, a member of the extended band family's had a rough run the past year, and he's ready to walk away from it. Let's be clear, all right? He not only authorised us to discuss this with you, he's the one who asked us to check out the facility to see if he and his wife would be able to make a go of it while he dries out. From what I've seen here today, I'll tell him it's on. So yeah, hold that slot, and tell whoever handles the bookings, or whatever they're called, that sometime over the next couple of days, they'll probably be getting a call from a Mr. or Mrs. Mancuso."

When I'd told Robert Mourdain I had no clue whether Blacklight was ever likely to tour again, I hadn't been dodging the question. I honestly didn't know.

The Book of Days tour was a couple of years in the past, now. Everything about that CD, about the tour we'd done to support it, had been completely out of our experience. We'd put out a nice little double CD and something about it had caught, big and hard. Next thing any of us knew, we'd been two and a half years dragging ourselves to every damned continent that had a venue big enough to hold huge crowds of screaming fans. It was nuts: the CD had swept the Grammy Awards, made us the first act to ever simultaneously hold down the number one, two and three spots on the charts, got us a gig at the Superbowl Halftime Show, and, thanks to his guest stint with Blacklight, had made Tony Mancuso into a multimillionaire with a drinking problem he hadn't had before. It had also turned Bree's hair mostly grey, courtesy of the massive heart attack I'd had the night of the tour closer.

So it was just as well no one in the band or our management seemed to be in any hurry to hit the studio or the road again just yet. The idea of another Blacklight tour hadn't crossed my mind in a good long time. Now that the subject had come up, though, I found myself looking at it. The idea wasn't thrilling me much, for quite a few reasons, not the least of which was the question of how in hell could we possibly top a CD that had not only shattered every existing record, but set a few of its own that weren't likely to get broken in my lifetime.

Also—hard to admit, but no more than the truth—we're not the kids we used to be. My local band at home in San Francisco is called the Fog City Geezers, but Blacklight's the same age.

Christ, I'm the youngest member and I'm up near sixty. Touring's hard work, yeah? Doesn't matter how luxe the hotels are, or whether you've got the band's name painted on the nose of the private jet, or any of that rubbish. If you're on the road, you're working, and working hard.

Still, if I said I wasn't missing working with Blacklight, I'd be lying. I love working with the Geezers, but they're different on every possible level, including the music itself. Blacklight's been making music as a band for over thirty years, and that's a good long time. Hard habit to break, yeah?

Bree and I held hands in the hire car. We weren't talking, just hanging out—that's one of the nice things about being together as long as we have, we don't have to constantly be talking. Bree actually dozed off; no surprise, really, since we were both coming off some serious jet lag.

She got a nice little nap, because it took a while to get back to our South London rental. We could have stayed closer to the Centre, if we'd wanted to: we still own our house at 18, Howard Crescent, just down the road from Muswell Hill, at the edge of Camden. It's quite a nice house, roomy and comfortable and close to the main business we were dealing with in London.

For Bree, though, the house wasn't so much a house as it was a nervous breakdown with built-in cupboards and cream paint. She hasn't got a single memory or association with the place that doesn't leave her shaking. Mac Sharpe, Blacklight's lead singer, had christened 18 Howard Crescent the "Villa Priscilla", and while that had got a laugh out of me, it wasn't really funny, because he'd nailed it; in Bree's head, the house belonged to my first wife, and Bree herself was always going to be miserable if we were anywhere near it. I was damned if I was having her upset, not if I could avoid it.

Besides, we'd both got quite fond of the mews house in South London we'd rented our last two visits. It's not huge or fancy, just a not too chichi little furnished holiday let with three up and three down, plus a functional kitchen and stairs that aren't too steep for me to deal with on a bad MS day. The furniture's dead simple, the garden at the back is tiny but very restful, and the place has got one loo and one bath, split in half. It's a nice location too, walkable to Knightsbridge and Sloane Square, quite close to Mac's place.

Mostly, though, it's what it hasn't got that we both like, and that's baggage. So far, the only personal history we'd had to cope with there had been the fallout from a nasty surprise left over from my first wife's drug habit. Bree'd accidentally jabbed herself with one of Cilla's old needles at the Camden house, during our honeymoon; we'd got the news that she hadn't caught AIDS or Hep C off it during our first stay at the mews house. We've got altogether too many shadows at our shoulders, me and Bree, and a few too many of them have something to do with 18, Howard Crescent.

Sitting in the car on the way back across the river, I slipped my hand free and got one arm round my wife. Bree made a gentle little noise, adjusted herself so that she wouldn't press up against the heartbeat regulator I've got implanted just under my left collarbone—and yeah, she's trained herself so that it's instinct now, and she really can do it in her sleep. She stayed nestled against me, breathing light and even, until the driver pulled up at the mews house.

"Wow." She gave a huge yawn. "God, how rude. Sorry about that. Stupid jetlag. Are we here?"

"Safe and sound. Got your key handy, love? No, not to worry, I've got mine." The driver was holding the door open for Bree; I slid out after her, and tipped the bloke. "Shit, I think the weather's got even worse."

"Well, we're closer to the river." Bree had her coat pulled tight. "I think I want some tea. It's that kind of day."

Once we'd got the door closed behind us and the weather shut out of doors where it belonged, I turned the central heating on and Bree headed for the kitchen. Funny thing—the kitchen here at the mews house was small, serviceable but nothing fancy. Back home in San Francisco, Bree's got a kitchen with top of the line everything: hanging racks of All-Clad cookware, big restaurant range with six burners, a Sub-Zero fridge. No expense spared, yeah? A professional chef's wet dream, basically. But she loves the mews kitchen. She says she can get comfy in there.

While Bree was setting out cups and pulling things out of the fridge for supper prep, I was checking the time. It's eight hours time difference, London to San Francisco. That meant it was nearing ten in the morning back home in California. Tony and Katia would be up by now, and anyway, I'd promised I'd ring as soon as I'd had enough of a look-around at the Centre to put an opinion together. No point putting it off.

Tony picked up on the second ring. "JP?"

"Oi, mate. Yeah, it's me." I watched Bree measure leaves into the tea ball. The poncey little shop in Kensington High Street had sworn this stuff was decaffeinated, and that had damned well better be true. I really didn't fancy being awake half the night, and these days, straight tea has the same effect on me as coffee does, after about three in the afternoon. "We're just back from being given the Grand Tour round the Centre. Nice little place I seem to be paying for."

"You don't like it?" His voice had sharpened up. *Shit.* He must have caught something in my tone.

"No, it's not that. It's just that I've got my own memories of rehab, and there's things I'd rather remember." *Yeah, like a couple of heart attacks and my last three MRIs. Or maybe a root canal or finding a dead body in a washroom.* "Actually, Tony, the place really is brilliant: everything top of the line, and a really competent bloke running the show. It's not a twelve-step thing, not at all. I

12

was really specific about that when I first got this running. This is much more one on one. Seems to be more—I don't know, maybe holistic's the wrong word. I sent you the link, yeah? What's that motto thing they use?"

"'Meditation, conversation, realisation'." Interesting, that Tony seemed to have that one by heart. "I'll be straight with you, JP, I thought that sounded really corny—you know, some New Age woo-woo 'let's all contemplate our belly buttons and groove with our Inner Child' bullshit. But I got into reading what they offer, what their system's all about, and it reads really straight-up. Katia thinks so too." He paused, just long enough for a good long breath; I heard him inhale, coming across eight thousand or so miles and eight hours and the Atlantic Ocean. "So, be upfront with me, man. You think maybe these guys can help me clean up and get my shit back together? Because right now, I've been dry about three weeks but I'm not enough of a dumbass to think I can keep it up without help."

The electric kettle had boiled, and Bree'd got a nice little china pot loaded up and steeping. The kitchen filled up with a gorgeous smell, hints of Earl Grey and whatever else was in this particular blend. Outside, the wind was doing its best to get in round the edges of the window casements. If I owned this place, I'd pay someone a decent bit of dosh and let them do some serious work on the glazing...

"JP?"

"Yeah, still here." Bree was watching me, her chin propped in her hands. The kitchen was warming up around us, filling with the fragrant steam of tea, almost ready to drink. "We talked about this before, Tony. I'm not a doctor. I'm not even close to being any sort of expert. The only cred I've got is the fact that I've been through this myself, and all I can give you is what I think. For what it's worth, yeah, I do think they might be able to help you work it out. They seem to be into the whole body-mind-spirit-psyche deal, that you've got to feed and nourish all of it, because it's all connected. That just strikes me as commonsense, really."

"It's a solo thing, right?" He sounded anxious, suddenly. "I mean, it's not couples counselling or anything? I'd be in there on my own. Katia wouldn't be able to check in and be there with me. Right?"

"That's it, yeah, at least for the main part of the programme. I gather they do couples stuff after you've come through it. Makes sense, you know? Part of that whole 'heal the whole package' deal."

"Okay. Cool."

He sounded edgy, and I suddenly found myself wondering if the anxiety I'd heard was because he was afraid I'd say *no, not solitary, she'd be in there with you.* I could understand that, weirdly enough. Since I'd made myself look back at the month I'd spent in rehab all those years ago, I'd tried imagining how much harder it would have been with my old lady there with me. A thousand times, maybe ten thousand times harder. I couldn't even wrap my head around that idea: going through all that with Cilla, or Bree, sitting there watching? Not enough *oh fuck no* in the world for that one. Of course, it was possible Tony was at the other end of that, that he felt he needed Katia there for strength and support and backup while he was going through it. If that was it, I just hoped it wasn't a deal breaker.

"So do they have an opening right now? Should I call them?"

"They do, as a matter of fact. Soon as I'd had Blacklight Corporate ring them about it, they blocked off a spot. I think they thought it was for me, but not to worry, they know you're probably going to ring. The bloke in charge is called Robert Mourdain. He'll get you set up."

Bree pushed a cup of tea across the table at me, and got back up again, heading for the pile of foodstuff she'd got out for cooking. Not very interesting, only being able to hear my end of the conversation, but she knew the score, and she knew I'd fill her in. I keep as few secrets as possible from Bree, and I wouldn't on this one, anyway. Katia's her best friend, and knowing Katia as well as I do, there was no way in hell she'd be waiting back in San Francisco and flying out at the end of the month, or however long it was going to take. She'd be in London the whole time, and that meant Bree would be there as backup.

Listening to Tony filling Katia in, my phone suddenly beeped. "Tony, look, I need to go, it looks like Mac's on my call waiting. Ring me and let me know what we need to do at this end to get it together for you, all right—oi! Mac? That you? Damn, I've missed the call."

"He'll leave a message." Bree was chopping a bunch of fresh greens from Harrods's Food Halls. The knives here at the mews house hadn't been up to her standard—she's got a full set of Henckels, back in San Francisco—and she'd spent some serious money on decent cutlery. She says good knives are the first thing a cook has to have, to get the job done. "How's that tea? Do you need a refill?"

"No, I'm good. Still a bit too hot to drink—ah, there we go." The message tone chimed. I took a mouthful of tea and punched in my voicemail.

"*(beep) Johnny? Damn! I was rather hoping you'd be home and up for some conversation. Look, something's come up and I need to talk to you—well, to the entire band, actually. I've just got a call from Ali al-Wahid. He's about to open his new Emirates party palace or whatever it is, and he's offered Blacklight an ungodly amount of money to come out there and play the opening.*"

Chapter Two

In over thirty years of playing with Blacklight, I've been to more band meetings than I'd want to try counting.

Sometimes they're mellow, sometimes they're nuts, and sometimes you just turn up when they've told you to turn up, without the first clue as to what the fuck's going on. There's usually food, and generally a good bit of noise, not arguing, just making sure we all get heard. We're not much for rowing—the only one us with a temper worth mentioning is our drummer, Stu Corrigan—but we're rockers and we're not quiet, either.

The "all hands on deck, get your bums round to Fallow House at half past six sharp tonight and be next to a telephone if you're out of the country, and no argy-bargy about it from you lot" message that went out from our manager, Ian Hendry, the morning after the call from Mac wasn't new, either. He'd sounded almost as frazzled during the Book of Days tour, as it kept getting bigger and madder and the numbers kept climbing through the roof. But this, what Mac was proposing—Gordon *Bennett*. Yeah, definitely in the "what the fuck is going on" class.

Because Mac really was proposing it, or at least, that's the way it felt. I'd rung him back straightaway, once I'd got my wits back and stopped making gobbling noises at the phone.

That name he'd dropped, *Ali al-Wahid*, would have tripped every warning wire for anyone who'd been near the Book of Days tour. Ten people that we knew about, and possibly more, had died across a double handful of countries because of the bloke, or rather, because of his twin daughters. Nasty little bits of work those two were, Azra and Paksima al-Wahid. They were all dimples and flutters and coos and demure little headscarves and big soft eyes, and all the time they were getting up to things that managed to nearly shock even Mac. Top of their list seemed to be indulging their taste for rough sex. Not just basic rough, either; it wasn't about the "this is consensual, let's explore the limits" thing. We'd found out later their nasty little games had got people killed. They'd attached themselves to the tour, and while they were hitting the wrong sort of parties, they'd nearly taken Luke Hedley's stepdaughter Suzanne down with them.

The worst of it was, they had enough money to pay for what they wanted, and more than enough to climb into a bullet-proof limo and leave a huge sodding mess behind them for someone else to clean up. You don't run short of funds when your doting papa owns his own damned Emirate. They'd been banned from any access whatsoever to any future shows we did as a band, something that had been made clear to their dad by his old school chum, our lead singer, Malcolm Sharpe.

Of course, I'd told Bree about Mac's message. Me sitting there mumbling to myself, *is he joking, what the fuck, what, he's gone off his head* was unusual enough to get her attention in a hurry. I'd managed one short explanation—*remember the Tahini Twins, yeah well their dad wants to hire Blacklight to play the opening of his nasty little resort*—and that had been enough to get Bree gawking and muttering, right along with me. Like I said, there's no one did the Book of Days tour who wouldn't tense up hearing that particular family name, and that includes my old lady. So yeah, I'd rung Mac back straight away.

"Johnny, oh good, you're there."

"Yeah, I'm here. Mac, what the fuck, mate?"

"Oh, wait for it. You haven't heard anything yet, believe me." Odd thing—he didn't sound as if he'd suddenly gone off his head or anything. I mean, the whole tone of that voicemail, he'd sounded as if he actually wanted the band to do the show. And if he did, he'd have to have lost his mind. But he just sounded really focused and energised. "Let's keep it brief, all right? You're the first person to ring me back about this, and I expect everyone's pulling themselves off the floor right about now. My phone's probably going to light up like the doorway over a Vegas strip brothel, any minute."

"Okay." I settled myself back at the table. Bree'd abandoned any attempt at dinner prep for the moment; she'd slid into a chair opposite me, still looking stunned. "Mac, hang on, I'm putting this on the speakers. Bree's right here with me and I'm not having this conversation without her hearing it."

"Of course not. I wouldn't expect you to." He sounded amused. "I've got it on speaker at my end as well—Domitra's been sitting here asking if I know any good quiet hotels where I can go draw on the walls with crayons, since I've obviously left Victoria Station without the train. Ready? Good—Bree, angel, I'm probably taking you away from supper, but this won't take long. Now. Let's save some time, because I suspect that Ian's going to flip out and demand a full band meeting tomorrow anyway, and we can go over all the details then. Here's the abridged ver-

sion: Ali al-Wahid rang me—not Blacklight Corporate, me personally—and asked if Blacklight would consider playing two
shows, back to back, to celebrate the opening of Give-Me-Your-
Dosh-You-Stupid-Punter Island, or whatever he's christened this
masterpiece of his."

"Bloody hell!" I remembered thinking, when we'd confronted
al-Wahid, that he had all the arrogance that comes with money
and power, but this was a mindfuck even by those standards. The
bloke had the bollocks of a tyrannosaurus rex, to pull a stunt like
this. "Mac, for Christ's sake, please tell me you told him to fuck
off, all right?"

"I didn't. I was laughing too hard." Mac really did sound
amused, but there was an edge to it. It suddenly occurred to me
that he was just as pissed off by all that arrogance as I was. Nice,
considering that Mac comes from money and prestige himself.
"When I got my breath back, I told him that, in the first place,
any offer of that kind should be made to our management and
not to me directly, and that I didn't much fancy the Old School
Tie rubbish. That in the second place, Blacklight was still on hia-
tus anyway, working on personal projects at the moment, and
that we had no plans to change that status in the immediate future. And that oh, by the way, there's a third place and it's really
the major consideration here, which is that the last time we had
anything to do with him and his cultural stuff, we'd ended up
with a drinks cooler full of severed hands from his little brats'
fundamentalist bodyguards."

Across the table, Bree suddenly shuddered. I could see her remembering that night; it was right there in her face, that memory. I remembered that night myself, much too clearly: the roar
and press of the crowd at Raymond Jones Stadium in Tampa as
we'd done our two songs at the Superbowl Halftime Show. The
plane back to the hotel in Miami. Everyone's phone suddenly
lighting up with an anonymous link to the online version of Al-

Jazeera's English edition, about the mutilated bodies of two men having been found outside a nightclub in the Emirate of Manaar, with their hands missing, execution style. And then, getting back to the hotel, what we'd found waiting...

"He offered us five million pounds." Mac didn't sound quite as amused anymore. "I told him he might try cleaning his ears or maybe hiring some bodyguards to do it for him, assuming he had any left with hands still attached, because he would have to make that offer through our management, and by the way, I had no desire to play for someone who'd damaged my friends or the people I consider my family. Then I ended the conversation."

"Mac?" Bree was very pale, but she was smiling. "Just in case no one's told you this recently, you rock."

"Bree, angel, what a nice thing to say." Was that a snort I'd heard in the background? Right, Domitra Calley was there with him, his own bodyguard. She'd not only be snorting, she'd be rolling her eyes. "He rang back, about fifteen seconds later. Not a man who grasps being told to fuck off very easily, is Almanzor, but he's not completely stupid. He knows damned well the damage his misbegotten twins did, not to mention their damned bodyguards, and he's smart enough to have sussed out that it's Luke he'd primarily need to convince."

"Shit. Yeah, you're spot on about that. He's bloody arrogant, but he's not dim, not at all." I had an uneasy feeling in the pit of my stomach, suddenly. "Mac, you wanted to keep it brief. What's the upshot?"

"He doubled the price." Nice and crisp. "Ten million pounds for two nights work, all expenses covered of course, the lot. I said something quite rude and told him I was ringing off again, and then he made a very interesting offer to go along with the ten million quid. And unfortunately, it's not an offer I get to refuse out of hand, because it doesn't affect me. It affects Luke. And in any case, I've got an idea that's been moving round in my head for awhile now, and this actually—damn, and right on schedule, three incoming calls, oh lovely, it's Luke, Stu and Ian, bang bang bang. Johnny, I've got to go. Look for either a tight-arsed little message from Ian or else nothing at all, depending on how this goes. Cheers, bye."

He clicked off. Bree and I sat there, staring at each other. She was ash-pale, her hands locked together, her shoulders hunched hard. I reached across and covered her hands with mine.

"Bree, look." Her hands were chilly again. *Shit.* "I honestly do know how you feel. I promise, I do. I don't want to get within two time zones of Ali al-Wahid or his little opening night rave-up. But I tell you what, there's no point worrying about this one, not until we know more about it. Besides, I can always dig my heels in and tell them no, you know? How's your appetite doing, love? What were you thinking for dinner…?"

Mac had been right about the tight-arsed message from Ian, and the next evening, Bree and I headed over to Fallow House. Both of us were cold and both of us were hungry, since we hadn't really eaten after an early lunch. I hoped I'd been right when I told her not to worry about food, that the staff at Fallow House always made sure there was a meal brought in.

"Wow, what a nice house." Bree, wrapped up in her favourite cashmere coat, was standing on the pavement, staring up at Fallow while I paid the driver. "Georgian? Victorian? It looks so—I don't know, I guess festive is the word I want. All shiny and lit up. It's kind of Christmas tree-ish."

She was right. Heading up the front stairs together, I realised something: all the years we'd owned the place, I'd never done a night meeting there before. It had always been afternoon affairs, somewhere between one at the earliest and five at the latest. Ian was scrupulous about that, never expecting the band to give up their lie-ins every morning, and not wanting to drag us out of evening sessions or gigs or commitments. This meeting was a first.

21

There was a nice spread set out on the long mantel in what had once been some 19th century industrialist's posh dining room. I got myself a plate, made sure Bree was happy with the hot soup she was loading up on, and found us a couple of chairs. Half the band was already there, and while it was nice seeing Cal Wilson and Stu Corrigan, I was keeping my eyes open for the other half. I had the feeling that, whatever was about to go down, the beat wasn't getting set by the rhythm section this time. This whole thing, whatever it was, was centred on Mac and Luke.

Ian had already got Carla Fanucci, Blacklight's US Ops and PR manager, on the phone in LA. He was looking twitchy and cross though, and while I was listening for more arrivals, I got him to sit and talk for a moment. Turned out I'd been right about him being edgy: neither Patrick Ormand nor Tony had checked in, or responded to the meeting message. I had no clue what might be up with Patrick, but Tony was another story.

"Well—Tony might be travelling, Ian. He might even be in London by now, in fact."

"Tony's coming here?" Ian raised his brows at me. "What, that thing with your recovery centre, that worked out for him, then? Glad to hear that."

Right then, I gave up trying to be delicate about Tony's situation. If the band was thinking about asking him to do anything, we were all going to need to know what was happening. That's how Blacklight works. "Yeah," I told Ian. "That's it. Now I think about it, he's probably not here yet, because Katia hasn't rung Bree. Thing is, Ian, I'm damned if I see why it would matter. From what I heard last night, talking to Mac, this thing with Ali al-Wahid is all rubbish anyway. The bloke fucked us over. Shit, we lost family because of him. We don't need the money. Why would anyone even be considering playing a show for this self-entitled pillock?"

"I don't know, JP." There it was, the core of why his knickers

22

were in such a twist: lack of information. Ian's entire gig is based on him being not only on top of every detail of the situation in question, but having at least a few strands of things yet to come under control. He doesn't like not knowing things. "All I know is that Mac is considering it, and so is Luke. Mac says he'll tell us everything when—right, they're here. Brilliant. Let's get this started."

As soon as the band's two founders walked in, I knew something major was up. Mac had brought Dom with him—he rarely leaves home without his bodyguard—but Luke was alone, and that was a dead giveaway as to just how iffy this was likely to be. He rarely leaves Karen behind, and the idea that he'd left her out of this meeting in particular brought it home, good and hard: her daughter had got into some serious shit because of Ali al-Wahid. So something was up, it was tricky, and it was big.

"Hey." Domitra nodded at us, and made for the food. She's a carb-loader, mostly; she says she needs a lot of carbohydrates to keep her fighting weight up. You'd have thought raw meat would be more her style, but no, she likes rice and quinoa and things like that. "Good, they've got hot food. Shitty weather out there. You maybe going to try to talk some sense into my boss? Because I can't get anywhere and he's pissing me off."

"Kind of tricky, since I don't know what he's going to say." Bree'd finished her soup. She was watching Mac. Luke was right behind him, and I'll tell you what, I'm closer to Luke than I am to most people, but I had no clue what he was thinking or feeling just then. He was completely on guard.

"Thank you, Bree. Rather nice, not being screamed at or called a lunatic. It's the first time today—well, almost the first time." Mac had everyone's attention. He's good at that, but no surprise; it's his job. "Look, let's get this out and at least into everyone's mental circuitry, all right? You all know that Ali al-Wahid rang and offered Blacklight ten million pounds to play two nights to open

23

his sheikh casino, or whatever it is. I told him to fuck right on along, and he came back with an addition to the ten million. He's offering matching funds—ten million quid, not exactly pocket change—to the Foundation for Research into Diabetes."

Oh, bloody hell.

That explained why Mac had felt this one was over to Luke to decide. It also explained why he'd left Karen at home. Luke's second wife has diabetes, and not Bree's kind, either. Bree's got type 2. She takes pills and watches her diet; her pancreas is impaired. But it's not dead, and Karen's is. Karen's a type 1 diabetic, no natural insulin produced at all. She's always hooked up to her pump, having her insulin and blood glucose levels regulated by this little portable machine she has to stay attached to. And Type 1 comes with some really scary side issues, like an increased risk of things like liver and pancreatic cancer. Bree's is bad enough, but it's nowhere near as bad as Karen's.

The Foundation was the charity Luke had founded to raise awareness and money for research, specifically into Type 1. And he'd just been offered ten million quid as a donation, with the only strings attached apparently being that the entire band showed up and played the opening party.

I caught Bree's eye. We had one of those moments of marital synchronicity, both of us thinking the same thing and knowing it: *no wonder Luke didn't bring Karen. It would have made it impossible for anyone to say no...*

"There's a bit more." Mac wasn't done yet, and Luke wasn't interrupting, either. "I've had an idea in my head, just the seed of one really, for a few months now. I didn't want to bring it up while Johnny was launching the Geezers' first CD, and of course not while he was touring the band. But now that we're all here, and all off the road, here's the thing: am I the only one who thinks we really ought to play a few big free shows, as a thank-you to the Blacklight fan base? Because let's face it, we're not

24

getting any younger. I've got some new material and I quite like it, but it would be well beyond miraculous for it to do something that hit the way Book of Days did. I've got no desire at all to do another major tour at this point, but maybe something like three or four free festival dates, one here, one somewhere on the continent, and one in North America—opening acts, the whole thing. Anyone?"

"I like it." That was Cal, and when I turned his way, I saw Stu nodding as well. "So long as it was planned out well in advance, and so long as we all agreed it would be just a few dates. I don't want a major tour either, but yeah, I've been thinking about the fan base recently. The website's getting more questions about that from the fans every day, I'm told."

"I'm good with it, as well." I'd got hold of Bree's hand. "No major tour for me either. Not saying that's forever, but for now, no tours. Still, a kind of private prezzie to the fans? Fuck yeah, I like that. What I don't see, though, is what this has to do with playing for your old mate from university. Care to clue us in, Mac?"

He grinned suddenly. It was a damned good thing none of the fans were there to see that grin, especially the female fans. It was as dark and as cheeky as it gets. Behind him, Luke had a grin on that was a good deal darker. Whatever Mac had in mind, Luke already knew all about it, and approved.

"Clever lad, Johnny. I've costed out three weekend-long festival dates, three specific sites in mind. With full outdoor rig, permits, the usual facilities and then some, paying our people and everything else, it works out to right around nine million pounds." He must have seen the light going on for the rest of us, because the grin got even cheekier. "I say let's tell Ali we'll do it for twelve million, one show only. Plus, he makes that ten million gift to Luke's foundation, and agrees to put another two million into the Kinkaid Recovery Centre, to make it an even twelve million in matching funds. He gets to make himself feel better about what his little twin hell spawn did, we get to do something good for the fans, and everybody wins. I say let's get him to pay for the whole damned thing."

"So this idea of Mac's—do you really want to do it?"

"I'd rather do you, actually."

"Smartass." She was practically purring. "But seriously, John…"

"Yeah, I know, I just did. Give me a few minutes, maybe we can try for an encore." I had both arms draped over my wife, and her naked back up against me. I planted a lazy kiss on the nape of her neck, and tasted salt. "You taste like a potato crisp. You talking about this little do in Arabia, Bree?"

It was late, well past one in the morning. The BBC weather service had said there was a hard freeze likely, and maybe some snow as well. That was easy to believe; outside the bedroom window, the moon had a sort of icy nimbus round it. It looked colder than usual, somehow. There were a few stars out, and they looked like frost points out there in the distance.

"An encore sounds good, but you might have to wake me up first, unless you've got some secret necrophilia thing I don't know about. I'm as limp as overcooked vermicelli." She wasn't joking; she was thoroughly relaxed. "No, not the thing in Manaar. I know you're not thrilled at the idea of doing that. I kind of got the impression that no one was, except Mac. Would it really be that hard to turn down the money?"

"Not for me, it wouldn't." Between the blast-furnace heat the small of her back was giving off and the duvet we were snuggled under, I was getting rather drowsy myself. Of course, some of that was pure physics: there'd been a very intense half-hour of slap and tickle in there, as well. "I mean, right, it's a lot of money. But if you want the truth, I think the idea of making al-Wahid pay

26

through his posh self-entitled nose for the privilege is what's turning Mac on. If you weren't talking about the Manaar deal, what were—oh, right, that whole thing about doing a few festival dates for the fan base. That what you meant, love?"

"Mmmm. Yep." She rolled over, facing me. "I hate to say it, but when Mac was talking about it, it sounded like something most of you wouldn't touch with a barge pole. I mean, I guess it's possible that I'm picturing something that doesn't have any resemblance to what Mac's suggesting…" Her voice trailed off; I'd got one hand on a sensitive bit of her, and tweaked lightly. I know where her buttons are, and right then, I was more in a mood to take her places than to talk. "Wow. Um. Okay, maybe I'm not as limp as overcooked vermicelli…"

"Good job," I told her, and pinned her on her back. "As it happens, neither am I. Here we go…"

Fifteen minutes, and that turned out to be quite a nice little encore. You'd think that with me being sixty, we'd be less intense about this part of being married, but not at all. I think I get a bigger rush from feeling her holding on to me like a drowning woman than I did when she was twenty. Not the way most romance novelists and whatnot would have it, but there you go. We've never been typical, me and Bree.

"Hello, darling." I bit her ear, a tiny little nip. Nice thing about being belly to belly horizontally instead of vertically is that the height difference, her being two inches taller than I am, doesn't matter. Lying with her under me, I can reach her earlobe just fine, and I did. She wriggled a bit, but this time, she really had gone pretty limp. Good. That's part of my job, getting her there. "So what were you seeing? Woodstock or the Us Festival or Glastonbury?"

"What was I—oh, right, Mac's thing. I forgot." Even in the darkness, I could see her eyes had gone cloudy, with sleep or pleasure, or maybe both. "Sort of, I guess. Just a lot of mud, and dirty port-a-potties, and what happens if it rains? I mean, the fans probably wouldn't mind too much, or at least they'd put up with it for a chance to see a free Blacklight show. But, well, you'd mind. Wouldn't you?"

I grinned down at her. "Fuck yes. What, you think I'm sleeping out with the mice and the bunnies in an unplanted alfalfa field somewhere in Belgium? At my age? Not a chance. We'd have a good hotel booked and helicopters to take us there—what, Bree?" She'd twitched a bit, and made a noise. It wasn't a particularly happy noise, either.

"That's nice for us. But what about the fans?" Suddenly I wasn't quite so relaxed anymore, myself. I knew the tone in her voice: it was Bree's Conscience, that fierce crusading thing she gets. "Isn't the whole point supposed to be that you guys would be doing this for them? I know a lot of the fan base is younger, especially after *Book of Days*, but a lot of them are our age, John. I'm only just about to turn fifty and the idea of sleeping in the middle of a muddy field for the weekend—oh hell no. Really not. How would people in their sixties cope with that? And is it fair to even ask them to do it?"

"Good point." I rolled off her. The tickybox in my chest, the weird little device that keeps the electrical impulses to my heart where they're supposed to be and keeps me out of a coffin for the time being, ramped up, settled, and then eased off. "That, well, I couldn't tell you, love. The logistics aren't handled by the band—never have been. That's management's call. We get input, of course we do, but we're not in on the details, how things like the facilities get handled."

She was quiet. There wasn't much light in the room, but I didn't need it. I'd know she was worrying, even with a blindfold on. Time to ease that up; otherwise, she'd sleep badly and I wasn't having that, not over something like this.

"No point in worrying about that, Bree, not yet, anyway. Right

28

now, it's just a pretty idea that's being looked at. And have a little trust in the band's brain trust, okay? They've never let the fans down before, and I don't see Ian or Carla or David Walters doing that now, you know?"

"True." She sighed, nice and easy. Good, that was tension on its way out. "Damn, I'm sleepy. It looks really cold out there—there's something about this weather that just knocks me sideways. It makes me want to sleep and sleep and sleep." She leaned forward and kissed the back of my shoulder. "'night, baby."

Yeah, well, maybe she was sleepy. Unfortunately, that question she'd put up, about being fair to the fans, had got into my head, and it wasn't giving an inch. Mulling it around in my head, ways to throw a huge free outdoor festival party for a couple of million people and have them remember the music instead of the smelly chemical toilets and the mud, cost me a good hour's worth of kip. That happens quite often at our house. Bree's conscience kicks in, she gets fierce, I get soothing or practical, she agrees with me and passes out, and I'm the one left lying awake, listening to the gears in my head churning on about whatever she threw out there before she went off to share a kitchen with Julia Child in Paris in the 1960s, or whatever she was dreaming about.

She let me sleep in next morning, which was just as well. The multiple sclerosis doesn't like temperature extremes, or humidity, either. Even if the weather isn't causing a full-on exacerbation or relapse, it makes its presence felt: the ataxia gets worse, for one thing, the shakes in my legs and hands getting much more pronounced. Things that are normally reasonably easy to cope with, all the small background pains and tingles, get sharper. They're more there, somehow.

And of course, there are times when I get caught in a combination of things—time zone changes, weather, exhaustion—when the disease says *right, you fucking clot, you've bummed this up completely and now you get to be useless and miserable until I say*

29

otherwise, so grit your teeth because I'm going to get on with it. So when I did wake up, just after ten next morning, I probably shouldn't have been surprised when the first tentative stretch of my right leg and foot left me swearing under my breath and reaching for my right calf. The entire leg had reacted to the stretch by pretending it had been doused in petrol and hit with the business end of a blowtorch. That's what it felt like, anyway.

I lay there for a few minutes, gritting my teeth, waiting for things to settle down enough for me to suss out where the rest of the bad bits were likely to be. It didn't work, that strategy—the whole body seemed to be in an uproar. And Bree'd gone down-stairs, probably a good hour before.

Shit. I needed my meds, and an extra hit of painkiller probably wasn't a bad idea, either. I also needed a piss, and right now, I wasn't sure my legs were getting me across the room into the split loo. Right. Call her, let her know...

"Bree?"

Yeah, well, that was a mistake. My jaw had locked up on the left side, trigeminal neuralgia, one of my least favourite side ef-fects of this bloody disease. I could barely talk, and I wasn't trust-ing my legs, either. The only thing that seemed to be working was my damned bladder.

Ring her, Johnny. She's got her cell with her, she always does. Ring her. Yours is right there.

I managed to fumble the cell off the table and into both hands without dropping it. The noise my bladder was making was put-ting pictures into my head, of things like tsunamis and hurricane storm surges and very large dams. I got the phone flipped open and spared a moment of gratitude for speed dial. All I had to do was punch in the number 1...

"(beep) This is Bree Kinkaid, I'm sorry but I'm unavailable at the moment, please leave a name and number and a brief message at the tone, and I'll get back to you as soon as I possibly can —"

It was almost funny, you know? She was right downstairs, probably in the kitchen, and probably on the phone with someone else. And that meant I was going to have to get across the room and into the loo somehow, because the bladder had run out of patience, or room, or both.

I was halfway between the bed and the door when I heard her coming upstairs, and heading for me. The fates had decided to cut me a break, apparently, and thank Christ for it.

"John? Are you awake? I just got a call—oh shit, shit, shit, baby I'm sorry, why didn't you call me!"

"Did." My jaw was locked up tight, but she was here, and helping me into the loo, and getting my meds together. I know she couldn't possibly have done all that without ever letting go of me—she's not Superwoman, not really—but it felt as if that's what she'd done. I sat, and winced; the toilet seat was chilly. "Voicemail."

"I was on the phone. Katia called." She handed me a small pharmacy's worth of pills and a cup of water. "Here, take these while you're sitting. I'll help you back to bed when you're done. Okay? Do you think you could handle some breakfast? Maybe something soft, or a cup of tea…?"

We got me back to bed, finally. The meds were helping a lot faster than they usually seem to work, and I got a hand out just as Bree looked to be getting up, and rested it on her arm.

"You said—Katia? Tony here?" The words came out almost slurred. Christ, I sounded like a fucking stroke victim, but inside my head, the brain was going rapid-fire: *need to let Tony know about al-Wahid's offer, no not yet, need to check with the rest of the band first and see if they want to ask him, he's not really a member of Blacklight but for this gig he should play, bloody hell Johnny, you're not asking anyone anything until this little lot eases up.*

"They're both here. Katia said their plane got in last night. Tony hasn't checked himself into the Recovery Centre, though, not yet." She took a long breath. "He says he wants to talk to you about it before he does that. I don't really know what's going on—Katia was being sort of careful, and cagey. You know the way she gets, when she's talking about Tony and doesn't want him to know it?"

"Yeah." I'd nearly nodded, but stopped myself in time. When the trigeminal thing hits, nodding leaves me feeling like Marie Antoinette about a nanosecond after the executioner let go of the lever. "And?"

"I'm not really sure. From something Katia said, Tony actually went over there this morning and spoke to the director, the guy we met, Robert Mourdain. And I don't know what's going on, John, but from what I got from Katia, there's some kind of complication, and Tony says he isn't checking in until he talks to you first."

Chapter Three

During the past thirty years, we've had Tony and Katia over to dinner more times than I can count. This time, though, we had a couple of firsts: Bree'd never cooked for them in London before, and usually, when the MS is giving me grief, she keeps people out of the house as if she were that pissy three-headed dog thing, the one that guards the gates of Hell. That night, though, we broke the usual rules, and a couple more besides.

Middle of the afternoon, after Bree'd rung Katia back and got them to come over for a meal, we'd done another first: I'd asked Bree to please talk to Ian for me, and get some details about what was being discussed by the band and our management. Bree spent most of her life shying away from the working end of my life, and even now, married and settled and nothing to keep her from it, she's still not comfortable with it. I hated having to ask the favour, but I hadn't got a choice: I needed the information before I talked to Tony about anything at all, and talking to Tony or anyone else meant giving the neuralgia a shot at dying down before Tony and Katia got here.

Bree agreed to do it, without any sort of fuss. She didn't even ask me why. It was right out of character for her, but she knew what was needed, and why I was asking her to do it. She just nodded, and reached for my phone. She doesn't keep band management numbers programmed into her own cell.

It was a short conversation, without one wasted word. She got Ian on the line, explained what was happening with the MS and why I wasn't ringing myself, and then just got on with it.

"Ian, look. John's worried. Tony and Katia are coming over here later, to talk with John about Tony checking into rehab." She had her eyes fixed on my face. I nodded, a tiny little movement of my head, pushing the pain away, not letting her see it: *good, yeah, keep going love, you're doing great.* "Hold on a second, I'm putting the speaker on, so that John can listen in. The main thing is, is there anything we ought to know about the show in Manaar?"

"You mean, about whether there's been any decisions made?" Ian sounded gruff and harassed, but he usually does. "Or about whether we'd ask Tony to come play the show if it does go down? Oi, JP, hope you feel better soon."

"Both." Like I said, Bree wasn't wasting words.

"Nothing's decided." Ian wasn't wasting words, either, apparently. "I'd have rung JP or emailed him—we'd need his yea or nay. That's how Blacklight works. I got the formal proposal this morning. I can tell you Mac and Luke are both up for doing it as a one-off, making it contingent on matching donations from al-Wahid to JP and Luke's non-profits. One thing I can say definitely is that, if it does go down, we'd be asking Tony. The proposal's very clear that the personnel who played the Book of Days tour is the lineup wanted. Anything else?"

Bree looked me. I mouthed one word at her: *when?*

"Ian? John wants to know when that show would be happening, if it does go down. And is it just one show? Because Mac said two, originally."

"One show, New Year's Eve. Manaar al-Wahid opens New Year's Day. And no, don't ask me if he named his little boogie palace after himself—Mac says his name means 'lighthouse' in Arabic."

I blinked at Bree. The thought must have been pretty clear in my face; I didn't care a rat's arse about what the place was called, it was the timing that was worrying me. New Year's was just about seven weeks away, and the full course at the Recovery Centre, including the couples counselling, ran about five. And we hadn't even officially decided to do it yet...

"Okay. Ian, John's gesturing at me, and I'm guessing that means he's thinking the same thing I am, that things are going to get shaved really close." Her voice went crisp, suddenly. "And that means he'll stress over it, which makes the MS worse, which makes everyone's life harder. So let's save some time."

I was watching her. I had no clue, honestly, what was going on in her head, or what she was going to say next.

"John?" She'd turned to face me, getting us eye to eye. "I don't want to push, but can you give Ian a thumbs up or thumbs down right now? If the rest of the band says yes, are you up for doing the show, without or without the insane time scheduling? And after that, I need to get off the phone and go get some groceries. I can't cook dinner with nothing in the house."

"Yes." Bless those painkillers, they're good stuff. I could almost talk without wincing. Not much volume in there, and not a lot of breath, but it was easing up. Ian and Bree could both hear me, and that's what mattered just then. "Thumbs up."

"Good. I'll let the rest of the band know." He paused, just barely, but enough for us both to notice. Same old Ian, gruff and

35

to the point. "Thanks, Bree. Saves us all a lot of time and work, you ringing me. Feel better, JP."

He rang off. Bree and I were left looking at each other. Neither of us was saying anything, not yet.

New Year's Eve. That meant seven weeks for the band to agree to do it at all, sign contracts, get our crew together, agree on a set list, get into rehearsals. Seven weeks for Ronan, our sound designer, to get out to the site, scope it top to bottom. Seven weeks to get a set designed, get the gear over there, get the fucking thing built.

And for five of those weeks, it looked as if Tony wasn't going to be available for anything at all, not even to approve or disapprove of things. That was part of the deal. Mourdain had made it clear: the first few weeks of the process, Tony stayed in and the outside world stayed out. No exceptions, not even for Katia, and if Katia was excluded, so was the band.

Bree kept dinner, and the shopping for it, really simple that night: she rang for a hire car, had the driver wait while she hit the Food Halls at Harrods, and came straight back again. By the time she came up to get me at a quarter of six, the relapse had eased enough for me to get up on my own and even get a quick hot shower. I'd dried off and got dressed, and was actually putting my shoes on when she opened the bedroom door to tell me Katia'd rung to say that she and Tony were planning on getting here right round a quarter past six.

The smell of supper cooking hit me full-on as I got to the head of the stair. I've spent a lot of nights in a house that smells like Bree's cookery, but that smell, that night, stopped me in my tracks.

"John?" She'd stopped as well, right behind me, sounding worried. "Are you okay? What's the matter?"

"No, I'm fine." I closed my eyes and inhaled, savouring it, wondering why the smell of something in the oven should be

36

having this effect on me, and having it this strongly. I could talk now, not much pain in there at all. "It's just something about whatever you've got in the oven, that's all. I was about ten years old for a couple of seconds, there. Brought me straight back to my mum's kitchen, Christmas or Boxing Day dinner, I think. What are we having, Bree?"

"Best Scotch topside roast. Roasted potatoes and Yorkshire pudding. Runner beans. I didn't make the puddings from scratch—no time. They'd better be decent or I swear, I'll take them back to Harrods and throw them at the cashier."

"They'll be brilliant, not to worry."

I started downstairs. Funny thing, how what you smell and where you smell it can play off each other. Bree'd probably done a hundred roasts in the big Viking at home in San Francisco in her day, maybe more. A roast smells like a roast, you know? Somehow, though, none of them had taken me this way, dragging me back fifty years to our tidy little house in South London, me knowing there'd be roast beef for supper, listening to the sizzle of my mum's Yorkshire puds in the hot fat, smelling the meat and the potatoes, wondering if I could hide the soggy boiled runner beans under something without letting on I hadn't eaten them, and still get a sweet for afters.

We didn't have a lot of money, back when I was a kid. My dad was a sign maker for a local firm, non-union, nice people but they couldn't pay him much. Me being an only child, after my baby brother died, was probably the only thing that kept decent food on the table night after night, at least until I was fifteen and started playing sessions, with my dad signing official approval for me to do it.

Not a big family, just the three of us, and not a lot of money for fancy touches. A roast in the oven, when I was a kid, meant either a birthday or a holiday. It was a treat, something special, something to be remembered.

Maybe you have to be where you first started, physically that is, for the smell to hit that hard. Either that, or there's some difference in the way the meat smells on either side of the pond. Whatever—I don't know. But I was still feeling warm and mellow when Tony and Katia arrived, a few minutes early.

Bree was paying attention to the runner beans, tossing them in a pan with a steamer piece in it, to make sure they stayed crisp and cooked evenly. She's never served up soggy veg in her life. I headed down the hall to let the Mancusos in. The mews house hasn't got anything in the way of an overhang, so whatever the weather was doing, it was doing it all over them until someone let them come indoors, out of the night.

A cold blast of wind hit me as I got one hip against the door, and it damned near pushed the pair of them inside. I got a quick hug from Tony, which surprised me. We're not touchy sorts, either of us.

"Oi mate, you're looking bedraggled. Not exactly the best time of year for London weather."

"Yeah, I noticed." He slid out of his topcoat, and watched me dig out a hanger for it. Katia had already murmured a fast hello, and headed down the hall towards the kitchen. Even not having been here before, she knows that, when the house smells like food, just follow the smell if you want to find Bree. "Man, last time I was someplace this cold, it was back in Moscow, for Book of Days. Fucking icebox out there, except iceboxes don't come with wind. You stay inside all day? Smart move, JP."

"Not much choice, really. Most of the day, I was down with the MS." I lifted an eyebrow at him, and lowered my voice. "Tony, anything you want to talk about privately, just you and me? Because now's the time to do it."

He met my eye, and I felt myself relax. That look was a question answered, one I hadn't fancied asking myself. Because yeah, he really did look bedraggled, but not the way he'd looked when he'd walked into our suite at the Beverly Wilshire earlier in the year, the wrong side of a two-day drunk, reeking of stale tequila, on his own because Katia'd broken under the strain and walked out. He was tired, a bit puffy, but his eyes were clear. This wasn't stale-drunk, it was just jetlag and stress, and yeah, believe me, I know the difference.

"No," he told me. "Everything I need to talk to you about, I've already talked over with Katia. And if Katia gets to hear it and you get to hear it, so does Bree."

I waited. Down the hall, I heard the murmur of the women's voices, and the funny little *clack* the oven door gives, if you let it bounce on its springs. Bree must have taken supper out of the oven, and was letting it settle, or rest, or whatever it's called. If this was our London house, properly ours and not just a rental, we'd be replacing that oven with a decent one...

"Katia's been amazing." The words came out in a rush, and I jerked my head round towards him. "She's been right there, no judgements, no bullshit. She's been nagging my ass when it needed nagging and letting me cry all over her when it got too rough. She's been a rock. What the fuck, JP, how long has she been doing this, and how come I never noticed before? What are you laughing at?"

"Nothing. Just a bit of *deja vu*, that's all. If you're good to go, let's have some supper. There's something I need to talk to you about—band business."

Supper tasted as good as it smelled. We ploughed through the meat, the potatoes, all of it—no bread, not that night, because we had the Yorkshire puds, and really, that's what they are, a kind of biscuit cooked in drippings. The roast was done to a turn, nice and tender, which meant I could actually chew it; after an MS relapse, it's a toss-up. Everyone ate quite a lot, including Tony. He had a third helping, in fact. That was more confirmation, if I'd needed it, that he was still dry.

"Oh yum." Katia was trying not to belch. "Was that Ye Olde Roast Beef of Olde England? Because if it is, then I don't get all those clichés about how bad English food is. *So* good. Bree, is there a dishwasher? Do you need help cleaning up?"

"No, that's okay." Bree'd started loading dishes into the sink. "I'll let them soak until later. I want to get you guys back to your hotel early—you said you were still jetlagged."

"Seriously." Tony yawned suddenly. "Wow, I'm full. Killer dinner. Thanks, Bree. JP, you said you had band business you wanted to talk to me about? Which band? The Fog City Geezers?"

"No. Blacklight business."

I caught them up on the story, all the details right through Bree's call to Ian. Bree was setting out teacups and filling the kettle. "…and yeah, if this is happening, you'll be asked to come play it. I don't know how a share would work out, since Mac's looking to take most of the pile and use it to throw a few parties for our fan base, but I'm sure something could be worked out. That's if you wanted to come play, of course. And that's if it even happens."

"I'm not worried about the money." His brows were bunched. "I'm just—did you say New Year's?"

"Yeah, I did, and yeah, that could make the timing tricky. Even assuming you got started at the Centre tomorrow, it would be shaving things right down to the bone for time. But first things first: do you want to do it, if it goes down?"

He grinned. "Fuck yes. Are you nuts? I wouldn't miss it. And boy oh boy, how devious is Mac?" The grin faded. "But I haven't signed in to the Centre yet. There's—there might be an issue. Look, JP, I know you put a lot of money into this thing, but I need to ask you: Can you absolutely vouch for their discretion? Are you positive, I mean really positive, about the privacy factor?"

Bree had set cups out, and poured boiling water into her favourite pot. The women had gone quiet, listening. Whatever had got Tony asking me that question, of any question he could have put to me, Katia knew all about it.

"I can't vouch for that absolutely, Tony, can I? I'm not God, or something. I can tell you privacy's a high priority there, one of their highest, that they emphasise it, that it was something I insisted on when it was being set up and when people were being hired. The entire thing would fall down without that. And Mourdain gets it, about the celebrity thing. Why?"

"I went over there today." He was stirring his tea, choosing his words, being very careful. "I met the director. Nice guy, scary smart, all the right stuff, just like you described him. He showed me around the place, the rooms, the gym, everything, even the garden."

He stopped. Bree and I were both watching him. Katia wasn't—she was watching me, weirdly enough.

"There was someone out in the garden." He took a mouthful of tea. "Katia'd gone to use the bathroom, it was just me and Mourdain. Mourdain got me back inside in a hurry—I guess they weren't expecting anyone in their right mind to be out in that weather, freezing their ass off. Obviously, it was one of their clients, someone who's resident at the moment. But it was too late. We'd seen each other."

"Wow." I shook my head. Inside, I was swearing. I was going to have a few pointed words for the director about that one. "Sorry about that, mate, but I don't see how Mourdain could have helped that. You afraid that whoever it was recognised you?"

"I know damned well he did." Tony took a breath. "We recognised each other. You'd have recognised him too."

It was probably just as well that, even with a lot of my head concentrated on Tony's situation, I'd already sorted out and accepted that Blacklight was going to play the Manaar show. Considering how tight the timing was, it wasn't as if I had a lot of room to dither about it.

If it had just been a question of getting a show together, seven weeks would have been no problem at all. Blacklight's got one of the best crews on earth, and the most stellar sound and stage design teams you could hope to find, in Ronan Greene and Nial Laybourne. We've done short-notice gigs before, quite a few of them. Mac's always been big on fundraisers, and those tend to be last-minute affairs. That makes sense, since it's usually some sort of emergency prompting the need for them in the first place. Hell, I'd met Bree for the first time at a hurricane relief benefit in San Francisco that had been pulled together perfectly in about three days. And more recently, just a few years ago, Ronan and Nial had got the band onstage for a free show at Frejus, in the South of France, in less than a week.

But this was a different situation entirely, in a different league, and there was no point trying to pretend it wasn't. I didn't have the projection numbers yet, those were probably coming at tomorrow's meeting, but there was no getting away from the bottom line. Almanzor al-Wahid wasn't about to hand over twenty four million quid unless the show he was expecting was fucking huge.

Then there was the issue of rehearsals. When we'd done the Frejus gig at the Cannes Film Festival, the band had just come off a few weeks working in the studio together, eight hours a day. We'd had our timing down, and everything was fresh and tight. But Blacklight hadn't done anything as a band since Book of Days had ended, and that meant we hadn't played together for a couple of years. Doesn't matter how much of a pro you are, or how long you've been playing together: once you lay off gigging and rehearsing for a while, there's going to be some rust that needs to be polished off the edges.

But the biggest issue was the situation with Tony. The last thing he'd told us, before he and Katia had climbed into the hire car, was that he was signing himself into the Centre in the morning. He'd actually been waffling about it, and what had happened during his tour of the premises had left him seriously wavering. But finding out about the Manaar gig tipped the scales, and tipped them good and hard: there was no way in hell he was missing this show. Besides, al-Wahid had made it pretty clear that he wanted everyone who'd played the last tour.

The sleet had eased up by the time the Mancusos were ready to head off, but it hadn't stopped. Bree and I had bundled up in our cold weather gear, and gone out to their car with them.

"Jesus, Bree, are you crazy, coming outside if you don't have to?" Katia, wrapped in a huge quilted coat, looked cold just thinking about it. "It's about ten degrees out there and breathing in is like sucking on a popsicle the size of a baseball bat. You're going to freeze to death. Are you trying to get sick? Like having to get this thing together in seven weeks isn't going to be crazy enough even if everyone's healthy?"

"It'll be fine." Bree'd wrapped herself in her cashmere coat, and was slipping on a pair of gloves and a hat. "John has this cool new coat. It's got a lightweight zip-out lining that feels like you're wrapping yourself in a down comforter, except that it doesn't bulk him up like a bear. It's the perfect coat for a horrible winter." She shivered. "And it isn't even winter yet, technically. Brrr."

"Bree's right, this thing's brilliant. Leather jackets don't keep the cold out, not the way they used to. But yeah, we're coming outside—not sure we're going to get much chance for talking for the next little while. Depends on what you decide to do." I moved the curtain aside. "Looks like your car's here."

We didn't actually say much, after all. I watched Tony climb in; round the other side of the car, Katia was already clicking her safety belt. I heard Bree's voice, a low murmur: *Remember, we're right here, call any time, I don't care when or why, I'm right here if you need me,* and Katia, sounding really calm, especially for her: *I know. I will.*

They drove off, east towards Central London. Bree and I watched their tail lamps disappear round the corner, tiny ice crystals dancing about in the wind, and headed indoors, shedding the coats and the gloves.

"Crikey." I watched Bree get the gear up on pegs, so that the central heating could dry them out. Even five minutes out of doors had left things damp; her cashmere looked to have a layer of frost on the shoulders. "It's cold enough the freeze the bollocks off a brass monkey out there."

"It won't be in Manaar, will it? Arabia's warm, right? I suppose that's something to look forward to." She sounded deadpan, no way to tell what she was really thinking or feeling. "I think I want something hot to drink—what time is it? Oh good, plenty of time to have some cocoa or something and not have to get up five times during the night. This getting old thing sucks."

"Yeah, I know what you mean. But it's only half past nine. We should be fine. Did you say cocoa? I wouldn't say no to that. Have you got any of your sugar substitute, so that you can have some as well…?"

Nice after-dinner conversation, the sort of thing any couple might talk about as she did the washing-up and he dried things and put them back in their proper places. Bree scraped a vanilla bean and seethed it in milk, beat some bitter dark cocoa into it, added some sweetener, and poured us each a cup. Over the rim, she looked at me.

"John, you've got that look on your face. There's something you want to say, isn't there? What's wrong?"

"You've got good eyes, lady." I took a deep breath. "Nothing wrong, but yeah, I've got a straight question. And feel free to tell me it's none of my business, all right?"

"Katia doesn't know who Tony saw. He didn't tell her." She smiled, a faint smile but a real one. "Was that it?"

"Sorry, love. Yeah, that was the main thing. I'm actually glad about that. Asking you to keep that sort of secret would have been a bit much, even coming from your best friend. But there was something else. Are you really okay with the Manaar show? And don't look at the wall or the clock or your shoes, love, please. Because I get the feeling you're not okay with it, and you know what, Bree, you get a vote. The way you feel about it, that matters to me. Just, let me know now, all right? Not later."

"I'm fine with it." She wrinkled her nose suddenly. "Shit, okay, maybe *fine* is the wrong word. I'm not fine with it. I'd rather not have anything to do with that guy, and the idea of you having to be somewhere where people's hands end up in picnic coolers isn't the happiest thought in the world. But I think you should do it anyway, John. I really do."

"You sure, Bree?" I was watching her face, trying to see what was going on in there. What she was saying was upfront, it was straightforward enough; the problem was, I wasn't entirely sure I believed it. There was something else happening there, something she'd shuttered, something I couldn't quite sort out. "Because you don't look happy, and if you're not –"

"I'm sure." She tilted the mug suddenly, and drained it. *Shit.* She hadn't lost the old talent for hiding things, not entirely. "It's fine. I wonder where I can get a bathing suit in London in the middle of November? Or is Manaar one of those places where women are supposed to cover up everything…?"

Katia rang Bree the next afternoon, to let her know that Tony had checked into the Recovery Centre. The women went off to shop for warm weather gear together, which was just as well. I'd got a call from Ian rather earlier in the day than he'd usually ring, to let me know we had another sit-down meeting at Fallow House that afternoon, dinner would be provided, this was going to be the "here's the details and you lot have all got to vote on it" deal, and had I heard from Tony?

So I was able to tell him that, yeah, Tony was here but he was officially out of circulation for the next twenty nine days, non-negotiable. I let Ian know that Tony wanted to do the Manaar gig, and Katia would probably be happy to come along to the meeting to hammer out details on Tony's behalf, if Ian needed that to happen. Of course, Ian had dealt with Katia handling Tony's stuff for him before; she's like a laser beam when it comes to his finances, and if you fuck with her, she can get just as scary as Domitra. So I wasn't surprised when Ian told me no, not at this point in the proceedings. Just before we rang off, he cleared his throat.

"JP, half a tick, please. There's something I need to ask you, and I don't want to do it in front of the band. Fuck, I don't want to ask it at all." I could practically hear him bracing himself. "Look, you know Tony better than any of us. And you've been down this road yourself. So I need to know. You think he'll be ready? Clean enough to handle it?"

For a moment, I felt myself stiffen up. Stupid, really, that reaction was: Ian wasn't trying to insult anyone, he was doing his job. It was a fair question, considering how much money was on the table here...

"JP? Sorry." He sounded worried. "Look, not trying to offend you, but I've got to ask."

"No, I know. I really do get it, Ian, and yeah, you do have to ask. Short answer? He could probably do it tomorrow. He's been dry for a few weeks now, and sticking to it, and yeah, I'm sure. Like you said, I've been down that road. But he needs time and space to sort it out and get it together. Rushing him won't do any good. We've got seven weeks. Barring something no one can control, Act of God or whatever, he'll be ready."

"Good." Back to being basic Ian Hendry. "That's one thing off my list of shit to worry about, then. See you in about an hour. I'm sending a car for Mac. Do you want your own driver, or should I tell him to come get you as well? And is Bree coming along today...?"

That first meeting had been short and not too tricky, mostly because the rest of us had been busy gawking after the small tactical nuke Mac and Luke had dropped on our heads. This time, with the proposal on the table and some hard information to kick about, things were a lot more complicated.

For one thing, everyone showed up without their old ladies. Of course Dom was there—if Mac's someplace, so is she—but she was the only band woman on the premises. That set the tone early on. Like it or not, when the band wives are there, the vibe is different, and so is the language.

I could tell the moment I walked through the front door at Fallow House that Ian was twitchy, wanting to get down to business. He's not an idiot, though; we got fed first, and warmed up, and then the two blokes who make up the night janitorial staff cleared everything away except the pile of paper in front of Ian.

"All right." Ian wasn't wasting time or breath, and that by itself was enough to clue me in to how big a deal this gig was. He'd booked us for the Superbowl Halftime Show and hadn't looked as piano-wire taut as he did right then. He jerked his head towards the phone on the sideboard. It's got a video hook-up, but they'd been left off. "Carla? Patrick? Roll call."

"We're both here." Carla sounded her usual self. "Patrick was actually finishing up a case and his client was in Glendale, so he just came here for this instead of heading north to San Francisco. Hi, guys."

"Brilliant." Ian was back looking at us. "Here's the basics, and do me a favour, will you, don't say a word until I'm done. After that, I'm going to want all the input I can get. All right?"

Silence. Ian's done that before, but not at the beginning of one of these things—it's usually after we start shouting at each other, trying to give us all a time-out. This was a new twist for him.

I looked sideways at Luke, who'd pulled up a chair and parked himself next to me. His eyebrows were a nice deep vee. Whatever Ian had, Luke didn't have the details.

"This arrived this morning, by diplomatic special courier. We've got a formal offer, a contract, a series of riders, a date, and the tech specs. The offer is just what Mac proposed: twelve million pounds for one show, New Year's Eve, to be held on some sort of municipal open grounds in the Emirate's capital city. Once the contract's signed and the rider details sorted out, there'd be a cheque for ten million pounds made out to Luke's non-profit, and a cheque for two million to the Kinkaid Recovery Centre. The braintrust for the resort would liaise with our people to make sure we've got everything we need, soup to nuts, tech to reservations. Carla, you and Ronan and Nial would be the ones doing most of the dealing on that. Security would be our baby, with cooperation from the palace, so there's Patrick and Dom with some major coordinating to do."

He stopped. Right. He'd asked for silence, and he was getting it. He tapped the papers in front of him.

"One more thing, and we're off. The projected audience figure is a quarter-million people."

Yeah, well, so much for the babble and blather he'd expected. You could have heard a fly die, the silence was that absolute.

Cal Wilson got his voice back first. "Um—yeah, okay. Leaving aside the question of just why that nutter al-Wahid is so desperate to get us out there to play, I want to make sure I heard you right. Did you say something about 'open grounds'? Can you clarify that? Because that doesn't sound as if there's a venue in place. Where would we be staging a gig for a quarter million people, in the middle of the local park? Or maybe on a sand dune?"

"It might as well be the local park, from the looks of it, apart from it being huge." Ian slid a stack loose from the pile. "Fuck, I'm an idiot. I meant to pass these round—here, there's copies for everyone. Carla, you have the one I faxed? Good. The site photos were taken just a couple of days ago, so this is the current gen. They're at the bottom of the stack. You tell me. Is this doable, or should I tell him to take his twenty four million quid and sod off? Nial? Ronan?"

"Oh, it's doable." Nial didn't quite shrug. "Since we won't have a handle on the physical layout and whatnot until we get out there, I'd want a really stripped-down design for this, something literally straight from the can. A call to Tait Towers would do it—I'd have them send over whatever they've got as the current flavour of basic stadium end stage. Ronan?"

"Yeah, straight front of stage line arrays, a handful of remote towers, extra generators, bob's your uncle. Nothing like Book of Days—even if we fancied it, there's not enough time. I'm with Nial: let's keep it simple."

Of course, right then, it was a done deal. Ian let the conversations bounce about for a few minutes; from the looks of it, it was business as usual, him taking mental notes on what we wanted and the best way to get it done, and right round the time he'd sorted all that out in his head, he brought us back to it.

"Right. An official yea or nay vote's probably just a formality at this point, but before we do it, oi, Patrick! You and Dom have been quiet. What about the security for this do? You okay with this, or what?"

"Dom, ladies first? No? Okay." Patrick Ormand sounded just the way he always sounds. Hard to know what he's thinking— he's a former DEA bloke and homicide cop, and he does poker voice as well as he does poker face. The only time you ever get a real shift in there is if he thinks something or someone is bleeding upwind. "Personally, I'd like a few things added to our end of the rider. I'm looking at the stuff you faxed Carla, and I'd want a really delineated backstage area. Not only that, but considering who's hosting this shindig—not to mention paying for it—I'd want absolute control of the band areas, and that includes the hotel. I don't want any incidents with these people. One picnic basket of body parts was plenty for me. Dom? Did you say something?"

"Just rolling my eyes and snorting, that's all." She was, too. It takes something special to knock Domitra Calley off her balance. "I agree with Patrick. Need to know who handles what, right down to the molecules, yo. Band and security, we handle all of it. No one gets in or out of the designated band areas without our say-so. The rest of it, how should I know? I don't vote. That shit, that's up to my boss."

"Dom, what a peculiar thing to call me, especially when we both know perfectly well you could fold, spindle and mutilate me before I got enough air in my lungs to ask you what I'd done to piss you off." Mac peered around Luke and caught my eye. "I think we're ready for that vote, but can we clear up the question of Tony's availability? I hate to sound intrusive, but this is band business and after all, Ali specifically wants the Book of Days lineup for this. Johnny?"

"Tony's in. I've already hashed this out with him—he's sequestered, no outside contact, for four weeks starting this morning, then a week of couples counselling with Katia. He'll be done with the Recovery Centre in five weeks, the gig's in seven. He told me to tell you he wouldn't miss it."

"Good." Ian stood up. "You lot know the drill. Hands up if you think Blacklight ought to do it. Crikey, not a single nay vote? Right, then, makes my job easier. I'll get hold of al-Wahid's people in the morning, and we'll have drafts of our own riders done by end of business tomorrow. Meanwhile, I'd ask that you please read what they sent us. Read it really carefully and yes, Mac, I mean you especially. You know him, we don't. If there's anything in that pile that twigs you wrong, let me know. We'll talk about rehearsals tomorrow."

Chapter Four

"(beep)...JP? It's Ian. Look, I hate to do this to you, but we need to do a fast run out to Manaar, and have a sit-down with al-Wahid and his people. Patrick wants a look at the security issues before he starts hiring staff, and we really ought to get a feel for the site before the gear arrives from Tait. No need to drag Bree along if she'd rather stay in London, this is really just band personnel signing off on a few things. Carla's got a private plane reserved for us out of Heathrow. She's flying out tonight, and Patrick flew out this morning. They'll meet us there. I'll have a car at your place tomorrow morning at half past ten. Sorry it's that early, but it's a seven-hour flight and a four-hour time difference. Be ready to go, will you? Call me if you've got questions. (beep)"

"Oh bloody hell!"

"Uh-oh." Bree was busy kneading dough—she'd said something about wanting a decent loaf of egg bread—but she turned round at that. "That doesn't sound good. What's wrong?"

"I'm being dragged off to fucking Manaar tomorrow, is what." The look on her face got me hurrying into an explanation. "Not to worry, Ian says you don't have to go. He just needs the band to sign off on some things. It's just the band."

"Oh, shit." She sat down, hard. "*Shit!*"

I blinked at her. "Bree, what? I know it's a drag, but I'll only be gone a couple of days."

"Did you say the band needs to sign things?" She sounded resigned. "Doesn't that mean Tony? Because he can't, can he? Katia's his designated representative."

I opened my mouth, and shut it again. I'd got the reason for her swearing now, good and clear.

If anything needs band signatures, it means the entire band has to agree. That's Blacklight's policy, ironclad, the way we've always done things. As a hard policy, it's worked for us from the beginning, and we've never seen any reason to change it. And for this gig, of all gigs, it was vital. I reached for my phone.

"Right. I'm ringing Ian, make sure he's thought about that. Wait, is that yours ringing?"

It was Katia, and listening to Bree's end of the conversation, I put my phone down again. Ian had thought of it, all right. From the pitch of Katia's voice at the other end of the phone, she was right at the edge of flipping her shit.

"No." Bree's shoulders were mauls of tensed muscle, but Katia wouldn't know that. It floored me, that she could look so tense and sound so Zen. "That's silly. You're not deserting Tony if you go to Manaar, you're helping him. What? No! Katia, would you please take a breath? No, I am not being condescending and I'm not talking down to you, either. I just don't think you're thinking this through all the way. He can't go anywhere himself and anyway, it's not like you can visit him or anything, right? You'd be acting as his agent, so why are you freaking out?"

Katia's voice crackled through the phone, higher pitched than usual. I knew what was being said—it was obvious from Bree's face, and of course, we'd both seen it coming. It was about the last thing in the world she wanted to do, but she'd made a promise to be there for Katia. And Bree doesn't break promises.

"Of course I'll come too, if you want me there." Nice calm voice, eyes as bleak as the weather outside. "Look, let me get off the phone so that John can let Ian know. Try and get some sleep. We'll see you at the airport tomorrow morning."

She clicked off. Before she could put the phone down, or smash it against the wall, I was up and across the kitchen, with both arms wrapped round her tight, talking into her hair. She was rigid as a wrought iron railing.

"You know what, love, you're a good friend. Best friend Katia could have, now or ever. It'll be all right. It'll be two days at the most, nice private plane, a break from this crap weather, and back again. We're not hanging out there for fun, just business and back. Bree? Gordon *Bennett*, are you crying? Love, what is it? What's wrong?"

"I'm sorry." She pulled back, just enough to get a hand free and dash tears off her face. "I'm being a total pill. I just—I don't want to go, I don't want you to go, I don't want Katia to go. The idea of having to go be polite to that man makes my skin crawl. I just hate the idea and yes, I know I said I think you should do the show and I meant it, John, I swear I did, but I really need to figure out how to deal with this."

I know my wife. I understand that she gets wound up, sometimes about stuff I wouldn't think twice about. Sometimes she's dead right, seeing things about a situation that I've missed. But this was about as extreme as I'd ever seen from Bree.

So I held on and stayed quiet. It didn't seem a moment for

pushing it, and I wouldn't have known where to push anyway. If she was really sorting it out in her head, the best thing I could do was shut my gob and wait. Pushing wasn't going to get much done beyond muddying up what she was trying to get clear.

"It's on his turf." She was speaking slowly. She'd pulled back from me, not withdrawing, just enough so that I could see her face. "When we saw him before, dealt with him before, it was on our turf. We had home court. Mac apologised to me for that, for inviting that man to my house without clearing it with me first, but he did the right thing and I told him so, John. It was absolutely the right move. Ali al-Wahid really didn't like having to cope with that situation somewhere where he wasn't in control, did he? He hated having to apologise at all, but he really hated having to do it on our turf, where he had no control. He's used to having control."

"Yeah, he did." I was remembering that encounter, and Bree was right—it had been there in the way al-Wahid had changed colour, the way he'd tightened up. "He really didn't fancy being surrounded, either. That's what's freaking you out about this, Bree? That we have to go there, because us being there means he gets to call the tune?"

"It's part of it, anyway." Her eyes were clouded. "I just keep remembering that he has more money and power than anyone has any business having, and that he's not too careful about what he does with either thing. Either that, or he's a fucking idiot, and that makes him pretty damned scary. I mean, Jesus, John, he hired a pair of traditional Moslems to watch his twin tramps. Would anyone with half a brain do that?"

"Damned if I know." She was right, dead right. If he'd been that arrogant in our parlour, half a world away from the safety of his own ground, how bad was he likely to be while he was sitting in his favourite armchair or throne or whatever, in his own palace overlooking his private bit of oceanfront property? *Shit.* "But it's not so much about his brains, is it? It's his judgement that's the problem. I'm not convinced this little face to face is going to be that bad, Bree. For one thing, I don't care how many harem guards or eunuchs with swords or dancing girls he's got at his back, we've got the whip hand."

She blinked at me. "We do?"

"Hell yeah. Strength in numbers, love. All it would take is one of us getting pissed off enough to say right, that's rubbish and I'm not playing the show, and the rest of the band would walk. And yeah, that goes for Katia saying it, as well. She's standing in for Tony, and her vote is his vote. And there's something else, Bree. I've no clue why he wants us to do this, but he does, enough to pay out all that dosh. That gives us damned near all the power. We can deny him what he wants, you know? We don't even have to know what it is."

She was quiet, watching my face. I bent a knuckle and chucked her under the chin; that's a gesture I use a lot less often than I used to, when we were both younger. This time, it surprised her enough to get a smile out of her.

"No worries, Bree, all right? We don't owe Ali al-Wahid a damned thing, and however it goes down, I'm not taking any shit from him or anyone else."

I'd been half-expecting some drama from Katia on the flight to Manaar, but in the end there was nothing, and thank God for it. She'd pulled Bree aside for a fast conversation that looked to be pretty much to the point, even though it was all done in whispers. Bree listened and nodded, and then she stepped out of the way because there was Ian, taking Katia under his wing, settling in next to her on the plane, clueing her in. No idea what he told her, but whatever it was, it did the trick. When the pilot set us down at al-Wahid's private airstrip, Katia was herself again: not calm, because calm isn't her thing, but level-headed and ready to deal on Tony's behalf.

That was a load off Bree's mind, I could tell. She'd finished that *tete à tete* with Katia all tensed up, but Ian moving in and taking over, that took care of it. It took so much weight off my wife's shoulders, she actually dozed off in the seat next to me for the last two hours of the flight.

Yeah, well, that didn't last. The plane's engines hadn't throttled all the way down before, and Bree'd woken up and was stretching, when the pilot's voice came over the speakers.

"Ladies and gentlemen, I've been asked to tell you that there will be a short delay in getting you off the plane." He sounded nervous. "The Emir has a personal envoy en route to greet you. Apparently the official limousines were a little late leaving the Palace, but they'll be here shortly. They've—requested that everyone stay on board until then. Thanks for your understanding and patience."

Oh, bloody hell.

Next to me, Bree was stiff. Envoy from the Palace, yeah, right. *Shit.* If Ali al-Wahid was trying to remind us that we were on his turf now, and had to play by his rules, he'd made a brilliant job of it. I hadn't missed that nervous little hesitation in the pilot's voice, before he'd said the word "request", and what's more, neither had my wife. Bree went from sleepy to stone-faced in about ten seconds.

Request, my arse. That was an order, a display of power, and no argy-bargy about it, either. We hadn't even got off the plane yet and this trip was already completely fucked.

We only had about ten minutes wait before we heard the portable stairs being rolled up to the door at the front of the plane. It might as well have been a year. Bree and I weren't the only ones reacting badly to al-Wahid's heavy-handed rubbish; that ten minutes had been completely silent. Even with no one saying a word, though, there was no way you could miss how pissed off everyone was. The silence in the cabin was so thick, the damned plane felt as if it were seething.

Right around the time the pilot came back on to tell us the doors were opening, welcome to the Royal Emirate of Manaar and he'd hoped we'd all had a nice comfy flight, Mac got up, and Domitra with him. He'd been at school with al-Wahid, so maybe he had a better clue about what the protocol was supposed to be. More likely, he'd just got bored with sitting about, or with the idea of humouring his old school chum. Personally, I didn't give a toss what this particular lot wanted us to do. What I'd told Bree was true: if one of us decided to say *sod it, not playing this gig* and walk, we all would. Just then, I was narked almost to the point of saddling whoever the envoy was with the job of telling his boss or master or whatever *right, fuck off then, I'm not playing, the gig's off...*

"Ladies and gentlemen, the stairs are in place and the representative from the Palace is ready for the official greeting." The pilot sounded seriously shaken up. Made me wonder how often he'd done this run, London to Manaar, and what they'd threatened him with if he cocked it up. "Your cars are waiting. If everyone is ready to disembark...?"

Bree and I were second down the steps, right behind Mac and Dom. Bree was in front of me—ladies first, yeah?—which is why, when she stopped dead halfway down, I nearly broke both of our necks running into her. She said something under her breath, but I couldn't quite make it out. Behind me, Luke said something a lot easier to understand. He hadn't brought Karen with him, which was just as well; she blushes easily, for a redhead.

Our cars were there, all right, four bullet-proof jobs. There were liveried drivers standing next to each limo, doing that whole "stare at nothing and don't blink" thing they do, as part of the gig. Our escort was there, as well.

It was Almanzor al-Wahid. The Emir had come himself.

"Malcolm." He made straight for Mac. He wasn't waiting to see what anyone else was going to do. Explained why the pilot

57

had sounded so twitchy, yeah? "I am pleased to see you all. I had intended to send staff, but it seemed best to greet you myself. I hope your flight was a good one?"

I opened my mouth, and shut it again, swallowing the words that wanted out: *oh please, mate, you don't give one single damn what the flight was like, or about anything else, either.* Yeah, it was his turf, his rules, all right. He wasn't saying or doing anything we could actually object to, but it was there in the tone of his voice, the set of his shoulders. He just stood there, face smooth and unreadable, completely in control.

I suddenly remembered him standing in our front room at 2828 Clay Street. His face hadn't stayed smooth that day, because Luke had verbally taken him to pieces, peeling long bleeding strips off al-Wahid's ego.

That wasn't happening today. If I'd needed a clear example of why Bree wanted this sort of encounter on her own home ground, this was it.

"The flight was fine, thanks." Mac had hit the tarmac, with Dom at his side. I'm quite familiar with her body language, the way she moves in particular situations. This was an interesting moment: she was watchful, but she wasn't on high alert. That meant she was ready to kill someone if they needed it, but she wasn't seeing the need, at least not yet. It also meant she wasn't actively expecting it.

The luggage was being unloaded from the plane, and into an SUV with blacked-out windows. Mac was looking around, at our luggage from the looks of it, making sure it got into the truck. What he wasn't doing was offering a hand for his old school friend to shake. That was peculiar, considering how formal this whole set-up was. I watched the Emir look at Mac's hands, watched his eyebrows go up, and I suddenly got it: Mac knew there was a game to be played, and he was on it.

Right. If our frontman was going to handle Ali al-Wahid and

his tree-pissing bullshit, I could relax and give my attention where it was needed, which was making sure nothing happened that triggered Bree into any kind of meltdown.

I got a hand in the small of her back. She was wearing a light shirt; we'd checked the weather for Manaar before we'd left London, and she'd changed into something that worked better for the 80-plus degrees Fahrenheit Manaar was enjoying than what she'd had on in London.

The small of her back is where she keeps her moods. I can always tell how she's doing by getting the palm of my hand right there, and just then, it was flaming hot. *Shit.* Not good. I was damned if I was having her made nuts, not by Ali al-Wahid or anyone else.

"Can we move on, love? We've got a queue behind us."

She glanced at me over her shoulder. Whatever she saw in my face, it did the trick; I watched the tension go out of her upper body. She went down the ramp and stood off to one side, looking past my shoulder at Ian and Katia.

Even in December, the temperature was too warm for my taste. I had a moment of thinking that, if all of Arabia was this hot, it must have taken some kind of sadist to have dreamed up all those veils and layers they seem to want their women to use as gear. Of course, coming from not quite freezing and a sky full of sleet back in London, it probably felt hotter than it actually was.

"When you are all ready? Your bags are secured." The Emir had gone back to being smooth and unreadable. Sod it. Not my problem, whatever the game was between him and Mac.

But he wasn't watching Mac, not anymore. He'd moved on to Luke. I don't know if he expected Luke to do something, or say something, but if he did, it wasn't on. Luke nodded at him, and looked over his head. Luke's over six feet, and al-Wahid was my height. Home turf isn't the only advantage out there, you know?

"Good, the limos are here. I hope they're air-conditioned." Ian had hit the ground with Katia at his heels, and unlike Mac, he held out a hand to shake. He sounded as gruff as he usually does, and he wasn't bothering about any protocol rubbish, but I thought al-Wahid looked relieved that someone wasn't actually snubbing him on his own airstrip, for a change. "Any sign of Patrick and Carla? Because they're the reason we're here, and we're not really scheduled to let this visit go long."

"Your head of security and operations manager are already here. They arrived this morning, and are my honoured guests at the Queen's Palace, as you all will be." He gave Katia a smile, pleasant enough. "If you are ready...?"

The liveried drivers were all at full attention. It was rather like watching some sort of Christmas display in the windows of the Regent Street shops, except in pantomime: they looked like clockwork soldiers, windup toys all moving together. I saw something move across Bree's face, distaste maybe, or just being uncomfortable with all of it, wanting to get the hell out of it and go home. I got one arm round her waist, and turned us towards the nearest limo.

"Here we go," I told her. "Let's get out of the heat, all right? Sun's giving me a spiker of a headache."

We climbed in, Bree going ahead of me. The limos looked to be designed for no more than four, and Cal and Stu had already climbed in. The driver shut the door behind us, and a moment later, we'd pulled off and away into traffic, past shiny steel skyscrapers glinting under a hard sun at the edge of the water, heading off towards Manaar's royal compound.

I had hold of Bree's hand, not talking, letting Stu and Cal natter. I wasn't telling her that, as she'd got settled in, I'd got a nice clear look through the window, at our host.

He hadn't been watching Mac, or Luke, not anymore. He hadn't been keeping an eye on his own people, either. He'd been staring in through the window of our limo, and his eyes had been fixed firmly on my wife.

I hadn't really given any thought to what our digs in Manaar were likely to be like. I mean, right, I'd expected comfort and probably luxury; for whatever reason, he seemed to be sucking up to us as a band in a big way, and he didn't strike me as the sort of bloke to deny himself anything he fancied. And yeah, I'd heard him say something about Carla and Patrick being put up at some queen's palace. But I'd been too busy trying to sort out why our host had been looking at my wife as if she was something he'd need to call in military manoeuvres to cope with to wonder about where we were going to be sleeping tonight.

Still, he was all about luxury, and not doing anything on the cheap. So when the limos pulled into the compound, and we got our first look at the Queen's Palace, I probably shouldn't have been quite as floored as I was.

"Bloody hell, is he joking!" Stu, peering out the window, snorted. I couldn't tell if he was snorting at the design of the thing, or at how over the top it was. There were peacocks and hens wandering about, giving the limos dirty looks. "We sleeping in a fucking *seraglio*, or something? We get regulation folding cots in this bloke's harem?"

It was nuts. We drove through a set of arches that would have put the gates at Buckingham Palace to shame; they reminded me vaguely of something, I couldn't quite sort out what, but after a minute, I realised I'd been thinking of the Taj Mahal: similar shape, a lot more colour. The gates were the same blue as all those peacock tails out front, and they were trimmed in what was probably liquid gold. Nothing would have surprised me at that point. It wasn't until later that I sussed out that the liquid gold paint had been used in a way to make the patterns on the gates look as if they'd had those peacock tails posed in place.

61

Inside, we pulled to a stop in a courtyard. The liveried driver got out and opened the door for us. Bree was first out, and just as she reached for the driver's hand, to help her out, the bloke was brushed away as if he were a gnat or something.

"Please allow me. I claim a host's privilege."

al-Wahid was smiling at Bree, one hand held out. There was no way for her to refuse, not without a level of rudeness that was probably beyond her. I know fuck-all about protocol or any of that rubbish, but there was something about this place that felt formal, and ancient, as if they took this stuff really seriously and had been doing it for a really long time, as well. And it was his limo, his courtyard, his turf.

Poor Bree was stuck, and she knew it. She glanced back at me, and I felt our usual line of marital thought-reading kick in hard: *I know, but we're guests.*

And she got it. She turned back again, and let the Emir get hold of one of her hands, and help her out.

"Thank you." Her voice was completely neutral, and so was her face. She's usually rotten when it comes to hiding things, but just then, she must have felt a major need, because even I was having trouble sussing out what she was feeling. "That's very kind of you. John...?"

"Right here, love." I was already out, no help offered by the owner of all this luxury. Something in me was kicking hard against that whole formality thing. "Nice digs you've got here, mate. Queen's Palace, you said? Didn't know there was a queen. She all right with us parking our bags in her sauna, then?"

I heard a snort from behind me. The other limos had pulled up and emptied out, and Mac had come up, Domitra glued to his side. Mac was just Mac—not sure if he'd ever been tense in the first place. Dom, though, she hadn't relaxed.

"There is no queen, not today." al-Wahid was matching my wife in being inscrutable, but he was looking straight at Bree again. It was very weird—he wasn't being gallant, and he wasn't attracted either. Trust me, I know when a bloke's hitting on my wife. But she wasn't the only woman there, and he was basically ignoring Katia and Dom. "The queen for whom this was built was my great-grandmother. She has been dead these many years, but she would not begrudge its use in any case. She is legendary among my people for her love of music, and musicians. My people will bring your belongings to your quarters—Ms. Fanucci and Mr. Ormand are resting, but will join us for dinner, at my personal table. I would be honoured to show you more of the Palace, if you will allow me…?"

Next to me, I saw Mac's lips purse up in a whistle. Not stupid, Ali al-Wahid. He was still talking directly to my wife but he wasn't offering a hand, or talking down to her. She wasn't unbending at all, but she shot me a fast look. This one was dead easy to read: *what the hell is this guy's trip…?*

I shrugged back at her: *no clue.* It was true. I couldn't sort out why he was taking so much trouble over Bree. She had no power to sign anything, she wasn't playing the gig, and she was here as the ornament on the man's arm, a band wife in a culture where wives aren't valued much to begin with, except as property or producers of little boys. I couldn't make sense of any of it.

Meanwhile, al-Wahid was giving us a sort of spoken Grand Tour, talking about his grandmother's digs. He waved an arm towards a series of pools that looked like something you might see in a Vegas hotel on the strip, or maybe that was the wrong way round. There were nine of them, nice and big.

"These pools are for the use of my guests—they are heated by the natural hot springs beneath Manaar. The minerals in the water are considered very healthy. My great-grandmother lived into her nineties. They are for your private use. I believe you drive a Jaguar, Mrs. Kinkaid. Is that not correct?"

We all stopped, just blinking at him. The question was so unexpected, it surprised Bree into an honest response.

"How the hell did you know that?" She blurted it out. "And what does my car have to do with anything?"

"Only that, if you wish, I am happy to put any of my cars at your disposal." One point to the Emir; he'd scored, and he knew it. "If you have a love of speed, perhaps my Bugatti would please you? Our roads are straight and uncluttered, and can be closed to other traffic should you choose. Let me know if this would suit you. Ah, here is the Queen's Kitchen. It has been made rather more modern than my great-grandmother would have recognised, but as you can see, it is not yet ready for full use; there is still work to be done. Our chef in residence is Paris trained..."

I missed most of the history lesson he dragged us through, because my brain was elsewhere, trying to suss out what he was up to with Bree. He wasn't flirting, and it wasn't a come-on, either. She had no power in this situation, none at all; Christ, that was why she hadn't wanted to come in the first place, knowing she was going to feel powerless on his turf.

I glanced over at Mac. Any hope that he might know what was going on went out the window; he was looking at his old school chum as if he'd only just met him.

We followed al-Wahid through arches, down between the hot mineral pools. I wasn't paying much attention to the tour guide thing he was doing, but I did notice that all the windows were high up in the walls, and very small. They also all had grilles over them, and a thought popped into my head: *I wonder if his great-grandmother was trying to keep people in, or keep people out?*

Eventually, either al-Wahid got tired of showing off the columns and pools, or else he'd run out of things to show off, because he finally led us through the one set of arches we hadn't been through, and into a corridor that was shaded, and dark, and looked to be made of limestone or marble or something. There was also a series of proper doors. Turned out the doors had proper rooms behind them.

"Forgive me. I take so much pride in sharing my home, I forget my manners. I am sure you wish to rest. You are my honoured guests at dinner tonight. I will send equerries to escort you. This section of the Palace is entirely at your disposal for as long as you are here—each suite has the name of its guest on the door. I ask you to forgive the simplicity of these accommodations, but the suites I commissioned are not yet completed. When you are next here, there will be comfort at a higher level."

He nodded at Dom, gave Katia a smile of sorts, bowed over Bree's hand again, and left. We stood there, the lot of us, totally silent, listening to his footsteps die away. From outside, I could hear birds singing, and the water in the pools bubbling away.

"He's right about one thing. I could use a nice nap." Mac's eyebrows were up, and he sounded as bemused as I've ever heard him. "Bree, angel, if you don't mind my asking, what in sweet hell was all that about? Why was Ali sucking up to you? And yes, in case you were wondering, that was a complete and thorough suck-up. He offered to let you drive his pretty shiny Veyron, and that bloody car cost over a million quid. What in hell?"

"Shit, he offered to close down the motorway." Dom was watching Bree as well. They all were. "He in love, or what? What's up with Ali Baba offering you the keys to the kingdom and the keys to the car, yo?"

"You tell me and we'll both know." There was trouble in Bree's face. "I don't get it. It's not like I have anything he wants, or anything I would be willing to give him if I did. I don't know. And right now, I think I want to take my shoes off and lock the door and lie down for awhile, because I am so damned creeped out, you can't begin to imagine. I hope there are real beds in there, and not just stupid floor cushions and bowls for peeled grapes. John? Please tell me one of those doors has our name on it…?"

If the rooms were anything to go by, the eastern notion of simplicity is rather different from mine. Turned out the Hotel Harem, or whatever al-Wahid was actually calling his granny's blue and gold pleasure palace these days, not only had proper doors, it had proper locks on them and hot Jacuzzi tubs in the bath, as well.

That was just as well, because my wife was frazzled as hell. She was so freaked, she was actually mumbling to herself. I could hear her while I was getting the water in the tub good and warm, and dumping in some of the fancy salts from the bottles on the edge of the tub. The room was actually on the cool side. No idea if it was the thick stone walls keeping the heat of the sun out, or whether it was really effective air conditioning, and I didn't give a toss, not just then.

"...his Bugatti?" She'd shed everything she was wearing and headed straight for the tub. "I don't even know how to drive a manual. John? Why would he offer me his Bugatti?"

"Bree, I don't even know what a Bugatti is. Here, you get in before that water cools down too much to do you any good."

"It's a car. A very pretty, very expensive car. It's the fastest car in the world. Does he think I'm Michael Schumacher? Do I *look* like Michael Schumacher?" She slid all the way down. The water was up round her chin. "What the hell is going on? John?"

"I don't know who Michael Schumacher is, either. I'm betting he doesn't look half as good as you do, though. Especially without his clothes on, yeah?"

I turned the Jacuzzi on, and parked myself on the edge of the tub. No idea what it was made of, but it looked like marble. I could feel the chill of the stone, straight through my trousers. "Bloody hell, that's got better bubbles than your favourite champagne! Bree, look, I've got a suggestion. Why don't we just skip all the imperial intrigue rubbish, and ask the bloke what he thinks he's on about? Want me to have a go?"

She'd settled down in the tub and closed her eyes, but they

popped open at that. "Wow. Would you really do that? Just go ask him, I mean?"

"Fuck yeah. Why wouldn't I? The bloke may think he's in some Hollywood flick about Lorenzo de Medici or Lawrence of Arabia or something, but that doesn't mean we've got to go along with it." I got up. "You have a nice hot soak. I'm off to find out why Sheikh Moneybags is sucking up to my wife."

Of course I got lost.

I suppose it wasn't surprising. I hadn't really been paying attention, back in the limo, coming in under those huge blue and gold arches; I'd been too busy gawking at the arches themselves. So I hadn't noticed that the road we'd come in on wasn't the only one in. There were five more just like it.

I stopped a minute, trying to orient myself. Right. Had those pools been off to my right? No way to tell; from the looks of it, the place was a quadrangle. I suddenly had a picture in my head: walking down the corridor at the recovery centre in London, scoping it out for Tony. There'd been a gardener out there in the sleety downpour, deadheading roses and looking miserable.

I looked up and around. The place was bloody confusing, and I was getting overheated too quickly for comfort. The MS doesn't like extremes in weather, you know? It's not wild about stress or time zone changes, either. And yeah, there were probably half a million people shivering back in the UK right now who'd have swapped places with me in a heartbeat, but the fact is, standing about in one place triggers ataxia in both legs. Doing it with eighty degrees of sun beating down on my head, in a disused harem too close to the equator for my comfort levels, just made it worse. And I'm not much for palm trees, anyway.

I shook my head, and sweat ran down into my eyes. It stung, and I lifted a hand to wipe it away. The hand was shaking, a sharp nasty little tremor. So were both legs.

Right, Johnny. Time to get the hell out of it. Just pick an arch with a road and see if it leads to Almanzor al-Wahid. Just pick a direction, and go there.

I took a step forward. A vicious little jolt of myokimia ran straight up from my left ankle to my hip, and both legs went out from under me.

It wasn't a bad fall, but it was a fall. I went down on both knees; in that situation, most people put a hand out to try easing the impact, but I'm a guitar player and I've trained myself not to do that. I need my hands. So I let my knees take the hit. They didn't enjoy it much.

"Shit!"

Weird acoustics the place had; I heard my own voice echoing round the courtyard, *shit shit shit.* It was still echoing when I heard a splash, definitely the sound of water moving in one of the pools behind me, off to one side, and the slap of bare feet on the tiles.

I took a breath, and started up off the ground. Not very dignified, but fuck, false pride about the MS does me sod all in the way of good. Having someone help me back to our room was worth having had someone watch me take a header. At least I hadn't done a faceplant; a state dinner with two black eyes would have just about put the tin cupola on what was shaping up to be a visit I was already planning on forgetting as soon as I feasibly could.

There was a hand under my left elbow, and another one under my right. Not much help, really, just sort of holding me while I pushed myself up. Small hands, they were, and very soft.

"Thanks." I was on my feet now, shaky but upright, brushing off the knees of my trousers. "Sorry about that. Can you tell me which way –"

Behind me, someone giggled. It was answered, call and response, just like two guitars echoing each other, by another voice, another giggle. I froze in place.

I'd heard this before, two little gigglers, fluttering and cooing. The tickybox in my chest was working overtime, kicking high and hard.

"Azra, he fell down! Should we call for a doctor?"

"But Paksima, if we do that, our father will know we were here. When he's angry, he's mean!" Her hand under my elbow tightened, ever so slightly. She was smiling, dark eyes nice and bold and very easy to read. "You're not so much hurt, are you?"

I looked down, left then right. They were both there, Ali al-Wahid's little blessings, his twin daughters, one on each side of me. The last time I'd seen these two, they'd been waving their arms, trying to seduce some poor roadie backstage at one of our shows, complete with their dimples and big dark eyes and modest spangled headscarves. Most of the roadies they'd managed to hook had ended up dead. They were bad news, those two.

The dimples and the eyes were present and accounted for, and all of it was being aimed straight at me. The scarves weren't, and neither was anything else in the way of actual clothing. One of the girls had a towel wrapped round her middle. The other one—I couldn't have told you which was which—was stark naked, shining with pool water.

"Right. Thanks. Cheers." *Right, Johnny, get the fuck out of here and don't waste any time about it, either. And whatever you do, don't touch either of them.*

I slipped between them, making damned sure I didn't so much as brush against either of them, back towards the safety of my nice chilly room and my nice warm wife. I didn't look behind me—I didn't need to. I knew just what they'd be up to: watching me, heads together, whispering.

Any conversation with their dad would have to wait.

Chapter Five

I'd thought the whole bit with Grandmother al-Wahid's soaking pools and peacocks and whatnot was decadent. But that was before I got dumped into the Emir's idea of a formal meal.

I don't know if the bloke ate his supper this way every night, or if he'd just had it laid on to impress the guests, or what. Either way, it was completely over the top. The only trick he missed was half-naked dancing girls feeding us figs, and he probably considered that. Mac said later he was surprised we hadn't been offered sheep's' eyes on a skewer by the pick of the local belly dancers. It was completely over the top.

Even with my own frustration at not having made it as far as al-Wahid's front parlour, I'd probably have enjoyed that dinner a lot more if both knees hadn't been making noise at me. It's always been a puzzle to me how you can fall, not tear the fabric of what you're wearing, and still come up with raw patches on the skin underneath. Doesn't matter how old I get, I don't fancy pain.

Back in the shaded corridor outside our room and safely out of the twins' line of sight, I'd actually hung out for a few minutes. I was waiting for my legs to stop shaking, but more to the point, my head was busy, coming up with rationales to convince myself it was all right to stay quiet about the twins: *Bree's already worried enough, the last thing she needs to hear is that the Persian Princesses are swanning round the seraglio naked just under our bedroom window, she'll flip her shit, no reason to give her more to worry about.*

It didn't take more than a minute to cop to the stupidity of that particular idea. Truth is, I gave Bree grief for years over her keeping things from me, the way she was making the pits we'd kept falling into with each other deeper and darker and dirtier by not being upfront with me. The last time one of us had kept a major secret, I'd been the one doing it. Her finding out about it—even though I'd had no choice—had nearly cost me my marriage.

So, right, not an option. I was going to have tell her.

I let myself back inside just as she was getting out of the bath. She was wrapping herself in a pricey-looking bath sheet; it reminded me, not very pleasantly, of the girls out there in the pool. "That was quick—John? Oh shit, babe, what?"

I told her what had just gone down: heat, ataxia, myokimia, naked and mostly-naked princesses, the lot. And of course, she ignored the Tahini Twins thing entirely. She was too busy using the house phone to demand that someone bring some stuff for my knees. You'd think I'd know my wife by now.

We got a nice comprehensive first aid kit delivered to our room within ten minutes. The bloke introduced himself: *Hello, my name is Nordine, I am your personal equerry for as long as you are the guests of Manaar, you have only to ask* and all that. Very nice manners, but I'm afraid Bree was a bit short with him. She just wanted to cope with my knees.

A few hours later, when he showed up to drive us to dinner, Bree apologised, and of course the bloke smiled politely and said something vague and waved it off. She was done up to the nines; I had both knees bandaged and was shakier than I liked under that particular set of circs. I'd had a short rest, but it hadn't helped much. Everything hurt like hell, legs, knees, even my back. There was an MS exacerbation just waiting to nail me. I could feel it ramping up.

I didn't fancy coping with dinner. I didn't fancy coping with Ali al-Wahid, or his horny giggling brats. All I really wanted was to get through a plate of something edible, get whatever band business that might come up taken care of, and head off to bed. Fortunately, I had serious backup on that one. When I get this messed up, Bree turns into a Valkyrie. She's especially fierce with the outside world.

"Hang on." She was sounding militant. Nordine had taken us under the arches and out along one of those gleaming white roads, towards a totally different pile of stone than the one we'd just come from. It was just as well I hadn't tried sorting out where to go before I'd fallen. "We're going to get some food and then we're getting the hell back to our room, and don't even think about arguing with me, John. Did you remember to pack some painkillers? I think I have a couple of TyCo with me."

"Not sure." It came out a bit slurred; as if the rest of it wasn't enough to have to cope with, trigeminal neuralgia was kicking in, creeping up along my jaw. *Shit.* I saw Bree's face tighten up, and tried to sound normal. "Doesn't matter. We can get something from the Emir."

"Like what? Opium? Morphine?" She sounded as tight as her own shoulders. I saw Nordine shoot her a look in the rear-view mirror. "Swell. I wouldn't trust a painkiller from this part of the world to be anything that wasn't designed to be shot straight into a vein. We're in Poppy Central, remember? That's how half these people got rich. The last thing you need is a bottle of highly addictive Silk Road pharmaceuticals. I think we've arrived. Whoa, is this actually someone's *house?*"

Nordine opened the door for Bree and stood off to one side, completely expressionless. I climbed out after her, and we just stood there, gawking.

I'm not sure what I'd been expecting. Something out of the Arabian Nights, probably, all marble and minarets and fancy gilded bits everywhere. Yeah, well, my mistake. The Emir had done a one-eighty. If he'd wanted an antidote to his Gran's peacocks and pools, he'd built himself the right house.

There were no mineral pools out in the front yard of this one, and no peacocks, either. This was four floors of exposed steel framework and gleaming white concrete that looked like something out of some futuristic sci-fi flick about New York. The windows looked to be taller than I was, but there was something about them, the dullness and lack of shine, that made me think they might be bullet-proof glass. We'd actually driven through security gates; they stretched off into the distance, and the damned things looked to be studded with laser triggers.

The Emir of Manaar's personal digs were about as modern as modern gets, and in completely the wrong way. The compound was about as unwelcoming as it was unappealing. Something about it was weirdly familiar, too. I couldn't quite pin it down, but whatever memory was being triggered at the back of my head, it wasn't good.

"Damn." Bree muttered it, under her breath. "It looks like a prison. Even without any bars on the windows, it looks like something you'd want to escape from. It's like bad science fiction or something. Horrible. Why would anyone want to live in that, if they didn't have to?"

"Damned if I know, but you nailed it. Place really does look like a prison. I could even tell you which one."

There it was, that memory: Herlong Prison, northeast edge of California. I'd spent a couple of hours there as a visitor, and even knowing I could walk out whenever I damned well wanted to, even with the warden being a huge Blacklight fan and going out of her way to make it tolerable, the only word I could find for the place was 'awful'.

My knees were throbbing, a sort of dull sting. So was my jaw. I reached out and got hold of Bree's hand.

"I'll tell you what, love, I'm betting the harem guards for this lot aren't eunuchs. Probably macho as fuck, with AK-47s or whatever, unless Ali decides that old-school swords work better with the scenery, or something. Sod it, let's get some supper and head back while I can still chew, yeah? I want to get the weight off my knees."

Nordine came round in front of us, and cleared his throat. "His Excellence is waiting. If you are ready...?"

He waved one hand towards the oversized front doors. No idea what they were made from, because they were open, but from the way the edges glinted where the moonlight hit them, I'd have bet on bronze.

Nordine offered his arm to Bree. I got a flash, a really strong feeling off him, that he really didn't want to, that he was only doing it because it was part of his gig. And Bree really didn't want to touch him, either; she doesn't fancy that sort of contact with strangers. But she took his arm.

Close up, the Emir's place was just as off-putting as it had been from the other end of the drive. We passed through the shiny doors and into a big open reception area. We went past that and into another open area. Beyond that, under some of the steel framing that made the place look as if it were wrongside out, we were led into a tall atrium done up as a dining room. There was a long table set with linen and crockery and whatnot, nice and formal, but in the western way—none of those fruit bowls for peeled grapes Bree'd mentioned earlier. There were two empty places at the table, side by side; every other chair was taken. From the looks of it, we were the last ones in the door.

Bree let go of Nordine's arm. He cleared his throat, and pitched his voice to carry. "Mr. and Mrs. Kinkaid."

Ali al-Wahid was sitting at the head of the table, about half a mile away it seemed like, with Carla at his left side and Patrick at his right. Carla was leaning across the table, getting in on the conversation, but she saw us and waved. Ali had been talking to Patrick and a bony pale bloke I didn't recognise, but that got his attention. He said something to the others, got up and headed our way.

"Thank you, Nordine." He was back to staring at my wife. This time, he at least remembered to swivel his head my way when he was actually talking to me. "I was told of your injury, Mr. Kinkaid. Your wife informed my staff doctor that no more than basic first aid was required. Still, I was concerned. I deeply regret that you have injured yourself while under my roof. Please, come and sit, and we will dine. Patrick Ormand and Bengt Ekberg have been going over requirements for your concert—Bengt is my own chief of security. I trust Nordine got you here in comfort?"

"Yeah, he did, ta. Nice comfy limo. Besides, it's not as if we had far to come, you know? If I hadn't trashed my knees, we could have walked."

"Indeed." He waved off a servant and held Bree's chair out for her. He'd seated us halfway down, between Luke and Domitra. "How did you come to fall?"

"Tripped over a peacock. There's quite a lot of them about, you know?"

Oh, bloody hell. I'm not sure what it was about al-Wahid that made me not want to admit a weakness, but there it was, and the words had come out with more of an edge than I'd planned. I saw Bree shoot me a look, and catch her lower lip between her teeth, biting back a faint smile.

Right. Time to get things back to some kind of normalcy. "Oi, Luke, how goes it, mate? Katia, that's a brilliant dress."

"Indeed. Well, so long as you are recovered." Ali nodded over one shoulder and headed back to his own end of the table. Luke opened his mouth, probably to ask me *never mind how I'm doing, what's all this about tripping over a peacock* but he didn't get the chance, because we got swarmed by a small regiment of servers with carts full of food. Bree was talking to Dom, but when she saw the food, her eyes got wide.

"Whoa." She leaned in so that I could hear her. The noise level in the room, all conversation and explanation of what was on the various plates, was insane. "Four kinds of caviar on one plate? Holy shit, those are black truffles! And this is just the first course. Who's he trying to impress?"

"Don't know, love. Maybe nobody. Maybe everybody." *Yeah, or maybe just you.*

I shook my head at the caviar, and Bree did the same; her feeling about getting salty fish eggs caught in her teeth runs pretty close to my own. I made sure she'd got something that worked for her—it turned out to be figs and pressed duck—and then got a few mouthfuls myself. Meanwhile, the trays just kept coming, and the food got more pricey and rarefied and fancy with every platter they trotted out. Not my thing, yeah? As soon as we got back to London, I thought, I was going out for a nice big plate of fish and chips or maybe even wrapped in newspaper, with malt vinegar on the side, and sod the bad weather.

It was a good ninety minutes before we'd belched our way through about eight courses and finished up with some sort of local sweet, with honey and nuts. Ali's army of uniformed servants whooshed through the room in a cloud of competence, clearing the table, pouring everyone tea out of huge steaming copper pots, and disappearing somewhere into the house, presumably to do a metric fuckload of washing up.

It was obvious our host wanted to give a speech, because he was standing up, tapping on his wineglass. I just hoped he'd keep it short; the stinging in my knees had gone from background to full noise, and I wasn't liking it much. They also felt damp, as if they might be leaking or oozing. Not pleasant at all, and definitely time to check the bandages…

"If I may?" Ali glanced down the table, making sure we were all paying attention. He knew how to pitch his voice to carry, I'll give him that. "I know that you are all tired. I hope you are all satisfied with your meal. I wished to say only that we are looking forward with great eagerness to the concert, and to introduce you to Bengt Ekberg. He is my Chief of Security, for anything to do with my house and my safety, here in Manaar. He will liaise and cooperate with Patrick Ormand. They have decided on the security arrangements to be put in place. Security for my old friend Malcolm is entirely at the discretion of Malcolm himself, and of course Ms. Calley. Mr. Hendry has given our grounds-keepers his list of contract requirements, in terms of space and equipment. Ms. Fanucci has signed off on the housing arrangements for all band and supplemental personnel. If there are any questions, or any objections…?"

He was looking straight at me when he asked that, and he wasn't alone, either. Most of the table had turned my way.

So, yeah, quite a lot had apparently been going on behind the scenes while I'd been getting my knees taped up and taking the nap I'd needed: the band business was taken care of, everything signed off on. Just so long as no one in the band decided to say *fuck it, don't think so mates, I'm staying home*, we were ready to rock and roll.

There was a time when not being woken up and asked for my

vote up front would have left me pissy enough to object out of pique. There was a time I'd have felt left out, the new kid, not important enough to ask. There was a time it would have hurt.

Those days were well behind me. I could take that much for granted these days. Just knowing that saying no would be good enough for the band to walk away from whatever was in the works, that was enough for me.

Everyone was quiet, waiting on me. Ali's speech had made it pretty clear that he'd been told upfront what our policy was: *it's all or nothing, mate, everyone or no one.*

I stood up, feeling my legs shake; Bree was up as well, one hand under my elbow in case she was needed. It was time to get our driver back. "If everyone's in, I'm in as well. Let's do it. Sorry to eat and run, but I'm not in very good shape tonight, and I need to have a lie-down. Thanks for dinner."

"(beep) JP? Hey man, it's Tony. I just wanted to let you know, we're getting there tomorrow. Carla said Sheikh Moneybags built you guys a kickass studio to rehearse in. I can't wait to see what—hang on—What? Oh! Katia says, tell Bree that if she drove that Bugatti and Katia didn't get to watch, Katia's going to kick her ass from one end of the desert to the other. Anyway, see you guys tomorrow night, unless we're snowed in and the flights are grounded. The weather in London sucks ass. Manana, guys. (beep)"

"John?" Bree was stretching, getting some yoga in. "What was that snort for?"

"Just that Katia's got a thing about that fancy car you're getting to drive. She promised you an arse-kicking if you don't wait for her to get here before you drive it. They're getting in tomorrow."

She'd been tucking herself into a lotus, but that got all her attention, and she uncoiled in a hurry. "Was that Tony? How—did he—was he—I mean –"

78

She stopped, and bit her lip. I grinned at her.

"No need to be delicate about it, love. He sounds fine. Nice and rested. If that's the case, the Centre and Mourdain's whole 'meditation, conversation, realisation' thing looks to have done the trick. Oi!"

She'd got up and got my face between her palms. It was a serious kiss, tongue tip to tongue tip and a bit more. The girl meant business.

"Wow." I got my breath back; both arms had got themselves round her. "What was that in aid of, lady?"

"I don't know." Her eyes had gone very green, and a bit damp. "Relief, or pride, or whatever, I don't know. Do I need a reason? John, what are you—oh, *man...*"

I don't know about Bree, but personally I was thankful for the oversized ceiling fan. It wasn't a hot night, not by Middle Eastern standards, but we generated plenty of heat on our own. After my heart attack at Wembley, Bree'd got into the habit of wanting me hard up against her long after the actual slap and tickle was done with, and that made for even more warmth.

Besides, we generally got chillier weather than the mid-seventies, most Christmas weeks, no matter whether we were in London or home in San Francisco. We'd only got back to Manaar ourselves two days ago, and my bones could still feel the London winter in them.

"Hello, darling." I had my fingers laced through hers, feeling her wedding ring against my skin. My heart was doing the fandango, wanting to argue with the tickybox, but the tickybox was winning the argument. It usually does—that's its gig. I touched my tongue to the hollow in her collarbone. "Crikey, you're a bit of a salt lick right now."

She made an incoherent little noise. It sounded like contentment, but moments like these, I can never be sure; she was still rippling away, miles away in whatever happy physical reality I'd

79

navigated her to. I was about to try for another fifteen minutes, just taking her places and letting her ripple on, when my phone went.

I rolled off her and reached for it, and she let me. With the largest single audience we'd ever played for showing up in less than a week, I wasn't about to blow off phone calls. Bree knew that, and she knew why. The only reason I'd missed the call from Tony was because I'd been in that fancy studio Tony'd mentioned, getting some early rehearsals in and meeting with our sound and set designers about the tech. The venue for the gig was a huge park in the capital city, and with a quarter million people projected to be trotting in for this one, I wanted to know what the blokes in charge were planning.

"Hello?" I was watching my wife. She'd pulled herself upright and picked up where she'd left off on the yoga postures. This time, though, she was sitting on our bed and she wasn't wearing yoga trousers, or anything else.

"JP? It's Carla. I just wanted to let you know your interferon got here today. I'll send it over with Nordine in the morning, when he comes to pick Bree up for her lesson in the Veyron. Oh, and Tony and Katia will be here tomorrow afternoon—I told him to plan on meeting his equerry and let him know he needs to be ready to rehearse at ten the day after tomorrow. Are you okay? You sound breathless."

"I'm fine. Just a bit warm." Bree was on all fours, facing me, one leg up and stretched out behind her. The Spitting Cat, she told me that posture's called. She arched her back and lifted her head, just enough for me to see her smile through the curtain of hair. "Carla, sorry, I need to go do something. Thanks for letting me know. See you tomorrow."

I clicked the phone off and tossed it aside. Sod it. Anyone who wasn't Bree wanted me tonight, they weren't getting me.

This time, Bree actually got her land legs back before I did.

Nice to be able to surprise both of us at my age, yeah? I was still trying to get my breath back while she headed off to the loo to get my pills and one of the fancy carafes Ali's people kept us stocked with. We'd got a full suite this time, and Ali hadn't been joking when he'd told us things were being tarted up between our last visit and the show. Considering just how much tarting up had got done between the quick trip and now, either a lot of dosh had changed hands, or there was an overseer with a whip involved.

Life in the seraglio wasn't all bad, considering. Even without the peacocks, the place would have made the Four Seasons look drab.

"Here. Meds. Wow, it's nearly midnight." She pulled the silk blanket up around her waist and watched me get the pills down. "John, is it okay if I ask you something?"

That got one eyebrow up. Her feeling she needs permission to ask me questions, that's something I'd hoped had gone the way of disco and dinosaurs.

"You can ask anything you want, love. I'm surprised you don't know that by now."

"No, no, I do know." She sounded defensive, suddenly. "It's just that this is really band business, not mine. At least, I don't think it's mine. But..."

She trailed off. I waited, but nothing: she'd gone quiet. "But what? Bloody hell, your shoulders are halfway to the ceiling! What's wrong, Bree? Talk to me, please."

"Okay." She bit her lip. "We haven't talked about it since we got back here. But, well, has Patrick said anything at all about those two girls? About how security is planning on getting them to stay away from the band and the gig, I mean? I don't know if anyone even gives a shit except me, and I don't want to stick my nose in where it's got no business being, but I hate not knowing, John. I don't even know if they're still around, but every time I walk out

81

there, I expect to see them naked in one of the pools." She shivered suddenly. "And I really don't want to see them at all."

"I don't fancy the idea much myself."

She had a point. I hadn't given the twins a second thought since we'd got back to Manaar this trip, probably because I hadn't actually seen them. Out of sight out of mind, and all that rubbish. But Bree was right, and it was something that needed dealing with, even if the only result was to put her mind at ease.

"No clue, love, but I'll check with Patrick and Bengt tomorrow. I'd ring Patrick now, but it's rather late for that." I planted a kiss on her shoulder. "It's not as if we're expecting them to climb in through the windows. Let's get some kip. You don't want to be driving that scary set of wheels if you're groggy. I've got to head over to the site in the morning anyway, before rehearsal. I'll talk to Patrick then."

Nordine showed up at ten the next morning, and this time there was no nonsense about bullet-proof limos. He was behind the wheel of the Bugatti, the first time I'd seen the thing.

I don't know a damned thing about cars. I've never learnt to drive; I manage to memorise what model Jag my wife's driving at any given moment, and that's my limit. Still, you'd have to be an idiot to look at the black and orange monster Nordine had just slid up in, and not get that this wasn't something you'd leave in the carpark while you went for a quick pint and a kebab. It looked as pricey as it actually was, and even just idling, it sounded terrifying: not really loud, but deep, as if eight thousand bass players had all hit the same note together after doing a lot of blow first. I could feel the thrum of that engine, all the way down in my belly.

Carla had made a tactical error, and nearly sent the tickybox into overdrive, by telling me how much the Veyron cost and, more to the point, how fast it went. I'd had a moment of wanting to come the heavy husband, and telling Bree I wasn't having her driving anything at over two hundred and fifty miles an hour, but I'd muffled it. For one thing, she's not a daredevil—she's a safe driver, never had an accident or even a summons for speeding. And she's my wife, not my property. However much I might have wanted to flip my shit, I don't get to order her about, you know? If she fancies driving the local dictator's supercar down a closed road as fast as she can get it to go, I'll try talking her out of it, but I don't get a vote.

That didn't mean watching her climb into the damned thing wasn't going to leave me grinding my teeth, though. It was just as well Luke and his driver had pulled in right behind the Bugatti. I had a quick silent conversation with the tickybox—*right, do your thing, she'll be fine, she's not an idiot or a kid*—snatched a quick kiss off Bree, waved her off towards Nordine, and climbed into the limo, next to Luke.

"Oi, JP. You're looking well-rested this morning."

Luke looked pretty wiped, probably from missing Karen; Bree had come out with me, but she was the only band wife there. Karen's widowed daughter Suzanne had spent Christmas at Draycote, and the current plan had Karen flying out with the rest of the wives on Boxing Day. I didn't know what Suzanne had planned, and didn't much care. I'd have been quite surprised to see her in this neck of the woods, though, considering the bad history with the al-Wahid family.

"Yeah, well, a good night's sleep'll do that." I was damned if I wanted to rub his face in me having Bree there. He wouldn't have minded—he knows better than most people just how much she does to make my life possible—but I wasn't going there. "Did you know Tony and Katia were getting in tonight? I need a word with Patrick and Bengt before we get started on anything. What exactly do they need us for today, anyway?"

"Nial probably wants us to tramp about and see if we're okay with the stage. Or maybe we're just expected to gawk at the

83

magnificence, or something. Hell, I'm not complaining. It'll be nice to actually get a look at the venue, now that the stage is up. Besides, I could use a break from the rehearsal studio."

He yawned suddenly. "Sorry. I'm not used to the temperature difference and I don't sleep well without Karen anyway. I'll tell you what, JP, I think I'm getting old. Travel didn't used to fry me like this. Oh crikey, is this it? Are we here?"

According to all the brochures, Amina Plaza's the largest public gathering place in Manaar, and like the rest of the place, it's dead flat. As far as I could tell, Manaar's about a third the size of California, and it's shaped pretty much the same, long and skinny with a curve at the southern end. The upper part's unreclaimed coastal desert, with some oil deposits in it. Bree looked the place up online to get a better handle on it, and she'd said something about the Kalahari, in Africa.

The southern end, where the Emirate hooks out to the east, is rather different. There's plenty of sand, but it's also got things growing, and quite a sizeable freshwater river to go along with all the hot springs underground. It even gets the occasional rain shower.

The southern end is also where Ali keeps his capital city, Medin-Manaar. About a third of it's given over to a huge green park, and huge is the word: as an open space, it'll hold three hundred thousand people with some room to spare in case of a stampede. Just as well, too, since we were expecting a quarter million to show up on New Year's Eve. It was nice to know there was room for an extra fifty thousand or so if Ali had underestimated the head count.

The Plaza's only a few minutes from the Queen's Palace by car, so there wasn't time for conversation. This was our first look at the site with the stage up, and I wasn't ready for the scale of it. Blacklight sold out Estadia Azteca in Mexico City, a hundred and five thousand screaming fans, on the Book of Days tour. We'd packed out massive stadiums from Argentina to Barcelona, but Amina Plaza was in an entirely different league.

The car pulled into the plaza from the end at the farthest point from the stage. That probably added to the sense of enormity, but the fact that the stage looked tiny from this distance really brought home just how many bodies were going to be moving about the place in just over a week.

"Jesus." Luke had got the window down for a better look. "This is the plaza? It's bloody *huge*. Christ, the stage is three hundred feet across and it looks like a puppet theatre!"

"Gordon *Bennett*!" I had the other window down; we must have looked like a pair of dogs, heads out the windows and tongues hanging out. Taking in the scale of the thing, my mouth had suddenly gone dry. "Luke, we're having video screens, right? Really big video screens, and lots of them...?"

"Yeah, we've got those." We were rolling up a long paved stretch between what looked to be miles of green lawn, and the closer we got to the stage, the bigger the area behind us looked. "I'm more worried about the seating. I know why we went with a festival setup, much easier logistics, but that's going to be one hell of a crowd with nowhere to park their bums during the slow numbers. I wish Carla hadn't headed back to LA this morning— she'd have the information at the front of her brain."

"Yeah, well, Nial or Ronan should know. Not to worry, Luke, it'll be covered. I trust the staff, you know?"

We were close enough now to see the stage layout in detail: it was smaller than our Book of Days three-circle clean-stage rig, and a lot more simple. Rather than trot our own stadium rig out of storage, we'd hired what we needed. Besides, with the size of this gig, we didn't have enough in storage to cover all the remote towers we'd need. The bill for the gear was going to be astronomical, but Carla and Ian had made sure that the rider put the full cost for any hired gear in Ali's lap. According to them, he'd signed off on that without a blink. I found myself wondering, one more time, just why the bloke was so set on having us play his little do.

Ronan, our sound designer, was waiting for us as we rolled up, with our stage designer, Nial Laybourne, right behind him. "Good, you're here. Mac's just got here, and the Bunker Brothers are setting up. Any word on Tony? I'd like you lot all up here together, to get the feel of it."

"They'll be in later, unless Heathrow's shut down for snow." Ian had come up. "Everyone's coming in today, wives, techs, the lot. We looked at the weather service projections and decided to get them all out while the going was good. Oi, chaps, you two look slackjawed. It's just a stage. Not nearly as impressive as the last one we trotted round the world."

"That's the problem. Coming in from the far end of the plaza, this thing looks like a bloody shoebox, or a kid's puppet theatre, or something." I'd been craning my neck over the hammering and lifting. "Ronan, hang on a sec, yeah? Oi! Patrick! Bengt! Can I get a word with you both, please?"

Up to that point, my contact with Bengt Ekberg had been shaking hands when we'd been introduced by Patrick, and not much else. Ali's personal muscle coordinator looked to be lacking any muscles of his own; he was so thin, he might have been designed to press all Bree's *must-feed-him* buttons. First time we'd met him, at that state dinner a couple of weeks back, I'd been too sick to give him or anything else much thought, but Dom's comment—that he looked as if the Vikings had booted him off the longboat for not meeting the minimum weight requirements for sacking Constantinople—had stuck in my head.

Now here he was, sticking out a long bony hand. I took it and shook it: nice easy grip, not trying to prove anything. He really did look underfed. Crikey, the bloke was even skinnier than I was.

"Hi, JP. How can I help you?"

"I've got a question I need to ask, for my wife. Thing is, it might be a bit delicate." I had one eyebrow up. "Sorry, but I hadn't realised you were American. Southern California?"

He grinned at me. He was so damned bony, the grin looked like a death rictus. It should have been scary, or at least off-putting, but somehow, it wasn't; it worked on him.

"Good catch. Actually, I'm pure Swede, but my father was a professor of speech pathology at UCLA. His TA used to call him Professor Potato-Eater." He lowered his voice. "Do you want to find a quiet corner? If the question is delicate, yelling it over all this noise is probably a bad move. Besides, they're setting up the first portable toilets."

I left Luke and Ian discussing video screens, and followed Patrick back behind the stage and into a trailer. It was obvious we'd borrowed the office of one of the construction bosses; there were specs and blueprints and schematics all over the desk, but the real giveaway was the corkboard on the wall behind the desk chair. It had our contract rider pinned up to it, with the tech specs for the stage at the front, all highlighted in nice bright colours, very reassuring.

"So." Bengt leaned up against the desk. "How can I help you? You said this was sensitive, JP?"

"Yeah, it is." I took a deep breath. Patrick was watching me, and I'd have laid odds he knew just what I wanted to ask, or at least who I wanted to ask about. He wasn't opening his mouth, though. Ah, sod it—might as well just say it. "It's about the al-Wahid twins. We've made it part of the deal that they can't come anywhere near the band while we're here: show, personnel, lodgings, the lot. Problem is, when we were here last, I found them skinny-dipping in the pools just outside our window."

"What?" I'd surprised Patrick, after all. "When was this, JP?"

"The day we'd first got here, and I fell and bashed up my knees. They climbed out of the damned pool, one of them in half

87

a towel and the other one stark, and giggled at me. I got the hell out of it—sorry, Bengt, I told you this was tricky, yeah? I know you work for their dad, but the truth is, those girls are bad news. There's good reasons we don't want them around."

They were both listening, not saying anything yet. I was betting Patrick had already guessed just what was coming next. He knows quite a lot about the way Bree and I work as a couple.

"Thing is, I had to tell my wife about it. Right after it happened, she was concentrating on my having got hurt, but she's got to the point now where she's afraid she's going to turn a corner and come up against one of them. I want to be able to let her know it's all right, not to worry, that won't happen. Question is, *is* it all right? Are they about? Neither of us has seen them since, but I promised her I'd find out."

"Bengt, that's your purview, not mine." Patrick sounded completely neutral, but something had flickered in his face. "I haven't seen them since I got here, JP, but of course, that doesn't prove anything—it's a big compound and we've all been working. I've got over two hundred hired security people here, but none of that touches the royal family. Bengt?"

"The daughters of the house are in residence, at home in Manaar." Out of nowhere, he sounded a lot less American, and a lot more European, or maybe Middle Eastern. Formal, you know? "They are aware that they have been barred from anything to do with the band, or with the show. They have their own quarters, under their father's roof. That you have not seen either of them since your arrival this time is no surprise. They have been instructed as to what's expected of them. They know what their duty is."

We were all quiet. Outside, people were hammering, yelling, measuring, sawing, drilling, assembling, doing what needed to happen to get the hired stage assembled and ready. In here, Patrick was watching me, and I was watching Bengt.

Something had moved in that bony face. I couldn't have said what it was, maybe annoyance at having to explain, maybe being irritated at me calling him out on something he thought was a professional issue, maybe something else entirely. I couldn't read him.

He knew I was watching him, too. He straightened up, and moved towards the door. Both of Patrick's eyebrows were up.

"Please assure Mrs. Kinkaid that the princesses won't trouble her. And now, if there's nothing else, I believe you were wanted onstage."

Chapter Six

"So, you ready to drive that thing tomorrow?"

We were spending Christmas night in Manaar just the way we might have spent it at home in San Francisco, or at the mews rental in South London: having a nice quiet supper and a serious roll-around for afters. That roll-around's the nearest thing we've got to a family tradition: no gifts, except each other. As far as I'm concerned, being able to taste salt on my wife's skin is the best present anyone could offer me anyway.

"Mmmm. I think so." She moved under me, just enough to get the edge of the tickybox under my left collarbone back where it belonged. "Nordine's coming at nine. He says it's best to take the car up to speed before the road surface gets too hot. Are you in the studio tomorrow? Or is it an outdoor rehearsal?"

"Outdoors. Now that all those damned portable toilets are set up, Ronan want to make sure there's no bounce-back issue. But I want to watch you do your drive first." I rolled over and pulled her up against me. "Happy Christmas, love."

"Liar. You do *not* want to watch, and you know it." She smiled at me, one of those smiles she never seems to produce for anyone but me. One more present, yeah? "Thank you for being such a nice husband, John. I'm going to feel better knowing you're there. No, don't freak out, I'm not really scared. That machine handles like a dream—it's actually easier to drive than the Jag, especially since I can leave it in automatic and let it do its own gear shifting. I just like knowing you're there, watching my back."

"Yeah, well, at the speed that thing gets up to, I really will be watching your back. Disappearing down the road like a damned jet, probably."

We were quiet, just curled together. Outside in the courtyard, something was singing; I had the feeling it might be a nightingale, since we were in Arabia and they've actually got them here. The fancy blue and gilt-painted grilles over the windows to our suite were open, letting the night air in.

"John? What are you doing?"

"Just relaxing." Something I've noticed the past few years, with all the travelling we'd got done: the air tastes different in different parts of the world, especially at night. In San Francisco, it depends on the time of year, but mostly it tastes of the ocean, and the fog, clean and salty. In the South of France, it tastes of flowers, the kind that bloom at night and smell almost too sweet sometimes. Here we were in Arabia, at the end of December, and the night air tasted soft and light, flowers, but not the same ones that grow in France...

"Wow, that jasmine smells amazing. I can almost taste it." Bree was murmuring into my shoulder. "Tony and Katia were really kind of neat today, weren't they? Almost like newlyweds."

"Yeah, a bit shy and careful with each other." I was beginning

91

to drowse off; the physics of sex being what they are, I'm likely to drop off first. But she was right, there was a kind of delicacy about the Mancusos at the moment, as if, now that Tony had gone through the fire and come out the other end, they were having to relearn each other. "In a good way, though. Kind of nice to—Bree? What...?"

"Someone's in the courtyard, just outside." She'd gone stiff against me, and her voice was very quiet, too quiet. Suddenly, I wasn't sleepy anymore. "Listen."

I held my breath, keeping still myself, trying to sort out the different sounds. The nightingale was still there, singing its head off. I could hear the steady burble of the water, endlessly circulating in that collection of mineral hot pools, and the night breeze, moving in through the bars of the grilles...

"Yeah, I hear it." There it was, a soft splash, a faint quiet murmur of voices. "Sounds like someone's having a midnight dip. Could be anyone, Bree. Didn't Katia say something about wanting to make some time for a swim? Do you want me to throw some trousers on, go have a look? I will, if you want me to."

"No." She let her breath back out, and I felt her relax. Her voice was still low, but it was normal again. "Sorry. I'm being silly. You're right, it's probably Katia. If she and Tony are taking a midnight swim, I wouldn't want to disturb them. Whoa, I think I just hit the wall. Goodnight, babe."

When Bree falls asleep, she doesn't mess about. I get rather jealous of it sometimes, the way she can just decide *right, I need to be asleep now*, and off she goes, lights out and not quite snoring. I've never sorted out how she does that; even before the MS, I was iffy about sleep, and it's a lot worse these days.

So there was my wife, getting ready to drive something at two hundred fifty miles an hour in the morning, off to dreamland within two minutes of telling me goodnight. Unfortunately, I was nowhere near sleep. Maybe it was the taste of jasmine on the air, maybe it was too much coming up in the near future, or maybe I was more worried about the drive of hers than I was letting on to myself. Whatever it was, my brain was too busy to let go straight off. From the edge of sleep, I'd woken up.

Six days to go, and Blacklight would be playing the biggest show we'd ever done. We weren't the first band to headline a gig to a crowd this size, not by any stretch—the Stones had done it more than once. But I couldn't shrug and say, *right, just another gig*. It wasn't.

If I'd had any inclination to try and shrink the scope of the show in my head, the portable toilets had set me straight: there were over two thousand of the damned things, and tankers were being brought in to keep them usable. Stu Corrigan had taken one look at them being unloaded, lorry after lorry after lorry, and summed it up quite nicely: *Fuck me, that's a lot of crappers.*

Bree sighed and turned over, snuggling deeper into her pillows. The silk sheet was still down round her waist, but it wouldn't be long before she'd be reaching for it, pulling it up round her shoulders and burrowing in hard. The room was still warm, but it was going to cool off quite a lot over the next couple of hours. We'd learned that much about the Arabian nights: when the temperature drops, it goes fifteen degrees or more, and it does it quick.

Ali's interior designers had left his Gran's windows where they were, just slightly beyond what's comfortable for me to reach. All they'd done was touch up the paint and gilt, and added decent locks and a longish hook stick thing to pull things together with. They hadn't enlarged them, either—they probably felt long skinny short windows with shiny grilles on them added to the ambience, or something. Dealing with them was a nuisance, and normally Bree would have shut them, since she's got two inches on me and a longer reach as well. Tonight, we'd been busy making Christmas merry, and we'd both forgotten.

The chill of that desert temperature drop nailed me as soon as I slid out from under the silk. Funny thing: with the colder air, the taste and smell of it changed. There didn't seem to be quite as much jasmine in the mix anymore, and it wasn't as sweet, somehow.

I headed over toward the casement, shivering like a puppy in a thunderstorm. Right. Grab the damned hook, no fumbling about, pull the grilles shut and down and get the fuck back under the covers and next to my nice warm wife...

Maybe the room was quieter than I'd thought. Maybe the breeze had died down. All I know is, the splash from outside sounded too loud. It wasn't the soft light noise that had got Bree to stiffen up—this was deeper, fuller, heavier. And there were no soft murmurs now. What I was hearing through the open grille sounded more like the slap of bare feet against the ground. Someone was running.

I set the stick back down. Maybe I've seen a bit too much these past few years, enough to get paranoid, or maybe my sensors are just permanently cocked open. Whatever—I don't know. The bottom line was, my heart was pushing the tickybox into overdrive. Every instinct I've got was yelling at me.

I got into my trousers as quickly and quietly as I could manage it. Bree was fathoms deep. Good; I was damned if I wanted her waking up and having to deal with anything in the way of trouble. I got my shoes on, and threw on one of the silk robes that came with the suite. I must have looked a complete git, designer shoes and a bathrobe straight out of Central Casting's idea of a Rudolph Valentino film.

Room keys, lock the door behind me, out into the corridor. Odd thing, the way the shadows along the walls seemed to move so much out here...

"Johnny?"

"Mac, for fuck's sake!" I managed to keep it to not much more

94

than a whisper. "You trying to give me another heart attack? Oi, Dom, glad you're here. You heard that, then?"

"Somebody fell in the pool. They haven't climbed out. Mac, keep behind me and don't come outside until I say so." Dom was leading us down the hall, out into the courtyard, Mac trotting obediently behind her. I tucked in behind him. If Dom wanted to lead the charge, I was damned if I was going to argue.

We hadn't got completely out of doors before Dom changed her stance. I've seen her do it before—when something even looks like posing a threat to Mac, she basically becomes a killing machine with an *on* switch—but it doesn't get any less impressive over time.

"Stay here." She'd contracted somehow, but expanded as well: whatever she'd done with her muscles, she was tighter and more compact, but also a lot more menacing. Looking at her, you knew this was someone who could fuck you up without taking the time to blink. "Both of you, until I tell you it's okay. I don't want anyone getting in my way. Clear?"

"Of course." Mac usually manages to sound slightly amused when he's dealing with his bodyguard in full protect mode, but not tonight. He was tense as an overwound guitar sting. "Go."

Memory—what sticks with you and why, the pictures you retain in your head when things a lot more immediately important or personal fade out—is really peculiar, you know? There's probably a thousand small things I've forgotten in my life, things I'd like to remember, but the mental image of Domitra moving across the open courtyard, keeping low to the ground and looking from side to side as she went, is right there in my brain, and has been since it happened. If I close my eyes and bring it up in my head, I can actually hear the nightingale.

The moon was up, just starting to come down, a half-moon that looked a lot brighter than we get in Europe or America. It washed everything out except Dom, moving across the courtyard in the moonlight like Bree's Siamese, Farrowen, when she's stalking a ray of moonlight, looking to be made of liquid silver herself. I found myself crossing my fingers, holding my breath, wishing to myself the way a kid might hold his breath and wish for something: *please let her be disappointed, let there not be anything for her to find, let it all just be moonlight and no more than that...*

There were nine full pools in that courtyard, and she looked at every one of them. She went for the far side of the courtyard first, keeping close to the base of the outer seraglio walls, the side away from our suites. Mac muttered something under his breath, very quiet; I couldn't make out what he'd said, but it sounded anxious. We were both watching Dom, moving from the paths between the outer pools to the inner ones, through the centre and back out, ending up at the pools closest to our windows.

At the far end of that cluster of three pools, she stopped. That's the clearest memory of that whole bit of weirdness, Dom stopping, her shoulders tensed up the way Bree's do, her head locked sideways. She was looking into the third pool.

Mac took a step forward. That brought it home to me, just how rattled he was, because she'd told him to stay where he was and when Dom tells him that, he does it. That's what he pays her for. No point paying a bodyguard to protect you if you're not going to do what she tells you to do, you know?

"Wait." I put a hand out, keeping my voice low. "Mac, wait. She's found something. Look, she's heading back."

Another memory with total clarity, Dom heading back to us. She wasn't running, but somehow, in some way, she covered the distance in what seemed a few quick breaths.

"Problem." She was breathing through her nose, like a racehorse. "Big problem, yo. Someone in the third pool, face down. There's blood in the water. A *lot* of blood."

We stared at her like a pair of waxworks. Mac seemed to be holding his breath, and as for me, I couldn't seem to get my throat to work. She hadn't sounded dramatic, but the picture she'd brought up in my head was really vivid, and really unpleasant. Someone in the pool, face down, blood. Right.

"Domitra?" Mac had his voice back, and he'd forgotten about keeping it lowered. "Why in hell are we standing about? So we can wait for whoever it is to drown—Johnny, what are you –"

"Shit!" The path alongside the suite wing was suddenly bathed in a different kind of light. "That's our room—Bree's woken up. I'm off."

I turned back into the corridor, a few seconds too late. There were doors opening, people talking, movement. Luke was out, calling back in to Karen to stay put. Cyn and Stu Corrigan were both heading towards me. I could hear voices as everyone else woke up to it. And here came Bree, her hair tousled and her eyes wide, in her yoga clothes, and with bare feet.

"John...?"

"Dom's found someone in one of the pools. I haven't looked, but it sounds bad. No, Bree, damn it! Stay here, will you please? I'm going to see if I can help. Just wait, all right?"

The corridor was full now: Tony and Katia, the Wilsons, Ian. Karen had got enough clothes on to pass for decent, and come out. There was something very primitive about it, as if everyone was clustered together for some kind of tribal protection against who knew what, monsters or something.

"Where in hell is Patrick?" Katia sounded sharp, scared. "Isn't this a security thing?"

"Patrick's not quartered in the seraglio, remember?" Ian had gone just outside the doors to the courtyard. "He's got a first briefing with two hundred hired security professionals tomorrow morning at eight. He needs to be with the security details. Fuck! What are they doing down there? Hang about, people, I'll be back."

Bree reached out suddenly, and got hold of my hand. Her own

was cold, much too cold. I let go and got one arm round her, pulling her close up against me, the pair of us stepping out into the courtyard, watching the group at the edge of the pool: Mac, Domitra and Ian.

They were arguing about something, Mac and Dom waving towards the pool and gesturing, Ian shaking his head *no*. Whatever it was, Ian apparently won. He stood up and pulled out his cell. Words, bits of information and conversation, floated across to us.

"Patrick...? Look, mate, we've got an emergency...dead...in the pool...no, not drowned...throat cut...a fucking mess...get Bengt out here you too, yes I said Bengt....just get here now... royal family... five minutes, good..."

I didn't realise I'd let go of Bree, much less that I'd moved, until I was halfway down the path. *Royal family.*

Shit, shit, *shit*. If those broken sentences had meant what it sounded like they'd meant, there wasn't going to be a fan in the world big enough to cope with what was going to hit it.

Ian saw me coming. He met me halfway up the path, getting his body in front of me, like an American footballer. He shook his head at me.

"JP, look, you want to go back up and wait, please? There's nothing you can do and it's pretty grim down there." He sounded gruff. "No need to give yourself bad dreams over it, and we don't want Bree heading down this way either. No, trust me, nothing in hell to be done but deal with it. He's dead, all right." His shoulders sagged, suddenly. "God, what a fucking mess. I don't know what's going to happen now, about the gig."

"He?" The royal family, he'd said. He'd demanded Bengt. Oh Christ. If this was Ali in the pool with his throat cut, the gig was going to be the least of our worries—getting out of Manaar alive would be more like it. "It's not one of the twins?"

"The twins? No." He craned his neck, peering around me.

There was cars coming towards the seraglio, moving hard and fast, screeching into the drive, doors slamming, Patrick and Bengt and God only knew who else. The nightingales were still making noise out there in the dark, trilling like mad things, lacing the cold night air with birdsong. "It's Nordine. Sorry, JP, but I don't think Bree's driving that Bugatti in the morning."

Over the past few years, I've seen more late nights that involved dealing with coppers on the hunt, and dead bodies lying about, than I want to think about. But the hours of Boxing Day morning, what happened after Ali's people had come and fished what was left of our personal equerry out of the water outside our bedroom window, was new to me. It was completely outside my experience.

It was clear, straight off, that the people in charge were Patrick and Bengt. I was too freaked and too rattled at the time to give any real thought as to why that seemed so weird, but it would have been obvious if I'd been thinking straight: what were two heads of security, both foreigners, doing in charge of investigating how a dead bloke, one who'd worked personally for the Emir, had fetched up in a pool in Medin-Manaar? Ali had plenty of local rozzers, but Patrick and Bengt were definitely running the show.

I'd got hold of Bree again. The pair of us clustered near the suite wing corridor entrance with the rest of the Blacklight contingent, waiting for someone to tell us what needed to happen next. Just then, I was concentrating on being ready to get between Bree and the body they were fishing out of the pool. The shortest route from the pools to the ambulance that had just come screaming into the courtyard was straight past where we were standing. If Bree showed any signs of not doing what she was told when they carried that shrouded stretcher towards us, if she even looked like giving me any argument when I pulled her back indoors and away, I was prepared to get heavy about it. Ian had called it grim, and he'd mentioned nightmares. That was enough for me—I wasn't having my wife exposed to it.

"Patrick, for heaven's sake, what's going on?" That's another visual that's stayed in my head: Barb Wilson with her hair in a mess, her in fleecy pink pyjamas and a pair of shiny black stilettos. Turned out they were the nearest shoes she'd had to hand, since she hadn't unpacked her suitcase yet. "What do you need us to do?"

"I don't know any more about what's going on yet than you do, Barb. As soon as I get details, I'll report them, believe me. For now, it's just the bare fact: Nordine Benhamou's dead. As for what you need to do, I'd say nothing yet, except stay back and out of the way."

Patrick was watching Bengt, who'd left the ambulance people at the other end and come up to us. That bony Scandinavian face was locked down hard, but I could see his Adam's apple working as he kept swallowing. I wondered if he was actually trying not to have himself a sick-up. "Bengt, I'd like to get our people back to their rooms. It's a pity we don't have a space in the suite wing large enough to fit everyone, but if everyone's back where they belong, we know where to find everyone."

Bengt managed a nod; he really did look as if whatever he'd seen in the pool had left his supper wanting to come straight back up again. He kept staring off towards the city, then jerking his back towards us again. "Yes." The Adam's apple went all the way, held, went down again. "All right."

"Sounds good to me." Dom was in front of Mac. You'd think that, surrounded by everyone else and with what passed for Manaari security two feet away, she'd have relaxed a little and eased up being quite so protective of Mac, but no. "You guys want me up first? Since I found the dude?"

"I don't know yet, Dom. I don't think it really matters." Patrick was doing the same thing Bengt was: staring off towards the city, then remembering we were watching him, and jerking his attention back to us. Really bizarre, you know? I couldn't sort out what they were on the lookout for. It wasn't as if someone was going to show up with some way of getting Nordine's blood back inside, and bringing him back to life again. "Look, if I can please get everyone to go back to your rooms? That will make our job a lot easier..."

His voice tailed off. A car had pulled into the courtyard, a big bullet-proof job, the Manaari flag fluttering behind it. I suddenly got what Bengt and Patrick had been watching for.

For all that the Emir of Manaar had his own personal security chief, he'd seemed to me to be quite casual about his personal safety. He strolled about the place with only a single detail covering him; once or twice, visiting the studio, he'd actually come out with no security at all, just a driver. He really hadn't seemed worried about someone having a go at him, at least not since we'd got here.

Yeah, well, things had changed, and damned fast, too. Ali's usual deal was to wait for his driver to open the door and stand there like a stuffed waxworks dummy while Ali did his cock of the walk, it's-good-to-be-king thing. Tonight, the driver opened the limo door and four pairs of black boots, worn by four commando types, hit the pavement in a big hurry. The commando types were carrying what looked like serious firepower, and the firepower, whatever the damned things were, were pointed straight at the rest of us.

I looked up, and made a mistake: I locked eyes with the nearest commando. Next thing I knew, he'd moved, not just himself but the gun, as well; he'd gone from pointing it towards us to pointing it at us, and the muzzle of the fucking thing was aimed straight at my midsection. Next to me, Bree sucked in her breath.

"That's not necessary." Patrick had somehow got himself between me and the gun. "Everyone is right here, present and accounted for. Lower that, please. Your Excellency...?"

"Lower it. You insult my guests with your nonsense." Ali was out of the car, and I was getting my first look at just how opaque that cold smooth face could be. There was nothing there I could read, nothing at all. Behind him, the commando lowered the gun, and my stomach settled back into its proper place; it had been trying to crawl behind my spine. "Bengt. What is happening here? I will hear all of it, and at once."

Bengt told him. That's how we got the details of just what Dom had found in the third pool, and the more we heard, the paler Bree got. Bengt wasn't out for the shock value, but the thing was, he was taking his boss seriously, and Ali had said he wanted all of it.

I'm not going into what Bengt was telling Ali. It was bad enough hearing it the first time. Short version was that someone had done a very nice job severing our equerry's throat nearly from ear to ear. Even without anyone having time to take more than a fast look, one thing was obvious: whoever had nailed him hadn't been messing about. There was blood spattered for a few feet along the edge of the pool, and the water was full of it. In the meantime, I had hold of Bree's hand and I was keeping an eye on what they were doing down by the pool, lifting something weirdly limp and bloodless-looking out of the water, onto a gurney, pulling a sheet over it, strapping it down, turning the gurney round...

"Ali." I'd got his attention, and everyone else's with it. "Look, I'm not having my wife made to stand about watching the parade, all right? If that's a problem, sorry mate, but we'll have to argue it later. Bree, no, don't even think about arguing with me." I leaned up and kissed her. "I'll be along in a minute, I swear. You don't want to see this, and I don't want you having nightmares. Off you go."

She opened her mouth and shut it again. I had my back to the rest of the crowd, and one eyebrow up. I mouthed it at her: *Please.*

She turned, and went. Down the corridor, I heard the door open and shut quietly behind her. The rest of us stayed where we were, watching the blokes in the dark blue jackets wheeling the gurney along the path, directly at us.

No one was saying anything, not a word. As they got up close, Ali stepped out in front of them, and they stopped.

"Show me." He sounded completely alien, about as old school as I'd ever heard anyone sound. I was suddenly reminded, full stop, that this was another culture, another set of rules, another world. "He was my servant. I will see the wrong I must redress. Show me."

There was no hesitation, none at all. One of them held the gurney in place, and the other pulled away the sheet, down and off Nordine's face, halfway down his chest.

There was a moment of absolute quiet. Then there was noise, plenty of it, Barb Wilson saying something I couldn't make out, and Luke muttering under his breath behind me—*bloody hell oh bloody hell no don't Karen don't look*—and people shuffling and moving about, Tony whispering to Katia to shut her eyes for fuck's sake, and Domitra peering round me, focusing on Nordine's face, saying something about how much blood he'd lost to be that blue.

I'm not going into detail, but I was damned glad I'd got Bree to head back inside. I was going to have enough bad dreams over this one to do for both of us. Then he was decently covered again, and Ali had waved the gurney off towards the ambulance, and away to wherever they were taking the body.

"Okay." Even Patrick was rattled, and that's saying quite a lot. He doesn't rattle easily, and almost never visibly. It's not as if he hasn't see his full quota of dead bodies, either—Christ, he's a retired homicide copper. "Your Excellency, may I ask, how would you like me to proceed? My first responsibility is to our people, but I understand that this changes things. What do you want me to do? If this is over to Bengt, I'll be happy to –"

"No." Ali had been looking away, but he turned toward us. For the first time, with the ambulance headlights on full and brightening up the courtyard, I got a look at what was happening to his face, in his eyes. "You will find out, both of you. Your duty is to your people. This is understood. But before you leave here, you will find out. That is what you owe me."

Flat as a stone in one of those deserts in the north, that voice was, and just as cold. No argument was possible, not that I could see, and from the total silence around us, I got that I wasn't the only one thinking that way. Ali had turned, looking off down the trail towards the pool, taking a step in that direction. I suddenly thought *right, is he wondering how to drain the bloody water out of it?* The commandos still had their hands on their guns. My skin was moving on my bones, and it wasn't from the chill of the night air.

"What about the show?" Ian had got his voice back. "Is that still on? Look, I'm sorry, I know this is a loss and I don't want to sound crass, but we need to know, and fast. It's not a small question—there's a lot of gear and money and time invested in this at both ends. We still playing New Year's Eve?"

Ali turned back, and locked eyes with Ian. Neither of them seemed to be blinking, and no one else was making a sound, except the damned nightingales.

"The show will proceed as scheduled." His voice was dead calm. "To cancel now would serve no purpose. Continue as you have been—request what is required, and it will be provided. To tell a quarter million guests to stay away is too foolish an idea to consider, and the negative publicity would be impossible to control. My staff will handle all media contact. You will say nothing to the press, no word, without clearance from my people. It is understood."

It wasn't a question, and we all knew it. If I'd thought it was quiet before, I hadn't known the half of it. You could practically have heard hair growing, it was that silent.

"Sounds good to me." Ian's voice had gone almost as flat as Ali's. "I don't fancy dealing with the media on this one anyway, believe me. I'll send all the vultures along to your people, with pleasure. Excuse me, I need to ring Carla in LA. She's coming out the day after tomorrow and she needs to know what's what. We don't want any cock-ups."

He turned away, reaching for his phone. That seemed to break some of the tension, somehow; I could hear people letting their breath out, feet shuffling. Everyone had been standing about like storefront mannequins. Ali was still staring down the path, and I wondered for a moment if he was planning to trot along and have a look at the blood, the way he'd demanded a look at Nordine, but no. He jerked his head towards Patrick and Bengt.

"Do what you must. Bengt, the Guard are at your disposal—use them at need, and at will. I will meet with our publicity liaison and make certain this is kept as quiet as possible. There will be penalties for any media crossing what lines we choose to set: expulsion for foreign nationals, more severe for any of our own people foolhardy enough to disobey. Goodnight."

He turned on his heel. A moment later, the courtyard had emptied out of any trace of the Emir and his entourage.

"Wow." Domitra was watching the limo's taillights disappear. "The dude doesn't mess around. Patrick, you want to ask us questions tonight? Because if not, I'm going back to bed. I was all the way out when that murder shit went down. No? Cool. See you in the morning."

Chapter Seven

I know I've said it before, that everything to do with that gig in Manaar was a new experience. Weirdly enough, someone getting murdered basically under our windows wasn't new, but the follow-on was: having our sound designer drag us out of doors to make noise at two thousand portable toilets was a first.

Not only that, they'd called us out early. I got that Ronan was twitchy about the sound, but the thing is, Ian should have known better. There was no reason at all for Ian to ring everyone up at a quarter of ten in the morning and tell us that cars were coming to bring us out to the stage in half an hour, look sharp and be ready out in the courtyard and no backtalk from you lot, either. And that was nuts, because no one knows better than Ian that we don't do early mornings, on or off the road. Bree'd been seriously cross over it; neither of us had slept well, and I had a few ominous little twinges of myokimia letting me know I'd underslept.

I'd soothed Bree down as best I could, got a mouthful of breakfast and my meds, grabbed Little Queenie and stomped out into the courtyard to wait for the cars. I was just awake enough to think that something was off here because Ian had gone straight out of character, and just groggy enough to shrug it off and decide I was being paranoid.

When the limos hit Amina, we saw that the first two towers were in and powered up, and a lot of the trenching they were going to need for the wiring was already dug; there were blokes laying in cables. It turned out Ian wasn't even actually there. He'd left this up to Ronan.

It was right round that point that my feeling that something was going on stopped being foggy and got more immediate. Ronan's about as incisive as it gets, and just about as anal. When he gets a soundcheck going, he's got an invisible clipboard in his head and he's ticking items off as they get done the entire time. That morning, he didn't seem to know what he wanted us to do.

The longer we were out there, the more I woke up. The more I woke up, the more convinced I got that I wasn't being paranoid. Something was very weird about all this.

I wasn't the only one worrying over it, either. Standing onstage, noodling bits of the set list, the rest of the band was as edgy as I was, being pissy about things that wouldn't have normally caught their attention, and just generally being cranky.

"Bloody hell." Luke had come over to hang out next to my stool. The day was shaping up to be a scorcher, even with the breeze coming in off the sea. I'd promised Bree I'd take it easy and not let myself forget to take rest breaks; that promise was damned near the only thing that had stopped her ringing Ian back and telling him *sorry mate, fuck off, not happening.* "I don't know about you, JP, but I'm ready to call it and head back to the hotel. What in hell did Ian and Ronan think they were doing, dragging us out for this rubbish? And where is Ian, anyway? If he's dragged us all out for this and gone back to sleep, I swear I'll sack him."

"Right with you, Luke. Bree wasn't happy about it, either." I shifted on the stool. "Christ, it's warm out here. I'll tell you what, mate, I'm this close to packing it in and getting a lift back to the seraglio."

"Fuck it, let's call it a consensus." Stu had headed over, with Cal at his heels. "This is rubbish. We're not needed out here. Any of the techs could have handled this—we're not playing, we're just making noise to check levels."

"I'm not even doing that. They haven't got the vocal rig set up yet." Mac was looking about as pissy as I've ever seen him. He's a solid pro, Mac is. He works his arse off, he doesn't whinge and piss and moan about having to get the work done, but just then, he looked fed up. "I can't see a single reason we're out here. If I had a nasty suspicious nature, I'd be wondering if there was some reason they wanted us away from the seraglio this morning—oh, bloody hell!"

"Right." I was up on my feet. The bulb had lit up in my head, nice and bright, and apparently, it had lit up for all of us at the same moment. "I want a car. Where the fuck is Ronan? And where's Jas?"

"Here, JP." My guitar tech, Jas, had been dozing in a folding chair on one side of the stage. He uncoiled and headed over. "Last I saw, Ronan was out at the far remotes—I think he's checking levels. Is there a problem?"

"No idea, but we're going to find out, and properly quick, too." Mac jerked his head. "Get Ronan up here, will you, and it had best be in the next five minutes, or else there's going to be—ah, here we go, lovely. The man in the kilt has joined the discussion. Ronan, a word with you, and then we want cars. And let me clue

108

you in, right upfront, that dodging the question won't end well. What in hell is going on? Why were we all dragged out here?"

Ronan Greene's been with Blacklight for decades. This was the first time I'd ever seen him looking uncomfortable, or out of his depth. He's like most obsessive expert types: if something doesn't fit, he'll just shrug and pretend it isn't there. Not that day, though.

"I don't know." He swallowed, hard. "No, Mac, don't flip your shit at me. It's the truth, I don't know. Patrick and Ian told me to get you out here, and to make sure you stayed out here for a couple of hours."

He took a breath, and waited. Luke found his voice first.

"Patrick and Ian? What the fuck?"

"I told you, I don't know." At least he was showing enough sense to not twist about it. "I haven't got the first clue why. And if you think I'm any happier than you are about it, you're off your head. We've got a couple of dozen remote towers going up, plus eight 40-foot generator trucks and I have to..."

He stopped. We were all staring at him, even Jas.

"Hang on a moment." Cal sounded pretty normal, but both hands were balled up hard and tight. "Ian and Patrick had you drag us out here, and you didn't bother asking why?"

Right about then, I found myself wondering if maybe I hadn't actually woken up yet. This was so far beyond anything believable, it didn't seem real. Maybe it wasn't. Maybe I was still curled up back in our suite, Bree next to me. As ideas went, that wasn't any weirder than our manager and chief of security conspiring with our sound designer to get us off the premises for a few hours. And it certainly wasn't any weirder than the possibility of our bassist knocking Ronan off the edge of the stage with a roundhouse punch, which is what Cal looked about ready to do.

"Of course I asked." Ronan was keeping a wary eye on those balled fists. "Tried to, anyway. Ian said they needed the hotel clear for a few hours, orders from Bengt Ekberg, just shut up and do it and don't ask questions. He's the boss, Cal. Since that guy got slashed last night, I wasn't about to push the issue. Ian told us this morning that Patrick and Bengt are handling it. He told us not to ask any questions, just cooperate with them." He shrugged. "I cooperated. Ian, Patrick and Bengt all said, do it. I did it."

"Yeah, well, we're undoing it." Luke's mouth was a thin line. "Cars, Ronan. Right now. We're done here."

We had to wait about ten minutes for the two limos, and it felt more like ten years. I've been with this band, played with this collection of people, for over half my life. We'd gone through ups, downs, and everything in between. Christ, I'd nearly fucking died on them twice. But the tension on that empty stage, that day in Manaar, was like nothing I'd ever come across with these blokes. You'd have needed Bree's best chef's knife to cut that silence, and trust me, it would have dulled the blade.

"All right." Mac waited until both drivers were out on the grass, and he wasn't wasting words, either. "Back to the Queen's Palace, fast as you can. And there'd best not be any bullshit later about taking the scenic route, or claiming you didn't get what I just said. Where in hell is my bodyguard? Domitra!"

"Here." She'd been here all along, staying out of the way, keeping an eye on things. She sounded nice and terse herself—she picks up on Mac's moods, the way Bree picks up on mine. "Ready when you are."

The first thing we saw, when the limos rolled to a stop just inside the main gates, was a small tanker truck.

It hadn't been there when we'd left, but there it was at the far end of the pools, perched between the farthest two, on the widest bit of the paving. It looked as if the driver had got lucky; either that or he was really skilful, because the tires were right at the edges of the path. One inch either way and he'd have had the thing in the water.

110

There were two huge hoses, out and working. One of them was pumping the bloodied water out of the pool where Nordine's body had been dumped. It took me a moment to realise that the second hose was also pumping, but not from the same pool.

"They had to hocus us away for this?" Luke was out, squinting across the courtyard into the sun. "What the fuck, we're supposed to believe that Ian and Patrick were so worried about upsetting our delicate sensibilities with the sight of trucks pumping water that they tricked us the hell out of here on five hours sleep? Bollocks to that."

"Yeah, that's bullshit." Stu was staring at the tanker. "If they tricked us out of doors, where in hell are the women? Why are they cleaning out the second pool over? Was there another body no one bothered mentioning?"

"You sort it out, Stu, you let me know, all right?" I was heading for the suites. My heart was giving the tickybox a major workout, and the fact that I couldn't get air into my lungs properly wasn't helping things. The corridors were dead silent. *Where in hell are the women?* "Bree? Bree!"

Fumbling with the key, pushing the door open. My heart was trying its best to act like a bullet train, making the wrong sort of commotion under my ribs.

Of course she wasn't there. Nice empty suite, bed made, tray set aside to be put outside later for the staff to remove. Everything was normal, except that we'd been tricked away, apparently so that the women could be taken elsewhere, all of them but Domitra. And the whole bloody thing had been done by people we not only pay, but by people we trust.

I went back out into the corridor. There was a shot I was wrong, that Bree was out but Karen or Barb were where they'd been when we left, but as shots go, that one was as long as odds get. The Queen's Palace wasn't easily walkable to anything; if you wanted to get round the place, you rang for a car and a driver.

111

And if Bree'd rung for a car and driver just to go out somewhere on her own, then yanking us off to the venue on a pretext made no sense at all.

There were voices, coming from everywhere: Cal calling for Barb with some serious urgency in his voice, Tony swearing like a navvy, Stu sounding like blue murder. I pulled the suite door shut behind me. My palms were wet. Right. If anything had happened to Bree, there was going to be a second murder done, and maybe a third.

"Karen's gone. Suite's empty, both rooms." Luke was back out in the hall, and one look at his face made it clear that I wasn't the only one wondering if Ian and Patrick might not be on the next plane out of here, both of them looking for jobs, or else being wheeled out on gurneys. Cal's mouth was clamped into a thin tight line, and Stu was a dark mottled red, clearly about to lose it. "If anything's happened to my wife, someone's going to bleed."

"Get in line." Tony was breathing through his nose. "I'm going to kick some ass from here to Istanbul. Where the fuck is Katia? What kind of Arabian Nights bullshit is this!"

"Let's find out, shall we?"

We all jerked round to stare at Mac. He had his phone up to one ear and he sounded calm, but of course he hadn't got a missing wife to worry about.

"Fair warning, mates, I'm about to get really high-handed— Ian? Oh good, I was hoping you'd pick up. Let's make this short and sweet, shall we? We're all back at the Queen's Palace, and everyone's rather cross because their families have gone walkabout. Sorry, ducks, but Ronan played copper's nark. He split on you. I don't know what's going on here, but you're about to come back and explain yourself, aren't you? Oh, and you'd best bring Patrick along with you."

He stopped. We could hear Ian's voice, crackling away. Had he been able to see Mac's face, he probably would have just shut his gob and not argued.

"Ten minutes or less, Ian." Mac's voice had changed—there was steel in there, now. "Because if it goes to eleven, we're not playing New Year's Eve. Yes, that's what I said. You get back here now or the show's history. And you may be, as well. Cheers."

Right after Mac hung up on Ian, he'd offered up a fiver on how long it was going to take either or both of them to get there, with that ultimatum ringing in Ian's ears. Mac's own bet was that we'd get Ian in seven minutes, without Patrick.

If I hadn't been so frazzled by the whole mess, by the empty suite behind the door with our name on it, by all those open doors with no one behind them, I might have wondered why I was more pissed off than I was worried. Everything was wrong about that whole morning, and by all rights, the top of my head should have been blowing off. It wasn't. There was a part of me that knew, all the way down where you know things, that Bree was fine. I couldn't have told you why, though, not then.

No one took Mac up on the bet, either, and that was a pity, because it would have been a quick five quid in pocket. He'd actually got it wrong. It took Ian nine minutes, and Patrick actually got there first, on his own.

We'd headed out into the courtyard to wait, full band, a solid united front. The tanker truck was gone; it must have finished doing its thing while we were inside, flipping out and ringing Ian. I'd slipped off down the path for a quick butcher's at the pools; both of them were empty.

Going by Ali's taste in wheels, I'd expected Patrick to show up in some shouty little red thing that made a lot of noise and went like a scalded rat. Considering the Bugatti, that would have made some sense. Turned out the car Patrick had been given for his personal use was just a newer, meatier-looking version of Tony's old Range Rover, back in San Francisco.

It takes quite a lot to ruffle our pet detective, but he pulled into the courtyard so hard and fast, the tires squealed and smoked. He must have taken one look out the windscreen at the six of us, at least half of us looking like murder and any one of us able to give him the sack, and known he was for it.

But he climbed out and headed straight for us, no hanging back. If he was worried, either about me or Luke or Tony beating him to death with his borrowed truck or about losing his posh job, it wasn't showing.

"Sorry if I'm late, but the car had just been requisitioned about two minutes before you called. They had to bring it from the auto pool." He glanced down towards the pools. "I passed the tanker truck on the way in. Empty?"

"No, you're not late. But about those pools, you're asking the wrong question, Patrick." Mac had got his attention, and ours as well. "You ought to be asking whether or not we're pissed off enough to give you a week's notice and show you the door. First things first, and we'll save the rest for when Ian gets here. Where are the women?"

"Having lunch with the Emir."

There'd been no hesitation, none at all, but no surprise at the question, either. So yeah, he'd known it was coming, and he knew why we were narked. He was looking at all of us, going face to face. Somehow, though, I got the feeling he was really looking straight at me, maybe because he was doing the 'one eyebrow up' thing. We could have been alone out there; he might as well have said "Bree's having lunch with the Emir" and been done with it. And, right then, I suddenly got why I hadn't seriously considered that anything bad might have happened to Bree.

Patrick wouldn't let that go down, and I knew it. I may not like that he fancies my wife, and I may not like the bloke very much on a one on one basis either, but I trust him to take care of Bree. Nothing bad was going to happen to my wife, not while Patrick Ormand was about.

114

"Lunch with the Emir?" Luke was keeping his voice steady, but his jaw looked like a bit someone had chipped off Mount Rushmore for a souvenir. "Is that why you and Ian felt you had to lie to us, and get Ronan to keep us away for the morning? One more try, Patrick. We're not dim, we're not puppets for you to jerk about on strings, and we're not going to be talked down to by someone we employ. We clear?" His voice went up, sharp and hard and loud. "*Where the hell is my wife!*"

"Having lunch." Patrick was locked up with Luke, stare to stare. He seemed to be pulling out every old cop trick he knew; the eyebrow up, the steady stare, the answering only the bits of questions he wanted us to know. It was all very familiar, and it brought back the bad old days, when we'd been obliged to answer him, instead of the other way round. None of us were saying anything—this was Luke's to handle. "I wasn't talking down to you, Luke. The Emir phoned Bree personally, shortly after you left for Amina Plaza. He'd remembered that she was supposed to be driving the Veyron this morning, with Nordine. He offered to let her drive it anyway, with him accompanying her in the passenger seat. She declined the offer, and he apparently decided that, in that case, everyone was having lunch with him. So he sent cars. They were just starting dessert when your call came in to Ian. He said something about taking everyone and personally showing them the shopping district in downtown Medin-Manaar. Apparently, it runs from an old-school souk to an Armani boutique."

I opened my mouth, and shut it again. The words were there, and ready—*oh for fuck's sake, mate, try it on the dog, all right?*—but Patrick cut me off. We could all hear a car, heading for the seraglio, full throttle from the sound of it. Patrick jerked his head over one shoulder, towards the sound of the engine.

"And that's all I can tell you. But it sounds as if Ian's here. Maybe he can tell you more, if you aren't satisfied with my answer. And I do understand that you probably aren't."

Patrick might have been pulling out everything in his copper's arsenal. Ian had nothing to pull. He got out of the car, looking about as harassed and miserable as I'd ever seen him look.

Out of nowhere, I got hit with a memory: sitting on a hotel bed at the Four Seasons Brickell Key in Miami, not quite one in the morning after a show. Bree'd come up missing, and Ian and Carla had come up to help me find where she'd gone. They'd sat there, the pair of them, side by side, using their cell phones, ringing airlines, trying to find her for me...

"What were you thinking?"

It was there in my voice, that feeling of trust betrayed. There's nothing worse, you know? There's nothing that can cut you into pieces as small as that can do you. I hadn't planned on saying anything, I've always left the Blacklight band business up to the band's two founders, but there it was, and everyone shut up and let me go, and the words kept coming.

"Christ, Ian, have you gone round the fucking twist? We trust you, mate. We've always trusted you. You've never let us down, never. I'm not speaking for anyone else, but here's the thing: if we can't trust you, where are we, then?"

"I had no choice." He had control of his voice, but it wasn't going to last. Stressed as we've seen him get, I'd never seen him quite like this. "None. I got called in this morning and given orders, no arguments, this is how it works, period. I've officially had my access to anything to do with Nordine getting killed revoked. You want to tell me what else I could do under the circs?"

I don't know what I'd expected him to say, but whatever I'd been expecting, it wasn't that. I stood there gawking at him. The rest of the band was doing the same.

"Everything goes through Bengt, full stop." Christ, yeah, our tour manager wasn't happy. "I wasn't what you'd call in an ideal position to argue, not unless I fancied telling him to fuck off and tell you lot I'd decided we were blowing off the gig. Besides, he

116

had a double handful of his own rozzers backing him up. Like I said, not ideal."

He looked me straight in the eye, and took a breath. "And I tell you what, JP, I don't much fancy being accused of being a backstabber. I've worked my arse off, keeping shit together for this band for twenty years. I haven't got that coming, not from any of you lot. I deserve better."

"JP knows that." Luke was looking thoughtful. "We all do. Never mind that. He told you hands off? What the hell is he up to?"

"'He' being my old school chum, I gather." Mac was tight-lipped. "Remind me again why I suggested we come within a hundred light years of Ali al-Wahid and his high-handed bull-shit? Oh, right, he's funding two charities that matter to us. So let me see if I've got this, Ian: we went to bed with Ali's an-nouncement that Patrick and Bengt were jointly in charge ring-ing in our ears. Now you're telling us that sometime between then and this morning, our pet pasha did a one-eighty, put Bengt in complete control of the investigation, and locked you out?"

Ian nodded. He wasn't talking, not then, and I wondered if he felt he could trust his voice. Mac turned back to Patrick.

"So, where does that leave you? You're our head of security. The contract's nice and clear about that: all matters concerning band security are up to you, and of course Dom. I don't really think I want to let Ali or anyone else fuck with that—in fact, I know I don't. I'll walk away from the gig before I agree to that. Where are you in the New World Order?"

Patrick snorted, a sour, angry little noise, very unlike him. This was definitely shaping up to be a day of unknown quantities. "I handle anything that concerns Blacklight security. But that's all I'm officially allowed to handle. And before anyone asks, no, of course I don't like it. But I have to respect it. We walked into a situation where existing security was already in place. It's damned good security, too, very efficient. Bengt's a solid pro. You don't run security for three winter Olympiads unless you're at the top of your game. Besides, that's also written into the contract, that everything to do with Manaari security issues is Bengt's to call. But this is the main reason I wanted to wait for Ian. It wasn't my place to tell you about al-Wahid's little backflip, it was his. I wasn't there. I got my orders from Ian and I'm following them, unless and until someone tells me otherwise. So was Ronan."

We were all quiet, letting that sink in. I'd moved back into the shade of the corridor. My legs were beginning to shake. Brilliant, just fucking perfect. The entire time I'd been stuck out onstage at Amina, I'd remembered my promises to Bree: that I wouldn't stand about exacerbating the ataxia, that I wouldn't forget to take rest breaks to keep the MS under control. And of course, we'd got back here, and I'd been standing in place the better part of half an hour.

"JP, dude, you look shaky as hell." Domitra had noticed. She wasn't offering any help, that's not her job and not her thing, but she spoke up. "You want to park somewhere?"

"Yeah, I do." I had to talk over my shoulder—I was already heading down the corridor, key in hand. "Sorry. You want me in on the rest of this, it's happening where I can sit."

Back in our suite, I hit the fancy fridge and managed to find liquid for everyone. I'd barely got myself settled with my legs up when Mac spoke up. He'd obviously been thinking.

"Is anyone else getting the delicate aroma of fish off this situation? Because I am. JP's equerry got his throat cut in the pool— and I must say, the fact that we were all snoring gently just the other side of the wall when that happened makes me very glad that these walls are nice and thick, because the idea of some nutter roaming about with a machete or a scimitar or something isn't the stuff pleasant dreams are made of."

"Not in the pool." I'd actually found Patrick a beer in the

fridge, God only knew how it had got there. He'd got the top off in a hurry, and was taking little chugs. "At the edge of the pool."

"We sure about that?" Ian sounded as if he might be getting some of his balance back, now that no one was questioning his trustworthiness and threatening him with the sack. "How sure?"

"Completely. There was blood spatter along a broad expanse of both the paving and the edge of the pool. He either fell in or was pushed or lost his balance and fell in, and he died in the pool." Patrick got another mouthful of beer down. "He bled out in the water, but he wasn't killed in the water. I got a good look last night, remember?"

The picture was much too vivid. Mac shook himself suddenly, the kind of movement one of our cats would do if he or she happened to fall into the tub and wanted to get all that water off in a hurry.

"Oh bloody hell. Right, okay. Wherever he was killed, Ali told Patrick that he and Bengt were both in charge, absolute authority. We all heard that? I wasn't having some sort of nightingale-induced hallucination?"

"That's what he said." Luke was watching Mac, eyes narrowed. "What's your point? Go on, will you?"

"My pleasure." Mac wasn't smiling. "My point is that something must have happened this morning. Whatever it was, it got Ali to basically forbid anyone except his own people to even look at what happened to Nordine last night. And more than that, it's clear that he wanted the women out of the Queen's Palace as well. Fuck, he wanted it so badly, he bullied our own tour manager and our own sound designer into jerking us about and lying to us." His mouth thinned out suddenly. "And believe me, he and I are going to have a conversation about that at some point down the road. Count on it."

"It worked, too." Stu was a dangerous colour. "Used our own

people to fuck with us. That bleeding little shit!"

"He's all of that." Mac was up and pacing, nice and taut. If he brought this level of intensity to the stage at Amina in a few days, he was going to melt the remote towers and all the portable toilets, as well. "But that's not my point. We're missing something here. Whatever went down, it went down here. *Right* here. This was where he wanted everyone cleared out of for a few hours, enough to invite everyone to lunch—no, right, sod that, invite's the wrong word, isn't it? And whatever it was, we must have slept right through it."

My legs were throbbing, a dull nasty jangle of stabbing pain. I rubbed them, feeling them wincing away from even the touch of my hands against the skin and muscle. My brain was kicking into high gear, always a bad sign where the MS is concerned.

"That tanker." *Shit.* This was going to be a bad one, a major bitch of a relapse. I could feel it, roaring down the track straight at me; my jaw was numbing up. Hopefully it would be gone by tomorrow, assuming we were staying in Manaar long enough to play. "When we got back here today. Two hoses, two pools. Why did Ali need to get the water out of the second pool? Only one dead bloke. Just Nordine."

They were all staring at me. I managed to get to my feet. I'm not proud about the disease, I don't try to hide it, but that doesn't mean I want to flash the results at my mates.

"Sorry." I sounded like a stroke victim, and I was hot and cold, pain coming in waves. Yeah, this was going to suck. "Not feeling well. Need to lie down. Can someone go find Bree? I need my wife."

Chapter Eight

"JP, can you back off the reverb? No, not that much, it's just that I'm getting some wash. Right, that's got it—Ronan? What have we got…?"

It was a nice clear early evening in Amina Plaza. The sun was just beginning to ease off into something that didn't actually leave my eyes watering. We had three days left to work out the few remaining kinks from two years of not playing together, until we hit the stage for the biggest show we'd ever played, and God knows, there had been distractions for miles.

Still, it was business as usual, at least as far as the rehearsals went: Ronan tweaking things, Luke picking up ghost echoes from Little Queenie, Cal worrying about whether there was enough bass in the mix, Stu rolling his eyes, Tony being diffident about the entire thing because he was just a guest and not a full member.

"Okay, set list, where are we? Yeah, cool, does anyone think we need to work on 'Liplock'? No? Good, okay, so what's next, 'Long Day in the Hot Sun', Stu, you ready…?"

Onstage, rehearsing, we could forget about anything that wasn't actually connected to the gig. Offstage, things weren't quite so normal.

For one thing, I couldn't get used to those lines of toilets and tanker trucks, stretching down both sides of the park. Yeah, I know—that sounds nuts, letting myself get distracted by portable khazis. But there was something off-putting about them, and something scary as well: a mass of people is just a crowd, but a crowd needing all those toilets was something else again.

The small army of security people Patrick was deploying during the onstage rehearsals was another issue, at least for me. He'd told us he wanted to get them used to hitting their assignments while there was actual noise, making sure their headsets worked properly. There was no way to simulate what the crowd was going to do in terms of ambient noise, but at least we could rattle their headphones with music cranked up good and hot. And yeah, he had a point, and that was clear thinking and proper planning on his part, but it was still a reminder of just how big this gig was. I didn't really need the reminder. None of us did.

"Mac, hang on, I'm going to need you to run through that harp break again. No, not yet, hang on a minute. We're not picking it up on two of the channels—no, still not getting it. Can someone check those damned wires, no, damn it, behind me, second trench…"

I resettled the guitar on my shoulder, and shifted my weight from foot to foot. I thought about parking myself on the stool until everyone got their shit together; hopefully, the stage was high enough up and far enough back to keep Bree from noticing how shaky my balance was. That last MS hit I'd taken had been a corker, but it had been mostly gone by nightfall. That's one thing about the bad ones, they move quickly. Not much of a consolation prize, not considering the rest of the shit the disease dumps on you, but at least it's consistent.

That was another difference, something completely new. I generally make a point of not dragging my old lady to tech rehearsals. After all, rehearsals are long and boring even if you're actually involved in what's going on. If you're not doing anything for hours on end but watching your old man getting progressively more cranky and irritable, you're probably not having a good time.

But the women were all out there, sitting on the grass or—in Karen's and Bree's cases—on the folding chairs Luke and I had demanded the road crew find them. The rest of the women had waved away the offer of back support, and opted for the grass. Cyn Corrigan, who's very fair-skinned, had found a parasol somewhere; I could see both Barb and Katia, stretched out on the grass with their hands under their heads. They looked to be asleep.

"Hang on—what? No, I said we need to do some fine tuning on that piano. We're losing too much of the high end in the mix...what? No, not the bleedin' Strat, the Strat sounds fine. The piano, mate, I said the *piano*!"

Like I said, rehearsals are a stone bore, especially when they're tech-heavy. None of us want to subject our wives to that. Normally we don't have to, and under any other circs, we wouldn't.

But these circs weren't normal, and we all knew it. It had taken me knowing Bree was safe, back from whatever had got Ali to manipulate the band wives into vacating the seraglio, before I could relax enough into that short sharp MS-induced high-gear brain pyrotechnics thing the disease provokes in me, to sort out why things felt so bizarre. But I got it, finally.

The bottom line was, we'd got spoiled. We'd got used to having a retired homicide copper between us and the rest of the

123

world. Patrick Ormand might not be my favourite human being out there, but he's very good at what he does, and what he does best is ferret out information, and sort out the best way to use it. And right now, he couldn't. He'd been hamstrung, not only by the situation, but by the bloke who happened to own the country we were working in.

Ali had told Patrick and Ian to back off, no guest list privileges, the whole thing was Bengt's turf, thanks very much and we'll keep you posted if we fancy it. And while Ali might not have actually said anything upfront about trespassers being shot on sight, Patrick isn't any kind of dim. He had to know that that was just what Ali had meant, whether the threat was stated or not. Besides, one section of the contract that Ian had signed with our approval said, nice and clear, that we agreed to respect the authority of the Emir while we were on Manaari soil.

So Patrick was stuck. Unless Bengt felt like keeping us in the loop about what had happened and what was being done to sort it out, we were locked out. And so far, Bengt hadn't told us a damned thing. Not a comfortable feeling, for any of us.

I don't want to be a diva over it, but the way I saw it, Bree and I had reasons to feel more involved than the others. Nordine had been our personal equerry, our driver, assigned to make our time in Manaar easier, and he'd done just that. He'd shown up within minutes of any call, from bringing me bandages the day I'd bunged up my knees to Bree ringing him to ask where she could get a shoe repaired in Medin-Manaar. Under different circs, he would have made a fantastic concierge at a five-star hotel somewhere.

And yeah, I know, that was his gig. I get that Ali would have probably had him beheaded or thrown into a pool full of electric eels or something if Nordine had slacked off or been cheeky or done anything to piss us off, but in my head, that was irrelevant. The point was, he'd done it all, without a blink or a question or a word of complaint. He'd sat with Bree in that pricey chunk of automobile, side by side, sharing information, answering questions.

Christ, I'd trusted him with my wife's safety. We'd called him by his first name. And he died right under our bedroom window. I wanted to know who, and I wanted to know why.

"Ronan, is that better? Good, because I want to have another go at 'Hammer It Home'. I'm still not getting my voice round it properly. You chaps up for that? Brilliant, let's do it. Luke, do you want to do the full lead-in again? 'Aftertouch' all the way through? Okay, right. Ready? Fuck, I've gone dry, going to need some spring water—oh, thanks…"

"JP?" It was Jas, holding one of my lightweight chambered guitars. "You want the Paul for this? Here you go."

I handed Little Queenie over, and watched Jas get her safely in her stand. Of course the Paul was perfectly tuned and ready to go. No surprise there; Jas has been my guitar tech for a good long time now, and he really knows his stuff. More than that, he knows the way I want things done, and he makes that happen. Now that I thought about it, Nordine and Jas had a few things in common.

My effects array was on the floor in front of me, ready and hot. On the black stage we'd used for Book of Days, the effects had been set into the floor itself, and I'd had to learn which lights in the surface activated which stomp box. Since we were using a standard Tait end stage, rather than the invisible set we'd done for Book of Days, everything was right there and visible. While I was checking settings, Luke got his PRS Blue Waterfall off standby, and ready to go.

"Aftertouch" is entirely Luke's piece. It's a gorgeous instrumental, shimmery and light at first, but it's full of twists and surprises; the deeper you get into playing it, the denser it gets, and the more layers start showing. It runs between four and five minutes, depending on whether we're doing any jamming on it, and as it moves, it takes on weight, getting darker and deeper.

By the time we hit the final thirty seconds, the music's so ominous that the audience is probably jerking their heads round to make sure there's no demons jumping out at them from behind the towers. And then, right at the point where even playing it starts feeling too heavy to deal with, it takes one short sharp musical breath and becomes an entirely different song, because Mac steps up and opens his mouth, and suddenly bob's your uncle, here we go, we're off and away, and it's Blacklight's third-best-selling single ever.

"Every time the big man tries to nail you, every time the jackboot finds your door..."

We settled into it, and for a few minutes, I was able to push the imaginary picture of Ali cutting us off from what was happening all the way to the back of my head. Just as well, because that meant I could push the other picture away as well, the one that wasn't imaginary: what was left of Nordine, on that gurney.

"Every time your self-respect has failed you, when you think you can't take it anymore..."

Mac was working the vocal, playing with it, testing inhales and punches. If you'd happened to be out on the grass listening—and there were quite a lot of people out there, what with Patrick's security people, our staff, workmen, riggers, Ronan's crew—you'd likely have thought Mac sounded perfect.

The band knew better, though. We'd played that song for well over two hundred shows on the Book of Days tour, and we knew to a breath where Mac still thought the vocal needed tuning up. That was quite heartening, in its own way, because it meant we were finally coming together. The instincts were still there.

"You don't have to take it, you don't have to buy it, you can make that nail your own, just hammer it home, I tell you hammer it home!"

Mac let the instruments spiral off into quiet. "Ronan? Anything that wants adjusting, best tell me now. And can I get a consensus from everyone? Because that sounded quite close to where I want it. Tony, you haven't lost one fucking note off the piano on that, have you, mate? Absolutely brilliant, people, cheers. Anyone up for a break? Because I want a sit-down and something very, very cold to drink."

I handed the Paul over to Jas, and wandered offstage. Bree'd been sitting in her chair, probably dozing under the floppy sun hat she was wearing. She saw me coming, and hoisted herself upright.

"Wow, that was a really good version of 'Hammer It Home'. Mac's sounding better and better. Are we done for the night? What do you want to do about dinner? Cyn was telling me about this French restaurant she and Stu went to last night in town, down near the port." She lifted the hat off, got a good look at me, and her voice sharpened up. "John? You're shaky, hang on, here, sit –"

"No, it's cool, Bree. I'm fine." *Shit.* Last thing I wanted was having her shoulders hunching up, she'd been through enough recently, but there's no sneaking anything past her, you know? She was right, I was shaky; there were some trembles in both legs, just bad enough to be noticeable. "I just stood a bit too long, that's all. Not to worry, this isn't a relapse. Just the usual bullshit. But yeah, sitting down's probably good. And I need my meds—where's your purse, love?"

We had a nice little break, hanging out on the grass with the rest of the band family, watching the moon beginning to edge itself up on the horizon. There were people camping already, all the way at the back of the Plaza—we'd seen them the last two days as we'd driven in. They were mostly trying to stay out from underfoot. They were probably afraid they'd get turfed out of the park, and maybe the country, if they were too obvious about pitching tents and settling in. And yeah, we knew we were getting the wide-eyed stares, but again, they stayed out of our way and out of our faces.

127

I stretched out on the grass next to Bree, and closed my eyes. A nice lazy break was just what I needed. There was a warm breeze blowing, just doing its thing. It tasted of the sea.

"I tell you what, I think we've got the world's best fans." Mac sounded mellow and relaxed, himself. Next to him, Domitra was sitting with her ankles crossed. "Or the best-behaved, anyway. There's got to be at least a couple of thousand people back at the entrance to the plaza, and they've stayed damned near invisible. Civilised."

Stu snorted. "Fuck yeah, of course they're behaving. We've got two hundred people who look like they ought to be trotting round behind some head of state. Have you taken a butcher's at that lot? Whoever came up with that ought to have got the sack straightaway. Do these people think they're blending in with the crowd? Inconspicuous? Christ, they're wearing black suits and Ray-Bans. For all we know, they've got something with a full clip in it tucked under their arms or in their socks, or something."

"Well," Cyn pointed out, "you're assuming they want to blend. If I were doing their job, I'd want everyone within eyeshot to know what I was up to. Preventing trouble is a lot less trouble than coping with it while it's actually happening. Isn't it? Come on, Dom, some backup here, please?"

Dom shrugged. "Less trouble, sure. Less fun though."

"I'm fine with the security types. It's the Manaari police worry me." Cal was chewing on a blade of grass. "I'm not about to piss that lot off. The ones I've seen look like they get off on killing people. They wouldn't have to put a lot of welly into it, either, not with what they're carrying in the way of firepower. What are those damned thing? Uzis, or something? Scary as hell. Oh good, here's Ronan. I'm damned if I fancy going back up for more work tonight. I want my supper."

Ronan wove his way towards us through a small crowd of Patrick's security people. Stu'd nailed it, spot on: they were all wearing the sort of suits that made them look like Secret Service, or maybe extras from a James Bond movie.

"Sounding good, you lot." From Ronan, that was a high compliment; it was clear he'd meant the music, not just the tech, and he's not one to notice whether we're cooking musically or not. He lowered himself into Karen Hedley's empty chair and jerked his head past us, looking down the length of the plaza, away from the stage. "Four more towers up, two more to get done. That'll happen by end of business tomorrow. I wish Patrick would keep his hired bruisers off my patch, though, and nobody bother telling me they need to be here, all right? I already know. That doesn't mean I've got to cheer them on or send them flowers. They're in my way."

Mac opened his eyes and propped himself up on one elbow. He'd sprawled out in the grass, eyes closed and ankles crossed, almost touching hips with Katia. Since Katia makes no secret of the fact that she thinks Malcolm Sharpe is hotter than a blast furnace in Lucifer's kitchen, I suspected she was enjoying the moment. Tony didn't seem bothered, and neither did Domitra; she was sitting just at his other hip, watching the security people. I had no clue what they were doing, they looked to me as if they were just wandering, but apparently, there was more to it than that. Whatever it was, Dom seemed to have a handle on it, or at least recognised what they were up to.

"Ronan, dude, they're not in your way." She bent forward, stretching out like a rubber band. I swear, if I tried some of the moves she and Bree and Mac do with that yoga stuff they're all into, I'd probably snap like a rubber band, not bend like one. "There's, what, maybe two hundred of them total, and the plaza holds three hundred thousand people. You're just pissed off because you have to pay attention to them."

"Wrong. I'm pissed off because they're breathing my air. And they're in my bloody way." Ronan was still staring. "Okay, people,

129

I think we're done for the day. I'll want you back here tomorrow, but probably not until mid-afternoon. We should have the rest of the line arrays up by then, and we can set some marks and get some of the fine tuning done. Patrick! A word with you, please? Look, I can't have these people wandering about. I've got towers going up, and there's fans being allowed to sleep at the back of the plaza…"

"Right, that's us done for the day." I really had needed the rest break; my legs had stopped trembling. "I'm with Cal, I want some food, and then maybe a good long kip and a nice warm bath. We'll be back at work tomorrow."

The French place in the city centre turned out to be just as good as Cyn had said it was. Even Bree made happy noises, and she's fussy about French food.

We had a very nice dinner, relaxing over it, taking our time. Work was done for the day, and the cars were waiting outside to take us back to the seraglio whenever we were ready. Ian hadn't come out with us; he was trying to catch up on stuff long-distance, things that had got pushed to the back burner by the gig. Having the entire band in one place for a casual meal, with all the wives but without the braintrust turning food into something that's more about business, that's a rarity, you know?

They gave us a private dining room, away from the rest of the customers. That was necessary, because, as I've already mentioned, Medin-Manaar was already filling up and beginning to spill over with Blacklight fans, and apparently not all of them were checking their sleeping bags back at Amina Plaza. We got some double-takes and not very well-muffled gasps between the front door opening to let us into the restaurant and the door to the private room closing behind us. Heading out after dinner, we had to run the gamut again, with an entirely new set of fans.

Still, they were quite well-behaved, all things considered. I did

130

catch a couple of looks at Mac by a table of wall to wall women in what looked to be their forties, but nothing went down beyond the inevitable *oh my god it's Malcolm Sharpe!* whispers. They stayed in their seats, probably because they'd got a good look at Dom. It's not just outraged boyfriends with fake paternity suits he pays her to handle.

Back at the seraglio, we brushed our teeth, I took my night meds, and we curled up under the silk coverlets. Sex definitely wasn't happening that night; at my age, digesting that much dinner takes all my energy, and Bree, with her diabetes, is in the same boat.

"John—those people at the restaurant."

"What about them, love?" She'd snuggled up next to me, her hair fanning out across the pillows. She'd cut it quite short for awhile, getting ready to have to go deal with her cookbook being published, but the publisher had decided to bring it out in the spring instead of for Christmas, and now her hair was coming back in long again. I wouldn't have said so to her—she worries far too much about how I'm going to react to how she looks— but it made me really happy, her letting it grow longer again. All that hair swinging round her when she moves, that's always been something that can get all the blood deserting the north of me for the south. My first sight of her, still sixteen years old, she'd leaned forward and all that auburn hair had leaned right along with her, nearly to her waist. I've never forgotten that. She says full long doesn't work on her at her age, that it's better on girls than women or something, but I'll take as much as I can get.

"I was just thinking about the hotels here." She sounded not quite drowsy, but getting there. "I just can't figure out how this can possibly work. I mean, there's supposed to be a quarter of a million people at this show, right? But there can't possibly be enough hotel rooms for that many people here, can there? I mean, Medin-Manaar's only got about that many people actually living here, at the most. So where are all those fans going to sleep? Out in the plaza? Because I know there were a lot of them already hanging out right by the entrance when we drove in today, but I thought that wasn't allowed. There are signs everywhere, in about eight languages, pretty much warning that vagrants will be fed to bears or flogged outside the local Starbucks, or something."

"Yeah, I know, but they've suspended that rule, just for this gig." There was a light breeze coming in through the window—bloody hell, I'd forgot to close it again, and tonight the temperature was really dropping. "It was in one of Carla's emails, after she'd come out here that first time. Ali didn't want to, but you know Carla. She's barely old enough to remember Woodstock, but she knows what happens when you've got a shitload of people and nowhere to put them. She had the numbers, and that was that: not enough room for everyone, you've got to put them somewhere, end of story. She put it in as part of the rider. Ian told us he thought Ali was fighting the idea mostly because he didn't want a quarter million people having a piss all over his nice green park, but with the portable toilets in place, he finally gave in. And don't ask me what they're doing for showers, because I've no clue. There's drinking water being provided, but I've got the feeling most of the crowd's going to smell a bit ripe come New Year's Day."

"Except the ones who actually scored hotel rooms. I'm pretty sure there's no such thing as a room without a private bath in this town." She yawned, warm breath tickling up against my shoulder. "I bet Carla will know. She gets here tomorrow night, doesn't she? If I remember, I'll ask her about it then. Damn, it's getting chilly in here. Is the wind blowing straight in at us, or something?"

"Yeah, it is." I swung myself out of bed, feeling the cold air coming in through those high skinny casements, hitting bare skin. She was right about the wind direction. "Hang on, I'll get the things closed and—"

With one foot on the floor and the other not quite there, I stopped. Behind me, Bree was sitting up. I put a hand up to hush her, but it wasn't needed; she'd already heard what I'd heard.

Voices, outside the window. They were being kept lowered, all the way down; if the wind had been moving in any other direction than straight through the window, we'd have heard nothing at all. Somehow, even as close to inaudible as those voices were being held, I got a feeling of urgency, panic, something like that.

Shit.

Something had gone very tight at the base of my spine: the instinct for self-preservation, announcing itself. The last time we'd heard night noises under that window, Nordine had been slashed to death a few feet away, just the other side of our bedroom wall.

"Chairs." Bree had her mouth up to my ear; she breathed the word, rather than said it. "Under the window. I'm going to see."

She was out of bed, still nude, shivering and hurrying, keeping quiet. I was right behind her, reaching for a robe, throwing one over to her. She stopped just long enough to knot the belt round her waist, and headed for the window. There was a small ornamental chest in the way, not tall enough to be useful. If we wanted to put chairs there, the chest needed moving first.

I got my hands at one end, and she took the other, and I nearly dropped it. It was damned lucky I didn't, because we were both barefoot, and it would have broken a few toes; the bloody thing weighed as much as one of my Marshalls. It brought back years of pictures in my head, Bree helping me move amps and guitar cases from local gigs, or from room to room, or even just when I wanted to reorganise things in my basement studio back home in San Francisco.

We got two of the chairs out of the dining room and up against the bedroom wall. I had a bad moment, wondering if the caned seats would hold either of our weight. I got a hand on the caning and pushed as hard as I could against it.

It held just fine. That was just as well, because Bree wasn't bothering about being careful, or testing for strength first, or whatever. She just got one hand on the chair back and one up on the casement, and hoisted herself up.

I held my breath, but nothing happened: no crash, no foot through the caning, no broken ankle, nothing. She reached out her free hand and slowly, carefully, adjusted the ornate grille so that we could see out without being seen ourselves.

Right. If it was holding her, it would hold me: I'm not mad enough to ask her what she weighs, but she's a good stone heavier than I am, and maybe more. I took a breath, and climbed onto the chair next to her.

Moving the chest out of the way had taken about a minute, and as it turned out, that cost us any shot at a decent look. By the time I'd got up on tiptoe and craned my neck to see who'd been whispering, they were heading away from us. They'd already gone down the length of the pavement, all the way beyond the second pool and out past the first one. I saw their backs, no more than that: just three people, covered head to heels in the same dark loose clothes. I had a better view than Bree, but it still wasn't much of one.

"Who is that?" Bree's voice was low, but it was audible. There was no way they could have heard us: they were too far away, and the wind was blowing in the wrong direction. "John? Could you tell? I can't really see anything."

"Sorry, love, but no, I couldn't. I can't see which direction they went, either—which road they took, I mean." I pushed the grille slats shut, cutting off the cold air. "These casements are too deep to see off to the right or left properly. Let's get back to bed, yeah? I'm too old to be climbing about on caned chairs in the middle of the night. Besides, I'm freezing my bollocks off. No, don't bother about the chairs, all right? We can get them in the morning."

Back in bed, we curled up close, not talking. I'd wrapped my-self round my wife, and it was a good long while before either of us slept; my nerves were jangling and twitchy, and Bree was as rigid as an old tree trunk in my arms.

When she finally did relax enough to drop off, I lay awake in the dark, listening to her breathing even out, light and smooth. She made a small noise and snuggled in. No nightmares there, and thank God for it. I wasn't so sure I wasn't going to have a few of my own.

I'd told her the truth, about not knowing who'd been standing about having a tense conversation under our windows. I had no idea who they were: I couldn't even guess. They were just three shapes, all completely covered with black robes.

Whoever had been wearing them, the robes were probably the long black deals we Westerners always associate with Arabs. Djellabahs, or burnooses, or whatever they're called, big loose things with a lot of movement in them. I'd caught the movement of the cloth, billowing out behind them as they moved away, two smaller shapes and a taller one between them, hurrying to— where? I hadn't got the first clue.

That one in the middle hadn't just seemed taller. Even in the look I'd managed, that one had just seemed bigger, somehow. I'd have bet even money that the shape in the middle had been a man.

Chapter Nine

That marital mind-reading thing Bree and I do sometimes, it's really peculiar, as if just letting our eyes meet can get across what's going on in both our heads. We've had it going on for years, but it can still surprise me.

On 29 December in Manaar, with two days left before the big party, it kicked into overdrive. Not only that, it did it first thing in the morning, and that was a surprise. All I'm generally good for first thing in the morning is mainlining coffee and seeing what hurts, and how badly.

That morning, I woke up early. The suite was still mostly dark, shadows in all the corners—I could see across the bedroom, but only after my eyes got used to it. That meant the sun was still down a goodish way. I did my usual morning thing: flexing, testing, being careful not to disturb Bree while I tried to sort out what the MS was likely to dish out, and where it was planning to dish it. Nothing seemed too noisy that morning except my bladder, and that was just business as usual, first thing in the morning. Good. Any time I begin a day with minimal pain, I can cope.

I rolled over and got my eyes unglued all the way. The first thing I focussed on was that pair of caned chairs, still sitting side by side under the window casement, where we'd dragged them last night.

I lay there, ignoring the demands my bladder was making and the faint jabs and tingles in both feet. I was still staring at the chairs, but I wasn't really seeing them. Something was moving at the back of my mind, edging its way towards the front, wanting me to look at it. Right. We'd been standing on those chairs, me craning my neck round the casement, trying for a good look...

People, three of them, hurrying away. It hadn't been anyone from the Blacklight contingent, I'd have put a fiver on that; it's hard to mistake a back and a walk, when it's someone you know well. Whoever that lot was, they weren't ours. But what in hell was it, that wanted me to look at it...?

No car, Johnny. Wherever those three were off to last night, it was close by. No sound of a motor, none at all.

At just about the same moment that thought popped into my head, a warm hand landed on my shoulder, and rested there. Damn, I'd woken Bree—I hadn't meant to.

But this wasn't her soft light *are you awake, are you okay* touch. There was something imperative about the pressure of her hand against my skin. I turned over and found myself staring into a face about as wide awake as she ever gets that time of day.

"John—last night." The hand against my bare skin was nice and warm. That's always a relief; most mornings, her hands are chilly because she's got crap circulation, and the diabetes doesn't help. Her voice was low, and clear, as if she were trying to keep it pitched down quiet enough for just us to hear. Silly, really, because the seraglio walls were nice thick stone. Unless you'd planted yourself right under someone's window, and they happened to have the casement slightly open because they'd forgotten to close it against the chilly night air, no one was likely to hear what you were saying. "They were on foot, weren't they? They were walking. I mean, walking to get to—where? Somewhere. John...?"

"Yeah, I was just thinking the same thing. No car, was there? Just feet."

I got out of bed carefully; if the MS was going to oblige by not taking me out for the day, I was damned if I wanted to trigger anything. Bree's hair was tousled, and she'd sat up. "Means whoever it was, they've got to be right in the neighbourhood, doesn't it? And it was the same story the night Nordine got slashed, yeah? They were running, not driving. I don't remember hearing an engine, either time. Do you, love?"

She was already swinging herself out of bed, reaching for the clothes she'd pulled off last night. That was a sure sign we were on the same frequency: it takes a lot, a crisis or a brainwave or something along those lines, to keep her from her morning shower. And that was peculiar, all things considered, because really, there wasn't any urgency, not beyond us both having just realised the same thing at the same time, and both of us wanting to know what in hell was going on.

"No." She got one leg into a pair of knickers. "But what the hell, John? Aren't we supposed to be the only people in the Queen's Palace? Blacklight, I mean? No one said anything about other people staying in any of the other buildings, or at least, no one said anything to me. The other buildings are closed off—they're supposed to be empty. I haven't really gone and explored or anything, but the one right across from us is deserted. There are padlocks on the doors. I'm pretty sure the Emir actually said we had it all to ourselves, when we first checked in."

138

"Yeah, he did." I was thinking back, remembering. She was right, Ali had been pretty damned clear that we were all alone in the Queen's Palace. If I was remembering properly, he'd made rather a formal song and dance about how much he respected our privacy, about us not being bothered. "But now I think of it, that's three times we heard people under our window. That first time, we thought it might be Tony and Katia. Remember?"

She paused with the zipper of her jeans at half-mast. "You don't think it was them?"

"No way of knowing, is there? I'm just saying it's possible that first lot was also whoever our little night visitors were the other two times. Or at least, it's possible that one of them was, anyway."

She blinked at me. "Nordine was one of them," I told her. "And he's dead. So obviously it wasn't him last night. Look, hang on a minute, all right? I need a piss and if I don't get my morning meds, I won't be good for much."

I'd known it was still early, but I hadn't realised quite how far from full morning we actually were. We slipped out of our suite, and down the corridor towards the courtyard, with almost no light to speak of coming through the high grilles. There was no sound either, not from the courtyard or from behind any of the suite doors.

By the time we got out of doors, I realised we were tiptoeing. And while I wasn't sure about Bree, I was actually holding my breath.

"Wow." Bree had both arms wrapped round herself. Her voice was barely above a murmur, and she was shivering. "This place really is all about cold nights and warm days, isn't it?"

She was right. I'd noticed it before, that temperature differential, the way an eighty-degree day would suddenly drop into the mid-forties. Outside our own quiet breathing, the only thing I could hear were birds calling, perched somewhere at the back of the trees behind the seraglio walls. They sounded plaintive, somehow, as if they were in mourning for something, lamenting. I wondered what they were. Larks, or doves maybe…

"Wow, listen to those doves. It's like they're singing dirges, or something." Bree slipped her hand into mine. "Which way were those people going, last night? Were you able to tell at all?"

I closed my eyes, thinking back, trying to remember. It was amazing, how fast and how clear the picture was there in my head: Three black shapes moving away from me, the way one of the smaller ones had looked hunched over somehow, the way the fabric had flapped at the hems…

"John?"

"Got it." We'd reached the end of our own white path, the first intersection between the pools farthest from the Queen's Palace. Now that we'd cleared our own quarters, I wasn't bothering about keeping my voice down. "They turned right, hard right."

"Are you sure?"

"Yeah, I am. They must have done, because whatever the tall one in the middle was wearing flapped hard left just before I lost them."

"Okay." She still had my hand, and she wasn't showing any sign of wanting to let go of it. She wasn't moving, either. "Now what do we do?"

I'd started forward, but that stopped me where I was. It was spot-on, that question. Here I was, about to go roaring off, and I hadn't got the first clue what we were doing, never mind what we were actually looking for.

So I raised an eyebrow at Bree—*come on, love, help me out here*—and damned if the old marital mind-reading thing didn't kick in again.

"Maybe we should go see if there's anyone down that way." Her voice had dropped again, quiet enough so that no one was going to hear her but me. "Maybe we should go see if Ali was wrong about us being alone out here."

"Wrong, or full of shit," I agreed. "Come on, love. Let's go for a reccy, yeah?"

I know this sounds nuts, but neither Bree nor I had explored the compound beyond our own corner of it. That probably makes us both out to be as self-absorbed as all get-out, but to be fair about it, I was there to work, and when I work, the job gets all of me. We were on a really compressed schedule, with a massive show coming up; that meant the band had been largely split between Ali's state of the art rehearsal studio and Amina Plaza.

Still, I was surprised about Bree not wandering about. She's got more curiosity than I've got at the best of times, and a lot more awareness of her surroundings, as well. It made me wonder whether she was even more uncomfortable with being here than I'd thought.

We got out beyond the three sets of bubbling pools, and stood at the head of the crossroads, looking to see what might actually be visible off to the right. I'd already worked out some of the geography in my head: the right-hand road led west, and so far as I knew, there was nothing out there but desert, dunes and lizards, and the stretch of blacktop that Nordine had said Ali had deemed unsuitable and unsafe for Bree's drive in the Veyron—too curvy or twisty or something to work with the car's speed. So unless someone had got some tents set up or something, there was no reason for anyone to have –

"Whoa." Bree'd stopped in place, craning her neck, pointing with her free hand. "Have those been here the whole time? Or am I having a mirage moment, or something?"

I jerked my head back into the moment, and followed her pointing finger.

There was a small jumble of buildings over there, just beyond where the road curved out west to meet the desert: I couldn't quite tell how many, not at that distance. But there were at least four of them, low squat things made of the local sandstone, topped with what looked to be tin roofs. From where we were standing, compared to the minarets and curving arches at our end of the compound, they looked ugly and graceless. The sun was coming up, touching them with colour, but even the distance and the dawn light couldn't make them look anything other than dismal.

The sun was moving up faster in the sky now, full sunrise. Even though we were both looking west, the sand was reflecting enough of the day's first brightness to make anyone with normal eyesight wish for sunglasses.

Bree was squinting. "Holy shit, is that a *slum*? In Manaar? That's a pretty far cry from his grandmother's antique blue tiles and silk lounging cushions. John, are my eyes playing tricks, or does that little gulag over there actually have corrugated tin roofs?"

"Looks like it." There was something disturbing about her using that word, *gulag*. She was right: small as it was, all it needed to make it look a proper POW camp was barbed wire round the perimeter. Something about it made me think of old photos of Viet Nam in the sixties, those miserable little Quonset huts all over the landscape. "I'm just trying to wrap my head round the fact that I never even noticed it was here. Christ, I'm dim, some days."

She squeezed my hand. "If you are, then so am I. I didn't notice it before either—when I came out with Nordine, we went straight. And I'm not surprised you didn't see it. If you're heading into the city to get to Amina, it's in the opposite direction, and I bet it's invisible half the time, with the sun hitting it—it would be too bright to focus on. But I never even glanced this way. I was giving the equipment in the Veyron all my attention. Let's go check it out."

I'm not a particularly heroic type, but I don't actually spook easily, either. You need imagination before stuff can get to you that way, and the truth is, I just haven't got much imagination. Creativity's a different thing; I've got my share and more of that. But that whole 'distant early warning' thing that people like my old lady have, I'm missing out on that. She's got imagination. She thinks there really may be ghosts out there. She's sensitive that way, and I'm not.

But I'll tell you what: that morning, heading for that dull-looking huddle of sandstone shanties, something was tingling up and down the full length of my nervous system. No idea what it was, not then and not now, either; if it had been straight-up caution, that would have made sense. After all, we didn't know who or what was down this way. Besides, I'd seen what was left of Nordine.

This wasn't caution, though. It was something much deeper, something that felt a lot more primitive, somehow. Last time I'd got that kind of tingle down what was left of my nerve endings after all these years of the MS, I'd been walking into a federal prison. This felt a lot like that: *look sharp, Johnny, there's bad craziness out here waiting to jump out and nail you.*

From the crossroads to the first of the buildings took just about fifteen minutes of walking, and neither of us said a word the entire time. Bree had stopped shivering; the sun was climbing now, and the day was warming up. There was no one else out there on any of the roads, not a car, not a human being, not even any of the local camels. It was so empty and quiet out there, we might have been the only people alive in Manaar. And that was in spite of the number of people who'd already piled in for the party...

Down along the blacktop, hugging the edges, until the buildings came into full view. They really were dismal little holes, nothing more than square sandstone boxes with crap corrugated tin roofs. There weren't even any proper windows, just slits in the stone, not big enough to let anything bigger than a fly or one of the small desert lizards in or out. I couldn't make up my mind whether they looked more like old slave quarters or small individual prisons. The only thing that made it clear we weren't looking at some kind of prison colony outpost was how flimsy the doors looked.

"Man, this place is creepy." Bree has a good strong grip, and she was using it; my own hand was going numb under the pressure. She had her voice pitched all the way back down to low again. "It's like someone moved Viet Nam to the desert instead of the jungle. Or maybe some old nineteenth century plantation, those shacks where they kept the slaves. What was that look for? Did I say something wrong?"

"Read my mind, that's all. Bree, love, can I have my hand back, please?" I shook it and got the blood flowing again. "Okay. So, now what? I'm not really up for knocking up one of the residents and asking them if they've been flapping round the posh end of the seraglio in the middle of the night, you know?"

"Me either." She turned to stare at the huts. "But you know what? We walked all this way to check this out, and someone from down here was probably trespassing on our space, and, well, I want to know, John. Don't you?"

"Bree, what, no, wait –"

No joy. She'd already turned and moved, going fast and quiet, straight ahead. Before I could get my wits together and get the heart to stop slamming long enough to scuttle after her, she'd reached the first building, slipped up against it, and was peering in through one of the slits, calm as you please.

Brilliant, just brilliant. We were visitors on someone else's turf, probably trespassing. I had a sudden parade of nightmare visions: the Manaari police leaping out from behind the other buildings and slitting our throats the way someone had done to Nordine, or some hulking yobbo in a black burnoose kicking the door open from the inside and leaping out of doors brandishing a scimitar, or...

144

"Huh." She was back at my side. For a moment, I thought about throttling her for scaring me that badly, but she was back unharmed, no damage done, and I let my breath out. My hands were slick with sweat. "There's no one in there. That one's empty. I mean, totally empty—there's a bed and a table and a toilet and small chest and nothing else at all. There's not even any linens on the bed. Just like a prison cell."

I lifted an eyebrow at her. "You planning on having a look at the rest of this lot? Because if you're going back over there, so am I, and no argument either, Bree."

"I was hoping you'd say that." She smiled at me, but it was gone in a moment, and I realised that her shoulders were hunched up tight. "I think we should, John. Don't you? Do you want to check out the second one, while I go do the third? Okay, bad idea, don't glare at me like that. We'll stay together."

We'd gone on tiptoe out of our own quarters, and here we were, back on our toes again. I doubt, now, that anyone in any of those buildings could have heard us walking; there were no paved white walkways, not here, just the fine grainy sand of the Manaari desert. But we tiptoed anyway.

Peering in through the slit window in the second of the four shacks, it took a moment for my eyes to adjust to the dimness in there; if the slits weren't letting people in or out, they weren't letting any proper light in, either. This one had linens on the bed, and a coverlet spread over the mattress, but nothing else. There were no towels in the room, and no tissue on the holder for the toilet tissue roll next to the loo. Nothing at all to be seen in there.

That thing about there being no paper, that sealed it for me: this was just another empty room. You can live without blankets and pillows, but not without toilet tissue. I shook my head at Bree—*no one here either*—and we moved on, to the third shack.

This time, Bree got to the window first. She slouched a little under the low roof, getting her eye up against the outer wall, lining it up with the slit…

"Bree?"

I didn't think I said it out loud, but maybe I did. I was watching her from a few feet away, hearing her breath suddenly shorten up, watching her profile, watching all the colour drain out of her skin, leaving her face the colour of old parchment. The eye I could see looked about the size of one of our salad plates, back in San Francisco, stretched wide.

"Bree, what –"

She stepped back from the window. One hand went to her mouth, but she was a fraction of a second too late. A moment later she was down on both knees, losing the remnants of last night's supper.

I got to the window slit. My heart was making some serious noise, clattering behind my ribs. From down near my feet, I thought I heard her say something—*no oh god John don't look*—but I was there, and already looking.

When I was a kid—damned I remember when or where, or even why—I read a description of the room Jack the Ripper had used for his only indoor killing. I remember a phrase used in there, about what the rozzers found, about there being blood on the walls and ceiling. Whatever I'd been reading, a phrase had stuck in my head over the years, the way phrases do: *blood frenzy*. Looking into that third hut, that phrase came straight back to me. I don't know if there was blood on the ceiling—it was too dark in the corners to tell—but the rest of that description fit, much too well.

There were no linens on the bed in here, either. There had been, but they'd been stripped free and tossed in a hideous little pile on the floor. Even as dark as that room was, I could see that they were streaked and smeared with blood. I couldn't be sure, not in the bad light, but something about it, the colour or how dark those stains were, felt as if the blood had had time to dry awhile.

146

Recent or not, there was a lot of it. The bare mattress looked to be nearly soaked through. There were spatters on the wall next to the bed, as well. Through that thin slit, I got a waft of stale air, and felt my stomach tighten up, making me have to think consciously about not retching: the air was laced with a genuinely ugly smell.

Bree was still on her knees, down in the sand. She was staring up at me, not saying anything. Her chest was heaving. I stepped back and got both hands out to help her up.

"Right." I was speaking normally—I wasn't worrying about whether anyone could hear me or not, just then. For one thing, all the puking would have let on to anyone hanging about that we were there, and that we'd had a look inside. And for another, I was too rattled to think straight. "Let's get the hell out of here. I want a good hot wash and some coffee. And after that, we need to decide what to do."

That walk back took a lot less time than getting there had done. I don't remember much about it, not beyond the fact that I kept glancing behind us, wondering if whoever had left all that blood on the bed and the linens and the walls had got any bright notions in their head, about following us back. I remember that I had hold of Bree's hand, that I wasn't letting go. And yeah, we hurried.

We didn't meet a soul. Except for the sound of car engines in the distance, the road back was as empty as the walk out had been. We'd just made it back through the peacock-gilded gates and into the corridor when the door to Tony's suite opened, and both the Mancusos came out.

"Hey, guys, you're out early –"

He stopped, staring at us. Even in the dim light, we must have looked like hell. Katia took a good look at Bree's face, and one hand went up to her mouth. Both of Tony's eyebrows were up near his hairline.

"JP? What's going on? You two look like you just saw a dead

body or something." He changed colour. "Oh fuck no, man, not that. Tell me it's not that."

"Not a body." Bree let go of my hand, finally, and pushed her hair off her face. She'd gone sweaty, whether with the heat or the fear or just a delayed reaction to our morning so far, I didn't know. "Just the blood."

"Blood?" Katia looked to be having trouble getting words out properly. "Bree, what are you talking about? What –"

"Blood. Just what Bree said." Down the hall, other doors were opening; we'd attracted some attention. Stu was heading towards us, and Mac, with Dom right behind him. Out of nowhere, I got hit with a thought: *I wonder if the rest of the band is as tired as I am of mornings in Arabia.* "A lot of blood. I think someone else got themselves killed. I also think maybe we need to sit down with everyone. And then we're going to want Patrick."

"Every good story starts: Once upon a time…You listen to the rhythms, you scramble for the perfect rhyme…"

It was Blacklight's last full rehearsal before the show, and the only one we were getting under the full night sky. Tomorrow night, the thirtieth of December, wasn't going to be an option for rehearsals, or anything else; that was going to be dedicated entirely to letting the crowds in and getting all that sorted out and managed. There was no way we could possibly rehearse. If anything still needed nailing down, it was going to have to happen tonight.

What with the stage being a pre-packaged rental, there was nothing fancy or even particularly complicated going on, but Nial and Ronan were both edgy anyway. Even though the number of people in the Plaza was nowhere near what tomorrow night was going to look like, we still had an audience. Medin-Manaar had been steadily filling up with Blacklight fans; the crowds had begun spilling over into the Plaza, and there was quite a good-sized crowd already camping out on the grass farthest from the stage, near the park entrance. The headcount near the back, just the early arrivals who'd been let in already, was a big enough audience to make most stadium bands happy.

So yeah, thirty thousand people or so had pitched their tents and sleeping rolls and bits of blanket on the grass. They were being kept well out of the way, though; Ronan had thrown a serious tantrum and completely flipped his shit over the fans getting in the crew's way.

Ian had handled it. He'd told Ronan not to get his Utilikilt in a twist, and had got some of Patrick and Bengt's security troops to shepherd everyone away from the work area. I wasn't sure what the blokes in charge were using to keep the front of house clear—there was nothing obvious in the way of security muscle. Whatever it was, though, it was working. We'd been rehearsing the best part of two hours and I hadn't seen anyone near the stage except the people who were supposed to be there: grips, lighting crew, techs. Our lot.

Tonight, with all the towers up and all the wiring trenches in place and covered over, the rig was about as ready as it was going to get. The PA was getting its final tune-up. We were slamming through tweaks to the set list, getting the standards out of the way early on so that we could concentrate on a couple of songs that wanted a last minute rubbing up. That meant the early arrivals were getting a one-shot chance at something none of our fans had really ever had access to before: a good look at Blacklight in "work out the kinks" mode. We don't generally sell tickets to band rehearsals, you know?

"*So just what rhymes with 'cry'? And just what rhymes with 'why'? I'll tell you if you tell me why you never kissed me goodbye...*"

"Damn, Mac really works this one, doesn't he?" Tony had wandered over from the piano, and he was watching me watching Mac. "Heavy duty."

"Yeah, he really does." Mac was leaning into it, pushing his body against the vocal as if the song were something solid he wanted the contact with. Just then, it was Mac, Luke and Stu working out the intricacies in the tune; Tony and I had stepped back, and Cal had his Alembic bass ready to roll, if needed. "That's the cool thing about Mac, you know? Doesn't matter whether he wrote a song or not. He just brings it, every time."

"I noticed." Tony was watching Mac himself, now. He had a very odd look on his face. "Believe me, I noticed. But with this one, he really seems to want to nail the sucker. It's like he's going after a whole different thing when he sings it. I remember noticing that, back during Book of Days. I know we only did this one a handful of times, but it really seems to matter to him. That's pretty weird. Because isn't this the one Luke wrote about Solange's mom? I mean, about her dying?"

"Yeah, well, Mac probably wants to do it perfectly, for Luke's sake. Hell, Mac knew Viv as long as Luke did—they all met right round the same time, you know?"

Now I thought about it, Tony was right. Luke had been writing the music to most of Mac's lyrics for well over thirty years now, but he hadn't written lyrics much himself until Book of Days, and he hadn't written a word about what had happened to Viv until this particular song, at least not that I'd ever heard. "You Never Kissed Me Goodbye" was a stunner, straight from the heart, and very bittersweet.

It's actually rather tricky to play, just because there's so much feeling behind it. The song really did seem to hit some peculiar buttons for Luke's best mate. Tony was right about that: something found its way into Mac's vocal for this one that wasn't really there for anything else. For some reason, that line of thought was making me uncomfortable.

"*I see your ghost round every corner, trapped forever in the looking glass, I thought we were free but how can that happen when I can't tell the present from the past?*"

150

"Man, he's fucking nailing it. But like I said, he just brings it for this one, every damned time." Tony dropped his voice. "JP, you get a chance to talk to Patrick or Ian yet? About what happened this morning, I mean?"

Mac had his eyes closed, and both hands behind his back. It was almost as if he needed them wrapped round something, but with the mic system completely wireless, there was nothing for him to hold. It's not often Malcolm Sharpe doesn't know what to do with his hands.

"JP? Hello?"

"Sorry—I got distracted, there. No, I haven't, not yet. Neither of them were around this morning, and we haven't had much in the way of time to hunt them down. Bree said she'd look out for them, though."

Christ, that full-on band conversation that morning—yeah, well. Short, sharp and tense as hell, and that was even though we'd got the entire band crammed into our suite. That was a return to tradition, something I'd noticed during Book of Days a few years back: when Blacklight's on tour and Bree's along with me, the entire band family gravitates towards our digs, even if we've got the smallest suite in the place.

That morning, Bree'd got everyone some good strong coffee and some of the local pastries, filled with chopped nuts and soaked in honey; she can't eat them herself, not with her diabetes, but they'd gone down well as comfort food. We'd let everyone wait a few minutes while we got ourselves calmed down enough to not flip our shit. After that, with everyone wrapping their tonsils round their coffee, we'd dished.

The conversation, about what to do, had lasted all of two minutes, maybe less. The choices were pretty limited: tell Ian, tell Patrick, or tell both. The fact that we discussed it at all, that we'd asked for input on what to do, just shows you how rattled we were. When you came down to it, the band could do sod-all

151

about any of it. About the only thing they could do was tell us to tell Patrick and Ian, and of course, that was exactly what they'd done. The consensus on that one—all hands voting, one for all and all for one—had been a no-brainer.

But neither was answering their phones. I'd left short sharp voicemails for both of them—*um, chaps, went for a stroll this morning, found something I think you need to hear about, you want to check in, please?*—but no one had got back to me, at least not by the time we'd left for rehearsal. It was really frustrating, and I found I was even less happy than usual about leaving Bree behind while I went off to rehearsal.

"I'd give the world if you could come back and kiss me goodbye, oh baby..."

Luke took a lead break, all sharp edges and minor progressions, up and down the scale. The PRS sounded like someone's throat trying to cope with swallowing tears. It worked with the song, almost too well; that was something I'd thought from the first rehearsals, more than three years ago now. Something about the melody said pain, or maybe the memory of pain.

Right now, though, Luke's lead was nowhere near as sharp-edged or pain-soaked as Mac's vocal. If he could bring this to the stage tomorrow night, he'd have a quarter million people sniffling and reaching for their hankies. Christ, it was even having an effect on me, and it's not like I'm not up on everything Mac puts out there.

"I need to learn to let you fly, let our story just soar on high, but I can't let go because you never kissed me goodbye, come back to me, baby, you never kissed me goodbye..."

"Brilliant." Stu did a little flourish on the snare, and got up. "That sounds about perfect. I don't know about you lot, but I want a break and a nice leg-stretch and something cold to drink. How are we for time? Oi, Ian, there you are. We have room in the schedule for a stretch and a cold beer?"

"More than enough. You're running about a quarter hour ahead. And yeah, before you ask, the sound out in the house is good. Nice and crisp."

Ian had come out on stage, with Carla right behind him. It occurred to me that, right, this was one reason Ian hadn't been answering his phone—Carla'd only just got in and there was probably a fuckload of detail to be sorted out. "All right, lads, break time. JP, got a moment? I want a word with you."

"Yeah, I was just about to hunt you up. Carla, glad you made it in time for the gig. You all right?"

She was just coming off the better part of thirty-six hours on planes, and she had to have been jetlagged half off her nut, but it wasn't showing; she looked just the same as always. Patrick's got that same thing going on, and it makes me want to bash him sometimes; for some reason, though, it doesn't worry me with Carla.

"I'm fine, just a little sleep-dep." She yawned suddenly, a proper jaw cracker, sucking down air as if there wasn't enough in the world. "Wow, sorry about that. I'm having my floors refinished and I underestimated how strong the smell would be. Not nearly enough sleep last week. Can we go backstage for a few minutes? Hey guys—this is sounding really great. Excuse us, okay? I'll get JP back to you in a couple, I promise."

She led the way between the amps, offstage and down to where the road cases and the rest of the gear was stashed. Ian was right at her heels, with me trotting after them. I wasn't sure why I was so convinced, but I was: they knew all about what Bree and I had found that morning.

That particular mystery got cleared up as soon as we below. Patrick was waiting for us, and Bree was with him.

"Hey, JP. Sounding good up there." Nice conventional opener, and the only problem was, it was rubbish. There was nothing conventional about Patrick's voice, or the way his eyes had gone all over dirty ice. He'd gone into predator mode, and he wasn't

153

wasting any time trying to hide it, either. "Bree told me what you guys found this morning. Have you got a couple of minutes, so we can talk about it?"

"Hell yeah. I was hoping you'd get back to me." I headed over to my wife, and got an arm round her waist; she was looking worried, for some reason. Or maybe it wasn't worry. Whatever was going on, she was as tense as hell. "You all right, love? Glad Bree got hold of you, Patrick. I left you a voicemail this morning, but I didn't want to leave any details, not under the circs. And we've been nose to the grindstone all day."

"I know. That's why I called Bree. You guys were in full rehearsal mode and Ian told me nothing short of blue murder was acceptable for interrupting the band." He paused for a moment, choosing his words. "And while it's possible that murder is just what may have happened, we've got no way of finding out, at least not that I can see."

"Why do you keep saying that?"

My wife sounded furious. I got it suddenly, the tension, the look on her face. She wasn't worrying I'd be sniffy about her having given Ian and Patrick the gen without me there; she was worried that someone had got killed, and that whoever had done it might walk.

She went on in a rush. "That horrible little room was absolutely streaked with blood. Someone or something died in there. How can you say you can't find out? That's insane, Patrick. Just go look in the window. That's what we did. You'll see."

"I did look." Flat as a rock, that answer was, and it was pretty obvious that this was the first Bree'd heard of it. "I was on my way over there in the Range Rover even before I got off the phone with you. There's nothing there, Bree."

"What!" I was gawking at him. "Sorry, mate, but that's bullshit, all right? Unless you think me and Bree are both off our heads, or fucking hallucinating, or just straight up lying to you —"

"None of the above." He was watching me, nice and steady, and cold as January. Frost on the sidewalk in winter, those eyes were, just ready for someone to slip on, fall, hurt themselves. "I'm reporting, JP. I'm not arguing. I'm just telling you what I did, and what I found as the result of what I did. I checked the slit windows on all those huts, just to make sure I wasn't getting the wrong one. I checked every window, every hut, from every angle. There's nothing there, not in any of them. Those huts are nice and clean."

We both stood there, staring. His voice had gone careful. "One of them was much too clean, in fact, especially when I compared it with the other three. In the third hut from the road, there was no mattress at all."

"Yeah, I'd guessed that one already, ta." For some reason, my own edginess was ratcheting up to match Bree's, and it was taking my temper with it. I sounded about as pissed off and grim as I felt. "That's the one we were talking about, the one with all the blood. Nothing there? Someone already got in there and tidied up, did they?"

"So it would seem." Patrick was still being careful, and I was damned if I could see why. There was no one within earshot of us in any direction. "The question, absent any overt physical evidence, is what everyone feels the next step should be. Because I've got nothing to show any of the Manaari authorities, not a single piece of evidence beyond your statement, and Bree's. And I'm afraid that isn't enough. There's nothing in that room that would support –"

"My word not good enough for you?"

Patrick went quiet. I was staring straight into his face now, and Bree was white-faced, either with rage or with shock, I couldn't tell which. I was a bit too close for comfort to telling Patrick what I thought about an employee of the band telling one of the members that he couldn't be arsed believing what he was told.

Ian and Carla were still not saying a word, just watching and listening. "Bree's word not good enough? Because if that's the way it is, mate, I'm taking the rest of the evening off. If you're not up for believing me or Bree, we'll go straight to the bloody Emir and let him tell us he doesn't believe us. That do you?"

Something flickered in his face. "It would, if I were disbelieving your word. But as it happens, I'm not. I don't doubt for a moment that you and Bree saw exactly what you say you did. That's not the problem, JP. You're not thinking this through. Suppose I go find Bengt and tell him all of this. Don't any of you understand what the problem is, here?"

"We can't tell who to trust." Carla let her breath out and finally put her tuppence in. "That's it, isn't it, Patrick? Whoever cleaned that room up and got rid of the evidence, it could easily be someone high up in the royal family or in the Manaari security forces, or who knows who else. And if we stroll in and tell them what we saw – "

"Fuck!" Ian sounded harassed almost beyond what even he could deal with, and he can deal with quite a lot. "I'll tell you what, people, I don't have time for this. We don't have time for this. We've got the gig the day after tomorrow, and not thirty seconds worth of wiggle room anywhere between now and then. The way I see it, Patrick's right. We can't do a damned thing about any of this, not if they already know what's going on and decided to handle whatever it is themselves. And they must have, because otherwise who the fuck got in there and got rid of the evidence?"

Patrick was watching me, one eyebrow up. I wasn't saying anything. Neither was Bree. There was nothing to say. They were right.

Yeah, I could do what I'd threatened Patrick with. I could stalk into the palace with Bree at my side. We could demand Ali front and centre on the carpet right now, no backchat from the Emir's personal thugs, thank you very much and be quick about it. We might even get him; he had very nice manners, and a respect for guests under his roof that was almost as obsessive as Bree's.

And if we told him just what we'd seen and demanded he do something about it—then what? All we had was a wild story and nothing at all in the way of backup. Besides, if Ian and Carla were right, there was a good chance Ali knew all about whatever was going down anyway. Fuck, I was sure of it. No flies on the Emir, you know? I'd be willing to bet that damned near nothing went on in Manaar he didn't have an eye on, or a finger in.

Next to me, Bree's shoulders suddenly relaxed, and I let my own breath out. Whatever had gone down, whoever had been involved, however it tied in to what had happened to Nordine, we were stuck. Whoever had done whatever it was, they were going to get away with it. There was nothing to be done about it, nothing at all.

"I'm sorry, JP." Patrick had seen it, seen us reason it out. "If anything changes, I'll be on it. But right now, there's nothing to do."

"He's right, JP. You know he is." Ian sounded gruff, but there was sympathy at the back of his voice. He knows me very well, does our band manager, and he knew just how frustrated I had to be. "Look at it this way, though. Two days from now, it'll be a whole new year and we'll be on a plane home. And after that, whatever is going on around here can go right ahead and happen. It's not going to be our problem."

Chapter Ten

If you want to know who came up with the idea of tracking down Bengt Ekberg whether he fancied being tracked down or not, I couldn't tell you. I remember it being Bree's notion, she remembers it being either my idea or Ian's, and Ian says he remembers fuck-all about anything beyond the actual confrontation with Patrick backstage before I headed back out for another hour's worth of final fiddling and song tweaking and tech run-through. All I can tell you is, the whole time we were smoothing out those last few rough spots, I was getting more and more pissed off about the whole mess. And the more I thought about it, the more pissed off I got.

(*Cal, what happened to that tasty off-timing thing you were doing after the second chorus? No, I mean that thundery rumble trill thing, the one that comes right before the bridge, I'm not hearing it. Luke, sorry, that Strat's out of tune. JP, can I have an A...?)*

I hit the harmonic on the A string, and Luke tuned his axe. Conversation, people talking, tech and tweak and all the stuff that gets done. And unless someone was calling my name, I wasn't hearing any of it. My head was elsewhere.

Right off the bat, from that first phone call from Ali to Mac, this gig had been a piss-poor idea. Nobody had wanted to do it, no matter what they'd said. And what's more, we'd all known it. We'd all known that any dealings with the al-Wahid family were going to mean trouble.

Bree hadn't wanted to come. Katia hadn't wanted to come. No one had wanted to do this gig. So what in sweet hell had all of us, any of us, been thinking? The money?

Yeah, twenty four million quid was a lot of dosh. Truth is, we had enough to cover that ourselves, if we really needed to. The Book of Days tour had been the most profitable tour in industry history, and not just in Blacklight's history, either: in anyone's touring history. A few years after the CD's original release, we were still getting royalty cheques that left me blinking, and left Bree looking for charities to send some of the money to, because it was more than anyone would ever need and having that much coming in after the fact sent her "all wealth is greed and all greed is evil and up against the wall, motherfucker!" needles redlining.

(What? No, we're going to need to do something about Mac's harp right there—it's getting washed out. Yes, I know it'll sound different when the venue's full. I'm not dim, mate.)

Why had we agreed to do this? It wasn't as if we hadn't known the al-Wahid connection was septic. We'd lost staffers and family because of it. We didn't need his twenty four million quid, we didn't need his horny little brats, and we didn't need his moneyed privileged bullshit.

We didn't need to play his opening party, either. Christ, we could have been back in San Francisco, hanging with the cats, spending New Year's Eve with the Fog City Geezers playing the 707 Club. So what in hell were we doing here –

"JP?"

I jerked my head back into the moment. Luke was watching me, the Strat at the ready. He knows me quite well, does Luke, better than most people out there, and besides, he's one of the shrewdest people I've ever met. I'd have bet my last royalty cheque that he knew just what I was thinking. "Check in, mate," he told me. "Keep in touch. You've got a guitar solo right there, last I looked."

"Sorry." I settled the Paul against me, ready to roll. They were all watching me, just waiting. "Here we go. Luke, you want to give me the last eight bars…?"

Why had we agreed to do this damned show? Right, of course, there'd been another reason. It hadn't been just the money for my recovery centre, or Luke's diabetes research foundation. There was also Mac's idea, wanting to put a few gigs on for our fans, free festival dates, a thank-you thing. He'd liked the idea of bending Ali over a barrel for double what we'd been offered initially, and getting Ali to end up footing the bill for the festival dates. I remembered just how dark Mac's grin had been when he suggested that; he's not usually malicious, or vengeful, or any of that.

Now that I was actively thinking about, I found myself wondering if Mac himself had even really wanted to play this gig. Hell, maybe the idea that Ali would agree to what was being demanded hadn't occurred to him; maybe he'd thought Ali would balk at the kind of numbers Ian had thrown at him. Christ, had that meeting really been only a month ago? It felt about twenty years had gone by.

But Ali hadn't balked. He hadn't even blinked. He'd just agreed to everything we demanded, and signed the bank transfers like some sort of indecently wealthy performing seal. What the fuck? We were back at the original mystery: why had the Emir of Manaar been so determined to have us play this party? For a lot less dosh, he could have had damned near anyone else in the world. Hell, for what he'd been willing to pay us for this gig, he could have booked the Pope to come out and do magic tricks, maybe pull a rabbit out of one of his hats. Apparently, though, only Blacklight would do. Why?

"Fuck me, Johnny, that was blistering!" Mac's voice cut through the noise in my head. "That little solo would have taken all the paint of the walls, if we were happened to be playing somewhere with walls. Seriously, what got into you? And can you do that again when we play it for real?"

I came back to the here and now with a thump. The rest of the band had stopped playing completely; they were all too busy gawking at me.

"Sorry again." There was a nasty little jolt of electricity up and down my right leg, deep under the skin, where the damaged nerve endings are. The pain wasn't doing my temper any good, not with me already feeling pissy and ready for a brangle. "I've got no idea what I was playing, none at all. The fingers were here, the head was elsewhere. Aren't we recording all this, though? I'll give it a listen tomorrow and see what's up. Look, what else have we got on? Because I've gone achy round the edges, so whatever's left to do, can we just get it done now, please?"

Another twenty minutes, polishing things, fine-tuning, getting it down and getting it done. My fingers knew the drill and just got on with it, and thank God for that, because no matter how much I tried to concentrate, I couldn't manage it. Pulling my mind off Ali's motives just wasn't happening, any more than shrugging off the idea of someone getting away with what looked to have been a really ugly bloodletting was.

"Time to call it a night, I'd say."

Ian had been watching from the side of the stage just behind Tony's piano bench. He doesn't need to waste his energy checking how we sound from out in the house. That's Ronan's thing, and he's very territorial over it. But Ian's not above reminding Ronan—or anyone else he thinks needs the reality check—that he's the manager, and that he's not having us get too tired out. "Brilliant job, mates, let's call this one and put it to bed. Cars are round back. There's a couple of restaurants offered to stay open if we fancied a late supper."

Bree was waiting backstage. It was late, and yeah, I was hungry; fact is, with her diabetes and my everything else, we can't afford to be missing meals. Used to be she'd be fussing over me, nagging me into making damned sure I got enough food to keep the MS hanging back. These days, since she got the diabetes diagnosis a few years back, we nag each other.

That night, though, it didn't go down that way. I hit the bottom of the stairs, we took a good hard look at each other, and well, yeah, there you go. Any ideas about plumping back in the limo, heading for one of the city's chichi eateries, and having a nice plate of goodies before bed went straight out the window. She was pale, and pinched; all that outrage, the same stuff that had been building up in me since that face to face with Patrick at the break, was reflected right there in her face. There are times when that marital mind-reading thing can be a proper nuisance, but there it was: neither of us was going to be able to enjoy anything at all until we'd done something, taken some kind of action, handled it as much as we could. And we both knew it.

"Ian." I jerked my head, and he was right there. Bree was at my shoulder. The rest of the band was already piling into the cars; I saw Carla, one leg already half inside the last limo, stop and turn to watch us. "If I wanted a shot at finding Bengt, where would I look? And don't even think about trying to talk me out of it. Where?"

162

"No clue, JP." He wasn't stonewalling me—he meant it. "You're asking the wrong bloke. I scratched Bengt off my list of people I needed to keep up with after al-Wahid ordered me off. You want Patrick for this one. Hang on, let me get him over here, or at least get him on the phone. I saw him about three minutes ago."

He'd already got his cell out, but it wasn't needed. I caught Carla, one arm waving in a *come over here* gesture and then pointing at us, and there was Patrick, coming up behind Ian. He must have been near enough to have seen us, and truth is, I'd have put a few bob on him knowing what we were talking about, as well. He knows me and Bree very well, does Patrick.

"Patrick?"

Bree had hold of my hand, and she'd caught Patrick's eyes with her own. Patrick likes to say he hasn't got a thing for my wife—he's been saying it so long, there are times I think he's actually convinced himself it's true—but that's rubbish. When Bree speaks, Patrick jumps, and I don't give a toss whether he's willing to admit it or not. Most times it drives me round the fucking twist, but there's no denying it can come in useful, and this was one of those times. Saves arguments, yeah? "We want to find Bengt," she told him. "Where should we look first?"

He opened his mouth, caught my eye, and shut it again. From the look on his face, I sussed he was probably just trying to sort out a good answer to Bree's question, but she can't read him as well as I usually can, and she misread him being quiet. "Please, Patrick? We don't want to get you involved in a turf war thing. We don't want to get you into any kind of trouble at all, but I'm not going to be able to sleep unless I do something, and I know John won't. We won't tell him you told us, I promise."

"I'm not worrying about that, Bree." There it was, that gentle note he gets in his voice at any evidence of Bree's warm-heartedness. It's one of the few things he doesn't seem able to control, or maybe he just can't be arsed to try. He was avoiding

163

my eye, though; too busy smiling and being gentle at my wife. "I was just trying to think of the likeliest place to start. What time is it? We can check the production office first…"

So, yeah, we missed the post-rehearsal supper. The limos pulled off without us, and we trotted along after Patrick as he headed around the side of the stage and off towards the little trailer where I'd first asked Bengt about whether the Tahini Twins were being kept off our patch, as promised.

No joy, not on the first try; the trailer was dark and locked. Bree made a frustrated little noise under her breath, and I got one arm round her waist. Patrick shot us both a look, and got his cell out.

"Let's see if I can get him on the phone." He smiled at Bree. "I know you guys must be starving—Bengt? Oh, good, I was hoping you were around. Listen, have you got about five minutes? I've got JP and Bree Kinkaid with me, and we need to talk to you about something. Where are you? Oh, at the Palace—do you want us to come there?"

He actually ended up coming to us. Looking back, I think that was probably a mistake; we gave him enough time to put a good mask over whatever he knew or didn't know. Or maybe the mistake was Patrick letting on that me and Bree were along for the ride. Either way, he showed up in his Range Rover about ten minutes later, and he hadn't even got all the way out of the truck before I knew it was going to be useless.

Forewarned, forearmed, all that rubbish. It was right there, in the nice careful blank look on his face. That look was so unrevealing, it might as well have been armour.

"Oh, *damn it.*"

Bree, muttering, hadn't managed to keep it low enough for Patrick not to hear. He shot her a look, and then one at me. Yeah, he'd seen what we'd seen. Waste of time. We weren't going to get told a damned thing Bengt didn't choose to tell, unless

Patrick had some way, some sort of cop-speak thing, of getting what we wanted to know.

"Good evening, Patrick." He smiled at us, and that smile set the tone: this wasn't the cheerful Southern California thing we'd got before, it was the formal European front, the same one he'd used on me when I'd asked whether the al-Wahid twins were really being kept out of our way. "And Mr. and Mrs. Kinkaid, a pleasure. Is there some way in which I may assist you?"

Patrick may have had some cop tricks up his sleeve, some way of getting Bengt to turn loose of the gen we wanted. I'll never know, though, because Bree'd apparently made up her mind that playing protocol games was going to get us fuck-all in the way of information. She just went straight for it.

"Yes." She was looking straight at Bengt, holding him with her eyes, making sure he kept his attention on her. She's lived with a European long enough to totally get where American and European manners are different. "We had a very odd experience last night, and then this morning…"

She told him, no whitewash, no frills, just the simple facts: people under our window last night where no one had any business being, no sound of an engine, obviously on foot, reasoning it out, and then what had gone down this morning. She kept her voice as even and uninflected as possible; she'd already sussed that giving him or anyone involved with the al-Wahid family any excuse at all for not taking her seriously would bury our chances at the start. Being written off as an emotional bird would have done it, and she knew it.

So she stayed calm. It got a bit dodgy near the end; talking about what she'd seen through the window slit, she had a bead of sweat along her hairline that had nothing to do with the weather. She got to the end of it, no interruptions from anyone, and waited.

"Ah." Bengt sounded completely neutral. "I'm familiar with those huts, of course. They were put up many years before my association with the royal family. If I remember correctly, they were mostly used for storage while the motorway was being completed, with the occasional emergency housing provided for a worker. But if you looked through the windows, you will have seen that they are very sparse in terms of accommodations. No one lives in them, these days."

"Maybe not." I was keeping my own voice level. There'd been just a shade of emphasis in that *if you looked through the windows.* "But someone was using that third hut for something, and whatever it was, mate, it left a lot of blood."

Bengt opened his mouth, but Patrick got in first. "I'm not primarily concerned with whatever happened in that hut. But the terms of our contract state very clearly that the Queen's Palace is Blacklight's, for the band's exclusive use, for the duration of our stay in Manaar. Then there's the specific rider, forbidding the al-Wahid daughters from interacting in any way with the band family. We already know Nordine was on the premises when he had no business there. JP himself encountered the two girls skinny-dipping in the mineral pools, right outside the palace. Both clauses have been breached, Bengt. I've already discussed this with Carla Fanucci and Ian Hendry. If band management chose to enforce it, we could turn around and go home right now."

Bengt and Patrick had locked up, eye to eye, and no one was saying a word. I was remembering, a bit too clearly, just how tricky it was hiding things from Patrick, back when he was a cop. I've always thought he'd make a brilliant poker player. There's no reading that face, not if he decides to keep it shuttered. But Bengt was matching him. Pair of stone faces, there...

"Yes." Bengt broke the silence, finally. "That is true. It would be unfortunate, however, and would cause a great deal of trouble to all concerned. It would also do some harm to Blacklight's reputation for reliability, if such things matter to your organisation. I would also remind you that the Emir has absolute say on

166

whether or not a plane leaves Manaari airspace. I do understand your position, of course. But whatever happened has already happened. What would you have me do?"

"We want to know what happened in that hut."

I jerked my head round to stare at Bree, and got a shock. Between outrage and frustration, she was about ten seconds away from dotting Bengt Ekberg a good one, straight across the chops. My wife doesn't play poker; she hasn't got the face for it.

"That's very natural." If he'd read it, he wasn't showing. "The huts, of course, are well beyond the grounds of the Queen's Palace. But I understand your desire to know. Patrick will understand, I think, when I say that I have nothing in the way of spare time until after the show. But I will look into it then, and keep you informed."

I got hold of Bree's hand held on hard. She was breathing through her nostrils.

Bengt looked at his watch. "And now, if you will excuse me, I have much work to do. Good night to you."

"Ladies and gentlemen, His Excellency the Emir and the Royal Family offer you warmest welcome to Medin-Manaar..."

"You ready for this?"

Tony had come up behind me, and he sounded shaken. That wasn't much of a surprise; yeah, we'd done crowds of over a hundred thousand on the last tour, but there's a difference between that and the decibel levels that come out of a quarter million people, you know? Just then, you could barely hear anything over the crowd noise. You couldn't really see where Amina Plaza ended, either. Something about all those bodies out there made the horizon look different, and of course it was getting dark. Good job we'd gone for all those audio towers and all that extra gear...

"Yeah, I'm fine." I had Little Queenie strapped on and ready to go. "Not a problem."

"We know that you have come to Manaar from the far corners of the world, and we have an extraordinary show for you..."

Of course that was bollocks. Truth is, I was nervous as hell, stomach fluttering, nerve endings jangling, the lot. I always get edgy on opening nights, even if the opening night is a one-off. I was damned if I was letting Tony in on that, though. He'd been through enough shit this past year. There'd been so much going on around us, it would have been too easy to forget that he was barely ten days out of a gruelling rehab, trying to get his life and his marriage back together.

I wasn't forgetting. No way I could, you know? I've been through that particular horror show myself. If dishing out a double handful of little white lies was going to make any part of it easier for Tony to handle, I was prepared to keep dishing until I ran completely out of the damned things.

"...to ring in a new era of entertainment and luxury in Manaar, and to ring in the new year..."

"Ready for this, Johnny? Tony, don't look so freaked out, mate. It's just a gig." Mac had breezed up next to me, running in place, loosening up, doing all the usual stuff he's been doing for forty years just before the spotlight finds him. If he's ever been nervous about a show, I've never once seen him show it. "Honestly, though, I still haven't quite wrapped my head round not having the ramp and the side stages out there. Not quite Book of Days, is it?"

"Bigger crowd, smaller stage." Luke was right behind Tony, and the Bunker Brothers right at his shoulder. "Jesus, listen to that audience. Everyone ready? What's the noise level out there, do you think? Hey, Bree."

I turned, just my head, and smiled. Bree was behind me, literally pressed up against me, one hand ready for her traditional way of wishing me a good show: snaking between my thighs and grabbing. She knows, and I know, that there's nothing like send-

168

ing the band onstage all primed for sex to get that out to the audience, as well.

I don't know what she'd been thinking since the encounter with Bengt, where he'd basically told us to fuck off and keep our noses out of their business. Whatever she was worrying about or imagining or anything else, she'd put it away and was apparently planning on keeping it put away until we got back to London, or maybe all the way back to San Francisco. She hadn't brought it up, hadn't said a word about it, nothing at all, since that backstage meeting. If Ian hadn't dragged the band off for a long last-minute full run-through in Ali's fancy studio, I might have spent more time worrying about what was going on in her head. As it was, I had no attention to spare for anything that wasn't the show. Probably just as well, yeah?

"...*one of the greatest bands in history, legends of rock and roll, in a once in a lifetime show...*"

"Dude, you've been talking for a year. Just shut the fuck up and let the band onstage, yo." Domitra was looking cross and concentrated, and she was muttering. The women were all dressed to the nines, but she'd gone the other way; normally she'd be in stretchy stuff and her Docs, but tonight, she'd apparently decided that being even scarier than usual was the way to go. She looked like a ninja from one of those Japanese black and white movies. Everything she had on was black.

"*Ladies and gentlemen...*"

The stage lighting shifted and flickered, a pool of gold and indigo, the logo that's identified the band for coming up on forty years, and of course the audience noise levels went up a few notches. Bree got one hand between my thighs and did her usual 'sending hubby off to the office' deal. She had her lips against my ear. "Do a good gig, baby."

"*...BLACKLIGHT!*"

That whole thing, about being a bag of nerves on opening

169

nights—I always forget that, as soon as we hit the stage and the lights find us and we hit those first chords together as a band, as a unit, the nerves get out of the bag and just let me do my thing. The Amina Plaza show was no exception.

We'd actually opted to do something unusual for us: we'd included a few numbers we don't do live, as a general rule. It could have been risky, that; it was Mac's idea, and he'd suggested we all brace for an argument when we let Ian know. But Ian was fine with it. He'd told us, usual gruff Ian style, that he was the tour manager and not the musical director, the set list was Mac and Luke's worry and not his, get on with it, play whatever worked for us.

So we opened the Manaar gig with a thing called "Locked Me Out Again", a B-side off our first mega-selling album, *Pick Up The Slack*. There was a good chance half the audience wouldn't know it, and yeah, you generally want to open a show this size with a standard or a hit. I wondered what was going on in Mac's head, but I hadn't asked him. I don't question him about this stuff often, or Luke either. Some part of me is still the new kid, still just being allowed to sit in, you know?

So, first chords—it's a sharp jumpy off-rhythm run on Luke's Strat. Cal and I played a call and response, Stu hit the kick drum, crashing low end of the piano from Tony, like distant thunder. Then Mac hit the spotlight.

"...*Same old movie, same old thing, here we go again, same reactions every time, been doing this since I don't know when...*"

I was holding my breath. I probably wasn't alone, either. Mac never shows nerves, but yeah, it was risky.

The crowd went nuts.

I glanced out over this endless tidal wave of faces and moving shoulders and hands in the air, a quarter million bodies swaying like rows of ripe corn in some field out there in the American heartlands. If there was anyone among the first few thousand people who didn't know the words, I couldn't see them. They all knew every word of a B-side that we've played live maybe three times ever, and which gets basically no airplay. They were all singing.

"...Same old story, same old song, it never seems to change, I make noise and you get weepy, I put myself right out of range..."

The portable toilets were shaking. Now that's what I call being on it, yeah? Even the crappers were dancing. I realised I was grinning, something I hadn't really been doing much of since we'd got back to Manaar. I wasn't the only one, either. The whole band was grinning along with me. I could see Tony's face over the long shining expanse of piano lid; the rider had specified a Mason & Hamlin grand, and Ronan had kitted it up with an assortment of internal mics. Tony's face—crikey, he was shining almost as much as the damned piano.

"...So I'm out on the porch and the sun is sinking, my key don't work, don't know what you were thinking..."

Bree was dancing off in the wings, my side of the stage. I had a fantastic view of her moving, and the rust-coloured dress she'd got for the show was moving right along with her. It had been too long since I'd had her there offstage, visible during a Blacklight show; the Book of Days set had been a revolutionary bare stage, 360 degrees open to the audience. That meant there were no wings for her or anyone else to dance in. This—my old lady shaking it, getting down and rocking out, just lost in the music, right there where I could see her and draw on that energy—was fucking brilliant. It was old-school Blacklight.

Right, Johnny, and there's you answer. That's what was going on in Mac's head.

That's why he'd wanted to open with a thirty year old B-side. All the tech, all the gear, Ronan had got us all totally twenty-first century, Brave New World stuff. And musically, Mac done a one-eighty. He'd taken us back to the band we'd been when we first crested, back in the late seventies: amps, light show, the lot. It

171

wasn't retro, any more than Book of Days had been. It was just another take on what we'd done with that last tour: Blacklight then, Blacklight now, here we are, rock on with us. The contrast was brilliant. It was like listening to an eight-track in that Bugatti Veyron Bree wasn't going to get to drive after all.

"*...Banging on the sliding door but it's double-paned, I might as well leave—you locked me out again!*"

So yeah, the opening night nerves were gone by the time Luke hit a scorching little solo three minutes twenty into that first tune. Some nights are good right out the gate. Some nights, especially when my body's playing Judas on me, I've got to go deep into the physical reserves and pull up stuff so that I can give the fans what they're there for.

But once in a while, we get the show where just a few bars in, everything comes together and you know, straight off: this one's historic. It's legend, magic, not something we can repeat. This is one for the ages. They aren't always the big gigs, either; some of the ones that get talked about longest are smaller shows. It's something to do with the energy, what happens when energy becomes alchemy: crowd anticipation and band and venue and maybe just the smell in the air come together and become one thing, and bob's your uncle: lead into gold.

I'm glad, now, that the crowd had something amazing to take away with them. They came a long way for that. They deserved it, the loyal buggers.

We finished the first set with "Liplock". It was a nice safe way to bring down the house, and it probably led to more than a handful of babies for some of that audience, nine months down the road; you give Malcolm Sharpe a song about oral sex, there's going to be rather a lot of belly-bumping by the time the night's over. Down the side stairs and straight into the tent that had been put up for the band's use, towelling off for a twenty-minute break, sucking down mineral water, hydrating.

"Damn, JP, that sounded fantastic!" Carla had glass of something bubbly in one hand. Right behind her, Bree was balancing two plates of food. "Way to rock the Kasbah, guys."

"Thanks." I'd headed for a chair straight off; my legs had gone shaky, whether from the adrenalin or the MS being pissy, I couldn't have said. My stomach was rumbling, as well—playing music is like good sex, the way it uses energy and burns off the calories. "Bree, is one of those for me? Great, because I'm hungry. We sound as good as I think we do tonight?"

"Better." She'd pulled over a chair and settled in next to me herself. I took a quick look at her plate—good, she'd gone for sensible food. Some show nights, she's so damned busy making sure I've got the right nosh, she just grabs whatever for herself. "John, you know something? I never realised until tonight just how much I missed dancing where you could see me. It feels like the good old days. And wow, I haven't heard some of those songs in years—actually, I don't think I've ever heard you do 'Locked Me Out Again' live, ever. Whose idea was that, the oldies stuff, I mean? Because it was totally kickass and I'm loving it."

"Bree, angel, how sweet of you to say so. My idea, mostly, with some input from Luke. But of course the entire band had to approve it." Mac was bouncing from foot to foot, shaking both legs and arms. "God, this lactic acid can just sod right along now. I feel as if I've just ridden three stages of the Tour de France. Ian, what have we got? Ten minutes…?"

We opened the second set with "Hammer It Home", Mac's pissy political monster of an anthem, and that pretty much locked up the way the rest of the gig was going to go. He always does this one edgy, but tonight he brought this weird sort of trembling concentration to it.

"…*Every time the Big Man tries to nail you, every time the jack boots find your door, when you think your self-respect has failed you, think you can't take it anymore…*"

173

I've got a really nasty guitar solo mid-song, and it came out dirtier and rougher than usual. Not a bad thing, that's what the vibe was that night, but as I was playing it, a thought popped into my head, maybe because I suspected Mac was envisioning Ali when he sang about the Big Man: I hadn't seen Ali anywhere, not before the show, not in the band's private tent, nothing. What the fuck, the bloke had coughed up twenty four million quid for the pleasure of having us come out here and play this gig, and he couldn't be arsed to actually watch it? It didn't make sense.

"*...Hit it hard, hit it fast, make them work if they want your ass, you don't have to take it, you don't have to play it, just make that nail your own, I tell you hammer it home...*"

I shot a look into the wings, both sides of the stage. Not there. Maybe he had a royal box somewhere, but even if he did, something was still off.

"*...I tell you, hammer it home...!*"

I had it now. Whatever I didn't like about the bloke—and that was damned near everything—he did have a huge respect for hospitality. Yeah, we'd been paid a metric fuckload of dosh to play this show, but we, the whole Blacklight family, were guests under his roof. And he hadn't come out to wish us good luck, hadn't sent someone, nothing.

I pulled my mind off it. I had to, basically, because two hundred and fifty thousand people were demanding our attention and that's where the attention had to go. So Ali, and why he hadn't come out, why he'd blown us off, that had to wait. The next hour and twenty minutes were all about the gig.

We closed the show with "Remember Me". That was hard, making that choice. It was one I'd written, words and music, a love song to our world, to the music we make, a way of saying thanks and a way of calling us all out on our bullshit. It was also a love song to my wife.

Unfortunately, it was what had been playing on the overheads at Wembley Stadium the night I'd gone into V-fib and flatlined. For Bree, that song is always going be about me on the floor, watching what she thought was me dying. She hadn't even been let touch me because her mum was busy using paddles to restart my heart, and she didn't need her daughter electrocuted in the process. The song is Bree's personal soundtrack to her worst nightmare.

But "Remember Me" is also one of the best-selling singles in music history, and our fans expect it. And the gig wasn't about Bree, it was about them. So, when Mac and Luke put it down as the closer, they did check with me first. Nice of them, you know? They didn't have to do that. But they were all at Wembley, and they all knew just how Bree reacts to it. I'd told them yeah, she'll be warned that it's coming, but I'm with you, this is about the fans, and she'll have to cope.

Halfway through the song, the entire stage and Amina Plaza and all those towers seeming to shake with how much music and feeling and magic and everything else was happening out there, I looked for Bree. This was the first time we'd played the song, the first time she'd seen me onstage with Blacklight, since I'd almost died at Wembley. I needed to know she was actually dealing with it, that she was okay. There was fuck-all I could do about it if she wasn't, but still, I needed to know.

She wasn't dancing. She was standing very still and watching me. Not the band—just me, I could tell by the way her head moved slightly whenever I did, following me movements. She was far enough back in the shadows to where I couldn't see her face. But she was there, offstage, still visible.

Arms around each other, bowing. Fireworks shooting off behind the stage; they were actually out past the city, being set off from boats out in the Medin-Manaar harbour. Offstage to towel off, letting the chanting and screaming and flickering cell phone display lights build up to insanity pitch. Back out onstage for a three-song encore, instead of the usual one tune. Lights up, announcement over the PA, and the largest gig Blacklight had ever played was in the bag, and done.

"Right." Ian was waiting for us in the tent. "Brilliant show, guys. That's quite a lot of happy people going to be going on about this one for good long time. I've got the cars just outside— there's a late supper waiting for everyone in the corporate suite, back at the Royal residence, if anyone fancies it. You lot ready? JP, what?"

"Just wondering about something." The show was over, and my brain was back in gear, looking at what I'd put aside for the past couple of hours. "Am I the only one thinks it's pretty damned rude that Ali never bothered to show? Or was he there, and I just didn't see him?"

If anyone had told me it was possible for silence to be that absolute just the other side of the wall from a quarter million people, I'd have thought they were bonkers. Maybe it was the look I got off everyone's face.

"Shit." Mac had gone very still, and Domitra, next to him, was reacting. "Good eyes, Johnny. No, I haven't seen him at all today. And if someone wants to reassure me that there's nothing ominous about that, I'll be delighted to hear it. I just won't believe it. Ali's got a very strong sense of what the host owes the guest, and if rudeness isn't a beheading offence in Manaar, it's bloody close. Ian? Suggestions? Because I've got a very bad feeling about this."

"Fuck!" Ian had gone even stiffer than Mac had. "No clue, Mac, and no, I haven't seen him today either. I was so busy concentrating on the gig, the Emir never came into my head. Look, let's get back to our digs. We can have the full confab once we're safe out of here."

"Safe?" Katia was staring at Ian. "You mean, you think we might not be safe?"

176

"I don't know, do I?" Ian turned and headed for the tent flap. We were right behind him; getting out seemed like a good idea, suddenly. "I just know I'd rather not be in a tent in the park if there's bad news no one's shared yet. Let's go –"

He stopped. There was noise, just outside the tent flap. Not voices—a different sort of sound entirely. A clicking, oily, a bit metallic somehow.

"Mac." Domitra was in front of him. She looked like a coil, ready to let go. "Behind me. *Now.*"

I didn't see Mac move, so maybe he didn't. Maybe Dom did the moving. But she was there, blocking him off. There were people in the entry to the tent, and they were heading in fast.

Uniforms. Ali's guard. They were all carrying guns, and the guns weren't in holsters. They were pointed at us.

I wasn't thinking, or anything else. It's a funny thing about moments like that—you don't think, you just do. I'd got one hand out and hard on Bree's arm, and I'd yanked her behind me before I'd even realised I moved. No one else seemed to be moving, not even the muscles of their mouths, because no one was saying anything yet. I had a mad thought: *might need a new ticky-box if we get out of this alive, Johnny, the old one's working so hard it's going to blow...*

"Excuse me. Let me through, please."

It was Patrick's voice, coming from the back of that swarm of armed guards. They let him through, but they weren't lowering the guns.

"Patrick?" I don't know that I'd ever heard Mac sound completely unnerved before. "What in hell's going on?"

"There's been another death." Dirty-ice eyes, cold cop looks, the smell of blood, of something wounded: everything I dislike most about Patrick Ormand. I'd never been so glad to see any of it. "And we've got one hell of a mess. It's a member of the Royal Family."

177

Chapter Eleven

I've been in a few crises in my day. I don't know about you, but I always think I'm right there in the moment, nice and calm, keeping it together, voice of reason. Then it's over with and I realise I was freaking out, losing it, flipping my shit. After that, the only way to suss out what really happened and how I really reacted is to ask someone else who was there.

I've been in the middle of a firefight in Cannes, in a club fire in Marin County, and saddled with a few too many dead bodies. I thought I was calm for all of that. But that New Year's Day in Manaar, I did a complete one-eighty: I remember myself being too freaked to put words together to make a sentence. Not my usual way of remembering how I handle the bad moments.

"The royal family? Someone's been killed?"

Ian had somehow got himself in front of the rest of the band, but the armed thugs didn't seem to give a toss about who was standing where. There probably wasn't any reason for them to worry; I don't know much about guns, but I was pretty sure that what they had pointed at us were the kind of things that could spray a hail of bullets before anyone could duck—automatic, or semi-automatic, or whatever. "Patrick, for God's sake, talk to us. The Emir? Has something happened to him?"

Patrick had his back to that collection of muzzles. I didn't know if that was some sort of show of courage or defiance or something, or whether he honestly didn't believe they'd open fire and shoot him in the back; either way, it occurred to me that our pet detective really has got glacial runoff in his veins. My own chest was thumping away like a bad drum machine track on some piece of eighties synth-pop rubbish.

"So far as I know, the Emir is unharmed. I don't have any of the actual details yet. All I have is the bare fact." He took a deep breath and looked around at us, frozen there in place like the Blacklight exhibit straight out of Madame Tussauds. "Princess Paksima has been killed."

There was noise behind me, murmurings, voices. Bree was still leaning up against me; I felt her let her breath out, realised that the reason my chest was throbbing was because I was hanging on to my own breath for dear life, and exhaled. The rush of air to both lungs made me giddy.

"I'm very sorry to hear that. I'm sure we all are. But I'm not really clear what it has to do with us."

We all jerked our heads. Carla had come up to stand at Ian's right shoulder, and she nodded her head towards the guard. She wasn't gesturing with a hand, not at that point, and I got why straight off: she wasn't pointing, or doing anything else that might get any fingers tightened on any triggers.

"Why are these people pointing guns at us? The band's been onstage for hours. They were in full view of a quarter of a million

179

people. Besides, most of us didn't know the princess—in fact, it was specified in the band rider that the al-Wahid girls would stay away from anything to do with the band while we were in Manaar. The Emir and I both insisted on that. It's pretty obvious that no one here interacted with the princesses in any way, at least not willingly. So I really don't see the point of this."

She sounded just the same as she always does: nice and calm, and completely competent. Not only that, she looked to have sorted out who was in charge of that lot, because she was talking to one particular bloke, forcing him to make eye contact with her.

She waved one arm, finally, a nice easy gesture. You'd have thought she was confronting someone blocking her driveway back in LA, or something. The gun in his hand wavered, lowering just a bit, just enough.

Carla had both eyebrows up, completely in control of the situation. She wasn't looking at Patrick, so I don't know whether she caught the tiny nod he gave her. I saw Ian reach for her hand suddenly, and hang onto it.

Funny thing, but with just that one gun not aimed at us any longer, the whole vibe in the room shifted and changed. For starters, Patrick suddenly found his voice again. He must have also realised what he'd been presenting his back to all this time, because he turned round, not too quickly. Most of the guns were still pointing our way.

"I've got a call in to Bengt Ekberg." He'd picked the guard in charge, as well, and he was talking straight at him. "I'm as puzzled as you are, Carla. I have no idea why the Emir or anyone else would send armed guards out here, or what their orders are. After all, you said it yourself: Blacklight's been onstage all evening. I'm guessing we'll have to wait for Bengt before we find out anything solid."

We were all quiet. Bree wasn't behind me any longer; she'd slipped out and come to stand right beside me. I'd been concentrating so hard on what was going on with Carla and the guards, I hadn't even noticed. Domitra was still planted in front of Mac, and she still looked dangerous as hell. So far as I could tell, she hadn't moved an inch the whole time.

And of course, Sod's Law being what it is, both my legs picked right then to get shaky. That was probably inevitable: the gig, the adrenalin, standing in place for too long. The MS is an opportunistic bitch of a disease. If there's any opening for it to ratchet up and give me grief, that's what it does.

"Excuse me."

Shit. Bree'd noticed. I know that tone. When my wife's voice gets that controlled and even, she's not taking no for an answer. Of course she'd felt the tremors start up in my legs.

"Patrick, can we get John a chair, please? He needs to sit."

Patrick opened his mouth and shut it again. He looked about as close to being confounded as I've ever seen him. Bree's tone got even sharper. "*Now*, please, Patrick."

The guard in charge went stiff around the shoulders. The gun came up, not all the way, just an inch or two, just enough.

Bree rounded on him. She fixed him with a stare worthy of that bird in the Greek stories, the one who turned you to stone if you met her eye—Medusa, is it? She looked like one of the Fates or something, assuming the Fates ever got tarted up in designer gear and high heels. For one really bad moment, I thought she was going call him *little man*. If she'd done that, he'd probably have opened fire. It didn't help that, in that particular pair of shoes, she was taller than he was.

"Is this your idea of Manaari manners?" She snapped it out at him. "Do you think the Emir would approve of you treating his guests this way? I have trouble believing he would be so discourteous, or send you to be so discourteous. My husband is ill. He needs to sit. Unless you're planning on shooting someone, lower that gun, please."

181

For a good long moment, the whole situation just hung there. I couldn't hear a damned thing behind me—for all I knew, the rest of the band, the crew, everyone else, had keeled over from shock, or slipped out the back of the tent, or been beamed up into some kind of alien ship or something. That device in my chest never had to do a harder few moments' work than it did just then.

He dropped the muzzle. This time it went all the way down, until it was resting on the floor. Behind him, the rest of the guard followed suit.

Someone, one of the crew I think, brought me a chair, and I sat down. My legs were shaking like the bloody San Andreas Fault about to let go, or maybe like all those portable toilets a few hours ago had done. I wouldn't have put tuppence on it being from the MS, either. The back of my shirt was plastered to my skin, soaked through with sweat.

With me safe in a chair, Bree went and got one for herself, and settled down next to me. I reached out and got hold of her hand, and kissed it. We've got some amazing women around us, and thank God for it.

I don't know how long we waited, but it felt like hours, or maybe years. I remember Luke getting Karen into a chair and bringing her a plate of food—when you've got Type One diabetes, the bad kind, you can't pretend you don't need to eat. I remember my guitar tech, Jas, bringing over a couple of bottles of cold Volvic water, handing one to me and one to Bree. That's my usual tipple, and of course Carla had made sure it was in the rider that all the band's areas be stocked with it. I remember Cal wondering out loud how many people were still in the park outside, how many were still camping out there.

And at the back of my head, I kept hearing something Bengt had said, during that useless confrontation we'd demanded with him. Patrick had pointed out that the contract had been breached just by the twins being in the seraglio in the first place,

182

that under the terms of the contract we could turn right round and go home.

And Bengt had said something about Ali having the last word on who got to fly out of Manaari airspace. I was wondering just how I'd been dim enough to miss that being a threat.

Because, yeah, it was a threat. It might have been no more than Bengt pulling a higher face card than Patrick's in the dainty little game of power poker that conversation had been, reminding us that we were on Ali's home turf and that gave Ali complete control, but any way I looked at it, that had been pretty damned ominous. He'd slipped it in there like the business end of a knife, and I hadn't sussed it.

I was so deep into thinking about that, I nearly missed the stir from outside. Then all the guards were standing with their backs straight and their eyes carefully not fixed on anyone or anything in particular and all the guns pointed straight at the roof of the tent.

Ali al-Wahid walked through the flap, and into the band's tent. And if I'd thought it was quiet behind me before, I hadn't known what quiet was.

For a bloke we didn't know well and didn't much want to, we'd seen him in quite a few different moods, you know? We'd seen him resentful when Mac and Luke called him out on his shit, back in San Francisco. We'd seen him calculating, nearly every time he'd had found himself around Bree since we'd first got here. We'd seen him doing his imperious privileged thing pretty much twenty four-seven, and of course, we'd seen him looking scary and relentless, the night Nordine had bought it. I hadn't really given him and his moods a lot of time; he just wasn't someone I thought much about if I wasn't given a good reason to.

That night, though, he just looked wrong. Different, stripped down, as if someone had peeled off flesh, taken everything inside out and then stuffed it back in again, but forgot to put all of it back. There was something indecent about it, I'm not sure why—it made me uncomfortable for a moment, as if I was look-ing at something through someone else's curtains. I don't do the voyeurism thing.

Next to me, Bree made a small noise at the back of her throat, but she swallowed it. Whatever it was that wanted out, sympathy or shock or whatever else it might have been, that wasn't the moment to be showing anything at all.

He came in, not looking around him at all, not looking at any of us. He looked as if he was seeing something maybe far away, something no one else could possibly see but him; no way to tell whether what he was looking at was brilliant or terrible, or maybe both.

The guards on either side held very still. A couple of them were visibly sweating, and that had me wondering until I realised the poor sods didn't know whether to risk moving to one side to let their boss through without interference, or whether moving and catching his attention was riskier than having him bump into one of them. They probably weren't sure which option was likelier to get them flogged, or maybe beheaded.

"Outside."

I had no clue who he was turfing off the premises, but whoever it was, his voice sounded different, as well. He'd never had much of an accent, not beyond that sort of moneyed-ponce modulated thing people get when they go to posh schools. Mac's got a touch of that in his speaking voice, as well.

I wouldn't have known that was Ali talking if I hadn't been staring straight at him. All the expression, all the body, had run out of his spine and face. It seemed his voice had taken a hit, as well. It was thin as wire. All the personality was gone out of it.

He hadn't sounded like this, or looked like this, when he'd stared down at Nordine's bloodless corpse, and told Bengt and Patrick to find out who'd killed his servant. This was a whole new level.

Since no one from our contingent was moving, it was just as well that Ali's personal guard got that he was talking to them. The bloke in charge, the one Carla and Bree had locked up with, shouldered his gun, and the rest of them followed suit. A moment later, they were on the other side of the tent flap. You could practically hear the sighs of relief, but that might have been in my head. We'd all gone quiet again.

The problem was, no one seemed to know what to say. The bloke had the power to keep us from going home, he had that troop of armed thugs waiting outside and a small army stashed somewhere else, and I was pretty sure that if he told them to slowly break all our arms and legs, they'd queue up and ask him whose fingers to start on first. But he was also a father, and he'd just lost one of his kids. None of the usual conventional rubbish was likely to work. Even Bree, who's got a nurturing streak you could park a tour bus on, didn't look to be able to summon up the necessaries...

"We're very sorry for your loss."

Bree and I both turned, and so did everyone else. Karen Hedley's got a wonderful speaking voice, good enough to give your ears a massage, very mellow and soothing. She was also the last person on earth to have any warm feelings for either of the al-Wahid twins, dead or alive, not after the damage they'd done to her own daughter; she dotes on Suzanne. But she wasn't putting it on—Karen's not capable of that. She meant what she'd just said. Maybe it was just being a parent herself, being able to feel what Ali must be going through.

"Thank you." Nothing was moving in that face, not a feeling or a muscle or anything else. "I regret my guards' behaviour. I gave them no instructions. They will be required to explain themselves, but this is not the moment."

"Your Excellency, is there any way in which we can help?" Patrick didn't sound as gentle as Karen had, but the official cop

185

voice probably did a lot more to get things moving than the conventional regrets Karen had offered up, however genuine they'd been. "I'm happy to offer any assistance I can give Bengt while we're still in Manaar, if that's appropriate."

Oh, bloody hell. Yeah, he'd slipped that one in nicely: *happy to help, experienced copper, you letting the band out of here and if so, when?*

"If Bengt needs assistance, he will tell you." Ali looked around, starting with Bree, moving to me, just looking. I got the impression he was making sure that he made eye contact with every person in that damned tent. "I have no reason to believe that any of you are involved, but I cannot know. And no one will leave Manaar until I can put a name and a face to the person who executed my daughter."

There were probably fifty people in that tent just then: the band, the family, the crew. If you asked me whether any one of us happened to be breathing just then, I'd probably say no, we weren't. There was something about that word, *executed*, something about the way he said it, that didn't leave much room for breathing, or anything else.

"As the head of the house of al-Wahid, I thank you for your performance tonight. I regret that my daughter's death made my attendance an impossibility." He had his hands in his pockets, and he was back to looking at something we couldn't see and probably didn't want to. "You are all tired. Go back to the Queen's Palace. If Bengt has questions, or desires your assistance in any way, he will tell you in the morning."

"John?"

It was probably not too far off daylight, New Year's morning, and Bree sounded wide awake. She was keeping her voice quiet, but she wasn't worrying about whether she might wake me; she knew damned well I hadn't slept more than a couple of minutes at a time. Neither had she. I doubt either of us had got within twenty miles of actual REM sleep that night.

"What, love?"

"Do you suppose those guards are still outside?"

I rolled over, and faced her. Sunrise was definitely coming up shortly; the light in the room was a chilly blue, but it was morning blue, not midnight blue, and there were birds calling outside. I could see her face, and the blue light wasn't nearly as dark as the blue circles under her eyes. She looked exhausted, completely wiped out.

"John...?"

"I don't know, Bree. Just guessing, but I'd say yeah, seems likely. Not really sure what they're up to, or why they're out there in the first place, though. It's not as if anyone's going anywhere." I got a hand out from under the cover and touched her cheek. "At least we won't have any midnight visitors under our windows, not if the Forty Thieves or whatever Ali's gang calls themselves are still patrolling the place. Why?"

"I just – " She stopped, and took a breath. She had her voice under complete control, but it was a visible effort. She was putting her whole body into holding it even. "Shit. John, are we prisoners?"

Even with her not letting her voice go up at all, keeping it straight up, that question should have sounded like melodrama. It says a lot about the situation that it didn't. It sounded terrifying and logical.

That was the result of hearing those boots out there all night. They weren't loud, but they were there, rhythmic, not stopping. We'd heard them echoing across the seraglio, back and forth between those damned pools, ever since we'd got back. The brief periods when we hadn't heard them had been even worse; both of us had strained, waiting for them to start up again.

There'd been no band meeting last night, no putting our heads together, no trying to sort out what the hell was going on and what we were going to do about it. That was a definite boot to the arse of my personal comfort zone. We'd had thirty years of dealing with anything that came up as a group, a unit, a pooling of brains and opinions and ideas. Last night, that hadn't happened.

So yeah, I couldn't answer my wife, and my comfort zone had gone walkabout. Not having that meeting was also a pointer as to how big this was, how much potential it had to fuck up our world: The cars had brought us back from the tent, motorcycle escort to cut through the crowds outside the venue, thousands of happy fans cheering when the limos went by. It was just like the post-show after any big outdoor stadium gig, yeah? Everything had been normal, right up until the limos got us through those peacock-gaudy arches and we'd seen Ali's guard, full uniform, and those damned guns.

Nothing was normal that night, not after Ali had used that word, *executed*. And Ian, who's so nuts for meetings that given half a chance he'd probably call a band meeting to discuss whether we were having enough band meetings or not, hadn't even bothered suggesting a huddle. He'd waved us off to our suites and told us to try for some kip, maybe things would shake out in the morning and he'd do his best to get some gen on what the hell had actually happened. He hadn't hung about waiting for anyone to answer him, either, just climbed back into the limo where Carla was waiting. They might have been going off for a management-level confab on their own, but if that was what was on, they weren't including us. Not exactly reassuring.

"John…?"

It would have been nice to be able to chuck her under the chin, grin, tell her to stop being silly, don't talk rubbish of course we're not prisoners. I couldn't. I didn't know, not for certain, and I was damned if I wanted to offer up soothing nonsense that might turn out to be a flat-out lie. It wouldn't do any good; she wouldn't buy it anyway.

"I don't know, Bree. Not sure if not being allowed to leave on schedule fits the definition or not, but –"

I stopped because she'd begun to shake. I pulled her up close, just holding on. Moments like this, only Bree will do me for comfort, and yeah, she feels the same way. The best I could offer just then was comfort, skin to skin, heart to heart.

"It's okay, baby." I was talking into her hair. "If we are stuck here, it won't be for long. There's a consulate right downtown— we passed it on the way to the restaurant. If there's any smell of us being detained here indefinitely, Carla will be down there handling it, even if she's got to get the bloke in charge out of bed. It's not as if we're what you'd call low profile. Besides, I didn't get any feeling off Ali that he was targeting us for anything, you know? So there's that."

She was quiet, but she wasn't relaxing. I kept both arms wrapped round her good and close, just holding on. I'm not sure what you call it, when that whole primal need thing kicks in and we just sort of slip back to wanting to do what our ancestors did, huddling together round the fires because something big and toothy is out there prowling in the bushes and wanting to eat us. Atavistic, or something like that? Whatever it is, that's where we both seemed to be just then.

Even if the reality of what was going on outside our bedroom walls hadn't been keeping me awake, the MS would have done the trick. There were little stabs and tingles everywhere. Both legs were twitching from heel to groin, to the point where the normal night dose of antispasmodics was barely making a dent; the twitches were becoming straight-up spasms and jerks. There were ominous little movements under the skin on the back of my left hand, as well, a sort of weird fizzing sensation. That was new to me. It was also painful as hell.

I could hide those from Bree, but I couldn't hide the small continuous case of the shakes. And Bree wasn't saying or doing anything that showed she'd even noticed. It takes something huge to get her attention so locked up that she hasn't got enough to spare for what's going on with me.

"I hate this place."

All of a sudden, her voice wasn't under control anymore. She sounded pretty damned close to the edge.

"Glad to hear it," I told her, and brushed my lips against her forehead. "I was worried you might want a little summer bungalow in the desert, or something. Seriously, Bree, once we're out of here, I'm not planning on coming within a hundred miles of this place again. He can have his tents and his peacocks and his mineral pools and the rest of it. I'm out."

She was quiet, and so was I, just holding on. We were both straining our ears, listening for that rhythmic footfall from outside in the seraglio, Ali's boys doing their thing between the pools. And either they'd got a lot quieter, or else they'd stopped.

My head kept trying to come up with a picture, any picture, of what might be happening back at the palace. Was Bengt there, burning the midnight oil, talking to people, coping, dealing? Had Ali slept, or was he awake, maybe staring at that distant thing he'd seemed fixed on, back in the band's tent? Was he pacing, walking the floor? I couldn't seem to bring up any kind of picture in my head; there was a just a blank, somehow.

"You know what?" Bree was muffled, her face up against me. Her voice seemed quieter than it had been; maybe she was getting sleepy, finally. I hoped so. "I'm worried about…"

Her voice trailed off, and I moved back a bit. "Sorry, love? I didn't quite catch –"

"The other twin." The sun was almost up, now, and for some reason, I found myself remembering sunrise, the two of us not sleeping, going out at first light, finding that blood-spattered hut at the edge of the desert. Christ, was that really just a couple of days ago? It felt like half a lifetime had gone by. "Azra. They were almost like one girl, somehow. Weren't they? Identical twins come from the same egg. She must be—I don't know. Destroyed. Ripped in half. She's lost the other half of the egg she came from. It's like someone smashed the other side of her mirror."

"Yeah, I know what you mean." She was right, of course she was, but I hadn't actually stopped to think about it until she'd brought it up. The way she'd put it was almost too vivid. "And them being almost like one girl, that's spot on. You couldn't tell one from the other, not unless you knew who was wearing which colour headscarf."

"Her sister's been killed. Her twin." Her voice was under control again, very quiet. "That's got to be so hard, John. Like losing, I don't know, half the person you were—hello?"

I'd heard it as well: a tap on our door, quiet, rhythmic. For some reason, we'd both gone stiff. Silly, really. It wasn't as if we were in any danger from anyone…

"JP? You awake?"

I let my breath out so fast, I got dizzy. Bree was already up, knotting a robe around her waist, heading for the door; I was rubbing my hands, shaking my legs a bit, trying to get the pins and needles out and get the MS to back off. I had a strong feeling that today, of any day, I couldn't afford to let myself fetch up incapacitated and helpless.

Luke was still in pyjamas, and he didn't look as if he'd slept much either. Neither did Stu or Cal, who were right behind him. Mac, just letting himself out of his own room with Domitra already on guard in the corridor, had pulled jeans and a tee-shirt on, but he was looking tousled and rubbing his arms. Tony was out in the hall, with Katia already waiting for him. I saw her glance over at Mac; if she thought he looked any less lickable in what he had on, she wasn't showing it, or maybe she was too busy shivering. That corridor was always chilly, what with the small high windows not letting the sunlight in, but that morning, it was bloody cold.

Bree held the door open, letting everyone in, peering out into the corridor to make sure no one else was coming along. I'd pulled on my own robe and swung myself out of bed. The floor felt as if small pins were sticking up out of it, straight into the soles of my feet. I could feel the nerves trying to squirm away from the source of pain, but of course, there was no place to go: the pain was entirely internal. You can't squirm away from your own body, even if there's days you wish you could.

"Can everyone hold on a few minutes, please?" Bree was keeping her voice down, but she wasn't whispering. Apparently, she was only worried about waking the rest of the band wives. She didn't seem to give a fuck whether the guard out of doors could hear her or not, assuming they were still there. "Are we expecting anyone else? No? Okay. Then could I get everyone to sit down while I put a kettle on? John needs his meds before we do anything. It's been a bad night. Stu, you do tea, not coffee, right? Dom, is tea okay? I don't think I have any of that drinking chocolate you like…"

So she'd noticed the MS was flaring, after all. For some reason, that made me feel better about things, more normal somehow. I caught her eye, blew her a kiss, and headed off for our posh khazi. I heard Tony say something about wanting a shave and a shower himself, as I was closing the door behind me.

I not only got my meds while my wife was sorting out who wanted what to drink, I actually managed a fast shower. I learned a good long time ago that when the brain gets into wide-awake mode but the body's reeling under the MS, a strong short hosing down can be just what the doctor ordered, and the hotter the better. I've run that one past my neuro, and the quack agrees: a good hot shower can't hurt. And one thing I could say for the

Queen's Palace: what with the hot mineral pools running underground, I couldn't whinge about not having enough hot water for a good wash. Besides, I'd snuck a fast look at the clock on my way into the bathroom, and it was twenty minutes of six. The rest of the band probably needed a few minutes of wake-up time, themselves. There was no need to rush.

By the time I'd got myself dried off enough so that the silk robe wouldn't glue itself to the wet patches, Bree'd got a second pot of coffee going, and the suite smelled brilliant. We'd also been joined by Karen Hedley. Bree was fussing over her, and one look at Karen was enough to make it clear why. She looked as if she hadn't slept at all, and you really can't do that, not with what she's got wrong with her. Even with Bree's less aggressive and serious form of it, sleep deprivation can mess with the levels and balances.

"All right." Bree'd saved me the rocking chair—it was more like a rocking throne, really—and I settled into it. "Bree, is there a cup for me, love? Great, thanks. So I'm guessing I wasn't the only one who thought we should have had a band meeting last night?"

"There probably was one." Mac likes his coffee loaded with sugar and cream, which means he can chug it while the rest of us are still waiting for ours to cool down. "In fact, I'd lay good money on it. What a pity the band wasn't invited to be there for it. Do you know, I'm rather cross about this."

Domitra snorted, and he gave his bodyguard a look. He wasn't joking about the mood he was in. "Well, honestly, Dom, can you or anyone else imagine that the braintrust wasn't up all night, figuring out what to do?"

"Of course they were." Stu got a mouthful of hot tea and swished it round like mouthwash. "Ian and Carla and probably Patrick, as well. I don't know whether I'm pissed off or glad we weren't invited."

"Don't you? I know exactly which one I am." Mac set his cup down, and Bree refilled it halfway. He didn't seem to notice. "I have to say, I'm not thrilled with this secrecy rubbish. In fact, I think I'm going to have a few words to say to our management on the subject. And yes, that includes Carla."

"I couldn't agree more. They do seem to be forgetting who pays them, don't they? It's not exactly a habit I want to encourage." Luke's voice was at normal volume, but had both of Karen's hands between his own, and he was rubbing hard. It reminded me of all these years I'd been rubbing Bree's in just that way, trying to warm them, get the blood circulating properly. "Hopefully it'll stop once we're the hell out of this bloody emirate and back home. It seems to only happen here. Bree? Is that someone at the door? No, you have your coffee, I'll get it—ah. Good morning, ladies. Sorry, did we wake you...?"

That was the only full-on band meeting I can remember where all the wives were there, and none of the management. Unusual, to say the least. Of course, we don't generally hold them at six in the morning in our pyjamas, either. But as I say, nothing about that night was normal.

Still, we did get a lot sorted out. It was interesting, because all the wives had opinions and they were all putting them out there, making damned sure they got heard. The one thing everyone agreed on was that, if we didn't have a definitive time by lunchtime for our plane getting the fuck out of Medin-Manaar Airport, management was going to be very busy.

"And I don't care how much it costs, either." Barb Wilson sounded pretty much the way I imagined her great-grandmother must have sounded during a suffragette march, back when Queen Victoria was still alive. Just the right tone to scare the hell out of generations of schoolboys, yeah? It would have been even more impressive if she hadn't been wearing paisley silk slippers that turned up at the toes, like something out of a 1920s movie about Arabia. "I'm not spending one minute longer than I have to in this place unless someone gives me a real reason to do it. If the Emir thinks he can keep us here indefinitely, he's got another think coming."

She stopped, because it was pretty obvious Karen wanted to say something. She'd opened her mouth and closed it a good four times while Barb was talking.

"Come along," Luke told her, and he was smiling. "No need to be shy, love. Put your tuppence in. What's on your mind?"

She'd gone bright pink. Odd, that, because she and Bree have almost identical colouring, but Bree goes white and Karen turns red. It might have something to do with the freckles—Karen's got masses of them, and Bree's got none—but whatever the reason, it's bizarre seeing them side by side.

"I do, actually. I just can't see why you don't call them and tell them to get over here. They work for you. They're supposed to be protecting the band's interests, aren't they? And really, they're quite good at that. But why should Ian be the only one who gets to call meetings? Can't you do it?"

"She's right." Bree was nodding, nice and fierce, her own hair bouncing against her shoulders. "You know she is. I get that they've probably been up all night, but tough shit. Shouldn't they be in on whatever we decide? I think Karen nailed it. Anyway, if we're going to bitch at them for not including us, we shouldn't be hypocrites and not include them."

"Bree, angel, how right you are. And yes, you've both nailed it." Mac had his phone out, and was punching in a number. "Besides, we've had one instance too many this trip of being separated as a family. I've personally had more than enough of—Ian? Good morning, mate. Mac here. Sorry if I woke you, but take comfort from the fact that you're in good company—I'm afraid none of us slept very well. We're just having a band meeting and we think you need to come play. No, we're in Johnny and Bree's suite. Yes, I know it's six in the morning. A pity we didn't do this last night—if we had, everyone might be getting their beauty sleep. See you in a few, and mind you bring Carla and Patrick with you."

Chapter Twelve

It turned out the guards outside actually had packed up their tents—or rather, their high-powered guns and whatever the hell else they'd had with them—and gone off to scare the shit out of someone else. We found that out when Patrick, beating Ian and Carla to the punch by about five minutes, stuck his head in through our suite door. It was a pity that was about the only good news he brought along with him.

Bree'd left the suite door propped open, letting everyone know to not interrupt the conversation inside by tapping on panels and waiting to be let in. I wasn't admitting it to Bree or anyone else, but I was edgy over that; between the guards charging into Blacklight's tent and having them stomping about outside our windows, I'd have felt a lot safer with any sort of barrier between me and the Forty Thieves. And yeah, I don't need to be told how much protection that flimsy little door would actually have been against a hail of bullets. I still would rather have had it shut.

We'd actually been quiet for a couple of minutes after Mac rang Ian, so we heard the Range Rover Patrick had been using since we got to Manaar pull up outside. Listening to his foot-steps, I wondered why they sounded so loud—he's a soft-footed bloke, is Patrick, probably thanks to all those years he spent as a cop. Then I got it: they were the only footsteps out there. The Forty Thieves had gone off and left us alone. So everyone was watching the door when he came down the corridor and poked his head into our suite.

"Good morning." If he was worried at having a dozen pairs of eyes fixed on him, it wasn't showing. On the other hand, it might have been the first time I've ever seen the bugger actually human enough to look the worse for wear. His eyes were looking nearly as puffy as mine get, and he needed a shave. "I'm sorry to see everyone up so early. Did anyone manage to get any sleep last night? Bree, that coffee smells wonderful. Would it be possible to snag a cup...?"

"Not much in the way of sleep, no." Luke was watching him load his cup with cream and sugar. "Personally, I find it tricky trying to sleep when you don't know if you're under some richer than fuck potentate's house arrest, or not."

"Not to mention having the potentate's personal goon squad marching back and forth under your windows all night." Bree was cradling her cup, letting it get cool enough to drink from. "Patrick, are they still out there?"

"Ali's house guard?" He'd gone very still, suddenly. "They were in the seraglio courtyard last night? They weren't there when I pulled up. Not a sign. How long were they here?"

"Bree just told you, mate." I was watching him. There was something happening there—finding out about the guards being here had flipped a switch somewhere, or maybe clued him in to

198

something. I've been around the bloke too often to miss that when it happens; everything tightens up, tautens, focuses. It's as scary as hell, even when you know why it's happening. When you haven't got the first clue, it's even scarier. "All night long. They were here when the cars brought us back from the Plaza, and they were still out there when Mac rang Ian. If they've gone, they've only just gone."

"Interesting."

He sounded nice and detached, noncommittal, whatever. And it was complete bullshit. Something in his head had opened, and let some light in from somewhere. I could tell.

"Interesting is one word for it." Bree had her eyes aimed at him as well. "But what I want to know is, why were they out there at all? I mean, why here? They had to know we weren't going anywhere, Patrick. We can't. So why were they guarding us? What did they think we were going to do, flap our wings and fly away home like a bunch of ladybugs, or something?"

She glanced at me, less than a blink's worth, and I got a shock, because it was there for me to see, even if no one else in that room could. She'd sussed it, figured it out. She already knew what the answer had to be.

Right then, the light went off in my own head, and I wasn't alone. You could practically here the bulbs popping, all round the room.

"Shit! They weren't guarding us, were they?" Tony was up on his feet. "They were doing something else altogether—or guarding something else altogether. What the fuck! This place is starting to piss me off. Anyone have any ideas?"

"You asking, dude?" Dom seemed to have gone as restless as Tony had, because she was on her feet, shaking her legs, limbering up, loosening muscles. "Because I think maybe it's got something to do with those damned pools. Remember when they got us all split out and shit, drag the band out for practice and every-

199

one else gets lunch with the Emir and no arguments, and we came back and found those tanker trucks emptying out two of those things? No? Patrick, you think it's something else?"

"Oh, you could be right, Dom." His eyes were dirty slits. "It does leave me wondering about something related to that, though. Why come here at all?"

Bree was nodding, and Mac seemed to have caught up, as well. The rest of us just waited.

"JP and Bree heard and saw people having some kind of rendezvous under their windows." Christ, yeah, our pet rozzer had gone into full homicide detective mode: his teeth were showing and you could see the gears meshing. "Nordine died under their windows. Something happened with the pool adjacent to the one Nordine died in, and no, don't ask me what because I don't know either. And last night, Ali seems to have sent the house guard over here before you ever got back from the show. But why here at all? What was Nordine doing here, or anyone else? There are mineral pools all over the compound. Why come to the only occupied area, and risk being seen?"

Back during the Book of Days tour, the morning our long-time security chief had been killed and I'd suggested Patrick Ormand as a replacement, I'd been functioning on not enough sleep and a bitch of an exacerbation. I remember Mac making a comment at the time, something about how, if this was how my head worked under circs like those, Bree needed to wake me every couple of hours during a crisis. He'd been joking, but I must have been in pretty much that same place New Year's morning in Manaar, because I heard my own voice coming nice and clear, and my own voice was the last thing I was expecting to hear.

"You sure about that, mate?"

Patrick turned to face me. "Sure about what, JP?"

"How do you know they came from somewhere else? Whoever they were, I mean? Because maybe they were right here all the time. Maybe they did their thing right here because it was the closest place to do it, whatever it was."

"Oh for fuck's sake!" Mac slapped his coffee cup down on the nearest flat surface. "Johnny, that's brilliant, and do you know, if you mean what I think you mean and you happen to be right, then I'm really going to want a few words with the bloody Emir, bereaved papa or not."

"I'm not following this." Cyn Corrigan, sitting on the edge of our bed in a pair of pale yellow pyjamas, sounded fuddled. She hadn't quite got all the lash goop off after the show last night, and she had a few streaks up high on her cheeks. "What do you mean, here all the time? How could anyone have been, and us not know?"

"Fuck! Are we idiots?" Stu looked ready to put the boot in with something, he was that narked. "We've never actually explored the rest of this place, is how. I can't speak for the rest of you, but I've never gone past Cal's suite at the end of the corridor. Anyone else? Yeah, that's what I thought. I never even tried that fancy painted door at the end of the hall, to see if there was anything on the other side of it. They told us we had the place to ourselves, I just believed it. JP's just sussed that we were probably wrong."

"Nits." Cal had his fists clenched. "Bloody hell, we're a bunch of nits!"

Stu snorted, a pissy angry little noise. He's got that Irish temper, has Stu. "That's one word for it. Cor stone the bloody crows, I feel a proper divvy right now. I don't know about you lot, but I'm off to have a butcher's and see for myself."

"Yes, let's." Mac held a hand up, and turned to face Patrick. "But before we go anywhere, I want to know just what happened last night. Why did Ali say his daughter had been executed? Because that particular word brings up a very particular picture in my head."

"He used that word because it was right word." Flat as the

middle of Manhattan Island, that voice. "It was an execution. The Princess Paksima was shot."

We were all quiet, all still, just waiting. It was so obvious Patrick was picking his words, being careful, that I had another one of those flashes, about what he was going to say.

"She took a single bullet to the brain, from close enough range to leave powder burns. I gather they think the muzzle of the gun was held against her temple." He cleared his throat, an odd little noise, very unlike Patrick. "There was an additional act of mutilation performed, that points to this being an execution, Manaari style. I assume all of you remember what happened after the Super Bowl?"

Oh, fuck me, yeah, we remembered, all right. Hard to forget a Styrofoam cooler covered with dip corps *do not open* stickers and with four severed hands in it, being left at our hotel. Ali had refused to turn his daughters' murdering bodyguards over to the New York police. He'd stood in our San Francisco living room and told us there would be punishment, or justice, or some damned thing. That was his definition, apparently. He'd sent his nasty little prezzie direct to Luke.

"Are you saying someone shot that girl in the head?" Bree was dirty-white, and I got one arm round her in a hurry. "And then cut her hands off? Oh god, *god*...Patrick?"

His voice was gentle. "I'm sorry, Bree. I only had about five minutes with Bengt last night—he's in charge of the investigation and he was pretty shaken up—but that's what he tells me happened. Of course he's worried, on several levels."

"No shit, yo. He's the guy in charge of keeping the family safe. One of them gets their head blown off and their fingers in a jar, that goes on the permanent record. And we already knew Mac's old school friend goes for the biblical shit, big time. Sucks for Bengt, but he cashes the cheque. Comes with the gig." Domitra was in the doorway, looking ready for trouble. When the girl thinks things ought to be happening, she doesn't stand about and natter. "Cool, so now we know what happened to Twin Number Two. I'm down with checking out whether JP's right. Anyone want to come with? Mac, stay behind me, and don't even think about arguing with me—yo, Carla, Ian, glad you could join the party. We're heading down the hall. JP thinks maybe we got some squatters at the back of the shack. You want to hang out and drink Bree's coffee, or you want to come along?"

"You trying to be funny?" Ian was even gruffer than usual, probably as much out of sheer exhaustion as anything else. I noticed that Carla had taken time to get dressed, right down to sensible shoes. So, yeah, she'd already sussed that some kind of action was going to need to be taken, and she'd dressed for it. No one's fool, is our Carla. "You're damned right we're coming along. Patrick give you the details? Right. Let's go."

So, right, there we were, band and management, together again. One big happy family, or at least back on the same page; whatever Mac had planned by way of schooling our braintrust on why leaving the band out of band business was a crap idea would probably end up getting shelved for a while, or at least watered down a bit.

Domitra and Patrick were heading up the expedition, side by side with Mac half an arm's length off Domitra's right shoulder. We went down the corridor in a single line, Bree behind me; behind her, Luke was filling Carla and Ian in on why we were traipsing down the hall like we were about to break out into a damned conga, or maybe more like something out of a Pink Panther flick.

We weren't bothering about how much noise we were making by then. No point to it; if someone had really been able to share the palace with us for over a week without us catching on, they probably knew every exit, hiding place and bolthole between the Queen's Palace and downtown Cairo. Still, it was a surprise to hear Cal, ahead of me, humming under his breath. It took me minute to track the tune down in my head, but I found myself grinning when I realised what it was: Robert Palmer's song, "Sneakin' Sally Through the Alley."

To be fair to all of us—as a group, I mean—we hadn't actually had any reason to go wandering down past the Wilsons' suite, or to push aside the gaudy hanging tapestry curtains and rattle the fancy brass hardware on the door at the end of the corridor. We hadn't had much time, either; we'd got there and gone straight into rehearsal and tech specs and build mode. Even Bree, who's got as much curiosity about her surroundings as anyone, hadn't had much time to go exploring; she'd spent a lot of what time she did have available before Nordine was killed learning how to drive the Veyron without killing herself in it.

And even though it felt as if we'd been there about a hundred years, it was actually less than two weeks. I'm not making excuses, but all that was just basic fact. Besides, Ali had gone out of his way to assure us we had the digs all to ourselves, for our exclusive use. That had actually been part of the contract rider for the gig. If we hadn't had the curiosity or the time to go poking about, we hadn't been given any reason to assume our host was wrong or lying to us, either.

What we hadn't known, any of us, was that the corridor we were all sleeping in was one of four arms. Turned out the Queen's Palace had been designed as a cross inside a square building, with only two of the arms having access to the outside world. That was probably part of the original design, back when you wanted to be able to keep an eye on where your naked dancing girls and your pet eunuchs were. The other two had windows, which was another reason we'd assumed Nordine and the rest had come from outside. After all, if whoever it was had walked right past our doors, chances are we'd have heard them.

So we basically had a quadrangle inside a big square block of a building. Dom, who got to the door at the end of the corridor perfectly ready to kick it down if that's what was needed, pulled the curtains aside, got a hand on the ornate brass bird's head that passed for a doorknob, twisted, and pushed with her full shoulder. She nearly fell on her nose as the door swung open in front of her. It hadn't even been locked.

"Oi! Steady on, brat." Mac knew better than to offer an arm or any physical support, but he was close behind, peering over her shoulder. "I don't remember Ali showing us this when he gave us that first Grand Tour. I don't even remember him mentioning it—of course, there was quite a lot of construction going on. What have we got here? The rest of the palace?"

"Looks like it." Patrick went through right behind Dom, straightening up and looking around. "I think this part of the place is clear. Ian? Carla...?"

So, yeah, a cross within a square. And there were doors the length of the two sides of the corridor than continued straight on past ours. The other two arms were solid wall, no way in or out to anywhere except to the other corridors.

"I wonder why they built it this way?" Katia was staring around, obviously fascinated. "Why waste the space on a hallway that doesn't go anywhere? That's just weird."

"Maybe so that whoever was on one side of the wall couldn't hear the screams. I wouldn't put it past them." Tony got hold of his wife's hand. He didn't look happy. "Let's check out the other end, the one with the door to the great outdoors. That one looks like it goes somewhere. I just wish it went to a fucking plane out of here."

Six doors, three to a side, leading to three suites a side, just like the six at our end. A mirror image, that hallway was, at least on the corridor side. I also got a question answered, something I'd been wondering about: those windows in the corridors, the ones high up that provided even the little bit of light? Those were slightly higher than the level of the roof over our suites. Ingenious bit of engineering that was, especially since it had to have been done centuries ago...

205

"Well, now. This is interesting."

Patrick's voice—pure cop—pulled me out of wondering about the architecture of the windows. Good job, too, because I'd nearly walked straight into Tony.

We all moved up, crowding together, peering through the door. It was the last room on the same side as mine and Bree's, the one closest to the gate that led out to the courtyard and the mineral pools. The door, unlocked like the rest of them, was standing wide open. I don't know whether it had been like that when we'd got there, or whether Patrick or Dom had opened it. Like I said, I hadn't been paying attention.

Ali had told us that, by the time we'd got back for the show, the suites would be completed and with every possible luxury, nothing left out. This wasn't one of our suites, but it was still luxurious, in a rather different way. It had the same basics as ours: a big bed, raw silk coverlet, wide-screen TV, minibar, the lot. The silk coverlet was rumpled, as if someone had got up and got out of the room in a hurry. But there were some personal touches as well, signs of someone who definitely wasn't one of ours: fancy antique scent bottles on every table. A pair of pricey-looking high heels for what looked to be a pair of small feet; one shoe was upright and the other one on its side, half-hidden under the bed.

There was also a rocking throne, just like the one in our suite. Over the back of it was a familiar-looking spangled silk headscarf.

"Bull's-eye." Domitra was inside, picking up the scarf, running it between her fingers. I got a whiff of something, not much, just a bit: perfume. "Or eureka, or whatever you want to call it. JP, dude, I'd say you called it. Looks like the twins were hanging out right here the whole time."

I've spent more than my share of odd mornings. It comes with the territory; when your working life starts after dark and involves the stuff a touring musician's job involves, you're going to

206

run into weirdness eventually. That's just the way it works. You add the last decade or so, all the effects of the MS on how I react to the rest of what the world throws at me, and weirdness takes on a few new definitions.

Still, end to end, that morning was in a class by itself. It went beyond basic weirdness, even by rock and roll standards.

No one seemed to know what to do about what we'd found out. Yeah, it was gratifying to find out I'd got it right, but there didn't seem to be any place to take the information, or any way to actually put it to use. Trotting round to Ali and waving his daughter's scarf at him wasn't on, not under the circs.

"Dom, do me a favour, please?" Carla was holding her fancy phone up close to her face. Whatever I'd thought about it, she obviously had a few ideas of her own. "Can you put that scarf back where it was, pretty much just the way you found it? Great, thanks. And can everyone move back and let me get some clear shots of this, and of those shoes? Because after that whole deal with whoever it was cleaning out that hut, I think we should avoid another 'proof, what proof' incident, if we can do it."

Right. Typical: while the rest of us were standing about like garden gnomes, Carla was getting to the core of whatever needed doing, and getting it done. It's why we pay her so much. We got out of her way, and let her get on with it.

She took at least a dozen photos, not just of the scarf, but of the scent bottles and the high heels, as well. There was something unsettling about those shoes, something pathetic and evocative.

Still, about half the pictures she took were of the headscarf, close up from different angles. I wondered about that, but only for a moment. It made sense, really: the shoes might have been anyone's, but that headscarf couldn't be explained away. We'd all seen it on at least one of the twins.

That done, she got the lot downloaded, sorted, and sent to

every one of our emails, as well as to David Walters' email back in London, all in less than five minutes. It hadn't quite gone seven in the morning yet, and we had hard evidence of the al-Wahid girls squatting in our personal digs scattered all the way through the Blacklight global network. There was no way Bengt or Ali or anyone else was going to be able to do the whole out-raged innocence thing and claim we were all full of shit. Raised eyebrows and acting as if we were mental wasn't going to cut it.

"There." She slid the phone back into her pocket. "I don't know if anyone's planning on confronting Ali's people with this or not. We might want to keep this up our sleeves until we need the firepower, assuming we do need it. In fact, that's my official suggestion. But this way, we're covered. If anyone at the Manaari end calls us liars, or drops any delicate little hints that we're all having acid flashbacks and hallucinating, send them over to me."

There was a definite snap in her tone, and I saw Mac shoot her an appreciative look. I had the feeling that quite a lot of his shirtiness at management's recent high-handedness had just been dissipated. I also got the feeling that if anyone at Ali's end gave Carla any aggro over it, they'd be shown a few different ways to regret it, and maybe regretting it in a few positions they hadn't known existed before. At the very least, she'd probably smile sweetly, show them the photos, and mention *Rolling Stone* and what a lovely cover story it would make. The girl earns her pay, every cent of it and more. I was beginning to get just how much she'd resented being jerked around by the Manaari contingent.

With that covered, we backed out of the suite and headed back to our own digs. No one seemed comfortable hanging about in there. Besides, there was no reason to hang about. We'd found out what we wanted to know.

There was something elbow-jogging away at the back of my head, though, and it was getting on my nerves, because I couldn't quite nail it down. It wasn't until we'd got back to our suite, and

Bree was putting up a third pot of coffee, that it suddenly came clear in my head.

"Oi. Dom, what you said back there, about the twins being here all the time. We don't know that, do we?"

"JP's right." Patrick had already worked out the problem in his own head. "Twin, singular, not plural. There was only one pair of shoes, and only one headscarf. At first look, the evidence supports the presence of only one of the girls."

"I wonder which one?" Bree's shoulders were up high and hard again. She saw me watching her, and visibly tried to relax. "Sorry. It just—someone was down there the whole time without us knowing they were there, and it just makes my skin crawl. I know I'm being silly, it's not as if anyone can do anything about it, but it's creeping me the hell out. I can't help it."

"I don't call that silly, Bree. I call it straight sense." Ian had made short work of his first cup of coffee and was already up and pouring a second one. "You want the truth? I'm feeling a right berk. Knowing what we already knew about the al-Wahid twins coming into this mess, I'll be buggered if I can sort out why we didn't suss it out straight away. I never even suspected it, but just look back at what we know about those two. Does anyone here really believe they'd be good little girls and keep off our patch, just because their dad told them to? Christ, JP found them out there skinny-dipping, and none of us thought past that. What, we all get the desert sand between our ears, to stop us thinking straight?"

No one said a word. Ian drained his cup, and sighed.

"Sorry. Truth is, everything about this show has been bad luck or bad news or both, right from the first. And there's no end in sight, not yet." He looked well beyond glum. "Everyone knows we're not likely to be getting out of here today, right? We clear about that? Even if Ali gave us the thumbs up, we've got problems at the other end."

209

That got a few heads up and some noise, especially from the blokes. Ian held up a hand.

"No, don't flip your shit, any of you. It's nothing to do with what's happening here—just your basic Act of God, that's all. I got an email late last night from David Walter, back in London. We've got a travel logistics nightmare. Turns out half Europe's under massive whiteout conditions, and it's the half we want. That blizzard that was supposed to blow in on Boxing Day blew in good and hard, and it's still there and still dumping snow. Paris and Rome are already under weather emergencies, and there's no trains moving in Southern England, either. Forget Scandinavia— even Scotland's locked down tight until the weather eases up. The North Atlantic's a solid wall of falling snow and high winds to go with it. So unless you fancy a week in Tripoli or Cairo, we're short on choices. The backup on flights is going to mean delays for days, no matter where we wanted to go. And that's assuming we could get a jet booked at this end, and clearance to fly out. I'm not holding my breath on any of it."

No one answered, or looked to have anything to say. Ian wasn't piling on the agony, but he wasn't prettying it up, either.

I took a quick look round at the band family. Mac looked disgusted, Dom wasn't bothering about trying to hide her irritation, and both the Wilsons were looking resigned. Cyn Corrigan made an unhappy noise and dropped her face down on her folded arms, and Stu got busy rubbing her back. I saw Karen close her eyes for a moment, but whether it was hiding her reaction from Luke or just being up so early catching up with her, I couldn't have said.

I spent a moment watching my own wife, or rather, her hands. They'd woven together, hard and tight. I had the feeling that, if I'd turfed everyone out and given her a chance, she'd have hurled the coffee cup, and possibly a few other things, smash into the nearest wall. Not happy, not happy at all.

"All right." Patrick had stayed quiet while Ian did his thing, but it was obvious Ian had said his piece. "So now we all know the situation. Until such time as we get some kind of word from the palace or from Bengt, the most we can do about the situation here is to see what can figure out for ourselves, and decide on the appropriate course of action. Personally, I can't see any point in talking to the British consulate, since about the only place we could actually get to is somewhere else in Arabia, and with the backup Ian mentioned, it would be days anyway."

He stopped, just waiting. Nice clear way of putting things Patrick's got. He always seems to get even clearer when whatever he's talking about is stuff I don't want to hear. He gave it a minute, but it was obvious no one was up for talking.

"My question for all of you is, do you want me to see what information I can pick up about what's happening with the investigation? It probably won't be too much, since I'll have to get what I can without actually asking Bengt about it, and he's going to be pretty busy anyway."

"Fuck yes." Mac sounded nice and definite. If there was any chance Ian or Carla had a different take, they were going to have to get through Mac first. He wasn't alone, either; Luke was nodding. "Do you seriously think you have to ask that, Patrick? Of course we do. It's bad enough being little birds in Almanzor's gilded cage. I'm damned if I want to do it with a blanket over my head."

"What about the American embassy, or whatever we've got here?" Tony had obviously been thinking. Right then, he was beginning to sound like old-school Tony: *I'm Italian-American, yo, don't fuck with me, my uncle was a Navy SEAL and I got friends in Jersey.* "I'm a US citizen. What about talking to them? Hell, we've got to have some clout, having an embassy here. I say we make use of—Carla, why are you shaking your head? Shit, you're an American citizen too."

"Not for this trip, I'm not. None of us are." Nice and crisp and to the point. "We're here specifically on a group work visa issued by the Emirate of Manaar. The work visa was stamped and okayed through the British office in London, and it includes the entire Blacklight party, British citizens or not."

"But we're Americans, goddamnit!"

"Not for purposes of this gig." She sounded stone flat patient. "Under the conditions of the visa, we're legally allowed to be in Manaar for six months, and we're here as visitors from the United Kingdom. It would be nice to call in the Marines, but Uncle Sam isn't going to be useful as a problem-solving device this time. Sorry, Tony."

"Shit." He doesn't do helpless very well. "Isn't that just fucking swell?"

Carla clearly had more on her mind. "I want to be honest here: I don't think that leaning on the Emir to let us leave is the smartest move at this point anyway. In fact, throwing a fit and demanding he get us a plane to anywhere that isn't here would be PR suicide. We've already cashed in to the tune of about forty million dollars at the current exchange rate, for one night's work, and that's what the rest of the world is going to see. Besides, where's our justification? Just wanting to go home isn't an excuse. It's not as if we're being treated as anything other than honoured guests."

"Except for that whole 'soldiers aiming guns at us' thing, true enough. And Ali did made it very clear he hadn't ordered that." Mac had gone from looking cross to looking thoughtful. "Carla, you've got an excellent point, there. We don't want to look a collection of cold-hearted shits, and if we're one breath the wrong side of clumsy, that's going to be how it comes off. Since we can't get home until the weather clears anyway, what's the next step? Public sympathy and offering whatever cooperation they want?"

She nodded. Ian was looking around the suite, taking the roll call of reactions; it was obvious he was getting ready to calm down anyone who disagreed. But there was nothing for him to do. Carla and Mac had both called it: Smile, close our eyes, and think of England.

"All right." Patrick rubbed the stubble on his jaw. "My God, I need a shave. The last time I got this bristly, I was staking out a drug lord in South Beach with DEA. Anyway, so you'll officially let the palace know the band is right here and willing to help in any way possible, and Carla will decide how much of that official stance is unofficially made clear to the world press. In the meantime, I can be a little less official with Bengt. It seems to me I've got two things I can use as starting points."

"That's two more than me." Crikey, Ian really was sounding glum. "Want to share, mate? Believe me, I'll take whatever you've got."

"The first thing might not be possible, at least not without being pretty blunt with Bengt. It might need a lot of pressure, and right now, I'm really not certain what I've got to use as leverage, unless you want to count those pictures Carla took. But I'd like to pursue the question of just why the guards stormed the band's dressing room with guns last night, and who ordered that action. Because as Mac's already pointed out, it clearly wasn't al-Wahid."

"Good call, if you can do it." Ian reached for a clean cup. "Bree, sorry, I think I've got the last of this. Patrick, you said there were two things. What's the second one? And is it likely to be any easier than the first one?"

"No." His voice changed suddenly. "No, it isn't."

I jerked my head round, and I wasn't alone. He didn't sound like Blacklight's head of security just then. That note, that tight quiet tone—that was the hunter, suddenly come front and centre.

"Dish, mate." I'd locked up with him, eye to eye, stare to stare. Just like old times, yeah? "Turn up the volume. What are you on about?"

"We had a dead man: Nordine Benhamou. We saw his body. He was killed on the path outside and bled out in the pool itself. We saw his body removed."

I got hold of one of Bree's hands. "Yeah, we did. What's your point, Patrick?"

"You and Bree both looked through the window of that hut. You both saw what you saw." He was watching me, very steady. "Someone died in that hut. It wasn't Nordine. And it certainly wasn't the Princess Paksima—for one thing, a single shot to the head would not have produced the amount of blood you both observed. The removal of her hands was post-mortem—Bengt told me that much—and could not possibly have produced what you described. For another, had she died that far in advance of the show, we would have known about it."

"Right." Bree's hand was paper-dry and very cold. Once we turfed everyone out, I was going to come the heavy husband and order her back to bed for a nap. Hell, I was going to try for one myself. "So the idea is to find out what happened out there, in that hut? That it?"

"Finding out what happened." He got up, and headed for the door. "And who it happened to."

Chapter Thirteen

The more I thought about Patrick's stagy little exit, the more I realised something: there was a damned good chance we'd get out of Manaar and back home without ever finding out what in hell had actually gone down. It wasn't a comfortable idea, for some reason, and I'd got the sense that the rest of the band was feeling pretty much the same way.

I don't know if Patrick had been trying to plant that in our heads, or not: trying to prepare us in advance for not ever getting the story, yeah? All I know is, we'd listened to the sound of the Range Rover as he pulled away and out of the seraglio, and no one had said a word since he'd left.

Dom finally broke the silence. "So, anyone else think maybe Big Boss over at the palace might have plans? Like maybe keeping the details about whatever the fuck actually happened all in the family? Anyone taking bets?"

"Not tell us, you mean?" The idea plainly hadn't crossed Katia's head, and it obviously didn't appeal to her much, either. "After we got put through all this bullshit? Oh man, Dom, if you're right, I swear my head's going to explode. All this crap, and never knowing what happened? That would suck like a vacuum cleaner on crystal meth."

"We may not get a vote." Ian was turning his empty cup round in his hands, over and over. He sounded grim. "I'm not sure what Patrick can actually do. Maybe nothing at all. But I want to get a consensus on something right now, just in case. Suppose we do get word from the palace? Suppose Ali or one of his talking heads shows up and says greetings mates, your jet's on the tarmac, diplomatic priority landing clearance arranged in Istanbul or Athens or wherever, thanks so much for a lovely visit, visa stamped, now get the hell out of it, effendi, and don't let the door hit your arses on the way out. What do you want me to tell them? That we're not going anywhere until we know what went down? Because if that's the way everyone in the band family wants it, I have to say I think you're all stone fucking bonkers, and I'm prepared to argue until I run out of air."

"Of course you are." Mac was watching Ian with his head tilted. I couldn't read what was going on in there; Mac had his face all the way under control. "Because the band's safety is the issue. That's the reasoning, Ian, is it?"

"You're damned right it is."

Shit.

Yeah, so, Mac had it under control. Ian didn't. The words had been snapped, and it looked as if our manager was just about to snap as well.

The pair of them were locked up tight, and something at the bottom of my stomach had locked up even tighter. Carla's face was a mask, totally unreadable; she was staying quiet, but it seemed to me she inched up closer to Ian's shoulder. That was a shock, for some reason, her being that obvious about where her loyalty was.

"If that's sarcasm, Mac, I'd appreciate you making it nice and clear." The vibe in the room had suddenly gone tense to the point of electricity; the suite was damned near crackling with it. "That way, we'll know where we all stand. I can tell you to fuck off, I quit, and we can be done with it. You think I've got some agenda beyond keeping you people safe, you might want to show a little bottle and say so. I've had more than enough of having my loyalty questioned. You've been doing it since that fucking over by Ali and Bengt, and I'll be buggered if I'm putting up with any more of it."

That might have been the longest three or four seconds I've ever been through during my tenure with Blacklight, and the most uncomfortable. No one was talking. I wasn't sure anyone was actually breathing. It seemed to go on for hours. It wasn't possible, the idea that we were going to have to get between Mac and Ian, choose one or the other, take sides…

Mac grinned. It was a real grin, too.

"Not a chance, mate. You try quitting Blacklight, I solemnly swear I'll personally chase you down and drag you back where you belong, which is right here with the band."

Ian's jaw dropped. Sounds like a cliché, but it's what happened—his whole face went loose and a bit soft, somehow.

"I'm sorry, Ian." Mac wasn't grinning anymore. "I know it's been iffy. Be fair, you did shake us up the wrong way. We had good reason to worry about it. From where I'm sitting, though, we've done with that rubbish, and it's time to move on. The thing is, you had to be the one to put it out there. There really was no opening for me or anyone else to say *oi, stop flipping your shit, you made a bad decision but you did it with Ali's gun to your head, we get that, not to worry, we're over it.* Now that it's out there, I can point out that the

217

situation has been about as unnatural as a nun doing a fan dance in a urinal. We've all been off our heads."

Ian seemed to be having trouble keeping his face under control. Odd, that was, because he doesn't show a lot of feeling, most days. Gruff is his usual thing.

"I'm really sorry, mate." Mac held out his right hand. "That's a genuine apology, by the way—I'm not taking the piss, or being sarcastic. You had to step into the biggest shoes that ever walked, after Chris Fallow died, and you've done it better than anyone alive could have done it. So I'll say it again, and I'm fairly sure I'm speaking for the whole band: we know this mess wasn't any kind of cock-up on your part, and we trust you completely. We good?"

"Yeah, we're good." Ian reached out a hand, and shook Mac's. His voice was gruff, back to normal. "Thanks."

I heard a soft exhale, then another one. For a moment I wasn't sure if it was Carla, or Bree, letting their breath out. Took me a moment to realise at least one of those was me.

"Good, because all this emo stuff is exhausting." Mac yawned suddenly. "Christ, I'm knackered. And by the way, I nearly forgot about that question you asked. I don't know about the rest of you, but if Ali hands us a plane and a landing zone anywhere on the fucking planet that isn't Manaar, I'm out of here so fast, I'll probably leave skid marks. If Patrick wants to ass about playing Sherlock Holmes, good on him. I'm gone."

"Mac, you said it, man." Tony was stretching, letting his joints crack. The air in the suite had suddenly got a lot cleaner and easier to breathe, I'm not sure how. "I'm with you, every fucking word. Guys, look. Is there anything we can do right now? I mean, is there anything we need to take care of? I'm beginning to feel like I'm in the middle of a football huddle, or something. If no one's calling any plays, why are we all hanging out, not doing shit?"

"Tony, dude, lose the passive-aggressive. It doesn't look good on you." Dom shook her head at him. "Spit it out. What you mean is, any reason for us not to go back to sleep for a couple of hours? Me, personally, I can't think of anything. But I do what Mac says."

"Dom, angel, you make me feel so macho sometimes. Very flattering." He blew her a kiss and got up. "Seriously, I've had too much of everything this morning, except sleep. Personally, I vote for going back to bed and clearing the cobwebs out of the circuitry. A hot soak before or after is definitely possible. Besides, I'm betting Johnny and Bree might like a bit of peace and quiet, and they won't get it with us infesting their digs. What time is it, anyway? Oh bloody hell, eight in the morning. Consensus? On the sleep question, that is? Because I'm off. Oh, by the way, a happy new year."

I didn't actually get back to bed straight away, but that was my own doing. Mac's mention of a soak in the tub had got itself lodged in my head and, having decided it sounded brilliant, I ran myself as hot a bath as I could do with.

The MS had settled into a rhythm, a steady miserable physical backbeat with jabs and jerking muscles everywhere. There was no way I was running the jets, not with my skin that hypersensitised, but I did use a double handful of Bree's mineral bath salts. She offered to run the bath for me, and hang out for a conversation, but I shooed her off to bed, after she'd got her morning meds. She might not have been copping to it, but she was wiped out, run off her feet.

She wasn't best pleased with me about that, but she went, after I promised I wouldn't go off and do anything mad without waking her up and giving her a shot at talking me out of it first. That turned out to be a good call all the way round; by the time I'd turned off the taps and eased myself down into the water, I could hear her snoring gently in the other room.

So, yeah, that was one of us conked out, at least. If I was hoping for my own brain to slow down, though, I was out of luck.

The body was happy to oblige, at least as much as the stabby little miseries in my legs and feet allowed for, but the engine running the show wasn't having any of it. A lot of it was probably the body getting the message to the brain that things were dodgy down below, time to sharpen up. It's just one more way this damned disease manages to never give me any peace. And of course the brain decided where it wanted to go, straight off: back to that hut, where someone—who?—had died.

I can't imagine why no one had done the math until Patrick brought it up, but from the reactions in our suite when he did, not one of us had put that together until he did. Whatever had gone down out there had left the place spattered with blood. Christ, the sheets and blankets had looked to be soaked through. I'd seen it, and so had Bree; lying there in the tub, up to my chin in hot water, I closed my eyes and felt my throat tighten up for a second, remembering the smell of stale blood carried out through the slit windows, and Bree on her knees, retching into the dust and sand.

That much blood hadn't just got there by itself. Someone or something had died in there. But Patrick had called it: everyone was present, accounted for, alive and breathing. Whoever had got taken out in that hut wasn't anything to do with Blacklight.

So there it was, a nice simple basic sum: someone had got taken out and we weren't short anyone. One plus nil, and there was no answer, just a huge question: who the hell had died in that hut?

I might have been fed up with Manaar and wanting to go home just as badly as the rest of the band, but I'll tell you what, if I could come up with a way to bring that amazing hot water supply back to London with me, I'd do it. Even our plumbing in San Francisco, the best money could buy, wasn't half as properly hot as what we'd got in the seraglio. What's more, the bathwater stayed hot longer than anywhere I've ever been before. Besides, the tubs were enormous; I was in up to my chin with room to stretch the legs, just letting the salts and the heat do their thing. They were working, too. Usually, when the body decides to back down, my brain's got enough sense to take the offer and follow. But that morning, the more the body relaxed, the faster and clearer my head seemed to be working.

Okay. So we weren't short anyone. That meant it had to have been someone on the Manaari end. And if that was the story, I couldn't see any way we were going to find out the truth unless someone decided to tell us. Patrick was wasting his time.

Bollocks to that, mate. Want to be honest? If that's the story, there's not much reason for any of us to give a toss one way or the other, is there?

Not a pretty thing to have to admit, but true enough: if someone we'd never heard of before had got themselves written off in that filthy little hut, it had fuck-all to do with Blacklight. Sad, okay, maybe even tragic; there was no way to know, because for all any of us knew, whoever it was had been a flaming berk and had got what was coming to them. That was the whole point: it was nothing to do with us.

It took all of about ten seconds to chuck that idea. It wouldn't fly, because if whatever had gone down had nothing to do with us, then nothing made any sense at all.

I settled down deeper into the water. The body was definitely lightening up, but the brain just kept ticking over.

What in hell had Bengt been playing at, lying to us about what we'd seen in that hut? Why would he, or his boss, think we'd have touched one hair under either of the twins' spangled head-scarves? Never mind what Ali had said to us—even if they knew we had nothing to do with Nordine dying, they had to have thought we knew something about the princess's death. The Emir's personal thugs showing up in our band room and holding us at gunpoint made that much pretty clear. They hadn't decided to wander over after the gig and scare the shit out of us because they hadn't dug the encore. They'd been sent.

And where did Nordine dying come into it? Because it must have done. There was no way I was swallowing three people who'd got themselves messily dead within ten days and half a mile of each other as some kind of coincidence. Bollocks to that.

The water was finally cooling off, just enough to make me have to decide whether I wanted a longer soak badly enough to risk waking Bree by turning the gushers back on. That's the one downside to pipes hooked straight into the natural hot springs: they're not quiet. There's a good loud gurgle goes on, there.

I had a quick look at the fancy clock over the sink. It was after nine. I'd been marinating in salty water over an hour, everything was going wrinkled and turning me into a prune, and the brain was finally beginning to slow down.

I got out of the tub and dried off, rotating first one ankle, then the other, testing for how bad the jabs were. The bath had been a good call: the pains were still there, mostly in the right thigh and foot, but they'd backed down enough to let me think about drying off and climbing into bed for some kip with my old lady.

Bree was fathoms deep when I climbed in next to her—she didn't even stir. Good. I had the feeling I wasn't going to get quite as far down into REM sleep as she'd managed, not unless I could turn the brain entirely off, but I was damned well going to try.

I did fall asleep easily enough, once my core temperature had come down far enough from the bath heat to stop me sweating. Unfortunately, I'd been right about the REM sleep being difficult; some part of my head just didn't want to let go of the waking world completely. It was probably some sort of survival instinct kicking in, yeah? That's the thing about deep sleep: Once you're out, you're vulnerable.

So I don't know how long it actually took me to get under, or how long I'd been dozing, before I started dreaming that I was back in one of my least favourite experiences in the world: stuck inside a metal tube, with rhythmic pulses being bounced off my skull.

Tap Tap Tap THUMP.

I turned over, trying to wake up, or at least shift it somehow. It had been a couple of years since I'd had an MRI, and thanks to the tickybox, I was likely never going to have to cope with that particular flavour of misery again. The last thing I needed was to be dreaming about it.

Taptaptaptap RATTLE.

Back when I used to get the damned things on an annual basis and sometimes more often than that, my tech had been a kid named Ramon. He'd used to snap at me because of course I'd dealt with it, gone Zen, by making music out of the pulses, and me humming would mess with the test.

This particular rhythm, the one I was dreaming, had just changed on me. It sounded urgent, somehow.

Wake up, Johnny. All the way up. That's not a pulse being banged off your skull. There's someone at the door.

It's a funny thing, really. Looking back at it now, I don't actually remember getting out of bed, or pulling a bathrobe on. I'm not sure I'd really woken up at that point. The only thing I remember clearly was being frantic to get the door before whoever it was woke Bree with their knocking.

I was biting back muttering, because I didn't want that waking Bree, either; she needed her sleep. And I hadn't really wiped the sleep out of my eyes or out of my brain, when I got across the suite and unlatched the door and realised that there wasn't much point in me worrying about waking Bree, not now, because staying asleep had just stopped being an option.

"Please." No headscarf and no high heels, not just then. She was standing there in our doorway, whispering. Her face was a clogged tearstained mess and her eyes were enormous. The Princess Azra was terrified, scared shitless. "Please help me. I am begging you. Please."

Awhile back, in San Francisco, I'd opened our front door to the wrong person.

I'd been expecting someone delivering our dinner from our favourite takeaway, and I'd opened the door without checking to see who it was first. Bad idea on my part: turned out the bloke on the front stair, with his finger on our doorbell, was a fugitive from a murder investigation in Los Angeles. He'd also been an employee of Carla's at the time, and I'd had to make a snap decision: to let him in, or not?

Yeah, well, *snap* was the word, all right. I'd pulled him indoors, shoved him into our front room, and told him to wait. I'd also told him that if he made any noise at all, I'd have the rozzers down to haul him away before he could blink. Not a brilliant choice, but it had been the only thing I could think of doing at the time: Bree and Katia were back in the kitchen, Katia was already a sobbing wreck dealing with Tony's meltdown, and I wasn't having either of them made accessories to a murder, if the kid had turned out to be guilty. Even if I'd been willing to saddle my wife with that, I'd got no right dumping it on Katia. She'd had more than enough on her plate just then. And turning him away wouldn't have been too bright either; one way or another, he'd had information we needed.

So I'd opened the door. That decision, letting him in and not telling my wife about it, had nearly cost me everything I care about; Bree'd found out about it, called me on being a hypocrite, and walked out. It had taken some very fancy dancing on my part to convince her to stay with me. I still break out in a chilly little sweat, bringing that memory up in my head.

Now here I was again, standing there gawking at probably the last person I would have expected to find in my doorway asking for help, facing another one of those *oh bloody fuck now what* moments. Part of my head was wondering why in hell they kept showing up at our place. You'd think we were trouble magnets, or something...

"Get in here. And close that door. *Hurry*."

I'd been so busy playing over the possibilities in my head, and being unnerved by all of them, that I hadn't heard Bree get out of bed. That whisper from behind me nearly stopped the tickybox in mid-beat. But there she was, awake and with her hair tousled. She was also completely stark.

She had one hand on the princess, pulling her inside, pushing the door closed with one naked hip. She'd got it bolted before either I or the princess could get a word out; I got the feeling that, if there's been anything like a deadbolt or a security chain, she'd have made good use of them.

"Thank you." The surviving twin found her voice first. She was keeping her voice low herself, just above a whisper, and she was watching Bree, not me. The thought went through my head: this was probably the first time in her life she'd ever given the wife her attention, rather than the husband. Still, it was just as well I'd got something on before I'd answered the door. "I am sorry for any trouble I am causing you. But I have no other place where I can go."

"Sit down, please." There was something about Azra that seemed to be keeping my wife formal. "I'm going to put some clothes on, and then I'm going to make some coffee, and maybe some breakfast, too. Have you slept? You look very tired."

"Where would I sleep?" Quiet as a mouse. "There is no place safe left here for me. There is no safe place anywhere."

"When was the last time you ate?" Something was happening to Bree's face; it was sharpening up, getting fierce in way I don't usually see, unless it's me she's getting fierce about. "Are you hungry?"

225

The thought popped into my skull and stayed there: she looked like a mother bear, about to put on a scary defence of an injured cub. Except that, when you came down to it, that was stone fucking nuts, completely insane. Azra al-Wahid wasn't her cub. There wasn't a single thing I could think of that the surviving twin had ever done to make my wife get that fierce look going on. The twins had been trouble from the first time we'd laid eyes on them, and the trouble had just got deeper and worse. So why –

"I ate nothing yesterday." Still quiet, nice and simple, none of the giggles or dimples or fluttering lashes. Maybe she needed her sister with her to pull that stuff off effectively, or maybe whatever had been going down had left her with no place to hide, the way she'd said. Whatever. I don't know. The point is, she was just answering the question, like a good little schoolgirl. "I could eat nothing," she told my wife. "I am not hungry."

"Well, tough shit, because you don't get a vote." Yeah, well, so much for that whole formality thing. "You're eating a decent meal. Sit down."

We were both staring at her now. She caught my eye, just long enough for her to see the *what the fuck is all this, then* in there, and turned back to the girl.

"Look." She was still keeping her voice pitched low; not whispering, but still low enough to where no one outside the door to the suite would be likely to hear it. She sounded reasonable, but pretty damned definite, as well. "I don't know why you came to us. For all I know, we were just the nearest door. But whatever made you pick this particular door, you're a guest here, and this is the way it works. This is my house and these are my rules, and you're going to eat some breakfast, so please don't argue with me. Nobody can think straight or get things done when they don't eat. Now sit down and be quiet, please. You can tell us all about it after you get some food down. John? How do you want your eggs, or would you rather I made you some oatmeal?"

"Eggs are fine." Right. If she was losing her mind, might as well go along for the ride. "Scrambled, boiled, doesn't matter. However you're doing yours, that works. Might want to put some clothes on first though, love, all right? You don't need to spatter yourself with hot oil, whipping up an omelette or whatever. Just give me a minute. I want to get dressed."

I headed for the bathroom at a fast trot. I wasn't admitting it to myself, not until I'd actually got my trousers on and zipped, but just the idea of having that girl within sight of my bed was enough to put me off my breakfast. That was one thing, and considering the past history of her and her sister hitting on me, it made sense. Next to the idea of having her anywhere near me, and me with nothing but a bathrobe on, though, that was nothing. That was actually making my skin pucker up with how cold it made me feel.

I'd got all the way to the point of fastening my shoes before I asked myself the obvious question: why should something as simple as putting a layer of street clothes between me and whoever might come looking for the girl make me feel safer? And of course the answer to that was right there, in the question: *Whoever might come looking.*

Shit, shit, *shit.*

It hit me, right between the eyes. Getting dressed in my street clothes wasn't going to appease anyone, or protect me from anything, and I'd been a bloody dimwit to think it might. Because there wasn't any room for doubt about it: if the cherished pampered surviving daughter of the ruling house was so frightened of whoever she'd pissed off that she'd knocked on our door of all doors looking for a hole to crawl into, then someone was coming after her. There was no safety for anyone concerned in this mess, not until it got resolved somehow.

Yeah, you clot, and you left her out there, alone with Bree. Brilliant.

I got my shoes done up, and that took longer than it ought to have done, because my hands were shaking. That was silly, really—I didn't honestly think the girl was getting up to anything, and anyway my wife could have folded her up with one hand and stuffed her through one of those tiny grilled overhead windows with no help from me—but logic wasn't coming into this one, not anywhere. Every reaction I was having just then came straight from the pit of my stomach, or the bottom of my spine, and every damned one of those reactions was telling me right, no slacking, and not good to be out of the action for a second longer than it took to get back to it.

There was also the fact that, the way things had gone in Manaar from the first, whoever showed up was likely to be armed to the teeth. I didn't ever need to hear that particular oily-sounding click again. Once had been more than enough.

Having escalated all that tension in my own head, it was a bit of a letdown to hurry back out into the suite and get hit with the smell of eggs cooking, and fresh coffee. There was another smell, more exotic, one I couldn't put a name to quite so easily: it took me a minute of just letting it percolate through the back of my taste buds to realise it was mint I was smelling. The Princess Azra was perched on one of the kitchen chairs with a plate in front of her. For all that *oh I couldn't possibly eat* nonsense, she was packing down my wife's cooking.

"John, good, ready for some eggs? I've been saving yours for last. And do you want coffee, or would you rather have some tea? There's some left in the pot."

Nice homey domestic scene, right out of some bad daytime telly drama thing, you know? Tasty smells, food cooking, coffee, pretty girl with big eyes scarfing down her breakfast and washing it down with mint tea. *Morning in Manaar*, or something. All we needed was a film crew to get it going. Everything you'd want for a show like that was there: the girl was up to something, her sister had been executed and her hands taken off, my wife's driver had been slashed to death, and who knows who or what had left blood all over a hut out there in the desert.

I couldn't wrap my head round it. The girl had been so flipped out that she'd come to us looking for a place to hide, and here was Bree, acting like a nutter, apparently buying into whatever Azra was up to and playing mother to this dangerous little bit of trouble who probably had men with guns looking for her –

"John?"

I jerked my head up and met Bree's eye. She can't do the "one eyebrow up" thing that I do—it's both or nothing. Both her brows were up, and there it was, that nice marital mind-reading thing, full throttle, and right that moment I decided I was going to let Bree play it any way she wanted.

My wife wasn't buying into anything. It was so clear, I could practically hear her say so.

The kid was in trouble and she'd fetched up here, right, but the big thing was, she was hungry. So she was getting fed and then, if I was reading Bree right, Azra al-Wahid was going to get asked a few big questions. And I was pretty sure that she wasn't leaving without providing a few answers. Fuck, I'd go stand with my back to the door, if that's what was wanted.

"John –?"

"Oh—sorry, love. Coffee, please." I settled in at the end of the table. "And two eggs. Scrambled will do me. Ta."

That had to be the weirdest meal I've ever eaten. Not your basic breakfast: me, the missus, and the potentate's surviving daughter who, for all I knew, might be hiding out from her dad's personal yobbo squadron, or maybe even from her dad. I ate my eggs and toast, I drank my coffee, I accepted a glass of cold orange juice from Bree, and all the time I had one eye on the Princess Azra and one ear tuned out of doors, listening for anyone or anything who might be showing up to break some hell loose. No one said a word the entire meal.

229

Bree finished first, ahead of me. She did just what I'd seen her do a dozen times before when we had guests for a casual meal: sit back and wait for them to finish before she got up to clear the table. Under normal circs, I'd have done just what I'd usually do as well, which is getting up and offering to help with the washing up.

That morning, I sat and waited. I wasn't about to do a damned thing that might interfere with whatever Bree had in mind for a nice after-breakfast chat, and besides, I wouldn't have known what to ask, or what to say. The truth was, leaving aside Bree's unwillingness to leave anyone in her vicinity feeling hungry, I didn't trust the princess as far as I could throw her dad's million-dollar supercar, with or without her dad in it. All things considered, it was best to leave the driving to Bree.

"Have you had enough breakfast?"

"Yes. Thank you." The girl had put her napkin in her empty plate. She looked less strained, a bit less like she was scared someone was going to use her for a coconut shy. Her looking more comfortable didn't make me trust her any better. "I am very grateful to you. The food was very good."

"Glad you enjoyed it." Bree was talking over her shoulder, putting plates in the sink, running just enough water over them to keep them easy to wash later. She hates dishes piled in her sink, but that morning, she had different priorities happening. "And now that we're all done with that, I sincerely hope you're up for a nice conversation, because we both want to know what in the name of hell is going on."

Azra was quiet. I could almost see the mask drop into place, see her get her head into game-playing mode.

"Azra." I heard my own voice, nice and sharp, a grownup talking to a kid. I didn't remember picking up my cell, but I must have done, because I was holding it. "You showed up here. You came to us, not the other way round. You've been fed. We don't owe you a thing, yeah? So here's the way it's going to be: you either come across with the answers to whatever we ask you, or I ring our chief of security and get him over here. And don't even think about strolling out the door. Get this into your head: You're not going anywhere until we get some gen."

She'd paled out, about as ashy as that deep olive skin was going to get. I couldn't tell if it was fear or temper, but either way, I'd got her attention. She whipped round to look at Bree. If she'd been hoping Bree'd be a softer touch, she dumped that little notion straight off. The girl would have had to be a complete idiot to misread my wife's face.

"You would not touch me." Maybe she was an idiot, after all. Either that, or she was trying a bluff. "You dare not."

"Touch you?" Bree smiled at her, and I jumped in my chair. I've never seen a look like that on her face before, and I don't much want to again. "Oh, honey. I'd rather touch a scorpion, but that wouldn't stop me. Hell, I'd just sit on you while John calls Patrick Ormand. You want to stop wasting time and knock off the bullshit now? You aren't going anywhere until you answer some questions. You might as well just lie back and enjoy it. You know, the way all those boys did, back when you and your sister were enjoying yourselves on the Book of Days tour, before your dad's bodyguards killed them?"

"I tell you nothing." Yeah, it had been rage, all right. Her English was slipping. "You cannot force me to tell."

"Like hell we can't." I was getting pretty pissed off myself. "Who died in that hut?"

Silence, nothing, not a word. She'd clamped her lips down to a single thin dark line.

"Fuck it." I flipped open my phone. "Bree, I'm ringing Patrick. It's his gig, not ours. I've had enough of this bullshit. Let Patrick and Bengt handle it—oi!"

She was on her feet. She'd moved too fast for either of us to anticipate, slapping the phone out of my hand. It hit the floor and skittered under the table. She was halfway across the suite before I'd got my head together enough to suss out that she was streaking for the door.

Bree was faster, though. She was up and across the room, with her back planted against the door, a half breath before the princess got there.

"You've got two choices." Bree was just about a foot taller than Azra was, and a couple of stone heavier as well. She wasn't moving an inch. "You came in here terrified, scared half to death. Either you tell us what we want to know, or you leave here with our head of security."

"Why are you doing this to me?" Her eyes were full of tears and her lips were shaking. She could barely get the words out. "If I tell you, I will be killed. Why would you do this?"

"Believe it or not, it's not all about you." Good. I'd had a bad moment there, wondering if Bree's nurturing thing was strong enough to take that kind of hit. "People are already dead— Nordine, your sister. Who died out there in that hut?"

"No one that matters." She must have seen Bree's face change, or maybe she caught how ugly she sounded, even thick-skinned and privileged as she was, because she hurried to explain. "Someone who was already dead, I mean."

She stopped, because Bree had held up one hand. A moment later, I saw the panic in the girl's face, and heard what they'd both heard.

Noise, coming from out in the courtyard: a truck's engine. It sounded like Patrick's Range Rover.

"Please." She was whispering, clutching Bree's sleeve. She was the colour of dirty chalk. "You must not give me up to them. If you do they will take me and kill me. You could not be so cruel. Please, please –"

A car door slammed. There were footsteps, not hurrying; I

could hear whoever it was walking across the courtyard, into the corridor. For some reason, it didn't sound like Patrick out there. Very light on his feet, Patrick is.

"Please." I don't know if she said it, or mouthed it, or what. I never got the chance to ask.

Behind Bree's back, I heard a click. Not the nasty oily noise I'd heard from the guards' guns; this was something else, the sound of a key in a lock.

A moment later, my wife staggered forward, straight into me. She hit me off-balance, sending us both backwards and into the side of the table. Bree stayed on her feet, but I went down. Whoever had put the key in the lock had shoved the door open as hard as it would go, with no warning and with all their own weight behind it.

I heard the princess scream, short and sharp and pitched to carry. The scream was cut off. And then there was that other kind of click.

"*There* you are." Bengt Ekberg had one hand wrapped good and hard in Azra's hair, at the back of her skull, jerking her head all the way back so that she was looking at the ceiling. The girl wasn't moving, and I didn't blame her. From where I was sitting on the floor, trying to get my wits and my balance back, I could see Bengt's other hand. The gun was pressed hard under her jawline, pointing straight up. "I had the feeling you'd come here. I've been looking all over for you."

Chapter Fourteen

I'm not sure how many people actually do get confronted with the chance to do something clever in a life or death situation. Not genuinely clever—that would be finding a quiet corner and climbing into it until the shit blew over and it was safe to come out. Self-preservation's what you do if you're actually being clever. Maybe the word I want is heroic.

Heroic, clever, whatever. All I know is, sitting on my arse on the floor and looking up at Bengt with his gun jammed into the soft underside of Azra al-Wahid's jaw, I realised that my phone was still on the floor, under the table, just out of reach.

It was a good bet Bengt couldn't see it from where he was standing. Besides, his attention was elsewhere. If I could just reach it, press the number 8, that would ring Patrick's phone. I wouldn't have to say a word—just having the line open, he'd be able to hear what was going on, and suss it out on his own.

I inched one hand under the table. *Right, Johnny, keep your shoulders still. You even let him think you're doing something to upset him, he might just go all Wild West and start shooting the place up.*

The phone seemed to have slid further under the table than I'd thought. I edged one finger forward, a fraction of an inch, slow and careful. I still wasn't finding anything but floor. Where the hell was the phone...?

"Sit down, please." He was talking to Bree. She'd been staring at him, not saying anything. Good call, I'd say; you don't want to piss off the bloke with the hardware. "That chair beside you will do fine. And if you'd help your husband off the floor, he ought to be sitting too. Where I can see both of you. Thank you."

Yeah, well, so much for Hollywood-style heroics. Probably just as well, really.

Bree helped me up and got me into the chair; I was off-balance and shaky. I glanced down at the floor, just for a moment, and she shook her head at me, nice and open. She was probably right—doing the action hero deal, managing to turn the phone on without Bengt's knowing about it and somehow letting Patrick know that something was going down in the Seraglio, wasn't going to happen today.

So we sat there, me and Bree side by side at the breakfast table, and Bengt stood there with the girl's hair in one hand and a gun in the other. We really must have looked a complete bunch of waxworks, because no one was saying anything and no one was moving, either. We just sat.

I had a really bad feeling, even beyond the obvious reason. Bengt hadn't been bothered about staying quiet. He'd driven the Range Rover straight into the courtyard—we'd all heard the motor. He could have left it outside on the road, but he hadn't done that. He hadn't worried about going on tiptoe, either. Our door had given a good loud bang when he'd thrown it open, not to mention that scream of Azra's, that he hadn't bothered telling her to muffle.

For someone who was about to get himself beheaded or worse for manhandling the boss's daughter, he was being pretty front and centre about it. So far as I could see, there was only one reason for that made any sense: he didn't give a shit who knew what he was doing. And that meant he was prepared to go down in a hail of bullets, to get done whatever it was he was planning to do.

"Bengt?" Bree sounded so normal, I had a mad moment of thinking she was going to offer him eggs and coffee. "Do you mind if I ask you something?"

He laughed, and my stomach tightened up even harder. It was a nice cheerful little laugh, but for just a moment there, he hadn't looked or sounded sane; he'd looked and sounded like what he was, a head case on the edge, holding a gun and holding us hostage. If we got out of this alive, I wasn't coming near Arabia again, never mind Manaar.

"Sure," he told her. "But I bet I can guess what you want to know. Want me to guess?"

"If you like." She had her head tilted, watching him steadily. Or was she? It seemed to me she'd glanced past his shoulder, the tiniest flick of her head for just for a second, as if something had caught her attention out there, just beyond the opened door. "I get the feeling you've known all about it all along. Am I wrong or right about that?"

"A little of both." She'd seen something, all right; even keeping my eyes on Bengt, I caught movement out there on the corridor wall, a shadow, something... "It took me too long to understand some of it. Didn't it, Azra?"

The girl was silent and pop-eyed. I watched the knuckles wound in her hair go white as he tightened his grip. "I said, didn't it? *Didn't it, you little bitch!*"

"You said you wanted to guess." How in hell Bree was keeping her voice so calm, I couldn't have guessed; the tickybox was doing a samba and I was having some trouble breathing around it. "But maybe I should just ask. Who died in that hut?"

"Well, now." Bengt moved, suddenly enough to make us both jump. He came all the way into the suite, dragging Azra with him, the gun never wavering. If he was hoping to provoke a noise, any noise, out of the girl, he wasn't making a good job of it. She was stone silent. "That's the big question, isn't it? Funny thing: it's what I came along to find out myself. Well—not exactly. It's the wrong question. I already know who died out there in that hut. What I want to know is who the father was. Once we have the answer to that, we'll be cooking with gas, won't we, Azra dear? There might even be a pop quiz later."

Oh, Christ.

I'd got it now, at least that part of it. Bree's shoulders were still down, still relaxed, but I could see the effort.

"Cleaning up all that blood." He sounded conversational, same Bengt we'd been dealing with the whole time. It suddenly hit me: he really was round the twist, completely off his head. "So messy and nasty. All those stinking sheets. Wasn't that nice of me? Of course, it wasn't as nasty as carrying that little blue corpse out of there and burying it in a pillowcase, out in the dunes. Really, Azra, you owe me. So just between you and me and these nice people here, before I blow your head off your shoulders, clue me in. Who fathered that baby? Was it me, or was it Nordine? I'm okay with not knowing which one of you girls actually killed him, but the rest—no. And don't bother telling me you don't know, that your miserable whore of a sister didn't tell you all about it. If she knew, you know. Whose baby, Azra?"

Silence. You'd have thought the girl was already dead, for all the response he was getting from her. And through the clang of the penny dropping and my own *fuck he's going to have to kill us,*

237

he can't not terror, I was aware of noise: doors opening, coming out, footsteps in the hall…

"Oi!" Someone was yelling, and that shocked the shit out of me, because it turns out it was me. I hadn't planned on opening my gob. Next to me, Bree sucked in her breath. "Bengt's in here and he's got a gun! Stay outside!"

He laughed. That laugh made it really clear: the fucker was off his nut. He didn't give a damn who walked in and who didn't.

"Azra." It was Bree, sounding gentle. She was getting her wits back. Mine still seemed to be walkabout, unfortunately. "Was that a miscarriage, or an abortion? Please say something. You have nothing to lose, not now. Bengt, if you want her to answer you, move that gun. She can't talk with it in her face."

He stared at her. "You know, you're right. I get the feeling you're right a lot. I would personally find that very annoying. But you make a good point."

He moved his arm down, until the gun was off the girl's throat and up against her ribs. Not much of an improvement from where I was sitting, but it opened the floodgates; she was talking, suddenly, babbling, and she wasn't stopping.

"The baby was dead. It was already dead. It died inside my sister but it would not let go." There were tears streaming down her face, splashing to the floor. "She could not live with a dead thing inside her, no one could bear such a horror. We could not tell my father. We asked Nordine to help us, my sister and me. And he took the dead thing out of her, but he was not a surgeon, him, and there was blood, too much. She was damaged inside. We did not know what to do."

Next to me, I heard a soft noise from Bree and with no conscious thought, I got an arm around her and pulled her close. Fuck Bengt Ekberg if he had a problem with it—he could sodding well shoot me, and have done with it. My wife had a painful messy miscarriage of her own when she was younger than the al-

Wahid girls, and she'd lost the ability to carry a child because of it. She was getting all my attention just then, and the crazy Swede with the gun could fuck off if he didn't like it.

Bengt ignored us. Holding on to Bree, I found myself remembering the day I'd dinged up my knees, taken that fall, and found the twins climbing out of the mineral pools. One of them, presumably Azra, had been completely stark. Her sister had been wrapped in a towel.

"That's fascinating, dear. But it doesn't answer my question." The gun was planted under her rib cage. "So Nordine helped you abort a dead baby. Whose dead baby? Mine or his? And you know, sweet-cheeks, I'm beginning to get annoyed having to repeat myself—oh, look, we seem to have company. Come on in. The more the merrier."

"Mac. Stay behind me." Domitra was in the doorway. I'd have expected her to have dropped into full battle stance, but she hadn't, and that surprised me. Presumably Mac was doing what he was told; I couldn't see him or hear him out there. Anyone with one good eye could have seen just how tricky this was for Dom, because she doesn't do helpless very well. She was jonesing to start something, launch a few good kicks, take Bengt down and rearrange his face for him—you couldn't miss it—but of course, he had the gun and the princess and all the cards, and none of us had a damned thing. Even if Dom hadn't given a rat's arse about whether the princess got shot or not, all Bengt had to do was move the gun a few inches and he could take out Bree, or me, or both of us. The only thing Dom could do just then was her job, and that meant protecting Mac.

Unfortunately, she seemed to realise that. "Out," she said, over one shoulder, and then backed out herself. A moment later, she was gone, probably dragging Mac and off to safety somewhere.

"How did you know she'd come here?"

Bree still sounded completely calm. She wasn't—I had one arm

239

around her and I could feel how cold she was—but you wouldn't have known it from her voice. She sounded curious, period.

"What?" The simple question had thrown Bengt off balance, for some reason. "What do you –"

"You said you guessed she'd probably come here." Calm, rational, almost relaxed. "When you let yourself into our suite. If you suspected she was coming here, you must know something we don't, because this is about the last place I would have thought she'd come. We were the ones who demanded that she and her sister be kept away from us in the first place. So why in the world would you think she'd come here?"

He laughed. That laugh settled it, for me. Bengt Ekberg was mental.

"Are you as naïve as you sound?" He was watching my wife, and the contempt in his voice was staggering. "Why here? Because you're as soft a touch as anyone this pampered little bitch here has ever seen in her life, that's why. Because she's been missing since she saw me kill her sister yesterday—probably hiding behind all those portable toilets. Suitable place for her, hey, Azra? Because she was scared and she was bound to be hungry. And you can't say no, can you?"

"Not to hungry people, no. Why should I? Feeding people is something I do. I'd have fed you too, if you'd wanted a meal. But you didn't ask." Bree'd probably felt me tense up—I'd taken a breath, ready to rip the bloke's head off—and her voice was a shrug, basically. "So was that why you sent the guards to our tent? Because you thought she might be there?"

I don't know why it took me as long as it did to sort out what Bree was doing. I swear, I must have been half off my head myself, for it to take so long to get through. Whoever was still out there in the hallway probably sussed it before I did.

Yeah, she wanted to know the answers. Yeah, she was asking genuine questions, stuff we all wanted to know, questions none of us fancied dying without getting the answers to.

And none of that had a damned thing to do with what she was up to. She was buying time, a half-minute at a pop.

That whole thing, about trying to be heroic, getting my cell out and somehow letting Patrick know what was happening? The entire rest of the band family, everyone out there in the hall, had probably reached for their phones as soon as they'd heard what was happening.

Bengt had to know that. He had to know Patrick would be on the way, probably with Azra's dad and the Forty Thieves and maybe a small army. And Bree had to know that, as well. So why was she stalling him...?

"Why do you care? Just curious?" Bengt let go of Azra's hair suddenly, and slid the arm around her waist, holding her up against him. The gun was still jammed up against her ribs. "Of course that was why. I wanted to find her before her father did. What a stupid question."

"Was that before or after you did that funky shit with the hands? You're a sick motherfucker, you know that?"

Bengt's head jerked towards the door. So did mine. Whatever was moving through Tony's voice, that was something I'd never heard in there before.

"Now there's a funny thing." There was a thin bead of sweat along Bengt's hairline, and I didn't think it had been there a minute before. "That business with the hands wasn't me. I was too busy trying to chase down her sister, when she ran off into the audience. I just put the bullet into Paksima's cheating whoring little skull. Someone else did that stuff with her hands while I was out hunting her sister. I found them on my desk when I got back."

"What?" It was Luke's voice, from out in the hall. I couldn't see him, but he had to be just the other side of the door. Staying out of range; I wondered if Karen was out there with him, refusing to leave him there. "Are you joking? Are you asking us to believe you shot that girl to death but you didn't mutilate her afterwards?"

"I'm sure this will come as a shock, but I really don't give a damn what you believe." He was definitely sweating now, and it wasn't because the room was any warmer. He had one ear cocked, listening to something we couldn't hear, or maybe listening for something he couldn't hear. I was listening too, wondering if that was actually a motor I was hearing in the distance: the hum of a single engine, getting closer by the moment. "But yes, that's what happened. I don't know who it was. I just know it wasn't me."

It was a motor I'd been hearing, all right, but just one. If there was more than one car, I couldn't have told you how many. Only one set of footsteps came down the seraglio corridor and only one person stood in the doorway, looking in at us.

The first time I'd ever seen Almanzor al-Wahid, he'd been toe to toe with Bree on the doorstep of 2828 Clay. At the time, I'd thought he'd looked too damned arrogant for his own good. He'd been perfectly polite, mind you, no bad manners or rudeness, but I'd got the impression that it was only because we were too far beneath him to bother being rude to. He'd looked at us as if he'd thought we were black-beetles, or something.

You'd have thought, under the current circs, that he'd have been a bit less cocky, carried a bit less of the toff about him. He'd lost one daughter already, the bloke who'd done her had the other daughter under the gun, but I'll be damned if he wasn't standing there with that same "right, you're all just the stuff I scrape off my shoes" thing going on. If he was worried about anything at all—including his chief of security blowing his only remaining child's head off—he wasn't showing it. He wasn't saying anything, either.

And he'd come alone. No guard, no backup, nothing. It was just him.

We hadn't moved, me and Bree. I had no clue who was still out in the hall, not beyond Luke and Tony; there was no way to see round the edge of the door, not from where we were inside the suite. Part of me was hoping they'd all gone, that if there were going to be headlines splashed all over the world press about members of the Blacklight family going down in a firefight in Arabia, it would at least be limited to me and Bree. Yeah, that would make it easier for the YouTube mashers to put together a fake video or two, probably with "Remember Me" as the sound-track, but at least we'd keep the collateral damage down…

"Good morning to you all." He was eye to eye with Bengt, and he sounded bored. "Ah, Bengt. I see you found my daughter, alive and well. Good."

I sat there and gawked. I'd thought it couldn't get any more surreal than it already was, but I'd been wrong about that. Next to me, Bree swallowed a noise at the back of her throat. I thought I was about to do the same, so the sound of my own voice was a bit of a shock.

"Don't suppose you happened to notice the gun? Or the fact that he's got your kid as a hostage? Not to mention me and my wife?"

The dark eyes flickered towards me for a moment, then went back to focussing on Bengt. He was ignoring Azra entirely.

"I did not know, until last night, why Paksima had been killed, or by whom. Once I knew—my surgeon told me that she had recently aborted a child—it was clear to me, of course, both the why and the who. I had long suspected her involvement with Nordine—what was found in the second pool outside these win-dows confirmed it—but so long as nothing came of it, there was nothing to worry me. My daughters enjoyed their dalliances. It has always been my policy not to interfere." He smiled suddenly. "But something did come of it."

Azra whimpered. No other word for that noise—she'd stayed

243

dead silent the whole time the crazy bloke with the gun had that grip on her hair, but she whimpered now. She looked so scared, she was pop-eyed with it. Her dad was still smiling, and my heart was seriously thinking about shutting down altogether, it was slamming so hard.

"I confess I knew nothing of your affair, Bengt. It is a pity that you were foolish enough to execute her—you could have left that safely in my hands. Of course you are a dead man, both for the affair and for the execution, but you know that already. Did you get my message? My orders were that it—they—should be delivered to you."

He waved one hand, very casual. He wasn't bothered about making the bloke with the gun jumpy, from the looks of it. "But of course, you must have, or you would not have come here. Would you?"

Next to me, Bree was holding her breath, and I was right with her. There didn't seem to be any air in the suite just then. Bengt had told the straight truth, when he said he hadn't mutilated his girlfriend's corpse.

"Father?" If I hadn't been standing there, seeing Azra trying to get the words out, I wouldn't have recognised the girl's voice. "Please...?"

Ali finally broke the stare with Bengt. He didn't answer his daughter, though, whatever it was she was trying to say. You'd have thought she was invisible to him, or as dead as her sister was. Whatever had happened here, it didn't look to be something Ali was going to forgive.

"I apologise for the intrusions into your privacy." It took me a moment to realise he was talking to us, to me and Bree. "I have learned, too late for any remedy, that my daughters were using the unfinished end of this palace for their trysting place. I offer my regrets. It was my chief of security's duty to prevent such things, but of course there were reasons he was derelict. Still, in

244

the end, the onus is mine. To let them remain at home was poor judgement on my part—I should have had them sent out of the country. To care for one's children too much is a weakness."

He turned back to his daughter. There were tears on her face, as if she knew what he meant, what he was on about, what he was going to say. She seemed to have forgotten about that gun jammed into her ribs, or maybe she'd just stopped caring. I didn't really know what was happening to that family, but one thing was obvious: whatever it was, it mattered to both of them more than Bengt and his weaponry did.

He and Azra had the same eyes, not just the colour, but the shape and the way they were set under those heavy brows. Hard to believe two pairs of eyes could look so much the same and so different at the same time.

The look I'd seen on Ali's face, last night in the tent, was back: smoothed out, as if he'd gone eye to eye with something and blanked himself out over it. If he gave a shit about whatever was behind those tears of hers, he wasn't showing it. He was off somewhere, behind high, high walls.

A phrase popped into my head, I don't know from where or where I'd heard it before: *all passion spent.* I'm not sure what it means, either, but that's what he looked like to me just then, talking about his daughters. You'd have thought Azra was as dead as her sister, that he'd thought about it and decided not to care anymore. "I have overlooked their bad behaviour in the past. It has cost many people. Some things cannot be overlooked. What this one's sister did –"

"*She didn't have an abortion.*" Bree was breathing hard, through her nose. "It was a stillbirth. That baby was dead. What kind of culture punishes women for stillbirths? Are you barbarians, or just insensate?"

I jerked around, to stare at my wife. So did Bengt. Azra kept her eyes on her dad's face. A weird notion popped into my head:

she was afraid that if she looked away, she'd stop existing or something, fade out like a ghost…

Ali turned, and met Bree's eye. There was nothing in that face, nothing at all. Emptied out, as smooth as glass.

"You are free to think so, certainly. Our laws are what they are. My daughter—both my daughters—knew they were breaking them. But even if they had not, there is the matter of Nordine's death to be paid for, and it is that of which I speak. It is not only our culture that claims a life as fair exchange for a life taken. Your own does the same, I believe, though I know many disapprove. My daughter Paksima killed her lover. Her sister aided her." He looked at Bengt. "As did you, by your silence. I am betrayed by my family, by those in whom I placed my trust."

"He threatened us!" Azra had found her voice again. "He said that Paksima must marry him or that he would tell you. He said he would lie, that you would believe him. He would not listen— he had no heart. Father –"

"*Be silent.*" Not a glance her way, nothing, but she stopped in mid-sentence. He was back to doing the locked-stare thing with Bengt. "I have no illusions as to Nordine Benhamou's character. He was a useful servant to me, from a family of long service to mine, but he was ambitious and greedy. I am unsurprised to learn him capable of blackmail, of threats, of anything he might have done to better his position. It does surprise me that he was enough of a fool to think he might marry my daughter without my approval. He must have known he would have faced beheading for daring such a thing."

His voice changed. I'm not sure I've heard anything quite like that before or since, and I don't much want to. Whatever it was that made him sound human suddenly blinked out.

"But his foolishness does nothing to change the truth. To have helped in the death of my servant is to forfeit your life." He raised his voice. "And so it will be."

He hadn't quite got that last word out when Bree finally moved. And all hell broke loose.

Time's funny, you know? The part of my mind that had got detached and was watching things happen was thinking *right, this flick needs an editor, much too long, they need to cut it back about half an hour*. The reality was just a few seconds start to finish, movie over, house lights up, please drop your empty popcorn buckets in the dustbin on your way out.

I had no idea what was happening, no idea why, no idea what was about to happen next. The only thing I was sure of was that something about what Ali had said, or maybe about the way he'd said it, had brought the situation to flashpoint.

I don't know that Bree'd ever moved as fast as she did just then. One second she was sitting in her chair next to me, and the next she was on her feet, kicking her chair out of her way, grabbing me by the shoulders and pulling me off my own chair. Mine toppled onto its side; hers skittered into Bengt's left leg. He loosened his hold on the princess and I saw her stumble forward, towards her dad.

Bengt turned, and the gun turned with him. It was pointing toward Bree, now, or maybe at both of us.

"Down, get under the table, John please, oh God God, John just *go!*"

Maybe it was just reflex, Bengt being trained to look at the source of whatever was suddenly different in his immediate vicinity. I don't know, now, whether or not he meant to put a bullet into me, or into my wife.

It doesn't matter anyway, not beyond basic curiosity, because he never took the shot. Someone else did.

I heard it, as we hit the floor and rolled under the table. It was nuts, how loud it sounded, the way it echoed—I couldn't tell who'd shot at whom, where it had come from, nothing. I knew Bree hadn't been hit, because we had our arms round each other.

247

But the floor where my chair had been was suddenly covered in a filthy spray of red mist. I could hear Azra screaming, finally, a long drawn-out noise that sounded as if she'd pulled it loose from some place inside that all of us have got, even if we don't want to admit it.

I must have got some of my reaction time back, and thank God for it, because I'd got one hand up at the back of my wife's hair, pulling her face hard into my shoulder and away from any chance at all of her looking at Bengt Ekberg and I hadn't known I was doing it. Bengt was slumping to the floor, knees first. There was something really graceless and lumpy about the way he was moving: horror-movie stuff, just not real, you know?

He slid all the way down, and onto what had been his face. He looked to be missing most of his head.

The floor of the suite just beyond Bree's back looked like a slaughterhouse. There was blood everywhere, droplets and splatters, and a few shards of bone as well. I had no clue what the fuck had just gone down; I just knew Bengt was as dead as dead gets. So far as I could tell, Ali had done a magic trick: he'd said *abracadabra* or something, and instead of a rabbit jumping out of someone's hat, Bengt's head had exploded.

I wasn't worrying about how it had happened—Christ, at that point, I was too confused and disoriented to give a shit. I just lay there, hanging on to my wife. The tickybox was revving like that bloody Bugatti, and I stayed where I was and let it do its thing. Nothing in the world seemed to matter just then beyond making damned sure Bree didn't look behind her. If she'd shown any inclination to turn round for a closer look, I'd have pinned her, but she wasn't going anywhere. It took me a few moments to figure out that she was doing the same thing I was: keeping me from trying to get up and go anywhere until the whole safety thing got itself sorted out. I felt her breath, short warm gusts, tickling the hollow of my throat.

248

Azra's screams had tapered off into sobs, with words lacing through them. I don't speak the local jabber, so I didn't know what she was saying, but the tone was clear. If she was hoping for comfort, though, she was out of luck. Her dad had already made it pretty clear that whatever he'd be offering his daughter, it wasn't going to involve petting and soothing and promising to buy her a pony.

Maybe she already knew that. In any case, she quieted down; the sobs became sniffling and hiccoughing, just quiet enough so that I heard the footsteps, coming down the long corridor. Whoever was heading towards our suite wasn't quite running, but they weren't taking their time about getting here, either: it sounded like a quick, purposeful trot. The footsteps stopped in our doorway.

I opened my eyes. Looking over the top of Bree's head, I found myself focussing on a pair of men's shoes. Halfway up the bloke's trouser leg was a familiar hand. It had a good grip on a really unpleasant-looking gun, much bigger than Bengt's and a lot more dangerous-looking, somehow.

"Is everyone okay?" Patrick might have kept his steps even, but he wasn't bothering about trying to get his voice to behave. That was the nearest I've ever heard him get to flipping his shit. "Ian, excuse me please, I need to get in. JP? Bree? For heaven's sake, talk to me!"

I let go of Bree and pulled myself out from under the table. Not easy, because I had to inch forward instead of taking the easy way and just rolling out the way I'd gone under in the first place. Problem was, that side of the table was where all the mess was, including what was left of Bengt. My stomach was already thinking about doing the fandango, and I was damned if I wanted to add my breakfast to all that gore.

"Yeah, we're fine, I think. Patrick, what the fuck, mate? You fire that shot? Where were you? Look, can someone find a sheet or

249

something? Bree, don't even think about looking at that, all right?"

She sounded pretty calm, all things considered. "Okay. But I really don't want to stay under the table. I promise I won't look, John, but I'm a little too close to it down here." Suddenly, she didn't sound quite so calm. "It—I can smell blood. And yes, can someone please cover him?"

"Go." Ali hadn't touched his daughter, or used her name. He jerked his head at her, as if she was an unsatisfactory servant he was planning on sacking, or maybe having flogged. "Go and fetch a shroud for your sister's lover. Bring a coverlet from the bed she used to seduce my servants."

Azra, her eyes cast all the way down, went. Meanwhile, Bree was pulling herself out, the same way I'd done. She wasn't looking at what was left of Bengt, and she wasn't waiting to hear Patrick answer my question, either; she was too busy moving him out of the way, gun and all. She'd remembered we had family, out there in the hallway.

Everyone was there, and from the general tone of my wife's questions and the answers she got, everyone was in one piece and no one was really flipping their shit, even if some of them were a bit freaked out. Sometime between us diving under the table and Patrick showing up and doing his Dirty Harry act, the whole band family had got themselves back into the corridor: even Carla and Ian had come over from the main palace. Ian was just outside the door, from the sound of it. I wondered how long he'd been there. Me, I was using the time to get my own breath back under some kind of control.

Mac and Domitra had joined the party as well, all the way at the back and well out of range. I heard Bree say something about it being all clear and then Domitra's voice, announcing that Mac was staying where he was until she decided it was all clear, thank you very much. Bree didn't wait for an answer. She was back with me in less than a minute.

Personally, I was still waiting for an answer from Patrick. The bare fact seemed obvious enough: someone had shot Bengt and here was our chief of security, on the spot, with a sodding huge gun in his hand. What I couldn't sort out was how it had been possible. I realised suddenly that I'd never seen him with a gun before, not even when he was a homicide lieutenant. If I'd ever wondered about it, I'd have said I thought he didn't much care for the damned things.

"Patrick? You want to tell us how you worked this one, mate? Because we've got all the shutters closed and the only other windows are up on the roof. So how…?"

He jerked his head towards the shutters, and I noticed he was wearing his Bluetooth in one ear. He's never been much for talking to hear himself talk, but he seemed even more terse than usual. "Shutters are closed, but not latched. And you left the window on the left open, about two inches. That's plenty of sightline for a clean kill shot, especially with this gun. I couldn't miss with a Desert Eagle at this range. But it's a good thing the window was open."

I turned my head for a look. Ali was going to have to spring for some repairs; there was wood missing.

"It was a little tricky." Patrick had looked back that way as well. "Standing on the groundskeeper's ladder wasn't much help. I'm just glad Bree figured out what was happening, or at least I assume she did, from how fast she moved. Not having to worry about hitting either of you made it possible for me to take the shot. Something else to be grateful for. Thanks for showing some good sense."

He wasn't smiling, and he wasn't bragging, either. I got the feeling—damned if I know why, but it was very strong—that something about having used that gun to kill Bengt Ekberg had triggered a very different reaction to what I'd assumed would happen.

251

From the day I first laid eyes on the bloke, I'd backed away from him for just that reason: the whole predator deal, the smell of blood in the water giving him a rush, all that. I don't like people who get their jollies off other people in pain. It's always kept me from actually liking him.

I wasn't getting that off him now; just the opposite, actually. It was obvious that he didn't want to talk about it, that he wasn't going to talk about it unless he had to. And that meant he hadn't wanted to do it. He was keeping those dirty-ice eyes completely away from the dead man on the floor. Not only wasn't he getting turned on from having done the shooting, he wasn't letting himself look at the results.

Someone must have left their own windows open, because there was a cross-breeze in the room. And out of nowhere, the clock rolled back and I was facing off with Patrick, toe to toe in a garden in the South of France, because he was using my wife as bait to catch a killer. Someone had killed a woman called Louise Goff, whom he'd obviously had feelings for, as well as his partner, back when he was DEA in Miami. What had he said? Something about one bullet to the head for each of them, and dumped on Patrick's doorstep like garbage, left for him to trip over...

"JP?"

Patrick was watching me. He'd seen me remember, seen me suss it out. And it was there in his face: I'd been right. This gun, this death, the smell of this particular blood, was going on the dark side of whatever the hell he used as a ledger. I wasn't likely to ever really know why, and that was fine. Fair enough. It wasn't my business anyway.

Bree had come back in, and Azra was at her heels. She wasn't looking at anyone except her father, and she only did that once more that morning. She looked up at him, eye to eye. If I've ever seen pleading in someone's face, it was there in hers.

"Cover him." Distant as the moon. "You aided in his death,

252

and in Nordine's. See what you helped bring about. Look at him."

"I did nothing to him. I did nothing to Nordine." She'd given up even trying to catch his eye. I wondered who she was trying to convince, while she was dropping the gaudy silk cover over what had been her dad's chief of security. "I will do as you tell me, but I am not to blame. I killed no one."

Nothing. Not a look, not a word, no acknowledgement that the girl was still alive or had even ever existed.

"I must thank you, Patrick, for your promptness in arriving and the precision of your shooting. We might have had more deaths, else. And there have been more than enough."

He was looking at the pile on the floor. The small pools of blood were already beginning to brown up, and I caught a faint smell. It reminded me of the morning we'd found that blood-soaked hut.

"My people have already left messages for Mr. Hendry and Ms. Fanucci, that the airports in southern Italy are opening to international traffic. I have arranged for a priority clearance. Your plane will be ready for you within the hour."

Chapter Fifteen

I can't speak for anyone else in the band family, but personally, I've never been happier about getting on a plane in my entire life. About the only person happier about it than me was my wife. If we could have got out of Manaar the day before last week, it wouldn't have been too soon for Bree.

I was saving my questions for the trip to the airport in Sicily; we were going to have a few hours in the air coming up. But yeah, there were going to be questions. There was still a shitload of things I wanted to know. Patrick might not want to talk about it, but he wasn't getting a vote, yeah? I wasn't the only one likely to be hitting him with it.

In the meantime, Bree was itching to get us packed and gone. Normally, if Blacklight's on tour, we travel with staff who handle all that. The Manaar gig had been a one-off, though, and very short notice as well. This gig, we were doing it ourselves; the only crew we'd brought along were band management and tech. All the housekeeping stuff was supposed to be provided by our host, but that didn't seem to extend to packing to get the hell out of the country. Even if it had done, I doubt Bree would have waited.

Under normal circs, my wife's got a nice clean easy way of getting everyone out of our digs when she's decided it's time they all left. Tony, who's been watching her do it for decades, calls it her "thanks for coming everyone please get the hell out and go home now" approach. It's about as subtle as a backhoe, but just then, she was going to have to be even less subtle than usual. She couldn't actually turf the Emir out, what with him owning the place. There was also the matter of the dead body under the silk coverlet.

"If our plane's almost ready, I'd like to start packing now." She'd apparently decided that straight and upfront was definitely the way to go. "Can someone please come and take Bengt off our floor?"

"Of course. I will have this taken care of at once." He turned for the door. "Azra. You will come with me."

"No, she won't. Not without your word that she won't be harmed in any way."

When Bree sounds definite, you can't miss it. The tone of voice means she's ready to go down fighting for whatever it is. I certainly wasn't expecting to hear it just then.

Ali stopped where he was. I could see his shoulders—they were as tense as Bree's own get. He turned slowly back, and stared at her. So did I, and my stomach went into lockdown mode. The green eyes were as fierce as they get. She wasn't going to back down an inch, not on this one.

"I beg your pardon?" Something was moving in that smoothed-out face of his. I had a bad feeling it was rage. "By what right do you demand such assurances?"

"Why did you offer to let me drive your Bugatti?"

It occurred to me that this was probably the last time they'd ever be in the same place again, and that Bree had sussed that out on her own. Even if he came out to the airport to see the plane off the ground, they weren't likely to be talking. This was the last shot at getting that one question answered. Ali had singled her out from the moment we'd got here, and no one had known why.

Still, the timing of her asking it was pretty dammed odd. She doesn't usually answer questions with questions anyway; she's too blunt and definite for that sort of game-playing. But I'm damned if Ali didn't answer her.

"You permitted me to cross your threshold, back in San Francisco. I was uninvited and unwelcome, but you allowed me into your home. You treated me with the courtesy you would have shown an invited guest. That is no small thing for a Manaari, in however low esteem you hold our culture. When I was told you would accompany your husband, I took the trouble to learn what might please you, and was told that you drive a powerful automobile. That suggested a love of speed. I offered the Veyron as a gesture in kind."

Yeah, well, score two points for the Emir. That answer had taken everyone by surprise, except for my wife.

"You just answered your own question," she told him. "Your daughter ate at my table. She was my guest, and she wasn't invited either. That's where I get the right. And if you have a problem with that, it's just too damned bad. Deal with it."

I'm not quite sure how it was possible, but my wife, the Irresistible Force, was managing to be the Immovable Object as well. And her voice wasn't taking any prisoners—that *deal with it* had been too close to being spat for comfort. If Ali hadn't known how little she liked him, he knew now. She might have been talking to a spider. Christ, even I hadn't realised how much she loathed him. She wasn't done with him, either.

"Don't you stand there looking down your nose at me. And you can lose that pushy arrogant tone, while you're at it. Considering that you mutilated your own child's corpse for the crime of not having a child of her own, you don't have a lot of credibility. So how about you stop wasting both our time? You either swear on the Koran or whatever you claim you believe in that your daughter won't be harmed in any way, or she doesn't leave this room with you. Got it? Clear now? Do you want me to write it down for you?"

I wonder, now, how long and how hot the desire to give the bloke a damned good hiding had been bubbling away. If things hadn't been so tense, it would have been almost funny: he was gawking at her, literally slackjawed with disbelief. Patrick was watching, ready to step in if things got out of hand, and he was still holding the gun. Azra wasn't staring at the floor anymore; her head was snapping back and forth between her dad and my wife. I remember thinking she was in for a bad case of whiplash, she kept that up.

"Oh, for fuck's sake, Ali, just get on with it, will you?"

Apparently Domitra had decided it really was clear, because Mac had got himself up to our end of the action. He was leaning against the door, and he sounded sardonic.

"She's right, you're wrong, and that's an end to it. Besides, I know Bree and you don't—such a fierce girl. If you argue with her, we'll miss our plane and that will make everyone cross. You'll lose the argument anyway, so why bother? I can safely promise you we'll all help her make sure your daughter's safe. That business with the hands? Not exactly delicious. All things considered, I doubt any of us are willing to cut you much slack right now. Just do it, Ali. Swear. Then we can all get the fuck out of here."

Ali's mouth was clamped so hard shut, he might as well have had no lips. He was breathing through his nostrils like some kind of pissed-off racehorse.

Bree shrugged. She walked right in front of him, dropped an arm around Azra, and planted herself. The girl's eyes were about the size of the cat dishes we use back at 2828 Clay. My wife's message was definitive: *This is how it is. Swear or she doesn't go with you.*

I had an odd passing thought: this was a new definition of that whole home court advantage thing my wife values so much. Ali might own the physical ground we were standing on, but Bree had just redefined the moral ground. And Ali knew it.

"Do it."

Ian had jumped the queue outside our suite. He slipped inside, in front of Mac and Dom. He was holding his phone.

"I should probably clue you in: Carla and I both recorded every word that just got said in here on our phones, and sent both recordings back to our own offices. I was out there in the hall with my phone getting everything from the moment you showed up. You walked around me to get in, remember? I've got the whole damned thing, including the bit where you said you cut your kid's hands off. We've got some pictures of Bengt, as well. I'm not squeamish and neither is Carla. You want that all over the English language edition of Al-Jazeera, you've got it."

Ian was keeping things icy, but Bree was smiling. It was clamped down, but I know every muscle in my wife's face, and there was a smile there, trying to get out. I'm guessing it was a sort of "finding a kindred spirit" deal, you know? Finding that Ian was just as pissed off at Ali as she was. And crikey, he was pissed off.

"You try any rubbish, anything at all, you'll have the whole story as a viral YouTube video. And don't bother wondering if I'd really do it, either. You jerked me around, you put a wedge between me and the band, and you nearly cost me my job. You tried to screw us and you put us and our crew in jeopardy. We don't owe you a fucking thing. What Bree said is dead right: you've got no cred."

Ali was grey with rage. Ian held up his phone, barely a foot away from Ali's face.

"Get on with it." There was a good hard snap in his voice. "Tell the world you've got no plans to damage your daughter. Say it nice and clear, no mistake possible, and crank up the fucking volume. Soon as you've done, we're off to pack and get the hell out of here. I want that plane on the tarmac and ready to go, and no arguments or excuses, either."

"As you wish." I don't know how Ali got the words out without choking on them, but there they were, and we'd all heard him say it. "She will not be harmed. I give my word."

"Accepted. For the moment, anyway." Bree wasn't smiling anymore. "If you go back on it, I'll call you a liar from San Francisco to Medin-Manaar and back. I'll shout it from the rooftops. But I don't think you will. And now, if you don't mind, I want to pack. If everyone will please excuse us? Mac, you're blocking the doorway. Patrick, be careful not to slip. There's blood on the floor."

Considering how many years Bree's packed for me going out on tour, I probably shouldn't have been surprised at how fast she had every last sock, pair of knickers and three-ounce travel sized bottle of hair product stowed away in our bags. She's packed for so long, she's got an eye for it, and getting all the gear and food she needs for the occasional catering gig back in San Francisco to fit into a rented SUV probably doesn't hurt either. But this was quick even by her standards.

You'd think the entire morning had been surreal enough, but it turned out Manaar wasn't quite done with us yet. Bree'd got nicely into her rhythm and was folding the last bits of my stage gear when we heard footsteps, more than one set of them, coming down the corridor. A moment later, someone knocked, a nice clean sharp rapping. Not the Princess Azra tapping away like a scared rabbit, not this time.

"John?" Bree had one of my jackets half folded. She wasn't slowing down. I suddenly realised, she was keeping her eyes away from the mess on the floor. "Can you get that?"

There were three blokes out in the corridor, waiting politely for me to stand back and let them in. These were definitely Ali's uniforms, probably members of the household guard, but there were no guns in sight. Instead, there was a stretcher, a mop, and a huge bucket full of what looked like cleaning supplies. I saw what looked like a dustpan, and the handle of a small whisk broom, poking out the top.

I'll give Ali this much: he wasn't a slacker. The Emir might have been having fantasies about having Bree strung up and flogged in the middle of Amina Plaza for insubordination or whatever, but he'd got right on his promise to deal with what was left of Bengt. He'd even remembered the pine-scented cleaner and the industrial strength rubber gloves.

There wasn't one word spoken the entire time, not by them and not by us, either. Bree kept folding, and two of them carefully loaded Bengt up onto the stretcher, silk coverlet and all. They got him off the floor and onto the stretcher in total silence. No communicating with each other, not a word to us, nothing. They might as well have been mutes. I just stood back and let everyone get on with it.

It was also really damned disturbing to realise just how good they were at what they were doing. I mean, we've got roadies who've been with Blacklight twenty years who aren't that smooth, yeah? And what the hell, how many chances did these blokes get to practice? I had a mad moment of picturing Ali training his people to load the headless corpses of his enemies onto stretchers without bothering the tourists, and wondering just what he used for the corpses.

They got Bengt off the floor, squared up on the stretcher and out the door without letting anything slip out from under the coverlet. There was none of that 'one limp hand dangling' thriller nonsense. I was quite thankful for that—we were already taking enough bad memories of Manaar with us as it was. Of course, by that time, he'd probably stiffened up anyway.

Before the first two uniforms had got the stretcher halfway through the suite door, the third one got down on both knees and got busy with the cleaning supplies. He used the small whisk-broom and got the shards of bone up and into the dustpan, and then went to work on cleaning up the blood. He was done in under three minutes, bob's your uncle, everything back in the bucket and out the door, with one small nod towards us. So far as I could tell, Bree hadn't let herself look anywhere near the proceedings the entire time they'd been here.

After I locked the door behind him, I found myself staring at the floor. There were already stains, and from the look of them, they were probably there for good. Ali was going to have to spring for a small pile of dosh redoing this particular suite, unless he fancied keeping it as it was and maybe renting it out to rich thrill-seekers as a haunted chamber or something. Maybe next time, he'd get the stones sealed before someone else bled all over them.

"Damn, my back hurts." Bree'd snapped the locks on the last suitcase into place, and was straightening up, slow and careful. "I wish I had some time to do a little yoga before we left. I'm too old to go without sleep."

"Rubbish. If you're old, what does that make me?"

I knew, we both knew, what she'd really meant: it wasn't a question of enough time, it was about a place to do it. Even with her yoga gear and mat already rolled up and packed, she could have pulled the coverlet off the bed and done a nice little yoga workout; if we got the call that the car was outside and ready, they'd wait for us. Hell, in the headspace Bree was in, she'd probably have enjoyed making them wait.

261

But she wasn't getting down on that floor. The stones were still dark and wet where they'd been scrubbed, still stained a really nasty blackish red underneath those damp patches. Like it or not, our suite had been the site of an execution…

"John?" She'd caught at my thought; the marital mind-reading was running hot and strong. "Would it be okay if we waited outside for the car? I'm sorry—this room is creeping me out."

We left the luggage just inside and headed out into the courtyard. Getting from one end of the corridor to the other, I could hear murmurs behind doors; everyone still seemed to be busy getting their own gear packed up. Out of doors, it was your basic day in Manaar: nice soft breeze, nice clean sunlight, the mineral pools sparkling in the sun.

"How soon do you think the car will get here?" Bree was staring towards the gates in from the main road, craning her neck. Her entire body looked to be straining to get the hell out of here.

"Not to worry—Ian'll text us first. We don't need to sit indoors. Anyway, it's quite pleasant out here."

I wasn't watching the road, or even listening for a car. I was busy reminding myself to ask Patrick about something Ali had said to Bengt, just before the shooting started. What had that been? He'd been saying something about how he'd already known or suspected that one of the twins had been involved with Nordine, and then something about what they'd found in the pool…

"I wonder what they found in that other pool? And when they found it?"

I did a double-take, and Bree hurried into speech. "He said something like that, didn't he? About suspecting that Paksima was having a thing with Nordine, and about how what they found in the second pool confirmed it? I thought –"

"Yeah, he did. You made me jump, that's all. I was just thinking that exact thing myself, but I couldn't remember what he'd said." I glanced out at the mineral pools, clear and shining in the sun. "No idea what they found, but I'm betting I know when they found it. Remember the day after Nordine got slashed, when Ali dragged you all over to the palace to have lunch, and he wouldn't take anyone's no? When we got back here from the band practice he tricked Ian into calling us out for, we found those two tankers. My money's on it being then. Must have been, yeah? They were emptying out both pools, not just the one, and bottom line is, Nordine only died in one of those pools. I'd lay a few bob on whatever it was being something Paksima's dad recognised as hers, straight off."

She was looking pinched, suddenly, and I got an arm round her shoulders. My arm was shaking a bit, just a tiny tremor, and I hoped to hell she'd put it down to nerves, or the warm weather, or not enough sleep.

"It's okay, baby." I had my lips up against her hair. "No point in letting it get to you, is there? We're out of here as soon as the car shows up to get us to the airport, and after that, fuck it, not coming back here again. But there's a few things I want to know, and what you asked, about the second pool, is right up there on my list. I hope Patrick doesn't think he's using the flight for a nice long kip. He's got questions to answer. As soon as we –"

I stopped, because the phone in my trousers pocket had suddenly vibrated. I pulled it out—Ian had texted, right on schedule. *Cars on the way, eta five minutes, plane ready, be packed.*

The limos showed up a few minutes later, along with Ian and Carla and a pair of SUVs for the luggage and guitars. The rest of the crew, Ronan and Nial included, were probably still working their arses off, back at the site: tearing down, checking shipping manifests, packing the gear. As loadouts go, Blacklight had certainly done bigger ones; the stage sets for Book of Days had been monsters compared to this. Still, everything had to be accounted for and crated up. I was just glad our staff wasn't responsible for all those portable toilets. They'd have been stuck in Manaar until midsummer.

Everyone had got Ian's text, and no one was dawdling or hanging about. By the time the cars showed, the suites were empty of people. Everyone had come out of doors to wait.

"Ian, what about our people?" Mac was watching Ali's boys get suitcases stowed in the Range Rovers; they were almost as fast doing that as our impromptu cleaning staff had been. "Are we sure there won't be any problems with them getting out of Manaar? I'm not exactly thrilled with the idea of leaving them behind, all things considered."

"Not an issue, Mac. We're not leaving anyone behind." Nice and gruff; our tour manager was sounding almost normal again. He had one eye watching Ali's people loading our stuff into the SUVs. "All of our people are on the same plane. Ronan and Nial have been onsite most of the night, working with the PA guys. The Clare Brothers staff's handling whatever's left to do. They couldn't head out yet even if they fancied a side trip to Sicily—the contract says they're ultimately responsible for the PA gear, so they've got to make sure everything's done. They're getting on with it. But Blacklight family, all of us, we're going out together. The crew's heading to the airport straight from Amina. They'll meet us at the plane. Everyone ready? Let's go."

Funny thing about that ride out to the airport. I'd got used to basically empty highways on our side of Medin-Manaar—after all, there was really nothing that side of the capital beyond the seraglio and Ali's own digs. That morning, the roads weren't empty. There wasn't much traffic, very few cars, but there were people, what looked to be an endless stream of them, walking along the main road.

"Holy shit, check out all the fans!" Tony was peering out the window on his side of the limo. He sounded a bit freaked, and I got why: the fans had obviously sussed out who was in the limos, and there was some commotion out there. "I never even stopped to think about how they were getting out of here. Are we even going to be able to get on a plane?"

It was a good question. There were a quarter of a million people looking to get to somewhere that wasn't Manaar. On top of that, today was an international holiday, and any flights would be dealing with the aftermath of really bad weather at the arrivals end of most of the destinations they'd likely be headed to. We were looking at a scheduling nightmare.

Even if our plane was the only flight off the ground today, the airport was likely to be buried under people waiting for a way home. I had no clue how we were going to get through the mob. I was about to ask Ian when, out of nowhere, we had company: a half dozen motorcycles on either side of the convoy, the Manaari flag fluttering off the back of each one, keeping a safety zone between the pedestrians and the limos. Next to Bree, Luke grunted.

"Efficient sod, isn't he? Nice little police escort—he thinks of everything. Tony, don't worry about the crowds. They'll drive us straight to the plane, the same way we handled it during Book of Days. I'm betting the yobs out there on the bikes get between us and the rest of the world. Does anyone want to take bets on whether al-Wahid comes out to officially wave us off? Or at least makes sure that we get out of his emirate?"

Next to him, Karen moved in her seat, sliding up a little closer to Luke. "Oh god. I don't want to sound rude, but I really hope he doesn't. I just want to go home to Draycote. I want to forget about this place."

We did the rest of the ride in total silence, not a word said by anyone. Karen sounded so stressed, so completely miserable and played out, no one seemed to want to say anything. Luke got hold of her hands and just held them. The bullet-proof windows made a good job of keeping noise out, as well. It was so quiet, we could have been in the middle of outer space.

265

Luke had nailed it. We were driven straight onto the airfield, two motorbikes leading the way and the rest forming a cordon behind us to make sure we weren't bothered. And yeah, it was needed. The fans were going nuts, yelling and pointing and cheering. It's something I thought I'd got used to over the years, but every time it happens, it feels new and odd. And the older I get, the more I find myself taken short by the whole thing, more surprised when I hear my own name come out of one of those mobs.

We climbed out of the limos just as the steps were being wheeled up to the plane. The cargo bay doors were open, and they were already loading luggage and gear. Patrick was waiting, and right behind him I saw Ronan and Nial and Jas. Ian, first out of the limo he was sharing with Carla, the Corrigans and the Wilsons, stood peering around. His lips were moving, doing a headcount.

"All present and accounted for." He jerked his head towards the plane. "Don't know about you lot, but I'm ready to get the fuck out of here. I see the Emir didn't bother to come out to kiss us goodbye. Everyone ready? The weather forecast has clear skies. We should be in Sicily in time for dinner."

Chapter Sixteen

As it turned out, Patrick did manage an hour's worth of kip on the way home, after all. We'd barely got ourselves strapped in for takeoff when he lifted his voice above the noise of the engines warming up.

"Hey, guys? Ian's suggested that I give my full report as soon as we're in the air. Is everyone okay with that?"

So, yeah, Ian had already sussed we wanted to know what in hell had just gone down, and that none of us wanted to wait to hear it. That was reassuring, in a way; after all, thinking ahead to make sure things get taken care of as smoothly as possible is what we pay Ian for. Comes with the job, yeah? Manaar had cocked things up badly, but it looked as if our tour manager was back to normal, and thank God for it.

I'd been expecting a bumpy flight, but there was no sign of

turbulence. Either we were behind whatever weather fronts were still messing up commercial air travel, or else we were out of the trouble zones. I didn't really give a toss, either way; I was too glad for a nice calm ride to southern Europe.

We'd only been up for about ten minutes before the little lights telling us it was safe to undo the belts went on. The flight attendant serving drinks and nosh did her thing, but no one seemed interested. We were all waiting on Patrick, and he knew it.

This wasn't the first time we'd heard him come across with an actual official report—he's had to do a few of them since we'd hired him on as Blacklight's security chief. But this was the first time he'd had the entire immediate band family there to listen: last time, it had just been the band and Carla getting the gen. This time, he had all the wives, and the full crew as well. Just as well he's not a shy bloke, you know? All those eyes might have put him off. As it was, he didn't look to have made up his mind about where to start.

"I'm not sure what the best way to handle this is." He was talking to all of us, but he was looking at Carla. "As much as I'd like to able to wrap this up cleanly, there are things I can only guess at."

"Really?" Funny thing—Barb Wilson had seemed just as wiped out as the rest of us, but now that we were safe off Manaari soil and headed for Europe, she'd perked right up. Hell, everyone was looking happier. "Such as?"

He took the question seriously. "Well, I don't have anything beyond guesswork for any of the emotional issues. I do have certain hard facts I can share, and of course I will. But all I have to offer, about what was motivating any of these people to do what they did, would be pure guesswork. I don't even know why Ali al-Wahid was willing to pay the kind of money he was willing to pay out to get Blacklight to play his show."

"Guilt. That would be my guess, anyway."

We all looked at Mac. He wasn't smiling. "It's not rocket science, Patrick. I was at school with him, remember. I've probably got a better look at how his mind works than you do. And I can tell you this much: he was writhing over the trouble his twin terrors' bodyguards caused during Book of Days—that whole 'shame of my family' thing is huge in his culture. I suspect this was his way of evening things out: reparation, or whatever he needed to make himself feel that debt was paid off in full. He was smart enough to know he couldn't simply offer us money and quiet down his guilty conscience that way, especially not after I hung up on him twice. The gig, and that ridiculous paycheque, were his way of coping. He did what he always does. He reached for his chequebook."

Stu grunted. "What, executing the bastards wasn't good enough for him? You're probably right about him writhing, but I don't think it was guilt. If he was writhing over anything, it was you and Luke taking him apart back in San Francisco, when he showed up at JP and Bree's place that day. I don't believe he'd have given a fuck one way or the other, if it hadn't been for that. It was the slap to his pride did it."

"He had it coming." Luke was stony-faced enough to give Patrick a run for his money. "And I'll cash his cheque. We earned it. We played the hell of a show."

"That sounds about right." Patrick was tapping on the table in front of him, that rhythmic thing he does with his fingers when he's eager for everyone to stop interrupting and let him get on with things. "Meanwhile, for the facts I do know, it all goes back to Paksima al-Wahid getting sexually involved with both Nordine Benhamou and Bengt Ekberg."

"At the same time?" Carla shook her head. "Wow. Just from the brief dealings I had with those two guys, I can't imagine how that girl thought she could handle both of them. Not a chance. Was she an idiot, or just too spoiled to care?"

"I don't know." Patrick sounded patient. "I could speculate about the emotional reasons, but if you don't mind, I'll stick with the facts. And the fact is that, a few months back, the princess discovered she was pregnant."

"She didn't know whose it was, did she?" Bree's voice was almost too quiet. I reached for her hand, but she had both of them clasped in her lap, out of reach. "I got that much from what her sister said this morning—at least, I think that's what she meant. And then the baby died. I wonder if Paksima thought that solved the problem of whose it was? Because Azra told us this morning that they didn't know what to do, that Paksima asked Nordine for help getting rid of that stillbirth. I can't believe she would have done that, if she thought even for one minute that he'd raise hell over it. She must have read him all the way wrong, if she did that. I only got to know him over learning to drive the Veyron, and even I could tell he wasn't the kind of man anyone could jerk around, not safely anyway."

"Yes, that's apparently what happened." I couldn't get a read on Patrick just then, what he was really thinking or feeling. He had the old homicide rozzer's poker face on. "I got confirmation of a few things from the Emir this morning, on the way over from the royal palace."

"What?" I was staring at him. "You mean Ali just let it bleed? Sorry, mate. Not meaning to be rude, but I don't think I'm buying that. Why would he share a damned thing with you or anyone else, especially if it made his family look bad?"

Patrick turned to answer me, and I got a shock. I'd seen that look on his face once before, back in the South of France. He doesn't show his personal weak spots very often, so when he does, I remember it.

"He shared because he had no choice." Flat as a rock, that voice was. "The information he had was my price for picking up that gun. I made it clear that unless I was aware of as many of the facts he had in his possession, I wouldn't take the shot. Excuse me a minute, I'm a little scratchy-throated."

We stayed quiet while he got a mouthful of cold water. It's like I said, sipping a drink's a great way of stalling for time while you get your shit together. After a minute, he went on.

"So Paksima was pregnant. I gathered from my conversation with Ali this morning that she'd visited her usual doctor, and that the doctor had come directly to him and told him the princess had aborted a foetus. I don't know how Ali convinced the guy to break his patient's confidence, and I don't think the knowledge is pertinent. I don't know when that happened, either. He wasn't forthcoming about it, and I didn't press it. There were things I was more interested in."

"He found out last night. Ali said that to Bengt, just before the shooting started. He said the doctor had told him all about the abortion. I'm betting that's what led to that sick bullshit with the hands. But hang on a minute, all right?"

I'd managed to get hold of one of my wife's hands. The way this conversation was headed was likely to bring up some bad memories. Something had just occurred to me, though, and it wanted out. I took a breath and turned back to Patrick.

"I don't know if you could hear Azra this morning, when she dished. She said they'd gone to Nordine to abort the baby, since it was dead anyway, and that he'd seen it as leverage, a way to marry into the royal family. She said he'd threatened to tell her dad all about it. And I'll tell you what, I think maybe everyone's on the wrong track here. I think we're doing that girl an injustice."

Patrick blinked at me. I went on, sorting it out as I talked.

"Where's the proof that Paksima was actually involved with Nordine? Because that's not what it sounded like, you know? Her sister said something this morning, about how they'd gone to Nordine for help, that he'd messed her up inside and then

271

threatened to go to their dad with it if Paksima didn't marry him. Remember, Bree? She said Nordine threatened to lie to Ali, and that Ali would believe him, yeah? But why in hell would he have to lie, if there was any shot the kid actually was his? Doesn't make any sense, does it? And another thing—the way Azra said it this morning, the way she put it out to her dad, it sounded like they went to him because they'd known him forever. Someone they knew, someone they thought they could trust."

"Oh man." Bree's breathing had gone choppy. "Oh shit. John, yes. And Ali said that Nordine's family had served the royal family for generations, or something."

I nodded. "I think that kid was Bengt's. I'm betting she was never involved with Nordine at all."

Dom had stayed quiet so long, her voice made me jump. "So, what? You think all that shooting and the stuff with the hands, everything that went down, all those people getting killed, it was just a mistake? Man, that's some sad shit right there."

"If JP's right, then yes. And I think maybe he is." Patrick was watching me. The cop face had softened into something else; I had the feeling he might actually be feeling sorry for everyone involved. Bit of a departure, that would be. "But in any case, there appears to be no doubt about the fact that Paksima killed Nordine. And yes, I'm sure of that."

"Why?" Katia sounded as if she really wanted to know. "I mean, why are you so sure?"

"Because her clothes, everything she was wearing when she killed him, were found by Bengt in the second pool the morning after the murder." Nice and impersonal. "Even after it had been in the water overnight, there was apparently still enough blood spatter to be obvious. The forensic evidence, in this instance, was very clear. There was also Azra's reaction. The evidence here would be enough to satisfy a jury. She killed him."

This time, it was Bree's hand tightening around mine. I won-

272

dered if she was seeing the same picture in her head as I was: the girl, all done up in her usual gear from the Paris runways, confronting Nordine, him issuing his threat, her doing—what, exactly? She must have had something in her hand, something sharp enough to do what she'd done to Nordine's throat. And that meant she'd come to that meeting knowing she might be wanting a weapon...

"We're never going to have all the details." Patrick was watching my wife, and he wasn't making any bones about it, either. This time, I didn't mind; she was pale as Manaari desert sand just then. "But clearly Paksima went into that rendezvous suspicious about what Nordine was going to do, because she went armed. And whatever he threatened her with, it was enough to get her to react by killing him."

"She went a little crazy." Bree sounded sad, but she was getting her colour back. Good. "Her hormones were probably off the charts. You're right, we'll never know all of it. But John and I may know a few things you don't."

Patrick lifted an eyebrow at her. "Bengt was—talking," Bree told him. "This morning. I was asking him questions, a little because I wanted to know the answers, but mostly because I thought he was going to have to shoot us and I wanted to be alive a few more minutes. So I kept asking him stuff."

She stopped, just to take a breath. No drama, she was just stating what she'd been up to, but right then, the plane's engines sounded louder than ever, because no one seemed to be breathing. I don't think she knew the effect she'd had, because she just picked up where she'd paused.

"He seemed to want to talk. He was totally whacked out—he must have been having a huge adrenalin rush, or maybe just the whole situation, knowing he wasn't getting out alive. I guess he knew he had nothing to lose, so he just answered things. He said he'd taken the baby's corpse, and buried it out in the desert. And he said he could live without knowing for certain whether Paksima had killed Nordine, but he wanted to know whose baby it had been. He was convinced Azra knew. I think that's why he killed Paksima—the idea that she'd have asked him to bury that baby, when it might not have been his. I don't know why I think that. I just know I do."

"I heard that bit, out in the hall." Ian sounded even gruffer than usual, but he leaned over and patted my wife's arm. Coming from Ian, that was mindblowing. He's the only human being I know who's got less time for stray pats than Bree does. "So he thought they'd been having it off. From all that shite the Emir said to his daughter, he seemed to think so too. But you and JP think he was wrong?"

Bree nodded. She seemed to have run out of words.

"I'm with JP and Bree on this one." Mac waved at the flight attendant. "I don't see that girl asking Nordine to do what she asked him to do if there was any way in hell that child could physically have been his. Oh, yes, I'd like some hot tea, please. Does anyone else fancy a nice cuppa? Because I want something comforting right now. What a hideous pointless mess this whole thing has been."

"Agreed. No, no tea for me, but I'd love a beer." Patrick stifled a yawn. "Where was I? More facts? Ali told me that Bengt was sent to make sure all traces of Nordine in the mineral pool were cleaned out, while Ian and I were told to find some way of getting everyone out of the seraglio. Bengt must have caught sight of Paksima's stuff in the second pool, and got the tankers to suction everything away. Of course he would have recognised the clothes—they'd been having an affair. He would have seen the significance immediately, since they'd been using the back end of the seraglio as their private little pleasure dome."

"He went off his head, didn't he?" I was thinking out loud. "Just lost it. He had a day or two to let it build up. He must have been right off his head. And in the middle of all that, me and Bree spotted the three of them outside our window and went out looking the next morning. That was when we found the hut where the mess with Paksima's baby went down. Wonder who the third person was?"

"Probably Azra." Bree leaned against my shoulder. It's always nice to know that, times like these, I'm who she reaches for. And when it comes to comfort, only Bree'll do for me. "Why did Bengt send the guard to our tent after the show? Or is that speculation and not fact?"

Patrick smiled at her. It was a genuine smile, gone a second later. It suddenly hit me, how tired he was.

"My guess would be to keep everyone's attention diverted while he went out after Azra. You realise, she must have seen her sister executed? There's no other reason for her to have been frightened, or to have run off into that crowd. He would have been desperate to find her and silence her before she could tell her father or anyone else what he'd done. Of course, Bengt couldn't have known that while he was trying to chase down the surviving twin, their father –"

One of the women, I'm not sure who, made a noise, and Patrick broke off. "Well. In any case, that's basically all I've got in the way of actual facts. Unless anyone has questions I might be able to answer, I'd like to try for a quick nap before we land. I'm a little short on sleep."

When it comes to weather, London in January isn't any less miserable than it is in December. Of course, that goes for most of Europe, really; it's probably just as well Bree and I'd honeymooned in southern Europe in warm weather, or she might have thought the entire continent was like this all the time.

We spent three chilly days decompressing in Italy and got back to about as cold a London night as I can remember: the entire city looked to be made of frost. It probably felt even colder than it was, coming from the desert. Letting ourselves into the mews house, I was psyching myself up to huddling with Bree, having a cuddle under a duvet on the sofa until the furnace kicked in. So it was a nice surprise to walk in and find the house a comfy seventy degrees.

"Oh thank heavens!" Bree headed straight for the kitchen, and I followed on. "I bet Carla asked someone at the office to come by and turn the heat on. Man, she's good."

"Yeah, she really is." I'd pulled up one of the kitchen chairs. "Is there anything edible in the house, or do you want to send out for something? Probably too much to hope for, expecting Carla to ask the staff to stock the fridge, as well."

Bree had filled the electric kettle, and plugged it in. "No, it's pretty bare in there. I cleaned the fridge out before we left, so we're basically down to crackers and some frozen stuff, but I can always—is that your phone?"

It was, and I'd left the damned thing in my coat pocket, out in the hall. By the time I got to it, it had clicked over to voicemail. I headed back to the kitchen, where the kettle was on the boil. Bree was dropping a mesh strainer full of decaf Earl Grey into one of the small teapots that came with the rental. She looked up at me, waiting.

"Ian," I told her. "No clue what he wants. Hang on, let me get this. Have we got any honey?"

"(beep) JP? Ian. Look, I know everyone's only just got home, but Mac wants a dinner meeting at Fallow tomorrow night, full band. This is about early planning for the 'thank the fans' gigs—no worries, there aren't any problems. But since you and Bree are heading back to the States soon, it makes sense to get it done early. Ring me back, will you?"

"John?" She sounded anxious. "Is everything okay?"

That startled me. She must have seen from my face that nothing much was happening, but that hadn't stopped her from tensing up, you know? I found myself wondering just how much damage the stuff that had gone down in Manaar had really done. Not just to Bree, either; I hadn't been sleeping well, not since the shooting in our suite. The whole time in Italy I'd kept waking up, never really getting too deep into real sleep, and I didn't think it had much to do with the MS, for a change. What was it soldiers got, after they've had too much shit going on around them, gunfire and being afraid all the time and too much death? Post traumatic something or other...?

"Yeah, everything's fine. Just Ian letting me know that Mac wants a get-together at Fallow House for dinner tomorrow night. He says it's about getting a jump on the planning for the festival gigs this summer. They know we're heading home in a few days, and they want to do it while we're still here. Probably going to be a lot of tossing ideas about, unless someone comes up with something straight off." I watched her shoulders loosen up, and patted her hand. "No worries, love. You can hang out here if you'd rather pass on it. I should go, though—at least they'll have a hot supper waiting. Speaking of supper, what are we doing about tonight...?"

In the end, we both went to the Fallow House meeting. That was just as well, because it turned out that between me ringing Ian back to say *yeah, we'll be there* and the hire car dropping us off at the front stairs the next night, someone actually had come up with something, and it was a corker.

Before we'd headed out, though, Bree'd gone off to get enough groceries to get us through the rest of our time in London. We had tickets booked to get us home to San Francisco at the end of the week. The minute she was out the door, I rang Carla's office in Los Angeles and left her a message.

There was something I wanted to book myself, that I didn't want Bree in on. It had nothing at all to do with Blacklight, and I was going to need Carla's help on this one; I knew what I wanted, but I hadn't got the first clue where to start getting it done, or who to talk to. I left her a nice detailed message, right down to remembering to tell her to not let Bree get wind of it. It was six in the morning in California, so she'd find it when she got there. No need to wake her up, you know? She'd only got home from Italy two days ago herself.

Time's a funny old thing, the way it telescopes itself. We'd been at Fallow House maybe six weeks before, but so much had gone down since then, it felt more like six months or maybe six years. At the same time, there was this weird sense of *deja vu*: big gas fireplace warming the place up, sideboard covered with hot chafing dishes, hired wait staff hanging about until they were wanted to do the clearing up, cars pulling up in front of Fallow House to drop people off and disappearing down the Kings Road to park somewhere until it was time to bring everyone home again. Just like the last big supper do we'd had here.

And this time, everyone was there. Ian had even got David Walter and Maureen Bennett, the London office's two honchos, out for this one, and everyone in the band had brought his missus, as well. Patrick had stayed in London, and he'd come along. It wasn't until the hired crew had bundled the last of the dirty dishes out of the way that Ian finally got down to business, and he wasn't wasting any time.

"Everyone have enough to eat? Good, because I told Carla I'd ring her as soon as we were done here. She says she's got a few things she wants to share with the band, and that it's got a direct bearing on the festival dates, and no, I haven't got a clue what it is. She said she wants to run it past everyone at the same time."

Of course she was ready and waiting for us. Marjorie, her assistant, picked up on the first ring and put us straight through.

"Ian?" If she was jetlagged, it wasn't showing. "Is everyone there? Can we get started? Oh, hi guys."

"All here, the lot of us. Half a mo, all right?" Ian said it over one shoulder—he was waving the hired help out through the main doors. "Yeah, thanks, good night. Carla? We're ready to rock. What have you got?"

"Three locations, with dates." Nice and crisp, and the truth is, having Carla and Ian sounding completely themselves again somehow put Manaar that much farther behind us. "Let's get Europe out of the way first. What would you say to two European shows? One in mid-June, one in late August?"

"I'd say brilliant, depending on where they were." Mac was sounding normal again, as well. "I wouldn't much fancy playing a goat pasture in Turkey somewhere. Want to share, please?"

Funny thing: Carla performs miracles on a regular enough basis to not even notice what she's pulling off. Just then, though, I'd have sworn I heard a touch of the smug in her voice.

"First thing is the June date. I just finished up with the organisers of Rock am Ring—that's June third through fifth, this year. They've agreed to Blacklight having an entire weekend at the Nürburgring two weeks after the official festival, acts of our choosing, the whole nine yards."

"Bloody hell!" Stu was blinking at the speaker. "Carla, how the fuck do you pull this stuff off? Have you got photos of all these people in bed with donkeys, or something?"

That got a laugh out of her. "Nice idea, Stu, but no, I don't. Does that work for everyone? JP, anything planned in California with the Geezers that might conflict?"

"No, nothing at all. Sounds brilliant." Inside, I was grinning ear to ear. Early or middle June, Germany, nice and close to Bree's birthday: yeah, Carla had got that phone message I'd left, all right. From the sound of it, she'd run with it. "I'm on. What was that about a second Euro show, though? Did you say something about August? What'd you pull out of your hat this time, Hyde Park or something?"

"Well—yes." Gordon *Bennett*. "The last Saturday in August, the twenty-seventh, is ours if we want it. I know it's a short lead time for getting two festivals together, but they're two months apart. Is that enough for planning and booking the other acts we want? And do the venue capacities work for everyone, or do we need two-day events for the kind of traffic you're thinking about?"

Silence. The entire room was just sitting there gawking, at the phone or at each other. Even Mac was slackjawed.

"Guys? Hello? Is everyone still there?"

"Um—yeah, still here." Ian got himself back together. "So you've got us the Nürburgring and Hyde Park, if we want either or both. People? Consensus, please, show of hands. Nürburgring show in June? Any reason to not go for it? I'm not talking tech stuff and prep, I'm asking about personal commitments. Is everyone open for the booking? Right. Carla, every hand in the room's in the air, so I'd say we're good to go for that one. Send me the contact stuff and I'll get it rolling from here. What about a Hyde Park gig? That one seems like a no-brainer—yeah, right, everyone's in? Carla, it's unanimous for both. We'll hammer out the details, no worries. Brilliant job. Was there anything else?"

"Actually, yes, one more thing. I got a call out of the blue about an hour ago, from a guy named Ryder DeWitt. Do any of you know who he is?"

"What, you mean the Las Vegas hotel guy?" Cal had both his eyebrows up. "Yeah, of course. We lent him two of my basses for an exhibition of classic instruments at one of his places, a few years back. What about him, Carla?"

"Apparently he's decided that one of his resort hotels, the Ra- venna, is too old to compete with the newer ones, and he's going to build a new state of the art replacement. The site's being razed flat. We're talking about sixty acres of prime land in the middle of Vegas, a nice level lot with nothing on it, as of mid-July." She took a breath. "He says that if Blacklight Corporate is willing to cover the costs of running the required City services into the site—water, gas, that kind of thing—we can have it for the North American festival dates. The only drawback is that he'd need to have the services in and done before the middle of October; something about his permits. So what would you say to a North American festival date in Sin City? Maybe the weekend before Halloween, when the weather in the desert has cooled off? There are no major events scheduled that weekend—I already checked with the Convention and Visitors Bureau. We can get it locked in early and get the Chamber of Commerce resources guaranteed."

Of course, that brought down the house. Everyone was talking, everyone trying to cut through each other's babble, while Carla and Ian just sat back and waited. I turned to Tony, who was sitting just to my left and looking about as happy as I'd seen him look since Book of Days. I was about to say something when Luke's voice came across the table at us.

"...Traitors Gate for the Hyde Park show? Because they haven't toured in a while, and they all live within half an hour of London. Remember the Hall of Fame show? Tony, you and Winston locked up that night. I'd love to play with those guys again. Maybe give Greg Carver or Winston Dupres a ring...?"

Tony went rigid.

There was no other word for it; Bree at her stiffest doesn't come close to how hard Tony closed up. Katia was next to him on the far side, and I watched her react to it, pulling back, staring at him. Whatever had triggered him, she didn't look to be clued in. I watched him gather himself, visibly try to control it, get a handle on it.

"Uh—" Tony's not usually stuck for what to say, but he was now. He was being careful, not just hunting for words but making damned sure every one he used was the right one. He'd got eve-

281

ryone's attention, too. The entire conference room listening. "I'm not too sure that's a good idea, Luke. They might not be—available."

I don't know what twigged it for me. Maybe it was the tone of voice, or maybe how uncomfortable he sounded. All I know is, I was suddenly back at the mews house, the night before Tony checked himself into rehab. My head brought the memory back, nice and clear: Tony and Katia, eating Bree's roast. They'd gone over to the Recovery Centre earlier that day, been shown around the place by the director, Robert Mourdain. Bad weather, sleety cold, the sort of weather in which no one in their right mind would want to be sitting out in a garden...Bits of the conversation, things Tony had said, came back to me, along with the taste of that roast, and everything else.

(*There was someone out in the garden...Mourdain got me back inside in a hurry...they weren't expecting anyone to be out in that weather...we'd seen each other...we recognised each other...you'd have recognised him too...*)

Winston? Greg? Was it blow, or crack, or booze, or maybe something worse? What in hell had happened, and who had it happened to?

My stomach was doing a slow crawl. I couldn't ask Tony, even though Winston, in particular, had become a damned good friend, even though we lived half a world away from each other. Anonymity's got to be respected—that's at the core of the whole recovery deal. Tony hadn't told us back before he checked into the Centre himself, and I couldn't ask him now.

I was staring at Tony, and he was busy making damned sure he wasn't meeting my eye. I jerked myself back to the here and now, but the talk had moved on. I'd missed some of the chatter, but in the end it was simple enough: Ian took an official vote, and confirmed we were unanimous on all three events. Patrick was asked to supply what he thought he'd need for full security for all three gigs, and said he would. Carla thanked everyone and rang off. For a meeting with that much important stuff going on, it was over in record time.

Afterwards, waiting just inside for our driver to pull up with the car, Luke pulled me aside.

"JP, look." His voice was all the way down. "I wasn't about to push Tony, but I got the feeling something was going on. You're good friends with Winston. Is something wrong with him, or Greg?"

"Don't know, mate." I met his eye. "And truth is, if I did, I wouldn't be sharing. That's not how rehab works. But there's nothing to share. I don't know. I'll ring Winston tomorrow—I was planning on asking him over for a meal before we headed home. But I don't know. Oi, Bree, that our car?"

Saying goodbyes, knowing we weren't likely to see most of them again until we got together for early planning and then first rehearsals for the Nürburgring show. Bree offering Karen a solid hug, heading down the hall to the small office where we'd stashed our coats. My phone pinged, letting me know someone had sent me a text. I pulled it out and flipped it open. It was from Carla.

"*Bree confirmed for Ehra-Lessien June 12 happy rocking early birthday mum's the word CF.*"

"John?" She'd come back, the green cashmere coat already buttoned. She was holding mine out to me. "Was someone on the phone? Is everything okay? What are you smiling about?"

"Everything's fine," I told her, and we headed out into the cold and frost, towards the mews house and another three days to get ready for the long ride home.

Epilogue

June 2011

"Mr. and Mrs. Kinkaid? I am Lothar Eichel, track director. Welcome to Ehra-Lessien. I hope your trip was comfortable. It is a great pleasure to meet you both. Please call me Lothar."

I've always thought of myself as a piss-poor actor. This time, though, unless Bree'd suddenly developed some serious acting chops of her own, I'd managed to get my wife out of bed at half past six in the morning and get her from the Grandhotel Schloss Bensberg in Koln to Volkswagen's test track just outside Wolfsburg without her sussing out what I was up to.

And mind you, that was with me giving her fashion advice on what not to wear for the two hundred mile plane ride, something I never do. You'd have thought me telling her *no, comfy clothes and leave the high heels at home today love, they really aren't suitable*, would have either clued her in or left her considering having me committed to the local corn bin; she knows how much I love her in high heels. But either she didn't connect the dots or she honestly didn't know why I'd have stashed her birthday present halfway across Germany.

Still, we'd got here, and the surprise looked to still be intact. I'd been ready to grit my teeth and put up with a helicopter ride for transport. Truth be told, I don't fancy choppers much—I mean, yeah, my head knows that they aren't actually sardine tins with pinwheels on top instead of proper wings, ready to fall out of the sky if the pilot sneezes, but that's got fuck-all to do with what happens to the pit of my stomach and the small of my back whenever I've had to ride in one. Besides, they're bloody uncomfortable.

But a last-minute back and forth texting session with Carla, after the band had checked into the Bensberg until the Nürburgring fan festival was done with, had got that particular worry taken care of. It turned out that Volkswagen not only owns the track at Ehra-Lessien, they operate their own air service in and out of the Wolfsburg airport for their guests. So instead of a couple of hours having my MS tweaked and my tailbone bruised rattling about in a chopper, we were driven from the hotel to Koln airport and settled in on a nice comfy plane. I spent the next hour checking the weather out the window. For what I'd paid for, the weather conditions had to be just right.

Once we'd landed, we'd climbed into another chauffeur-driven car and headed for Ehra-Lessien. Getting in had been scary; the guards at the checkpoints were carrying firepower and not trying to hide it. I found myself wondering if what had gone down in Manaar had left me with some deeper emotional ditches than I'd realised; even though the guards glanced at our driver's papers and waved us straight through, I clenched up so hard and tense, I was sweating. And Bree looked just as tense. There might be some trauma counselling in our future, if that didn't ease up. That could get tricky, because Bree really doesn't like shrinks.

But here we were, finally, climbing out of the car deep inside Volkswagen's no-fly zone, shaking hands with the bloke who'd put everything to do with Bree's birthday prezzie together. Carla had actually introduced us in email, just me and Lothar Eichel. I shook hands with him and grinned, watching the driver help Bree out of the car. Any moment now, the penny was going to drop, and I wanted to be watching her face when it did.

And right on cue, from the opposite direction we'd come in from, I heard the sound of an engine. Lothar, who was shaking Bree's hand, lifted his head and looked over her shoulder. "Ah, right on time. Lanzo has arrived with your car."

First time I'd heard that engine, I'd thought of a lot of coked-up bassists hitting the same low note at the same time. It still sounded like that. Bree'd heard the engine as well, and turned fast, and I caught the look on her face. I was grinning like an idiot.

"Lanzo! Come and meet Mr. and Mrs. Kinkaid. Mrs. Kinkaid, allow me to introduce you to Lanzo Caruselli of Bugatti. Lanzo is our Veyron specialist. Even if you were new to the car, he could show you how to drive it—it's designed to be driven easily, very intuitive. But we were given to understand that you are not completely unfamiliar with it, and that is even better. It will take less time for him to acquaint you with the track, so that you can take the car to its maximum—"

He got out of the way just in time. Bree's never really been the sort of woman who shrieks and clutches, but she was right there, both arms around me, so fast he barely had time to move his arse. If he hadn't, she'd have gone straight through him, and I'm pretty sure I heard something that might have been a stifled shriek, as well. I got a good hold on her; she was whispering under her breath, something that sounded like *omigod omigod omigod*, over and over again. I pulled back and planted a nice noisy kiss.

"Happy birthday, baby." The two techs were watching us, both looking approving. We must have appealed to their sense of sentiment, or something. "Yeah, I bought you a track day. Take the car up as fast as it'll go. I know you want to."

"John…" She bit her lip. "Are you sure? Because I got the impression you really didn't want me doing that. Are you really okay with it? This is the fastest car in the world."

"Yeah, I'm okay with it. Why wouldn't I be? You've been driving me around for thirty years." I patted her bottom. "Go drive the fancy car."

Of course, it wasn't that simple. There were liability releases that had to be signed first, and one that seemed to be Bree signing on the dotted line to admit that her training on the car had been in private one-on-one and not at some place in France where Bugatti usually wants their one-offs to train. There was a very thorough briefing that I basically understood about ten words of, and yeah, it was in English, supposedly. There was Lanzo telling us that, normally, she'd be taking the car out for the final run on her own, but that, what with what he called the slightly unusual nature of her training, they felt that having the ace driver with her for the last lap was best. If she was disappointed or insulted, she didn't show it.

It also turned out that she could have worn the highest heels in her collection and it wouldn't have mattered, because they weren't letting her drive in street clothes anyway. They'd got a fire-proof suit thing ready for her, and a crash helmet. If I hadn't been nervous before, the suit would have done it—it made her look like she was about to drop some comment about this being one giant step for mankind. Carla'd asked for Bree's measurements early on, and I'd sent them along and forgotten about it, and never actually asked what they were needed for. Turns out they even make you wear fireproof long johns, if you take one of these drives.

Ali's Veyron had been black and orange. Not this one; this was white and silver, end to end. I stood with Lothar, listening to the Italian explain things to Bree in nice clear English sentences, watching her visibly remember where things were in the beast, telling myself that it was okay, she wasn't going to crash the thing and get herself killed, it was going to be fine. She hadn't been wrong about how I felt about it. Bree risking her neck pretty much heads my 'oh fuck no' list.

The bottom line, though, is that I trust her. She's never given me any reason to not trust her, you know? She's the most capable human being I've ever known, and what's more, she hasn't got much of a secret death wish. If she doesn't think she can do something, she doesn't bother with it, even if it looks to be fun. And she obviously thought she could do this particular thing, because she put the helmet on, headed back over and climbed straight into the driver's seat.

Not being a driver or knowing anything about cars except where the doors and tires are, I couldn't make sense of the explanations Lanzo Caruselli kept offering up. I do remember one point, when he said something about dropping the car into race mode and how it needed a second key. I wasn't sure if Bree'd got that far with Nordine's lessons, but this part was new to me. I don't know that she was expecting the entire car to hunker down round her. I know I wasn't. I jumped a mile.

They went round four times all told, Bree at the wheel every time. Each time was faster than the last, and they'd gone round three times when they both climbed out and sent the car in for a once-over, and a look at the tires. That made me blink—I already knew that each set of tires cost over forty thousand dollars. I was hoping an extra set of new feet wasn't going to be needed when I realised that my wife wanted to say something, and wasn't sure how to say it. Unusual for her, you know? I jerked my head at her and we stepped away.

"John—listen." She'd left me keeping an eye on her purse while she drove; for some reason, she'd refused to check it with the rest of her gear. Now she'd picked it up and was unzipping one of the inner pockets. "I actually have something I want to give you, too. I just—I want to do it now."

Both of my eyebrows were up. My own birthday, back in early March, had been one of those milestone things: I'd turned sixty. I'd told Bree, flat out, that I was damned if I wanted to make a big deal over it, and I hadn't been joking, either. She'd thrown me a dinner party, close friends and music, all my favourite things that she cooks, with the real prezzie coming after we'd said good-night to the last guests and gone upstairs. So this wasn't a birthday thing, because I'd had that...

"I was going to wait until we got to London in August to give you this, but I think I'll give it to you now. Just because." She paused, just for a moment, not long enough for me to ask her what that *because* was in aid of. "Just in case."

She pulled out what looked to be a simple cream-coloured envelope, European size rather than American, and yeah, they're different. She wasn't smiling, but her face was soft.

"I've been carrying this around for the last two weeks, when I got everything signed off on. I couldn't give it to you on your birthday because you said you didn't want a fuss made, and anyway I didn't have it yet. I do now, though. Happy birthday, John."

For one wild moment, I wondered if she was handing me divorce papers or something: the envelope had a London solicitor's imprint in the upper left corner. It also had something heavy inside. I loosened the flap, and tilted what was inside into my palm.

Keys, wrapped inside a sheet of paper. The keys were familiar, but it wasn't until I unfolded the sheet of paper, and read my name on the freehold to the London mews house we'd been renting, that I realised which locks they belonged to.

"Right." There was some noise going on under my ribcage. I

got one arm round her, and pulled her close. She doesn't like London much—the balance of crap memories to good ones is tilted pretty badly in the wrong direction. I was born there, and in some sense it was always going to be part of what I think of as home. To Bree, a house is a home. "We'll have to get you a proper oven, and a couple of rocking chairs. Nice to put in some gear of our own, even if we aren't in London all that often. Oh hell, here's Lanzo and Lothar back again. Off you go, lady. I'll be watching from wherever Lothar puts us—probably the pit. That's where he had us for the practice runs. Do a good drive, baby."

Showtime.

I don't how many autos out there go by so fast that the wind pushes people watching from fifteen feet back on their heels, but the Veyron did. Lothar had given me a detailed explanation of what speed points Bree would have to hit and where she'd have to hit them, but truth to tell, he might as well have been speaking Early Martian, for all the sense it made to me. I remember that he said something about tapping some paddles and putting the car in cruise control. I did get that there wasn't any question of setting records; she wasn't experienced enough to try for that. Besides, they were quite happy with the record they'd already got.

"She will likely hit two hundred and forty at the midpoint of the straightaway. Perhaps slightly above."

We were standing together in the pit, behind the protective rail. We couldn't see the car; it was taking the big circuit and heading for the straightaway Lothar had talked about. Nice and flat, apparently, and that was where she'd be taking it as high as she could.

He'd sounded pretty damned certain. Of course, he'd watched the first three practice runs, and he must have seen enough drivers in his day to be able to guess straight off what their skills were.

I must have been looking worried, though, because he caught

my eye. "I doubt she will attempt to take the car up to its limit," he told me kindly. "She is not that style of driver."

"Yeah, well, that's my wife you're talking about, and two hundred forty miles an hour sounds quite fast enough for me, ta." I was craning my neck, watching the road. Nothing. But I thought I could hear something, the deep familiar hum of that coked-up bass-player engine. No, not possible. She'd pulled the Veyron out of the starting house and onto the track about three minutes ago, no more than that.

Time really is funny. Three minutes or three hours or thirty seconds, there was no difference in my head until the engine suddenly got even and clear and loud as hell. And there was the white and silver car going past us, and I staggered backwards in that wind from the speed. The damned thing had gone by too fast to even let me see Bree at the wheel. It wasn't a car, it was a blur.

But right after she'd gone past, the car began to slow down. It must have done, because the wing at the back came up. I'd done some reading up on the car before I'd decided to set this up, and one of the things I remembered was how well it actually stops, something about a special wing to help it brake. I'd got no clue what they'd meant—it's a car, not a plane, and cars haven't got wings, you know? But there it was, a big wing right at the back of the car, where I hadn't seen it up before.

And it did stop, finally, well down the road and out of sight of the pit. I heard the engine, and watched it come back towards us, at a normal speed this time.

Both doors opened and my wife climbed out. She was already pulling the helmet off. It would never have occurred to me that a woman shaking her hair loose from a racing helmet could be that big a turn-on, but it really was. I wondered if I could buy the thing as a souvenir. She'd look brilliant in just the helmet and a pair of her best heels...

291

We met halfway, at the side of the track. She'd actually turned pink, and she was trembling. She looked as if she'd just had some of the best sex of her life.

"Wow." There was heat coming off her in waves. "Sorry. Adrenalin. Wow."

"Gordon *Bennett*!" We were hanging on to each other. I honestly hadn't known how hard I'd been hoping nothing would go wrong out there, how worried I'd been. "How fast did you go?"

"I don't know." She'd started sweating, and her whole body was twitching. That damned thing wasn't a car, it was a sex toy on wheels. "Lanzo had a telemetry box on the dashboard, but it doesn't use miles, it uses kilometres. So I don't know." She shuddered, suddenly, a long ripple, head to heel. "*Wow*."

It turned out she'd actually got the thing up to two hundred and forty nine miles an hour on the long straightaway, so that was one in the eye for Lothar, who'd doubted she'd get it above two forty. That qualified her for something they called the 400 Drive Club; it sounded rather like having sex in a 747's loo, but Lothar explained that the four hundred in question was kilometres, that she'd hit 400 kilometres an hour. They told us they had a plaque for Bree. I'd rather have had the helmet—it really was having the same effect on me that driving the thing seemed to have had on Bree—but no go, and I made a mental note to just buy one, once we'd got home. Lanzo made some nice comments, complimented her on how good her driving instincts were, and kissed her hand. Of course, he was Italian, and Italians and Frenchmen always kiss the pretty lady's hand, but I got the feeling he meant it.

"Your flight will be ready for you at half past seven. You will only need a short time to get from here to the Braunschweig airport. If I may offer you a cup of tea, or perhaps some of our local beer…? Ah, you would prefer to get back to Koln? If Mrs. Kinkaid would like to shower before she changes back to her street clothes, I will have your driver bring your car."

"Yeah, we've got the big show next weekend—the whole band took the day off so that we could come do this." I offered a hand. "Thanks, mate. I don't know I'll ever be able to top this as a prezzie, you know?"

Lanzo was getting into the driver's seat of the Veyron, moving it back indoors for its next tire change. Bree turned for one last look; her eyes were about as deep and bright a green as I'd seen them in years, but I wasn't sure whether that was meant for me or the car. Lanzo waved out the window, and the car was gone from our view. Bree headed indoors for a fast shower. She got to keep the fire-proof suit and the special undies.

The day had been hot, but it was coming on towards evening and the air felt fresh and cool. Off to the west, the outlines of the sun had softened up. Our driver, the same chauffeur who'd picked us up at the airport on the way in, headed towards us with the same car.

"I am curious about something, if you will indulge me." Lothar had his cocked off to one side, looking at Bree. "I was told that you had already had some instruction on driving a Veyron, but I was not given any details—your people in Los Angeles communicated those facts directly with Lanzo. Surely you live in California? I am unaware of any place where taking the car up to true speed is possible there."

"Oh, it wasn't at home." She was waiting for the driver to open the door for her. "It was last year, in Manaar. I was learning to drive the Emir's car, but the driver –"

The words stopped halfway. Something was happening to Lothar Eichel's face. It might have been grief, or pain, or maybe regret. Whatever it was, it silenced both of us.

"Ah, the al-Wahid car. It is always a sad day for us, when we lose one of them. That will perhaps sound odd to you, but you must remember, there are only a few hundred of these in the world, and each is hand-built. To lose one is to lose a member of our family."

"What?" I had hold of Bree's hand, and she was holding hard. She seemed to be having trouble breathing. "Lose it? What do you mean, lose it?"

"I am speaking of the accident that took the life of the Emir's daughter earlier this spring."

Bree's mouth opened. She shut it again. I shot her a look, and watched that nice pink glow the Veyron had left her with drain out of her face.

Lothar saw it, as well. "You had heard nothing of this? The girl was alone in the car, apparently, and tried to take it to full speed on a stretch of road along the coast. I gather the Princess was untutored in driving such a car, because she lost control. The Veyron struck the side of a docking office, and then went into the sea."

I was breathing hard. Bree barely seemed to be breathing at all. Lothar shook his head.

"A great tragedy, even more so that I doubt she was given permission to use the car. It is not a vehicle to be driven carelessly, or taken lightly. I understand the Emir is now childless. We were told very little, beyond the bare facts. I believe the Emir has been in complete seclusion, seeing no one since the accident. Thank you both for coming today. I wish you a safe and comfortable flight back to Koln, and all success with your show next weekend."

I've never spent that long travelling with my wife at my side in complete silence. Between Lothar waving at us through the back windows and letting ourselves into our suite at the Bensberg a few hours later, neither of us said a word. We were offered food, but Bree shook her head at the flight attendant and so did I. I did open my mouth to say something, only once, but a quick look at Bree's profile kept me quiet. I know that look, and I hate seeing it there.

Back in the hotel with our door safely locked, Bree turned to me and finally broke the silence. I couldn't have told you what she was feeling just then. I'm not sure she knew, either. I watched her take the deep breath, watched her decide to say it. I knew what she was going to say, too.

"John—did he kill her?"

There was no point pretending I didn't know who she was talking about; there was only one person that "he" could have been. I'd been running it through my head the entire way back from Wolfsburg and I was seeing it now, too clearly: the father and daughter, how things must have been with them. I had my answer ready and I gave it to her straight.

"No. I don't think so, Bree. For one thing, if he was going to use that car as a murder weapon, there'd have been two of them in the car, you know? Main thing, though, is that I can't see him going back on his promise. He didn't want to make it, but he did, and that's a huge deal where he comes from. You want to know what I think, I'll tell you. It's not pretty, but it's not murder, either. I don't believe he lied to us. I think he cut her out of his life and his heart and she couldn't take it. And her sister was already gone."

"Suicide?" She reached out a hand, finding one of the upholstered chairs and easing herself into it. She looked tired suddenly, the kind of bone-weary she gets after she's done a full eight-hour catering event and forgotten to take the proper rest breaks she needs. "You think she couldn't bear to stay alive anymore, so she helped herself to her father's car? You think she got to the coast road and put her foot down and floored it and kept it floored until she lost control of it?"

I nodded. Bree sighed.

"So do I. Because there's no way she lost control of that thing, not unless she took both hands off the wheel and closed her eyes. It had to have been deliberate." Bree closed her own eyes for a moment. Her voice was bleak. "God. That poor kid. I wonder what Ali al-Wahid feels like?"

"If he's lucky, it hurts like hell. Better to feel anything than to feel nothing at all. But I'm betting he's not letting himself feel a bloody thing. He's good at that, numbing himself. And you know what, Bree, there's not a damned thing anyone can do about any of it."

For a moment, we were both quiet. A while back, she'd finally got fed up with thirty years of me telling her not to feel things because feeling them made her unhappy. She'd called me on it, and she'd been right. So I wasn't about to tell her how to feel, or whether to feel. She's quite capable of a lot of things, including knowing how she needs to react.

"True." She reached for the hotel phone. She was still pale, still looked tired, but the look I hated was fading out of her face, like the distant echo of a car engine. "God, I'm hungry. When did we eat last, breakfast? What would you like for dinner…?

JP Kinkaid

Photo by Nic Grabien

Deborah Grabien can claim a long personal acquaintance with the fleshpots—and quiet little towns—of Europe. She has lived and worked and hung out, from London to Geneva to Paris to Florence, with a few stops in between.

But home is where the heart is. Since her first look at the Bay Area, as a teenager during the peak of the City's Haight-Ashbury years, she's always come home to San Francisco, and in 1981, after spending some years in Europe, she came back to Northern California to stay.

Deborah was involved in the Bay Area music scene from the end of the Haight-Ashbury heyday until the mid-1970s. Her friends have been trying to get her to write about those years—fictionalised, of course!—and, now that she's comfortable with it, she's doing just that. After publishing four novels between 1989 and 1993, she took a decade away from writing, to really learn how to cook. That done, she picked up where she'd left off, seeing the publication of eleven novels between 2003 and 2010.

Deborah and her husband, San Francisco bassist Nicholas Grabien, share a passion for rescuing cats and finding them homes, and are both active members of local feral cat rescue organisations. Deborah has a grown daughter, Joanna, who lives in LA.

These days, in between cat rescues and cookery, Deborah can generally be found listening to music, playing music on one of eleven guitars, hanging out with her musician friends, or writing fiction that deals with music, insofar as multiple sclerosis—she was diagnosed in 2002—will allow.

Visit her website at www.deborahgrabien.com

CPSIA information can be obtained at www.ICGtesting.com
Printed in the USA
LVOW12s1526160114

369728LV00002B/436/P